ANYTHING

Full Murderhobo Book Two

DAKOTA KROUT

MOUNTAINDALE
PRESS

ACKNOWLEDGMENTS

To my Patreons who are supporting me directly, thank you all so much! Especially to William Merrick, Samuel Landrie, Garett Loosen, Zeeb, and Michael Matteucci.

And to my loving wife and daughter, always.

PROLOGUE

"*Bring out the Bard!*"

The chant was taken up by the utterly *stuffed* tavern. People outside were still attempting to push into the building, and all standing room had been filled, to the point that the barboy was unable to move through the crowd to deliver food and drink. He pushed and shoved the wall of flesh, knowing that the bartender would have his job, or tan his hide, if he didn't try anyway.

Vibrations from clapping, stomping, or banging on tables filled the establishment as the chanting reached a peak, and the bartender worried that tonight would be the night that his structure would collapse and kill them all. It was how he'd always dreamed of going, but at this moment, the daydream of a full house was looking more like a nightmare.

Just before the place shook itself to pieces, Zed rose to his feet from the exact spot where he had been telling his tale the previous night. Greeting the room with a grin, he let his words float to everyone in the building—and its surroundings—with perfect clarity.

"Good evening, everyone. Thank you all for coming tonight,

1

even knowing that my words are purest sedition, and perhaps even treason to the expanding Hollow Kingdom." His 'joke' was met with the appropriate chuckles and shaking of heads, though the bartender gulped down a draft he had just poured for a guest, in order to steady his nerves. Inquisitors never seemed to mind collateral damage when they were rooting out treason. "Would anyone like to guess what the topic tonight will be?"

"War crimes!" one of the earliest arrivals slurred, evoking cheers at the reply. "The Mindbender Special!"

Another bellow followed right on the heels of the first. "The implosion of the Dynasty of Dogs! They say that was you!"

"No… that was the Archmage." Both the requests and Zed's admission were met with excitement; tales of the actions of The Four during the war were always wildly popular. Even so, Zed shook his head and smiled as though he were telling children that it wasn't playtime just yet. "Perhaps tomorrow, after the Kingdom's troops arrive to haul me away! No, today we will discuss the first time The Four were sold out and left friendless, the creation of the Dryad, the restoration of the Hollow King-dom… and we'll get to the death of the *True* King tomorrow."

Overlapping conversations exploded: this crazy Bard was *actually* speaking treason.

"This again?" A familiar voice broke the atmosphere of rapt attention that had formed nigh-instantly. "You fraud! I don't know about any betrayal, but the Dryad are a *race* of people! They've been around forever, but they were *discovered* by The Four. The restoration of the Hollow Kingdom? Didn't you say last night that the world was about to be destroyed, or some other nonsense?"

"If I recall correctly…" Zed's eyes radiated a golden light for a bare moment, just long enough to be seen, but so fleeting that most took it to be a trick of the light. "Last night, I said 'The Ascenders have begun to lose hold of their power and authority. This world, this entire *civilization*, is ending'. Is that what you're referencing?"

"Uh… yeah?" The bold man withered under the combined attention of the room.

"Well, that might be a *teensy* bit my fault. How about this: I tell *my* version of events, and you can point out each place I'm wrong as we go along. Then you tell us the *truth*, because clearly *you* were there, and I'm most certainly the fraud in the room." Zed paused but received no reply. "Or perhaps you're yet another agent of the Kingdom out to discredit me? I saw you slip away and return last night. I'd say you were gone just long enough to… send a raven, perhaps?"

The man went pale, but Zed turned his attention away, uncaring of the man's clear guilt.

"Let's discuss the repercussions of the events I touched on last night." Zed was addressing the crowd at large again, and more than one drunk heckler was getting laughed at by their seatmates. "Defeating the Chimera allowed a small respite from war for the Kingdom, as the invasion had already overrun the Dynasty troops that had been stationed there. The mountainous pass was reduced to flat land, the *first* accomplishment attributed to Andre… as well as being the only one he hadn't actually *earned*."

This callback to the previous evening made the group laugh and glance at the outed agent, who sank into his chair and downed his drink.

"Returning successfully was *something* no one had expected. The Four returning at *all* was a shock to those in the know." Zed chuckled mirthlessly as he remembered the 'welcome' they had received. "Not only did they come back, finish the mission, and earn personal glory on par with some of the greatest war heroes of the time, but they brought back purified resources that could contend with the national assets of the entire Dynasty we were defending against. As I'm sure some of you are aware, that result should have *destroyed* our Kingdom. Yet, somehow, the True King managed to turn it into wealth, as well as enriching the Kingdom to the point where… flat out, others got lazy.

They got jealous. Dangerous. *Treacherous*, to the point of patricide and regicide!"

The entire room was still; all but the bartender, who was helping himself to yet another drink as sweat rolled down his face.

"Weapons, armor, structures which required rare *resources*." Zed snorted at an internal thought. *"Mercenaries* they used against their own people, defenses to protect the Nobility nearly exclusively, and turbulent-space monoliths that prevented Ascenders from casually popping into restricted areas. They believed those measures were sufficient... that mere resources were enough to ensure safety. If any of you had family near Scarrocco, you might recall the *thousands* that died because The Four were forced to follow the Kingdom's commands."

There was a long moment of silence, where even the drunkest among them took off their caps in remembrance. "Onward to... happier memories. Today, I'll start our story only a few days after where I left off last night. Tomorrow will be different, I'm afraid. Too much ground to cover, and too little time before... well. For those of you who don't know the truth of where our titles came from, we've had *many* throughout the years."

"Before Zed 'the Mindbender' came to be, I was called everything from 'Potentia Mooch' to 'Farmer's Friend' to 'Tornado of the Red Light'... ahem. Ignore that last one. This isn't a story only of my struggles; I'm merely an observer. Andre the Terraformer gained a second, less-well-known moniker during our travels-"

"Druid of the Flesh and Blood," a man missing an arm and an eye called from a corner booth, his outburst gathering the attention of the room. "I was *there*, Bard. I came after ye and was tossed in one of them abyssal flowers."

"Ah, you have no hard feelings with me, then. It was The Murderhobo and myself that lobbied for and secured your freedom, after all." Zed's words earned him a raised glass as the grizzled man wiped at his nose, a phantom pain that evidently still plagued him years later.

"As he said, Andre was known as the 'Druid of Flesh and Blood'. This is a title only spoken of along the border towns, and the story itself is a dark reminder of what occurs when forced to follow stupid orders." Zed shook his head sadly. "Ambushing the Druid on his land, not checking the enchantments on the Archmage, or attempting to keep the Murderhobo from murdering in Murder World? This *has* never, and *will* never… be a good idea."

"Let's talk about *why*." Zed raised his hand, sending gold-tinged mana racing into the fire, and the minds of everyone present fell back in time.

CHAPTER ONE

"Zone nine! *Finally!*" Luke stood at the edge of the territory in Murder World and slammed his knuckles into the ubiquitous blue grass near his feet. He gazed into the depths of the Zone and, for a very brief moment, considered making a plan.

Then he laughed and charged across the border screaming, "*Bum Rush!*"

His target was a small humanoid a few dozen feet into the Zone, and he appeared next to the creature in an instant, thanks to his Skill. He had *just* enough time to hear the witch-like creature cackle before it erupted into an explosion that tossed him back nearly the entire distance to the boundary and sent him rolling the remaining distance in a shower of blood and torn-up earth.

Simple Metal Pauldron has broken!
Simple Metal Cuirass has broken!
Health: 241/250.

You have entered Zone nine! While in this Zone, be careful when attacking the local population! Most of the creatures like to fight, but a few prefer taking you out at all costs. This Zone is devoted to training your ability to make good choices, and will allow you to explore and train new ranged-weapon options! After you feel like you have a good handle on your distance-combat ability, please feel free to continue onward!

"*Learn* to make good choices?" Luke was furious that he had taken the time to read *instructions*, but he blamed it on the fact that two parts of his armor had broken in an instant. "I make *great* choices! *Bum Rush!*"

The Murderhobo sprinted at the next creature that was wandering around. It, just like the previous foe, wore a pointed canvas cap, a thick black goat-wool robe, and bore a metallic staff. There were no instantly visible differences between this entity and the one he had exploded, but that didn't stop him for a moment.

One *tiny* fact he had overlooked was that he had lost the element of surprise: this opponent knew he was coming.

Boing!

A barrier appeared between the creature and himself, shimmering and blue, and Luke bounced off it as though he had hit a wall made of rebounding slime. The fact that a barrier like this could stop him, even *momentarily*, brought him back to the moment when he had finally gotten *this* close to taking his revenge on the Archmage for trapping him in this world alone for forty years… only to be stopped by a barrier exactly like this one.

His veins bulged as he dashed forward and slammed a fist into the energetic field, the effort briefly materializing his Battering Ram Knuckles as he vented his frustrations. His fist rebounded off the barrier and would have damaged him if he hadn't had such impeccable control of his body. A flash of inspiration caused him to swing with his left hand, and a Simple Steel Sword made of mana whipped out and sliced through the barrier as though it wasn't there, dissipating it in the same instant.

"*Die*, Don!" Luke hissed as he charged the creature. He took it to the ground with a flying tackle, then proceeded to punch its head into the grass until a notification appeared, along with a concerning lack of internal organs as the head broke like a porcelain doll.

You have killed a Bouncy-Boomy Mage of Doomy!
Etheric Xenograft Potentia gained: 25!
Current Etheric Xenograft Potentia: 4258/8900 to level 9!

"Mmh." Luke nodded at the surprisingly large amount of exp he had gained. Since he had needed to run through Zones six, seven, and eight to get here, he had made a good haul; but each new Zone held far more exp for each individual kill than the previous, especially after he had been stuck in them for a while. "Good to be back. Glad you're functioning properly. Now stuff a *sock* in it."

Set verbose messages to minimal mode?

"Ya." Luke ignored the confirmation message and sprinted along the landscape, bound and determined to make it to the end of the Zone within the next thirteen days. Since there had been a weak point in the universe back at the end of Zone five, he wasn't sure whether there would be one at the end of Zone nine, or ten. If it were *ten*, he was going to need to return and demand more time in his world if he ever wanted to be able to progress.

Either way, he needed to hurry. To that end, he took out every witch in his path, not bothering to go *too* far out of his way to kill the others that he saw. He *knew* it was a mistake to leave enemies behind him, but right now, he just didn't care. He could always return and destroy them later.

Luke hated being proved right.

He slammed his fist against the strangely effervescent boundary between Zone nine and ten. He had run into this issue back at the end of the 'Tutorial' Zones, so even though it was annoying to be blocked from progressing, it set a high expectation that getting through this boundary would allow him to access a new exit point. The annoying bit was that there was a *requirement* to getting past this Zone, an issue that he hadn't run into in subjective *years*.

Quest alert: Seven ate Nine.

Congratulations on reaching the end of Zone nine and finding a reward plinth! If you are seeing this message, you have not met the minimum requirements for stepping into Zone ten! Please make sure you have:

- *Kill at least 100 total Bouncy-Boomy Mage of Doomy: 18/100*
- *Kill at least 50 Bouncy-Boomy Mage of Doomy with a ranged attack (An attack from 5 meters+): 0/50*
- *Explode 25 Boomy Mage of Doomy without taking damage from the explosion: 0/25*
- *Had fun: 0/1*

*Save up your Skill Pearls for an **enhanced** skill at the plinth!*

"What is the metric for *fun?*" The Murderhobo pounded on the wall, each blow causing the air to fizz like an alchemic reaction and reverberate like a drum. An hour later, he stepped back from the wall and turned his eyes on the witches that had been lured into the area by the light and noise show he had been putting on.

They hadn't yet attacked, as the noise was dispersed over a large area when he hit the wall; but they were getting too close for him to ignore them any longer. The first thing he needed to do was differentiate between the 'Boomy' and 'Bouncy-Boomy' types of witches, so he took a short amount of time and studied the dozen creatures walking through the area. They looked very, *very* similar… but he finally saw it.

The eyes.

One of the witches had Cadet Blue eyes, or as his Sigil noted for him: '#5F9EA0'. The others had Blue-Green eyes, or '#088F8F'. Luke winced at the fact that, if he wanted to be able to tell them apart, he would have to let them see him. He much preferred clean, one-hit kills where he caved in his target's head from behind, when he could get them. Still… if he needed ranged kills, maybe it didn't matter *too* much.

To ensure that he had identified the difference, Luke *Bum Rushed* the solitary one with Cadet Blue eyes. His fist landed squarely in the center of its face, sending it tumbling back a half-dozen paces with a broken neck. He watched it, then spit to the side in disappointment.

Boom. Shrapnel flew from the spot where the creature had fallen, which Luke easily dodged.

Quest updated: Seven ate Nine!

- *Explode 25 Boomy Mage of Doomy without taking damage from the explosion: 1/25*

The corner of his lips twitched upward for an instant, and he turned his attention to the other witches. It might have been his imagination, but he was almost *certain* they flinched when his eyes swept over them. "Good."

A shard of ice the length of his arm, from finger to elbow, scraped off his mana-made paulron, the chill penetrating the armor, although the icicle itself did not. Cracks ran along the length of the piece before repairing in the next instant, thanks to the massive mana regeneration this world afforded him. Realizing he was standing still and gloating like a mid-sized goat instead of killin' like a large goat, Luke sprinted at the offending witch and reached out, intending to grab her neck for maximum leverage as he punched.

He abruptly turned and looked to the left, noting three witches standing and casting together, just as their spell circle completed.

A bolt of lightning, thicker than the meaty thighs of Old Man Sunny—a literal god from a different and specifically non-connected universe—jumped from the staff of the lead witch in the trio, blasting Luke into the air and hurling him nearly a hundred meters away. He crashed onto the well-groomed grass and bounced along before coming to a crumpled halt. He coughed once, sending steaming blood splashing on the ground next to him.

All armor broken! 62 lightning damage taken!
Health: 188/250

"Abyss. They can work together." Luke lurched to his feet and stared into the distance as the witches slowly drifted toward him. It appeared that they couldn't walk, and their movement speed was nothing to be concerned about. With a flexing of his will, his mana moved along Walking Arsenal's pathways and reactivated the Skill. His armor reconstituted piece-by-piece with a *fizz*, and he checked to ensure all of his power was distributed at ten percent for each chunk of armor and weapons.

"Nice." That reserved a total of eighty percent of his mana, leaving him with roughly seventy points to use in combat. Not a huge issue at all, as his only Skills that used mana were Goat Call, Open Up, and Bum Rush. Of those three, only the last was useful at the moment.

He calmly sidestepped an icicle, watching for any signs of other spells. More ice shot through the air, and Luke finally felt that he had a good handle on the capabilities of these attackers. "Ice at range, lightning at near-touch range when three are together, barrier if they see me coming. Can dodge ice, lightning is too fast; don't let them group. Cut through barrier, punch faces…"

Luke's brow furrowed in displeasure as he tried to calculate the most efficient kill method. He didn't *want* to change his fighting style just because the area *told* him to do it. The witches were closing in on him, and the ice was flying as thick as hail falling in a storm. Just before he charged in, he glanced to the right and noticed that even more witches were closing in on the site of the battle. He roared at the air, clutching at his head as he tried to *think* about the situation.

Then he noticed that one of the newcomers was an exploding variant, and that gave him an idea. He rushed out of the line of sight for the witches, observing how they reacted to losing him. They continued drifting for a moment in the direction he had gone, then grouped up and peered around suspiciously. "Perfect."

Not wasting a moment, he erupted from the long bluegrass

he had been hiding in like a tricky goat. His target didn't even get a chance to see him before the Murderhobo devoted a total of forty percent of his mana to his right hand and sent a Battering Ram blow to its hat-covered temple.

The air *screamed* as the witch flew directly at the group he was targeting. As his projectile of choice came within a few feet of the nearest witch, a lightning bolt struck and detonated the Bouncy-Boomy Mage of Doomy, supercharging the explosion to such a degree that it instantly wiped out the remainder of the group.

That counts!

- *Bouncy-Boomy Mage of Doomy killed with a ranged attack (5 meters+): 11/50*
- *Explode 25 Boomy Mage of Doomy without taking damage from the explosion: 2/25*
- *Kill at least 100 total Bouncy-Boomy Mage of Doomy: 31/100*
- *Have fun: 1/1*

Luke walked forward and collected the fallen Skill Pearls, a slight grin showing through his mustache and beard. "So *that's* how you have fun? I can get behind it."

CHAPTER TWO

Luke stood at the edge of the effervescent barrier once again, hurriedly and nervously depositing Skill Pearls into the plinth at the edge of the Zone. There were fewer than fifty minutes remaining before he would be forced by his Sigil to turn around and *sprint* to the start of Zone six. If he couldn't get through this space and out into his base world, he would need to battle through the last few Zones *again* the next time he came through.

He glanced at the details of the Zone quest one last time. *Quest complete: Seven ate Nine.*

- *Kill at least 100 total Bouncy-Boomy Mage of Doomy: 372/100*
- *Kill at least 50 Bouncy-Boomy Mage of Doomy with a ranged attack (5 meters+): 61/50*
- *Explode 25 Boomy Mage of Doomy without taking damage from the explosion: 26/25*
- *Had fun: 3/1*

This quest was making fun of him, he was *sure* of it. The last of his Pearls went into the plinth, and it gave him a notice that a custom Skill was being generated. Unlike the last usage in Zone five, this plinth didn't pretend that it was going to take a large amount of time. It also didn't spit out a super high-Tier Skill, so that may have had something to do with it.

He eyeballed the Pearl as it appeared and the barrier vanished, getting the feeling that this Skill was likely fourth-tier. Powerful, but with plenty of room to grow. To be fair, he hadn't deposited the equivalent of more than a quarter million lives this time around.

As the fizzy wall scattered in the wind, leaving behind only a refreshing tingle on his skin, a wavering white line appeared in the air. "An exit. Abyss, I was starting to get worried."

He took a deep breath and gulped down the Skill Pearl. It dissolved into power before it ever hit his stomach, flooding him with knowledge and the ability to use it.

Skill gained: Shockwave Cleave. T4, level 0. Mana cost: 50

Effect 1: You now hit so hard that your enemies don't just wince in sympathy; they actually feel the pain. Beings behind and within one foot of the target of a melee attack will take 10+5n% of the damage dealt, where n = skill level. Maximized at 55% damage dealt to additional targets.

Bonus 1, at range: the range of the damage spread is increased to three feet.

Effect 2: You can increase the amount of invested mana in order to deal a greater percentage of the damage to additional enemies. With each additional 50 mana devoted to the Skill, the damage percentage spread increases by 50%. For example, devoting 100 mana allows for 82% of the damage to pass through; 150 mana increases the percentage to 95.75%, and so on.

Bonus 2, Multitarget: Each enemy that takes damage from a shockwave releases a rear-facing shockwave that deals 50% less damage than the original shockwave.

Luke stared at the Skill he had just gained and ran through the possibilities. It *sounded* like a great way to take on an entire army at once and kill them in one blow, but the reality was slightly more disappointing. He *could* deal more than one hundred percent of the damage dealt to enemies beyond his original target, but that would decrease the amount of mana he could passively devote to his weapons, as well as leaving him open to taking damage.

Frankly, the total damage would drop too far to do more than inflict light bruises as soon as it reached the third rank of enemies. The *other* major issue was that it didn't specify 'enemies'. This was a great way to accidentally kill members of the Hollow Kingdom and trigger his Sigil frying his brain in retaliation.

"Where were ewe when I needed to kill goats for ten years?" Luke snarled as he studied the line in the air and the fresh, untouched Zone behind it. His Sigil was starting to *pulse* on his forehead, and his feet twisted of their own accord back toward the known exit as he tried to consider his options. He barely, *barely* managed to hold himself in place long enough to activate *Open Up* and tear through to his home world. The Sigil faded back into thin lines on his forehead as it detected a closer exit, allowing him to step out of Murder World.

His foot touched the ground, and the excess mana that clung to him poured out into the open air, burning away the vast majority of living things in his immediate vicinity. The small plants and bugs that managed to survive began to *thrive*, mutating into new variants in an instant. Luke glanced around and scoffed as Zed perked up and began frantically playing his trademark Ukulele at him as if trying to tame a wild animal.

"I always have a huge burst of inspiration when you show up, Luke!" Zed shouted over the gentle thunder that echoed around the area as the pure mana was assimilated into the natural environment. "Ooh! I think I can turn shouting encouragement and praise into a Mastery buff if I-"

Andre stepped through a green circle in the air, the Archdruid having timed his travel to return at roughly the same time as Luke. As far as Zed was concerned, Luke and Andre had only left just shy of two full days prior; the benefit of the time dilation being at fifteen in Murder World and six times base world for The Grove.

The Druid heard Zed's comment and sank into an inquisitive reverie. "Inspiration, you say? I wonder why that might be? Do you think being around him allows for a variant of some kind of minor mana baptism? If that's the case, there's a good chance that you'd benefit from more potent mana channels in the future, as your body grows more comfortable with the pure mana."

"There's an equal chance that his body will burn out, mutating or falling to the ground as a charred husk in a failed mana baptism. That's what happened to all those plants and insects that Andre's so interested in right now," Taylor the Archmage candidate called from the very edge of the pure mana bubble-nova's perimeter as it popped. "Especially when he stands three feet from the portal. You ought to be more careful, Zed."

"Your disapproval means *no~thing*," Zed sing-sang at her as he strummed his instrument dramatically. "Reality is always so much more *vibrant* around Luke! I'm not giving it up, and you can't make me unless you know for *certain* that it'll harm me! My Sigil agrees, and it will let me try my best to get more powerful at every opportunity!"

"Luke, you've had your time. Are you feeling better? Are you ready?" Taylor's cautious prompting made Luke remember the deal they had struck. One hundred percent of his mana surged into his ethereal helmet, causing the gear to appear exactly as it had when he'd first absorbed it. Each flaw, every scratch and dent, was perfectly preserved in the power. It also *buzzed* so loudly from the dense mana that it nearly drowned out Taylor's next words. "Hey! None of that; you promised that you'd come with us to tell your family that you're alive."

"It's the law to inform every family of a surviving Ascender candidate," Zed agreed easily as he strummed his Ukelele at a more sedate pace, then caused it to screech as he asked, "Do you *really* want to ignore them? Is there a good reason, or are you just... a scaredy-cat?"

"I don't know them," Luke answered flatly as he allowed his power to relocate across his six armors and two weapons. "Why put them through this pain when I have no intention of being a part of that family unit again? You know abyss-well that I'm not going to get the freedom to just relax and catch up, especially since I just don't care enough to fight about it. So why are *you* forcing the issue?"

"Wait... this means that you don't want to go because it'll cause *them* pain." Zed's music came to a stuttering halt. His expression grew joyous and delighted. "There *is* a real person with feelings in there!"

"Zed," Andre groaned as Luke tensed up. "Haven't you learned *not* to tease the abyssal *Murderhobo*? Of course he cares; somewhere really, *really* deep down in there. That's not the issue, and you know it. We all want to be out there doing amazing things for the world. Luke's just like us, but he's gone through even more than-"

"Talk like I'm not here, and I'll make sure I'm not," Luke abruptly snapped at the two of them before turning to Taylor. "Any word on my stuff?"

"Yes, in fact. Even though I think you're wasting your coin, it's yours to spend." She calmly ignored the latest in a long series of near-fights that had erupted among the team she was barely leading anymore. "Three master craftsmen Ascenders and their workshops have been hired to exclusively supply you with the highest-quality weapons and armor that can be produced. Two Enchanter Ascenders and their apprentices have also been hired to make the gear even more potent. I *also* hired you a personal butler that will run your estate, since I am *not* your errand girl."

"Not my fault they wouldn't let me into the city," Luke snorted as he turned away. He had the answers he had been looking for. "I *own* two banks now, and I can't even spend the the stupid money. Just another black mark against 'Master' Don. Won't even fight; he'll just revoke access to anything useful."

"At least *your* investments were wise." Andre tried to cheer

Luke up. "The 'Tornado' over here already spent his cut of all that money on buying and *using* the entire red light-"

"*Private*! That's my private business!" Zed yelped frantically.

"Teenagers," Taylor tutted jokingly, getting silence as her only reply.

"Well, uh. Let's go, then. We all have people waiting to see us for the first time in years." Andre paused and snuck an apologetic glance at Zed. "That is... we missed the first chance to return to our town of origin..."

Mood thoroughly awkward, The Four each heaved a sigh for different reasons and began walking the final mile that needed to be crossed to return to their hometown.

The signs of change were everywhere. The fortress had been completed; the power of wealth—and an influx of Ascenders from the area showing off to their families—had accelerated the construction to well-beyond-human capabilities. The Woodswright noble family had moved into the grand structure right away, consolidating power in the area by hiring dozens of locals and cleaning out the surroundings of dangerous animals, bandits, and deserters from the frontlines.

In short, the already-beloved family had become a force of great change in the area, and thus now had influence that stretched into the heart of the Hollow Kingdom. Not only had they become a key defensive resource, but the eldest daughter of the family was slated to become the Archmage. Even her younger siblings were beginning to show signs of Ascender potential. As far as the Kingdom was concerned, the Woodswrights were on the fast-track to success, and everyone wanted to be a part of it.

The Four walked through the gate of a new five-meter-tall stone wall that encircled the entirety of the village, just one of many unexpected structures that struck the group as strange. Many houses had been replaced, upgraded into manors for wealthy citizens; the massive estates were impressive structures that no one originally from the town would have been able to afford a mere two years prior. Yet, the Baron's decree that new members of the town needed to contribute to the area for a full year before being allowed to purchase a home had saved the original inhabitants from being displaced.

Instead of being cast aside and treated as second-class citizens, the residents became landlords able to charge a rate for rent that allowed them to increase their quality of life to an entirely new tier of society. Merchants, contractors, even the families of newly-recruited soldiers rented spare rooms, available houses, or long-term housing at the inn, which had quadrupled in size over the last two years.

However it had happened, the native citizens that had struggled alongside the Baron when the area was poor were now being well-taken care of. Zed noted every detail as they walked through the town and pointed out many changes to both the area and the people that The Four had missed—or forgotten, in Luke's case.

Finally, they came to an area that hadn't changed a bit. Luke studied his familial home and, with his enhanced eyesight, was able to clearly see the faces of his nearly-forgotten family. Luke grunted the names as if they were rusty nails he needed to gargle, eyeing his team to make sure he got them correct. "John, Joanne, and Cindy."

Taylor nodded and tentatively reached out a hand, cautiously resting it on his shoulder, where her flesh tingled against the energetic armor he never dropped. "I hope you'll be able to call them Dad, Mom, and sister."

Luke rolled his head to the side to grace her with a curt look. "Don't count on it."

CHAPTER THREE

Thanks to Zed being the first person to walk over and speak to the family, no one rushed at Luke to give him a hug. In fact, there were *very* few sudden motions whatsoever. Luke took a moment to appreciate how very *useful* a tool the Bard was, and decided at that moment to try and replicate his behavior... "Nah, I'll just keep him around. Yes."

The Murderhobo nodded as his internal monologue became external, interrupting the flow of questions from his family. Cindy was the first to open up again, pure excitement in her voice. There were still tears of joy running down her and Joanne's faces, which made the Murderhobo more uncomfortable with the situation every second. "Was that a 'yes' to me asking if you're staying here? Or was that for taking more missions right away?"

"Wasn't paying attention. Zoned out a minute ago. I was nodding because I was agreeing with myself that Zed is useful," Luke admitted with a flat stare. It wasn't his fault that these people didn't really bother to listen when Zed had told them that they were strangers at this point.

"Aw." The Bard fluttered his eyelashes and pretended to be bashful.

"So you really…" Joanne took a deep breath and exchanged glances with her husband while stealthily wiping at her eyes. "Luke, all else aside, we're glad you're home. We missed you… *so* much."

"I don't want you to think I'm ungrateful for how you raised me. Many of your teachings kept me alive. Zed… tell them what they have now." The Murderhobo looked over his parents. They seemed so… young. Compared to him now, they actually were. He had twenty years more life experience than they did, which was ironically the exact number of years they'd had on him *before* he went into his portal. He shook his head and stood, making it only a single step toward the door before Zed launched into an explanation.

"Thanks for dumping this on me!" Zed actually sounded pleased as he dove into a detailed accounting of Luke's plans. "This filthy hobo… *ahem*. Let me try that again? The generous and *gracious* Murderhobo has found himself with more money than he ever cared to have, and has decided that he wants to gift a portion of his royalties to his family. He has also declined a higher title, instead passing it along to Lord John, though it will automatically revert to Luke later in life. Congratulations, Lord John."

The stunned family stared at the Bard for a long moment and waited awkwardly for better information. Zed coughed lightly into his fist and tried again, slightly less announcer-y this time around. "Luke has purchased your family a noble title, and there's a shipment of gold roughly the size of your house that has been deposited into the royal treasury in your name, as well as unlimited access to two new banking systems owned by Luke directly. You are now, legally, *Viscount* John Von Murderhobo."

"*Viscount?*" John sputtered furiously as he lurched to his feet and slapped a hand on the table. "I *outrank* Baron Woodswright? That… you can't… I don't want it!"

That reaction actually made Luke feel closer to his father for a moment, and he paused at the door to listen. Taylor took the opportunity to glide forward, receiving smiles and hugs as the ladies recognized her. The Mage's impeccable cleanliness and extravagant garb had made her unapproachable until she stepped forward, so they had been averting their eyes, so as to not give offense. "Don't worry about my father. Thanks to my position and a hefty donation, he was promoted to a Marquess. The fact that this has become an important border post made the choice easy for the Kingdom. I'm going to deliver the missive about his new rank when we are finished here, actually."

"I still don't want it!" John resolutely glared at his son, a mammoth, hirsute man that he only recognized thanks to the few surviving family features. It looked as though someone had taken his son and added ninety pounds of muscle, ten pounds of hair, a foot and a half of height, and then ritualistically scarred him across the entire surface of his body. "Just because you're bored with all your money and power? You can't just drop responsibility on other people like this! This will upend our entire lives!"

Luke whirled around and stared down at the man yelling at him. A benefit of the mana baptism that had occurred due to living in Murder World for decades on end was that the constant exposure had *perfected* his body, all the way down to his genes. Every time a cell died, it was replaced by a better version —one suffused with mana. Every part of him had been damaged at some point, including his brain. Had he not been constantly healed from drinking the 'water' of that world, he would have died within seconds after nearly every battle he had experienced during the first few years.

"It's too late. It's done. Take care of them the best way you can. Relax. Enjoy life. Get an education. I don't care." He shook himself, then turned and reached for the door that he had barely fit through. "I've repaid the debt of raising me, and given you the blood price for the son that was taken from you. That boy no longer exists."

He gripped the handle and took a single step out the door.

Cindy cried out in a plaintive voice, "I missed you. We…"

She trailed off, and Luke paused as a memory from long ago bubbled to the surface of his mind. He turned toward her and gave her a full inspection. He had been gone two years, and he found that the awkward fifteen-year-old that had once asked him inane questions had turned into a woman that would be beautiful by any non-Ascender benchmarks. She was unblemished, with very symmetrical features, and her skin was incredibly soft and supple from the work she did as a leatherworker.

"Take this." He reached into a pocket and tore out a small item so fast that the people in the room sucked in a breath in fright. His team nearly gagged, thinking he was attacking; they had seen what he could do. Only Cindy stepped forward, a question burning in her eyes as she watched Luke open a canteen full of water and pull out a strange strip of hide.

Pressure built in the room as the water turned to steam in an instant and pushed the air in the space away. As soon as no more water remained on the hide, the item *burned* in her senses. She could barely look away as it was revealed to be a stunningly beautiful necklace. "What… what is this?"

Cindy took the necklace in a daze, somehow noticing that Luke flinched back just before their hands would have brushed against each other. The leather that held the strange gem in place was intricately worked, filled with the most beautiful engravings that she had ever seen. This was clearly the work of *hundreds* of hours. The gem itself was almost perfectly clear, with just a *hint* of milky whiteness to it.

"Made you a promise before I left." Luke nodded at her, then John, who had been the person that had taught him to honor his obligations. "Promised you a birthday present. Told *you* that I'd keep working at my leatherworking. Oaths fulfilled."

"*I* was promised that my son would come back," Joanne whispered so softly that even Luke almost didn't hear it. His eyes locked with hers, and she didn't recognize the person behind them at all.

"Blood price has been paid." Luke shook his head and kept

his eyes on Cindy, intentionally not seeing the single tear that rolled down Joanne's face. "That thing shouldn't hurt you. Don't eat it."

"What... *eat* it?" Cindy's eyes shot up from the necklace in bewilderment. "Why in the world would I *eat* a necklace?"

"No idea. Just *don't*. It'll make your head explode." Luke pushed the door open fully and stepped out. "If you ever need to escape a monster, throw that and run in the other direction. If you need someone or something dead, convince them to eat the pearl. It won't be hard. Just don't stand next to them when they do it."

"Because... their head will explode." Cindy searched around the room helplessly as Luke marched off without looking back. "Would any of you eat this if I gave it to you?"

"Are you... offering, sweet lady?" Zed inquired as he swallowed with some difficulty. "Now that you mention it... it looks so, *so* tasty."

"Didn't you *just* hear him say it would make your head explode?" Cindy gaped at the Bard, who nodded vigorously.

"I did, yes. Sure; the thing is, just... I almost feel it's worth the risk? Is that really so strange?" Zed reached out for the trinket while slowly smacking and licking his lips. Cindy pulled it back and glared at him. The Bard shook off the strange hypnosis as Cindy fastened the necklace around her neck, and the aura of *want* covered her entire body, instead of being concentrated around the gem. "My Lady, please pardon me... I have no idea...?"

Zed trailed off in confusion, then shook himself again and handed a bundle of legal documents over to John to disguise his feeling of discomfort. "Here's your title, and all the documentation that goes with it. Congratulations again, Viscount Von Murderhobo."

As the Ascenders departed from the small house, John gaped at the documents in despair. "We finally get a last name, and it's 'Murderhobo'? What has he been doing these last two years?"

CHAPTER FOUR

The newly-promoted Marquess Woodswright settled heavily back into his ornate chair and took a hefty swig of his drink to calm his nerves. He skimmed through the documents which Taylor had personally handed him in a daze, then up at the Ascenders that had joined him in his meeting hall. "Do you have any idea what this means?"

"I'm guessing war," Taylor coldly stated before anyone else could speak, eliciting strange looks from her team and a flinch from her father. "The sheer amount of troops that you'll be expected to recruit and maintain as a Marquess will raise the suspicions of the Dynasty. As you increase the forces you have available, they'll increase theirs along the border, until someone accidentally sparks off a major conflict."

"I have time, but at the pace this outlines? Not much." The Marquess sighed and regarded the powerhouses he had sitting in the room with him, and a hopeful light appeared in his eyes. "I'm also allowed to maintain a stable force of Ascenders... what are the four of you doing in the near future?"

That gave the group pause. They had been having that very conversation previously, but the final choice was something that they had agreed would require further discussion. Taylor had lost the trust of the entire team when she had thrown herself into the belly of the beast, nearly dragging the others to their death against the Chimera threat... all for the 'safety' of the Hollow Kingdom. Zed was the first to speak, and even then he was hesitant, allowing room for others to interject if they disagreed.

"I don't know about the others... I kinda want a vacation? While we got a great story from our first mission, and also got great rewards... " Zed eyed his companions helplessly, "I haven't had a moment of relaxation in *years*. I think it's been even worse for them."

"Lying low might be a good idea," Taylor admitted as the room went silent. Most people were lost in thought, only broken by Luke licking the table and muttering that he 'knew this wood wasn't *local* wood'. "What does that mean for us? Where could *we* go to lay low or relax?"

Andre smiled helplessly as he lifted his hand slightly off the table. "We aren't allowed on the front after Luke's... incident... and we haven't been granted an official mission yet. I doubt we will for at least a *little* while, not after we dropped literal mountains of resources on the Kingdom. If it's okay with the rest of you, I'd really like to go take a look at the Scarocco Desert. I've been planning for *years* to get to work on fixing it-"

"Not a bad idea. That's about as remote as you can get." The Lord of the area nodded pensively as he set his cup down with a **thunk**. "Even so, I don't think you should go there. I think you should stay nearby and help protect this area. If I had you here, I'd feel better about supplying skilled troops to the front."

Taylor shook her head. "We can't. You have all four of the most politically-contentious Ascenders in the entire Kingdom in this room. If we stay, none of us will have a single moment of peace. We also don't want anyone to get restless here... again."

Everyone's eyes twitched involuntarily to Luke, who froze

like a rat in a corner, instantly ready to fight. "I needed the weapons and armor."

"You destroyed the guardhouse in one-point-two seconds. I had to tear it the rest of the way down and rebuild the entire place." It was starting to dawn on the Marquess why Taylor wanted them to go. "Zed also has a reputation in town... the more I think about it, the better the desert sounds as a destination vacation for all of you."

Zed appeared utterly scandalized. "Hey! I have a *stellar* reputation."

"People still spit to the side when they speak of you," the Lord bluntly informed him as he resettled himself in his meeting chair. "You're a mind-bender, no matter how passive the Kingdom swore to keep you. No one trusts *any* feelings they have toward you. Not only did you sneak into this town and live off the generosity of my citizens, but you stole from everyone after making them trust you. Worse than that, the ripple effect from there? Everyone is *far* less trusting of each other, because if *one* person can hide away and manipulate everyone to that degree, what is stopping a rogue Bard from doing the same?"

Zed looked crushed as the accusations were piled on mercilessly. Luke slapped the table gently to pull attention to himself as he stood up. "If we have nothing going on, I want more time away. Send me back to Murder World."

Andre shrugged helplessly. "You got ordered by the Archmage directly; you need permission from our handlers to go through. Only someone of a higher rank than the Archmage can allow you more time away. That's either the King, or the Crown Prince. If it's just about fighting, I hear the desert is infested with monsters. The reason it is the *Scar*-rocco Desert, and not the *Rocco* Desert, is because of all the open Scars in the area. If you want to kill things and earn rewards, there'll be lots of chances there."

Luke glared darkly at the Druid. "*Fine.*"

"Among the entire group, Luke has the most, um...

'straightforward' desires." Zed explained to the concerned Lord. "He wants to fight, and get 'Cookie'."

"A cookie? He wants... a cookie?" The Marquess gulped nervously as he eyed the hulking man that had destroyed an entire outpost just to steal cheap weaponry. "Not very... *present*, mentally? Is he controllable?"

Luke slapped the table again and walked out of the room, leaving behind a shattered wreck of wood and cracked stone beneath. Zed coughed into his fist and stood as guards flooded into the room. "He tends to take offense to people saying he needs to be controlled. I think we're off... good to see you again, M'lord."

"Wait... I have some small gifts that might be useful for you. Give this to him... it was the only thing that made me passable in society after *my* training period." The Marquess called just before they departed. He had clearly been debating with himself, but he handed over a book titled 'How to Make Friends and Not Burn Down Society' to Taylor, and offered a strange rock to Zed. "This text is the non-spellbook version, not the one that teaches necromancy or golemancy. For you, Bard; sometimes just feeling useful to those around us is what we need to be happy. With this firestone, you'll always be able to get the campfire going. Hit it on anything, and it'll start on fire for a few seconds. Nothing better than an instant fire no matter how damp or cold the wood is. Good luck."

"Oh, absolutely. Nothing like lighting things on *fire* to feel useful." Zed rolled his eyes, but he did take the stone and toss it into his pocket. "I've got eight instruments, and I'm a Bard in truth, but lighting a *fire* is gonna make me feel good about life.

Three people gave sketchy bows and hurried after a visibly fuming Luke, as did a half-dozen guards that tried to stay out of sight. Taylor wanted to let Luke work though his thoughts, but she also knew that he wasn't exactly someone who was forthcoming about their emotions and feelings. If one of them didn't break the silence, no one would. "Luke, he didn't mean anything by it."

"Huh." Luke acknowledged her with a noncommittal grunt. "Where we goin'?"

"We *are* going to the desert, I believe," Zed cheerfully explained, ignoring the trio of bloodshot eyes that locked onto him. "But first, I think you all need a nap and some water; you seem dehydrated. Not a great starting point when we're going to a desert."

A man came sprinting toward them, his eyes locked on Andre. Luke howled in excitement and lunged at the man, barely restrained in time by grass intertwining and yanking his feet to the ground, tripping him momentarily. The unknown person snapped off a salute and coughed out some of the road dirt that had entered his lungs during the run. "Messenger Friedrich number two-two-nine reporting. I have a top-priority message for the four of you."

Luke remained sprawled on the grass, staring at it as the blades danced in front of him and a flower grew from a seed in under five seconds. Zed nodded magnanimously at the messenger. "Go ahead. *Unless* it's orders for us to go somewhere. Then I'd like for you to pretend you missed us, and go away. M'kay, pumpkin?"

"I have orders for you... um. To..." The young man was flustered by Zed's words, clearly uncertain for a moment if he should continue. He finally shook his head and relayed the words he had been entrusted with. "For the high-risk bounty-hunting group of Ascenders that has recently returned from a successful campaign against the Dynasty of Dogs and enriched the Hollow Kingdom, you are cordially ordered to appear before King Alexander at the best speed you can manage as a group."

As soon as his pronouncement was complete, the man held up a document bearing the seal of the King, and all four of the Ascenders' Sigils flashed as one.

Mandatory order given. Begin to travel at once.

"Cordially... *ordered*. What did I *just* tell you, Friedrich?" A single sigh slipped from Zed's lips as they all adjusted the direction they were walking and started moving faster. "You guys are going to leave me behind again, aren't you?"

"I can carry you." Andre offered, and Zed hopped onto his back without even a moment of hesitation, taking both of them to the ground. The Bard looked just as surprised as Andre, who stood and took a moment to adjust his vines to 'walk' for them both.

"I... suppose the orders were for the best speed we could manage?" Zed's expression shifted toward downcast and troubled. "I hate that magic is so literal."

The messenger bowed at them as they began to speed away from the backwater border town. As he stood up, a rock whizzed by his head, and he jumped back while frantically searching for his attacker. Zed shook a fist at the man he had tossed a rock at. "I told you to keep your fat mouth *shut*! I wanted to *like* you, Friedrich!"

"Why are you even complaining, Zed?" Taylor inquired as Zed howled about the 'indignity of being carried along like an invalid'. "Isn't this a great chance for you to get into a populated area and start gathering experience and followers? We'll stop at an inn or two along the way, and there is no way that we'll get in to see the King as soon as we arrive. A power play will happen, and we'll be forced to wait for *days* after getting orders to go there 'right now'."

"You're saying we'll need to sit on our thumbs and *wait* after getting to the capital?" Zed eyed her suspiciously, though a smile was threatening to grow on his face. "You think they're *really* going to be so rude as to maybe not even put us in nice housing, and instead force us to pay for our own lodging after ordering us to go there?"

"Sounds like *exactly* what a bunch of stuck-up nobles would do, to me." Andre's murmur earned him a glare from the only person who had been a noble her entire life.

"*Yes!*" Zed bounced in place excitedly, causing Andre to stumble a little. "I'm gonna make sure we're the most well-loved team in the entire Kingdom by the time they make us go anywhere!"

"Just don't do *anything* stupid," Taylor ordered him shortly as the wind started to pick up. She glanced up, checking for rain clouds as she strolled along. "The capital is the seat of power for the King, and there will be people reporting on everything we do, and *especially* every word we say."

"My *best* behavior!" Zed smiled at her brightly. "I won't accidentally embarrass a soul!"

CHAPTER FIVE

"So there he was—his very first step out of training—and Luke punches the Archmage in the face!" Zed's story made the patrons of the tavern howl with laughter, even more so when he recounted what the Archmage had done to Luke directly after he had gotten over his initial surprise.

Zed would have left off the second part, but that might be *mistaken* as going out of his way to damage the reputation of an official. People kept tossing glances at Luke, who was taking up an entire bench at a long table by himself. Not a single one of them doubted the fact that this glaring beast in their midst would be happy to break them in half, if given the chance; lending credibility to the Bard's tale.

Luke was *not* happy to be the center of attention. His glare was entirely directed at Zed, who had terrible gooseflesh and shivers running up and down his spine constantly due to the rage contained in that stare. The Murderhobo scowled at Andre and hissed, "Can I leave yet?"

They'd been in the capital a full week already, and every morning had needed to appear at the King's court to see if he would have time to see them after the 'important affairs of state' that regularly took place during the day. Luke was getting *restless*. Every day that he couldn't get back to Murder World was another *fifteen* days that Cookie needed to wait for him to find her.

"Soon, Luke," Andre promised him as he ordered another plate of food for each of them. He had discovered, quite by accident, that he was able to entice his friend with food; the tastier, the better. So far, he had been completely unable to bring Luke to a point that he couldn't eat any more. "Today I'm having them bring in an entire cow, plate by plate, for you. Think you're up for it?"

Luke's glare lessened fractionally, and he even snuck a quick glance at the door that the food had been coming out of. His eyes whisked back to Andre a moment later. "You don't know what kind of game you're playing here. I once ate an entire berry bush, roots and all, just to try something new. Goats were working together too well for me to eat meat that day."

"I have just… no *idea* how those sentences relate to each other," Andre brightly exclaimed as a trickle of sweat started running down his forehead. He had plenty of coin to spend, but he didn't *really* want to buy an entire cooked cow for Luke. Zed swung over to their table a moment later, winking furiously at the Druid.

"Guys. Guys." Zed blinked owlishly as he leaned over with a goofy grin on his face. "Have you tried this moonshine stuff they make here? I got like… three extra wineskins of it for us to try later. Together. It never goes bad, they promised."

"You stink, Zed," Luke unceremoniously informed him. "Stay away from the fire. I think you might light up if you get within five feet of it."

"Speaking of things that are hot, I need that special flower that sings and increases stamina," Zed stage-whispered to Andre, jerking his head to the side to point out a local lass that had been giving him her *full* attention. Andre shook his head and produced a seed of the Mountain Willow Wind flower. He accessed his mana and handed over a softly chiming flower a moment later. "Thanks, buddy! You're a better wingman than a whole *host* of florists!"

Zed swayed over to the table confidently, engaging the woman in conversation for a short while before suddenly presenting the flower with a flourish. Luke watched the entire process while chewing on some overly-cooked steak, snorting in agitation when the two vanished into the dark stairwell. He stopped munching for a moment, looked down at his steak, then scanned the room for the person who had delivered the food. She was nowhere to be seen. "You shouldn't eat that."

Luke reached over and grabbed the meat off Andre's plate, then chomped down mercilessly as Andre gaped in shock. The Druid collected himself with a deep inhalation. "Why did you just steal my food?"

"I'm overhealing." Luke informed the other man, as if his words meant something profound, motioning for another cut of steak from a dumbfounded server that *did* work there. "Also, you should probably go save Zed."

"Pretty sure he doesn't *want* to be saved right now," Andre muttered as he waved for more food.

"Okay. I guess." Luke agreed with a strange glance and shrug at the redhead. "Taylor's back."

The door to the tavern nearly fell apart as the Namer slammed it out of the way while sprinting into the room. "Let's go! Our appointment is *now*; it got moved up suddenly! If we aren't there in ten minutes—where's Zed?"

"He was led away by some kind of assassin," Luke informed her as he chewed through his mouthful of steak. "Probably the same one that dosed this food with hallucinogens."

"*What?*" Andre yelped and leapt to his feet. "Why didn't you stop her?"

"*You* told me not to save him." Luke paused his chewing and stared up at the Druid. "You mean to tell me you couldn't smell the poisons she was carrying? They're mostly plant-based, so I figured you had a handle on it."

"Smell...? I'm all Capacity, Luke!" Andre closed his eyes

and concentrated on the upper floors. He felt one presence that had dozens of tiny plants with them, then pricked his finger and drew a circle in the air to connect with the plants at a distance. A scream of pain and rage pierced the air a moment later. The three of them rushed up the stairs, following the noise. Luke kicked in the door, turning it to dust and twisted metal, then watched passively as foam bubbled out of a corpse's mouth.

"I can get rid of this. Now that I'm looking for it, this is just a concentrated dose of mushroom spores. Mind-altering, but not deadly." Zed lay unconscious right next to the bubbling body, but Andre managed to clear the plant byproducts out of his body in only a few seconds, reviving the Bard, even if he was groggy.

"Trisha? Where'd you…?" He squinted up and found the remainder of his party hovering over him. "Oh, *not* cool, people!"

"How could a *Bard* fall for this?" Taylor scathingly gave the practically-naked man a once over. "We need to stop and think about this: I bet we were the *last* to know about our appointment with the King. The poisoner, the last-minute summon…? This woman was clearly someone specialized in discrediting political opponents. You would have been out of your mind, and *still* forced to go in front of the royal court. Get dressed; we need to go."

She swept out of the room, still fuming. Luke turned to go with her, continuing to munch on meat, which Andre regarded with concern before stopping him. "When you said that was bad for me and good for you…?"

"Oh, it's poisoned. For sure. Just something that would make your innards turn to liquid and run out your pants." Luke took a deep bite and let out a refreshed burp. "Just 'spicy meat' to me."

"Immune to poisons? Overheal; does that mean…" Andre trailed off as his guess earned him a cold stare for his troubles, which reminded him how rude it was to ask someone else about the powers to which they had access: it was the same as sussing out their weaknesses. "I thought we were past the suspicions and cold shoulders."

"Maybe after we kill a few hundred more things as a group, we'll all feel better." Zed hopped out of bed and swayed woozily. "Mostly okay… no lingering mental dizziness, just balance issues."

Andre watched Luke's retreating form, feeling resignation as he grabbed Zed and tossed him over his shoulder. "Hey, Zed. Do you really think that's all it's gonna take? Some more time together?"

"That's what all the stories say. The power of friendship grows through shared suffering." Zed shifted around to get as comfortable as possible, already used to this form of undignified travel. "Wouldn't be a cliche unless there was *some* truth to it, right?"

"I guess?" The group warned the staff on the way out that the food was poisoned and left the stricken tavern-goers to worry for their lives on their own. There was an important meeting they were going to be late for.

———

"The four of you are permitted to enter the Grand Hall," a royal guard finally announced, after they had been left waiting outside the doors for at least a full hour. Luke was staring at the man near-hungrily; he could practically *taste* the Etheric Xenograft Potentia surging through this man.

The others might have felt suppressed by the powerful aura of an expert that swirled around the guard, but all Luke wanted to do was test his mettle. There was something almost… *fluffy* about the high-leveled Ascender, as if his accumulated Potentia was cotton thread that ran through him—while the Potentia within Luke's own group was like steel wire. They accomplished the same thing, but the steel thread would be able to bear a massively higher load. "Why are you weak, like a suit of armor filled with feathers?"

"What did you just say to me?" The guard paused and looked at Luke, flinching involuntarily before rage filled his eyes as he registered the Murderhobo's near-hunger. Luke took a single step forward, towering over the guard. Luckily, before he could open his mouth and implicate himself further, the court herald announced them. They were ushered inside, and Taylor took the opportunity to sidle up to Luke and whisper a harsh reprimand.

"Every royal guard is at *least* level eighteen," she informed him while smiling brightly and waving to the surrounding crowd of nobles. "Please don't get us killed here. Let us do the talking; you just relax and ignore everything as best as you can. Do that for me, and I'll try to pull in a favor to get you back to your world a week ahead of schedule."

Luke fired a sharp glance at Taylor, making her realize that he now knew she had *always* been able to maneuver for a favor like that, and simply hadn't. She sighed and tried to get into the moment. Taylor knew she had lost a lot of trust back in the mountain pass when she had been willing to sacrifice everyone to save the Kingdom. Even so, she hadn't realized that meant that every single little action she took was going to be scrutinized by them from then on. "Gonna have to do something big to get them back on my side-"

"King Alexander speaks!" The herald's voice boomed across the room, stilling the voices and softly whispered schemes.

The King of the Hollow Kingdom gazed around the room and nodded, as if seeing something he approved of. His eyes turned and lightly rested on them in order, touching on Taylor, analyzing Andre, zipping past Zed, and finally landing on Luke, where most of his attention languished. "*Thank you.*"

The simple statement caused the Grand Hall to buzz with confused whispering. The King ignored the hushed commotion and leaned forward slightly. "Because of your efforts, this land is *sprinting* toward a golden new age. The sheer quantity of resources—not to mention the quality—recovered by the four of you will outfit our armies, build and rebuild our cities, and push our research capabilities forward by decades, at the *least*."

The room filled with polite clapping as the King paused. He allowed the applause to continue for a moment, then raised a hand a fraction of an inch. The onlookers fell silent once more. "As you know, a percentage of the value of those resources which your small group granted us has been turned to coin and a line of credit in recognition of your contribution, and I had hoped that-"

"*Peasants.*" A surly young man seated next to the King scoffed lightly, but not softly enough.

The King turned to contemplate the boy with calm eyes. "Did you have something to say, Crown Prince Vir?"

"You know my thoughts on this, Your Highness." Prince Vir observed the team with disdainful eyes. "They are merely performing their *duty*. Why award them with such high honors for simply doing what they are *supposed* to do? Do we laud the servants when they clean our bedpans?"

"An interesting view on the people you will *perhaps* rule one day." The King gazed into the distance and went quiet for a moment. Then his eyes twinkled as he regarded the four standing awkwardly before him, and winked. "You seem to think that these four Ascenders have only acted as they are *meant* to do. As if *exceeding* expectations was *the* expectation. In that case... tell me why no other *fifty* Ascenders combined in this Kingdom have... *ever*... done what they did?"

Before the Prince could say a word, King Alexander began listing their accomplishments. "As new Ascenders, fresh from initial training, they repelled an invasion. They *closed* a Scar. A literal mountain of resources was gifted to the Kingdom, instead of being squirreled away through a portal for personal use, as would have been their *right*. I think they've gone *far* beyond simply 'doing their duty', and I will award them accordingly."

"Wait, we could have kept *all* of that?" Zed whispered as he tapped Andre. Three members of the team turned cold eyes on Taylor, who began to sweat.

"I think *you're* being wasteful," the Prince scoffed. "They already got… their…"

King Alexander whirled on the young man with fury in his eyes, and the Prince knew he had gone too far. Before he could apologize, the King's soft voice issued a challenge. "In that case, how about a *bet*? I have faith that these four new Ascenders can crush any of your sponsored teams that have spent the same amount of time as an Ascender. Choose any of your teams with less than two and a half years in service to the Crown."

"Go on. What are the terms?" The fear that had jumped into Prince Vir's eyes vanished as the challenge was offered. He leaned forward as the King elaborated.

"If your sponsored group is able to win in a fair mirror match, I'll gift each individual with *all* of the total Potentia they have collected for the Kingdom. If your team loses, you'll need to offer these Ascenders full of 'farce'… let's say, *half* the Potentia they have collected for the Kingdom since the day they began training. Now, as we cannot use the Kingdom's resources for something of this nature, the cost will be taken from our weekly sponsorship resources until the debt is paid. What say you?"

"Against them? Right now; not after you equip them?" Prince Vir shook his head in amazement as King Alexander nodded grimly. "Absolutely. I look forward to bringing my team to loftier heights. Herald, bring out the Knights of 'Heaven's Earth'. We have a duel!"

The room erupted in cheering, and the four Ascenders waiting patiently glanced at each other with complicated gazes. Taylor leaned in to the others. "The King knew this would happen. Others must have guessed as well… now the attack against us in the inn makes sense."

Luke spat on the highly polished floor, earning a wince from the other three. "I don't *perform*."

"You know," Zed slipped into the budding argument before

anyone else could make Like dig his heels in further, "I've always wanted to know how much exp was being drained from us. I always knew it was a possibility, but…"

That gave Luke pause. He looked down, then up, and finally into Taylor's eyes. "How much have they stolen?"

"What? Why would *I* know?" Taylor appealed to the others for consensus, collecting only flat stares in return. "All I know is that they do take it as a small tax. They use it to pay for guards and people that can't go into their own world, since they are serving the Kingdom directly."

"That's an *option*?" Zed hissed at her, shocked that he had never even heard of it as a possibility. "That would *literally* solve all of my problems in no time flat!"

"Is that why that guy was fluffy?" Luke's grunt derailed the conversation, as the others weren't sure what to make of it. "Was it a lack of *earned* Potentia? Let's be careful not to use too much of that for gaining levels when we win."

"Not sure what you mean by that, but okay. Hey, at least the King said it'd be a fair duel, right?" Zed was interrupted by a small team entering the room. As soon as they arrived, pressure pushed the majority of the Nobility back. Their auras of the newcomers were powerful and wild, raging like unchained tigers. They smoothly approached the King and bowed with perfect court etiquette.

One of them—the team leader, if Luke had to guess—removed his shiny helmet to reveal perfectly coiffed golden hair. "Your Majesty. Your Highness. We welcome this opportunity to display our skills before the court."

"Feel free to humiliate them, Sir Edward," Prince Vir ordered casually. The team slammed fists to their breastplates in unison and turned as one to face Luke's group, who suddenly found themselves feeling very ragtag. Only Taylor looked as perfect as these Royal-sponsored Ascenders. Luke's and Zed's clothes were torn and stained—both for different reasons—and Andre's clothes were entirely natural; a mix of animal furs and plant matter.

Zed rubbed his chin and nodded sagely. "Oh, I get it. Their *interpretation* of fair. Not actually, you know, *fair* fair."

"Archmage, if you will." King Alexander nodded to another seat. Both Luke and Taylor's eyes snapped to that space, just in time to see Archmage Don nod and begin forming a spell circle in midair. The King took the few moments of needed casting time to explain. "The *Mirror Moment* spell will allow you to fight at full force until one team has been fully eliminated. Once a team has been wiped out, you will return to reality. All damage done in that time will be as a dream, so don't hold back. The winners will be granted bottled Potentia in the amount of half of the accumulated quantity taxed from them over the last two and a half years."

"I wish you luck." The King's voice echoed strangely as their surroundings faded. Only the four members of Luke's team and the five members of 'Heaven's Earth' remained. "Begin."

CHAPTER SIX

In the same instant that the King had ordered the start of the duel, an astral wind began whipping around all five members of Heaven's Earth. One of the men was chanting something, and he appeared to be creating a large-scale group buff. Luke glanced at Zed, then the Knights, then back to Zed. "Hey. Why don't you have something team-use like that?"

"The Kingdom had been intentionally suppressing my Masteries before I joined this team. Bards are just *so~o* scary, apparently." Zed sighed dramatically as they stood there and watched the opposing team power up, one after another. "Are we just going to let them keep dancing around and adding more auras to themselves?"

"It's fun to watch them get all excited. Kinda like watching a bunch of children pretend to be mages, or sword fight with sticks." Taylor snorted as one of the knights held his wrist at eye level and spun in place, resulting in his armor being coated in energy and thickening slightly. "I'm gonna get started. Andre?"

"I already killed them; you can show off if you want." Andre leaned his back against his staff, which somehow fully supported his weight without budging even slightly. The others looked at him askanse, and he shrugged. "King said not to hold back, right? Luke, they're worth a lot of Potentia, if you want to take it."

"I can go all-out on them? I have a new thing I want to try, and I really want to see if they're actually as weak as I sense they are." Luke glanced around just to ensure his Sigil wasn't about to stop him. Taylor nodded stoically, and Luke's head snapped forward so he could focus on his opponents. He eyed them for a few long moments, then began muttering his evaluations. "They were called 'knights' and sponsored by the Prince. I feel like they're at least level... fifteen? But... they have that same fluffy feeling the Royal Guards did."

He glanced at his own stat sheet for a quick comparison.

Cal Scan
Level: 9
Current Etheric Xenograft Potentia: 3,333/8,900 to level 10!
Body: 30.1

- *Fitness: 40.2*
- *Resistance: 20*

Mind: 18.6

- *Talent: 16.3*
- *Capacity: 20.9*

Presence: 14.5

- *Willpower: 23*
- *Charisma: 6*

Senses: 22.4

- *Physical reaction: 27.5*
- *Mental energy: 17.3*

Maximum Health: 250
Maximum Mana: 324
Mana regen: 5.43 per second

"Okay. I'm at a disadvantage because they're all ready now, right? *Bum Rush!*" Luke dropped all of his armor and devoted eighty percent of his total mana to his Battering Ram Knuckles, spent ten mana on Bum Rush, then used nearly the entirety of his remaining mana on activating *Shockwave Cleave* for the first time. He covered the distance between the two teams in an instant, releasing his pulled-back fist.

Warning! Mana dangerously low: 4.85/324.2 mana.

Space distorted around his brightly glowing clenched hand; his mana was packed so densely that the light actually *bent*. To the Knight Captain's credit, he pulled a glowing tower shield between himself and the incoming fist in that bare instant. Sir Edward braced himself, fully confident in his team's protections.

The fist landed.

Metal screamed as the shield was bent inward, and the arm holding it steady broke in an instant. Edward's eyes widened fractionally as his gear failed, then narrowed as he pushed back as hard as he could.

Damage dealt: 599 blunt damage!

Edward activated a burst of his own damage-soaking Feats, dropping the total damage he received to a fraction of what had actually landed. If he could have seen the notifications that Luke received at the same moment, he would have spat blood from gnashing his teeth so hard.

Damage dealt: 299.5 blunt damage x2!

Damage dealt: 150 blunt damage x2!

The Knights had been standing in a wedge formation, and it was typically considered the best defensive formation in small-scale battles. Unfortunately for them, it allowed Luke to damage each of the subordinate Knights at the same time. The two directly behind Edward failed to make any preparations to receive an attack beyond the buffs, and the shockwave that reached them utterly liquified their internal organs. The final two took heavy damage but managed to keep their feet.

Seeing two of his team die from the very *first* attack, Edward roared like a lion and swung a glowing sword at Luke. Luke snarled like a wolf in return and backhanded the blade, his strike causing the metal to vibrate like a gong. In the moment that Edward was forced to spend in bringing his sword back under control, Luke managed to redistribute his mana so that each item of his Walking Arsenal was allocated ten percent, his standard for combat.

The remaining Knights dashed forward, each of them wielding a variant of a sword in an attempt to suppress Luke fully. A claymore bounced off his seemingly unprotected chest, with only a hint of his *Simple Metal Cuirass* mana armor appearing; even that only lasted long enough to turn the blade before breaking. Plenty of force managed to reach Luke, as the twelve and a half points of armor was a joke in front of the heavy weapon.

Damage taken: 85 blunt.

Health: 165/250

Luke's body shuddered, and he coughed out a spatter of blood. His focus increased; he had stopped letting pain control him *decades* ago. He dropped into a horse stance as another blade whizzed by his head, then punched out with full force at the man wielding the two-handed claymore.

Damage dealt: 110 blunt damage!

The metal cuirass protecting the Knight was torn through as easily as if it had been made of tissue paper, dissipating the majority of the force, but it was unable to stop Luke's hand from piercing through to his opponent's chest and poking a hole in his heart.

The Knight died and vanished like fog burning away under the scorching light of day. Edward said a word and *pushed*, sending the Murderhobo tumbling away in a burst of divine-seeming light.

Damage taken: 110 solar.

Health: 55/250

Luke came to a halt only by hitting the wall and shattering it. His entire body was covered in a thick layer of charcoal, the first few layers of his skin ready to flake into powder from the lightest brush of wind. He peered at the battle though damaged eyes, barely able to make out the remainder of the fight.

Partially because his eyes were crisped, but mainly because combat ended a mere instant later.

A Flame Lance tore into Edward's damaged shield, carving through the warped metal and broiling the Knight from the inside, followed by a series of ice and force shards from Scatter Shot. Tyalor wasn't the only one that had been making preparations as Luke held the opposing team's attention. As the spells petered out, thorns erupted *out* of the Knights, and the sponsored team was unable to dodge the plants that had finished growing inside of them.

Between the two attacks, the remaining Knights vanished from the Mirrored Moment zone, leaving behind wooden constructions that could easily be repurposed as scarecrows. Clearly, the plants had been growing for a while, yet the Knights hadn't sensed even a *hint* of crisis before the barbs had erupted outward from every part of their bodies.

The dreamlike setting faded, and so too did the injuries which each of the four had accrued. In a blink, they were once more facing team Heaven's Earth. However, at least *one* major difference was immediately apparent: the overbearing and arrogant aura had faded away, leaving behind shaken and sweating Knights. The surrounding court was silent for an extended moment; clearly only one person in the crowd had expected that a group at least five levels weaker—and one member fewer—would prevail.

The King clapped gently, speaking loudly over the explosive curses that erupted from Crown Prince Vir at the same moment. "Very impressive! Your capabilities are a true testament to what can be achieved when *earning* your power through harsh training and true combat. If my information is correct, you are just shy of half of the total power allowed for remaining on this plane of existence. I truly look forward to seeing what you can achieve as you grow."

"There's no *way* they should have won! That is *bullsh…* that is… Your Highness, I feel that something is amiss with this result." Prince Vir coughed lightly at the intense stare he was subjected to when erupting publicly. "My Knights are undergoing strict Royal Guardsmen training, being instructed by the best of the best. How could *they* possibly…?"

"How indeed? Why… we may need to rethink our *entire* training methodology for *all* of our Royal Guard at this rate!" King Alexander allowed a smile to play around the corners of his mouth as he hushed his overexcited progeny. The defeated Knights winced as the full Royal Guards in the room glared at them sharply. "As for the winners of our little wager, I think we should certainly release their winnings to them, no?"

The King looked first at Zed. "By my authority, and the agreement of Crown Prince Vir, what do we owe you?"

"Well, about that, Your Highness…" The Bard opened his mouth to answer with pure uncertainty, but he was cut off as a low chime swept through the room, the noise originating from his Sigil. A number appeared on his forehead, magnified and projected to the Grand Hall at large. "Oh, well, nevermind, then."

Etheric Xenograft Potentia owed: 1,760.

There were a few impolite chuckles from various Ascenders in the area, and Zed flushed with shame for a reason he didn't understand. The King cleared his throat lightly. "As a… token of my appreciation for participating in this surely unwanted duel, I'll directly increase your reward to two thousand Potentia, taken from my private stores."

"Just two thousand? That's not even a full week's stipend. That's not so bad." Zed's highly trained ears twitched as he overheard one of the Knights of Heaven's Earth mutter. All the Bard could do was try to mask his fury, and he bowed to the King to hide his thunderous expression.

The monarch turned to Taylor. "For you?"

Etheric Xenograft Potentia owed: 25,850.

"*What?*" Crown Prince Vir shot to his feet and roared, "How could this weak *Mage* have possibly-"

"*Vir!*" King Alexander bellowed at his heir, slamming a hand onto his throne. "You *dare* act like this in front of me? The *Court?* You truly want to spit upon the honor of the direct Apprentice of the Archmage? This debt *will* be paid! Forcing this sort of act and reneging on your word, once given, would remove *all* of our authority, deactivating her Sigil and giving her free rein to leave our Kingdom! By the celestials above, I would *personally* ensure that she left to pursue her passions rather than remaining loyal to a failed future King!"

That announcement shocked everyone present to their core. Prince Vir was alternating between flushing with fury and going pale at the thought of insulting three *very* important people all in one go. "That's four *months* of resources for one of my sponsored Knight squads!"

"I'll add my own resources to increase the amount to an even twenty-six thousand. Perhaps, Vir, you'll learn to understand *exactly* what you are getting into before betting next time. Perhaps this lesson will one day save our Kingdom from ruin." King Alexander coldly cut down any arguments, then addressed Andre. "What is owed to you, *Archdruid?*"

The Prince, hearing that magical politically-charged word, groaned and fell back into his chair.

Etheric Xenograft Potentia owed: 37,630.

"How is this even being *calculated?*" the Prince wailed into his hands as he read the amount. "They haven't even been active for six months! They just got out of training!"

"Twenty percent of all Potentia they've gained has been given to us as a tithe," the King announced grandly, for all to hear and understand. "Half of that is going back to them. This will serve as an additional reward to them for the grand service they've accomplished for the Kingdom. Give them these resources with no ill will, and allow the proof that you promptly pay your debts to your subjects to inspire confidence in your future rule."

Many of the Nobles nodded at these wise words, and soon the only people wearing unpleasant expressions were Prince Vir and Zed. The King nodded at Andre. "I'll increase that to a full forty thousand, Archdruid. Luke Von Murderhobo, what is owed to you?"

The Sigil on Luke's head began to brighten, then spin and flash as numbers began to emerge. A line of text appeared in Luke's vision that no one else was able to see.

If these pigs want to continue to toy with you, let's see how fat they really are. Hope you like bacon! Source-cerer protocols are increasing your earnings… complete.

Etheric Xenograft Potentia owed: 130,035.

CHAPTER SEVEN

"What in the *abyss*, Luke?" Taylor gasped as the rest of the room collectively sharply inhaled. "Did you kill an *Archdemon* or something?"

Luke shrugged and watched the Crown Prince hungrily. If there was even a *hint* that the amount due wouldn't be granted, he was fully prepared to Open Up a portal and vanish forever. As soon as the magic binding him loosened…!

"O-one *hundred*!" Prince Vir's voice shook, and he looked like he was about to pass out. Even King Alexander was gawking at that number in shock. He knew it was impossible for an Ascender to monkey with their Sigils, else he'd directly accuse Luke of doing so. "So many… that's *years'* worth of… I… *refuse*…!"

Luke leaned forward, ready to make a break for it. The motion didn't go unnoticed. The Prince stared at the Murder-hobo with a feverish, intense gaze, then swallowed and amended his statement, turning green, as though he might vomit. "Forgive that lapse… I understand this lesson, Your Majesty. The Potentia shall, of course, come from my personal stock."

"Good." The King nodded proudly. He had been concerned with the company the young heir had been keeping, and it was good to see that his top choice to inherit had been able to recognize some of his flaws with such a small cost. The show was over, and it was time to move on to the meat of this audience. "As for you... that is, Namer Taylor, what is your team name?"

"Reporting to Your Majesty, we have... not really-"

Zed advanced with a wide smile on his face and swept into a dramatic bow. "Your Majesty! Lords and Ladies, please pardon my interruption. We, the prospective Archmage, the Archdruid, the Murderhobo, and perhaps, one day, the King's Own Herald..."

The True Bard trailed off and waggled his eyebrows at the King, earning a chuckle from the vast majority of attendees. "Though we have high hopes for our futures in the Kingdom, we know that the first rule of propriety is to stay humble and understand our standing. While today you truly make us feel grand, we hope you will allow our moniker to become an official designation. We are merely 'The Four', and desire to remain as such."

A smattering of applause rang out at this 'humble' display, and even the Prince managed a bitter smile at the Bard's antics. King Alexander nodded and waved his hand magnanimously. "Let it be done."

Achievement gained: Named by the King. Your party has achieved an official Royal designation. +500 exp.

Luke slapped away the notification that was buzzing around his head like an annoying fly. At that moment, a small platoon of Royal guardsmen pushed a cart into the room. As they uncovered the cart, the revealed contents glowed, a rainbow appearing around the displayed vials.

"If you will come into the private meeting chambers, there are a few matters we need to attend to that will assuredly bore the Lords and Ladies to no end. As for the rest of you, I hope you'll save your burning questions for the feast this evening. I suspect this Bard will have a good tale for us." King Alexander stood amongst the polite laughter, and everyone else scrambled out of their seats to offer a proper bow or curtsy as the King walked out.

A guardsman motioned for The Four to follow, and moments later they found themselves in a far cozier room. They sat at the King's behest, and Luke noticed that not even a single guard was present; only The Four, the King, and the Archmage, who stepped in a few moments after they did. Zed looked around the room, almost *vibrating* with excitement. "I can't wait for the feast! I get to speak to the entire royal court for an extended period?"

"The room is sealed?" the King murmured, getting a nod in reply from the Archmage. As soon as he got the all-clear, King Alexander deflated like a pierced waterskin and gazed at The Four with sorrowful eyes. "I'm *terribly* sorry for the position I've put you in. You need to vanish, likely for the next few years. The little play I put on today was the best that I could do to outfit you with the proper resources you deserve without causing an outcry, though I fear even *that* has earned you the enmity of Vir."

"So he wasn't a part of that?" Taylor questioned as the others frowned in confusion. "I thought he did very well, and I had been hoping he would be an ally in the future."

"Unlikely." The King sighed sadly. "The sad fact of the matter is that most people want your heads for drawing so much attention to us. The Dynasty of Dogs is already sniffing around in hopes that we will slip up and hand them a small hill of precious metals as a bribe to leave us be for a short time."

"Your Majesty... what's happening?" Andre inquired directly, growing very concerned when the King did not meet his eyes.

"A massive influx of wealth is often an issue for those who have never held responsibility before." Master Don was the one to answer as the silence stretched. "Simply *having* resources does not make things happen. Getting them into the hands of crafters, enchanters, architects—whatever it may be—also gets a portion into the hands of each noble house as they collect tax. All of a sudden, we have huge mercenary groups being hired, and… large bounties on each of your heads."

"You're joking," Zed denied instantly. "Why?"

"An Archmage is always a target. The *only* Druid in a kingdom? A weak Bard? A man that ran onto a battlefield and killed hundreds with no retribution?" The King listed each of them one-by-one. "Your achievements and growth in such a short amount of time point to the fact that we are on the rise once more. The Dynasty will *handsomely* reward your killers. The company that Prince Vir keeps? I'm certain they'll be pushing for him to go after you in some misguided honor-killing."

"You can't do anything to stop this? To help us?" Andre rose to his feet, his Livingwood Staff in hand.

King Alexander shook his head, then locked eyes with Taylor and enunciated. "I can give you a head start, and only the *legal protection* available to any other Ascender. Go somewhere remote. Archmage, assist their escape."

"Grab your rewards. The Scarrocco Desert is a good choice. A decade or so of work and making little progress should help the vermin infesting the capitol forget about your contributions." Don stepped forward, his power reaching out and beginning to pull at the fabric of reality. "You, Murderhobo. You're ordered not to attempt an attack upon my person."

"*Mother-*" Luke snarled as his thrown fist reversed and hit himself in the face, cutting off his cursing.

King Alexander spoke before any other questions could escape the group's lips. "There are many—far too many—who look at the vast resources you've delivered on a platter and are now *content* with our lot. You've given us the opportunity to have a golden age in our Kingdom, and many fear that any more growth will be what turns the full might of the Dynasty of Dogs upon us. They want their benefactors to vanish forever, or to discredit you to the point that *anything* else you do will be distrusted in the extreme. I will likely never see you again, but I thank you for all you have done for us. *Run.*"

A portal snapped into place, a strange purple light emanating from within. The others took a step forward, following the will of the King, but Luke resisted long enough to say, "I want more time in my world."

"The Archmage told me of your circumstances." The King stared at Luke levelly. "I can't give you more than you earn, but I can make sure you are *never* denied. I, King Alexander, decree that you are permanently allowed to enter your personal portal to Murder World every thirty days at the absolute minimum. If your handlers allow more time, that is acceptable. If you are in a dire situation, or if you have life-threatening injuries, and the best course of action is to enter your world, you have permission to do so without repercussions for up to a week of your subjective time."

"Good enough." As Luke walked to the portal, the last thing he heard was the Archmage instructing Taylor.

"Ambushes will likely be near-constant. If you are attacked first, I grant authority for you to deal with *any* attacker however you will. Do your best not to kill citizens, as that will still subject you to the Kingdom's scrutiny. This permission is backed by King Alexander's authori-"

Luke peered around this strange world that he had stepped into, his mind reeling from the alien… everything. Taylor appeared next to him several subjective minutes later; probably only a moment later for her. The portal behind them vanished, accompanied by the sound of static electricity discharging. She took a deep breath and gazed at their surroundings comfortably. "Welcome to 'mundi sunt nominibus singulorum'. This is my world."

"It's nice," Andre offered as he watched a book launch into the air and start circling them like a vulture. "Very… um… homey."

"Zed's dying," Luke tattled to the others as Zed tried once

more to take a breath, failed, and sank to his knees, lips already going blue.

"Son of a-" Andre grabbed the bard and tried to examine him, discerning the problem in an instant. "The mana in the air is too dense; his body is going to shut down. Even if he survives, he's going to be undergoing a mana baptism. We need to get him out of here before he burns out."

"We can't! The King ordered us to escape, and our only possible destination is the desert; at sprinting speed, it's still a week's travel away." Taylor shook her head grimly even as she wracked her brain in an attempt to find a solution.

"Seriously? *This* is too much for him?" Luke sat down and looked up at the sky, where a huge cloud was drifting. His eyes focused on it, and he realized the cloud was made of tens of thousands of words, each of them describing a portion of its existence.

Cloud. Wet. Floating. Dozens of words were written, erased, and rewritten each second, describing the distance to the ground, as well as the topography of the cloud itself. The entire structure was a constantly changing dictionary drifting along. "This is actually pretty relaxing. I can see why you like it here."

"Wait! What if he levels up?" Taylor struck on the concept as she noticed the light shining from their packs. "Zed! Absorb the Potentia!"

The Bard's face flashed with hope under the pain. He grabbed the vial he had earned and drank it. Wincing, he looked at the empty container in despair: he had nowhere near enough to level.

"Abyss, don't you both rush to help him at once," Luke snapped as the others simply looked on sadly. He pulled out a jug of light, which he uncorked and force-fed the Bard. "Here's ten thousand Potentia. Figure out how to survive."

The determination to live appeared in Zed's eyes, and the team could practically *see* the sudden Potentia windfall changing the man before their very eyes. His skin cleared up and became more vibrant, while his eyes deepened and held intense wisdom.

Finally, the restraint on his neck seemed to loosen, and he gasped in a deep breath.

"That sucked so *bad!*" He coughed heartily, seemingly forcing each inhalation. "This is a temporary measure; I can feel my insides melting."

"How long does it take for exterior pressure to fulfill the requirements of a mana baptism?" Andre looked first to Luke, then Taylor, when he got no reply.

The Namer shrugged helplessly. "It could be literal *decades.* It's different for every person, and it's entirely dependent on the quality of their mana channels. If they're low quality, the mana needs to not only widen the channels, but it might also need to open new ones and reinforce them; in the most extreme cases, it blasts them open. Very few have ever survived the process, and it certainly doesn't happen often enough to even have a good guess."

"Can you *help* me, somehow?" Zed's face was still pale, and his breathing was ragged. "Please? Any of you? Also, Luke, thank you for saving me. Now, I think I just need-"

"I can tell you that just gaining levels won't do more than delay your death," Taylor told him directly as he eyed the pack that her liquid Potentia was stored in. "This is an issue with how mana flows through your physical body, not an issue of pure power. There are *very* few resources that can nourish mana channels and allow them to reach higher heights."

"Was still nice to reach level eight in one fell swoop. Kinda like walking up to a mansion and buying it with pocket change, ya know?" The panting Bard managed to show an impish, if pained, grin. "How long will it take to get out of here? You won't... you guys aren't going to leave me here, are you?"

The Namer hesitated, trying to calculate the numbers. The pause had the side-effect of increasing Zed's anxiety to the point that he almost had a panic attack before she answered. "Rules on travel are strange here. For every meter traveled, we move close to four meters in the base world. That's why it's so important to return to the point where you entered, or through a known exit. The desert… I'd say a week and a half, if you walked; a week, if you're carried and we're running most of the time."

"Better than a month traveling in the base world," Luke grunted in displeasure as he stepped close to Zed, ready to carry him once he was done. The Murderhobo pulled out his bottles and began tossing back his liquid Potentia as if taking shots of the liquid mana. He paused at the twenty-three thousand, three hundred and thirty-three Etheric Xenograft Potentia mark, having already determined where he wanted it.

"Devote eighty-nine hundred into getting me to level ten." Power poured through him as he spoke aloud, his body primed for breaking his limits. At that point, he could use the remaining fourteen thousand to reach level eleven, but he knew that he needed to become harder to kill if he wanted to get stronger. "Dump the rest into Walking Arsenal until it won't be enough to reach the next level."

Skill and Level increase complete! Etheric Xenograft Potentia used: 21,200/23,333. Please choose sub-characteristic to increase.

"Resistance." Luke had another hundred thousand experience to toss back, but he hesitated as he stared at the remaining vials. His eyes brightened slightly as he gained a realization: he didn't *need* to use all the Potentia at once. He could devote it piecemeal, so that it didn't sit as one giant chunk in his status sheet. "Get Walking Arsenal one point away from breaking through to the next tier. Keep the rest in reserve."

He tossed back the experience, not wanting to leave anything to chance. These bottles seemed *fragile* for something so potent and precious. When he had finished, he looked at only the changes in his status sheet.

Cal Scan
Level: **10**
Current Etheric Xenograft Potentia: 91,169/14,400 to level 11!
Body: 32.6

- *Fitness: 40.2*
- *Resistance: 20*

Maximum health: 300

Walking Arsenal. Tier 8, Level 9. 10,999/11,000 to Tier 9, Level 0.

"Good. Tier up Innate Balance and Bum Rush." Luke watched as forty-five thousand and three hundred Potentia was gobbled up by the two skills, and they deactivated as he began to throb with rapidly undulating power. "Mm. Glad I didn't push to the next tier with my main battle skills. Also, I think I got around the issue those fluffy guards were having by sending it to my Skills, instead of applying everything to my level. Or maybe I just have a more firm foundation. Who knows? Food for thought for the rest of you."

The other three were watching him in horror. Andre sputtered as Luke began throbbing with multiple out-of-time reverberations. "How are you not exploding into little chunks right now? How did you absorb almost two hundred *thousand* Potentia and use it all at once without falling apart?"

"What do you mean *two* hundred? He only had an additional one hundred given to him." Andre's words had broken Taylor out of her stupor, and she settled into her favorite role as 'instructor of people that have incorrect information'. "Haven't you ever broken through a tier? You get to level nine, then use double that amount of Potentia to get to the next tier."

"*Double*? Xan told me it was *ten* times the amount of raising it to level ten!" Andre yelped in shock, thinking back over his conversation with his mentor.

"You can't get a Spell to level ten. You can only get it to level nine. I think this Xan guy was messing with you. Wait a second…" Taylor narrowed her eyes, realizing Luke had made an intelligent and decisive decision, then shared good information with the rest of them without being coerced. She pulled her vials out and started drinking as well, followed by the impassioned Druid.

"C'mere." Since the others were busy, Luke grabbed the Bard and tossed him over his shoulder. "Let's get moving."

"First he gets me drinks, then he carries me home? I didn't know you liked me so much, you should have said something earlier—*oof!*" Zed fanned at his flushed face, yelping in pain a moment later as Luke squeezed him hard enough to bend his bones.

CHAPTER EIGHT

"So what you're telling me is that I don't need anywhere *near* the amount of Potentia that I thought I needed, that when I *do* upgrade my Abilities, I lose access to them for a certain amount of time... and that you just deactivated two really important Abilities in an unfamiliar world when people are probably hunting us." Andre added on the last part when Luke stumbled and barely caught himself on the edge of the bookcase he was moving along. "Seriously, Luke, what's happening with you? Are you sick?"

Zed's head bounced off the wooden section of wall, and he grunted at yet another blow. Luke growled and lumbered along, finally pausing and turning to the Druid, bonking Zed's forehead once more. "Just so you know, I have 'Skills', not 'Abilities'. One of those Skills gives me perfect balance all the time. In any situation. Without ever needing to think about it, my body is *perfectly* balanced. I've gotten used to that, and right now, it feels like I'm walking with three horses tied to my feet that all want to go in different directions."

Finishing his explanation, Luke calmly turned and began following Taylor once more. Zed pulled himself close to Luke to narrowly avoid yet another injury, then began excitedly chattering. "See *that*, Andre? It's working! We're getting through to him! The stories were right; the power of friendship wins out, no matter the situation!"

Andre poked the Bard with his Livingwood Staff, the symbol of his connection to plants being used as a mere walking stick in this land that lacked all greenery. "You should focus on cycling your mana so that you don't burn out before we get you to a safer environment."

"It's not that I *don't* like you," Luke offered unprompted, and the others stiffened as if a butterfly had just landed on their nose and they were afraid to scare it away. "You're just… you're all insubstantial. I'm still waiting for you to fade away like a dream."

When it was clear that no more words were forthcoming, Taylor slowly turned around with understanding shining in her eyes. "Luke… who seems the most real among us?"

"Andre. Then you. Zed might as well be a soap bubble waiting to pop." Luke lifted Zed above his head a few times, showcasing the exact same effort needed to lift a leaf, getting mewling curses in return for his effort.

"Did anything change after he leveled up?" Taylor's line of questioning had Zed and Andre confused, but they could feel that she was building up to something big.

Luke shook his head firmly. "Nothing."

"It's *mana density*." A satisfied smile spread across the Mage's face as she made the connection she needed to understand the Murderhobo's mental state. "His world is so utterly mana dense that things are *actually* more real, filled with the energy that suffuses higher planes. It's not that he doesn't *want* to care about what happens here… in his mind, it just literally doesn't matter. We're the sketches of images that have yet to be filled in with color."

"Speaking of *sketchy*," Zed started frantically thrashing around in an attempt to escape Luke's grip, pointing off in the distance from his hoisted position, "random people running at us. They're casting spells at us! Guys! *Fireballs incoming!*"

"Shatter Shot!" Taylor barked her spell, instantly sending out shards of force and ice that zeroed in on and impacted the fireballs; prematurely detonating them. Seeing the weaker version of her own spell caused a hint of contempt to appear in her eyes, and she retaliated in kind. "Flame Lance!"

The hyper-condensed bolt of explosive energy appeared in front of her for a bare instant before howling through the air, arriving in the midst of the charging group and detonating. A series of screams and wails rose from the ambushers, and Luke dropped Zed and started running at the downed enemies.

"Bum Rush!" He kept running as hard as he could, only realizing after a short moment that nothing had changed in terms of his speed: the Skill was upgrading. He uttered a unique curse as he closed in. "Abyssal *goat* eyes!"

An arrow whizzed past him, taking one of the masked attackers in the throat just as he began a chant. His abnormal Ascender physiology allowed him to pull out the arrow, toss it to the side, and continue fighting. Zed's voice floated to Luke's ear, as if the Bard was standing next to him. "That guy is a Battle Chanter; that arrow was really effective at keeping him out of the majority of the fight. Nice shot, Andre. He's down thirty health and is bleeding heavily."

Luke's attention shifted when he heard that the battle capabilities of his original target had been cut down. He charged at a robed attacker, hearing the others begin to panic as he did so.

"Protect the Mage; he goes down, and we're all trapped here!" a Knight in slightly rusted steel plate armor bellowed at his compatriots. The Battle Chanter and Knight moved to intercept the Murderhobo, while the others circled around the heavily charred Mage. "Essence of Iron!"

A metal plate barrier appeared between Luke and the remainder of the group, reminding him of his most recent escapades in Murder World. His pride refused to admit that learning to use a ranged weapon to fight like Andre was a good idea, but his logic could definitely come around to the idea of being able to pick off enemies as he closed in on a group. The fact of the matter was that Luke *needed* to know that his enemies were dead for *sure*, and he could only guarantee that by using his fists to triple check.

Using his left hand, Luke punched into that magical metal plate. The mana-image of the Simple Metal Sword directly penetrated, causing those behind the barrier to gasp, but the remainder of the plate remained. Luke bounced comically off the wall with a roar, having expected it to shatter like the barriers of the witches in Murder World. By the time he had regained his feet, a crescent of condensed air was flying at him, aimed to take off his head. He lifted his arms and took the blow on his mana-made gauntlets, the force of the cutting gale sending him flailing backward toward his team.

"Fissure!" Taylor finished incanting her spell and released it in the same instant, the fifth-tier spell causing the ground around the attackers to shatter into hundreds of stone spikes that flew at them from all directions. Each spike that entered its target dealt ninety damage. As the spell ended, only the Knight with his powerful defense remained alive, and even *he* was breathing raggedly.

A weak hand reached up and pulled the helmet off the Knight's head. His words were barely audible, but a hint of arrogance still somehow managed to suffuse his voice. "I am Vanguard Kestral; by the authority of Captain Edmond of the Third Royal Knights, I order you to grant me mercy, heal me, and see me safely to an outpost."

Luke had started to approach the man as soon as he was able to get on his feet, and arrived next to him just as Kestral finished his statement. The Murderhobo's Sigil flared with a bright light, and a smile appeared on the Knight's face just before his head was gripped and his neck was snapped like a chicken going to the soup pot.

"No way to heal you. Mercy granted." Pulling the corpse upright, Luke rapidly stripped away the armor and weapons.

Then he went through the remaining carcasses and pulled out *anything* that could be used by his Walking Arsenal Skill. "Someone else carry Zed while I work on absorbing this stuff."

The abrupt shift from conversation to battle and back was something that most of them were used to dealing with. Yet for Zed, the shock was still enough for him to lose the focus he required, and he began choking in the dense air once more.

Taylor calculated the chances of his survival over the next few days and shook her head sorrowfully, but Andre ignored everything else and picked the Bard up, putting him in a vine sling. "Don't you worry, little buddy! I'll figure something out; you just go ahead and take big, slo~ow breaths!"

Andre watched Zed as his eyes closed and he drifted into a meditative state. Then the Druid used his exceptionally long legs to easily catch up to the others. "I have something I want to discuss with you both. I have my new Potentia, and... well, this is hard to describe. I really trust the both of you, and I hope this knowledge will never be shared to hurt me. Even though I reached the Third Circle... I actually only have, um, two Abilities. Everything else I'm doing is Circle magic, and it isn't something inherent to me."

"Is there a reason you're saying this out loud when someone might be listening from a distance?" Taylor sharply reprimanded him, her eyes rapidly scanning the horizon. Finding nothing, she turned her glare on the Druid. "How are you so powerful if you only have two things that are actually attributed to you?"

"Right; that's *Circle magic*, like I was saying," Andre griped at her, already clearly angry that he had bothered to share. "It allows me to essentially use brute force and lots of mana to control nature in various ways. There aren't really levels associated with Circle magic; just control, mana, and willpower. If you remember, I managed to reach the Third Circle, thanks to Luke, and transfer that mana into saving us and such, but my *Ability* to do more than that hasn't yet manifested. It will only appear after I manage to do a service for nature that allows me to bond with it at a more fundamental level. That's why most Druids manage to get an Ability *before* reaching the next Druidic Circle. I'm... well, I don't even have an Ability from the Second Circle. Never did anything grand that allowed me to commune with fauna."

"The point is *what?*" Luke didn't bother to get too invested in the long-winded back and forth between the two pseudo-intellectuals.

"Yes!" Andre took a deep breath to calm his nerves and control his rising anger. "The point is, I have enough Potentia to take the two Abilities I have to the next tier, or even higher. *Should* I do that? I'll be essentially useless, unable even to grow arrows for my bow or connect to anything."

"You're practically already useless here," Luke retorted bluntly as he tramped along, mana particles slowly moving between himself and the gear he was carrying. "Only plants you got are the ones you're growing. Just make sure there's nothing growing *in* you that you'll lose control of, grow a crapload of arrows that you'll carry, and make sure your bow isn't going to need your magic to use it."

The logical, if rankling, statement generated a slow nod from Andre. "You have a point, and I like it a lot. I'm doing it. Devote Potentia to Bind by Blood to break the Tier limit. Then Bloodthistle."

A shockwave emanated from his body, followed by a steady throbbing that battered at the minds of his companions. When they looked at Andre, the triumph they had been expecting to see failed to appear. The shamefaced Druid blinked at Taylor with watery eyes. "Did... did you drink all your vials? I'm four thousand and seventy short."

Taylor's left eye twitched, and she reached into a hidden pocket of her pack. She gritted her teeth into a smile and handed over her last five vials, a total of five thousand Potentia. "I didn't want to Tier up right now anyway. *Someone* should keep some of their firepower when we're all running for our lives."

"Perfect! Thanks!" Andre tossed back the liquid, grew a

huge quiver of arrows, and prepared himself. "*Now* break that limit!"

An out-of-sync energy reverberated from his body, and the Druid gave the others an excited thumbs-up as he temporarily became practically powerless.

Then Zed fell to the ground with a **thump** as the vines stopped supporting him.

CHAPTER NINE

- TAYLOR -

"I can't let them get to me... but they're driving me *nuts!*" Taylor let out a long, whispering scream-breath, releasing the tension in her shoulders and feeling Cleanse whisk away a streak of sweat that had threatened to trickle down her forehead. She strolled forward gracefully, watching as Luke plodded forward like a neanderthal. It boggled her mind that just an hour previously, the man in front of her had moved with the unceasing and disconcerting perfect grace of a predator.

When he walked in the forest, the only branches that would break were the ones he *hit*. He could step in a puddle and not leave even a ripple behind. Now... *now?* He would cause local legends about almost-human monsters roaming around if people could see him. "It's unbelievable that a 'Skill' can have such an effect on him. Is... perhaps he has a Skill impacting his mind, as well? Why wouldn't he improve those, if so?"

In all fairness, there were certain spells that Taylor would never upgrade. Cleanse and Purify were forever destined to remain at Tier one. Seeing Luke practically fall over with each loping waddle, because he hadn't needed to intentionally balance himself for who-knows-how-long, was a chilling reminder to the Mage that she had relied on these two personal grooming spells for over a decade, and had been able to completely ignore personal hygiene that entire time because of it.

Luke stiffened, and Taylor realized that she had been staring at him and critiquing his every motion for... she wasn't even sure how long. She cursed her lack of attention to the surrounding area and immediately began searching for what-ever signs of danger that had caused Luke to act in such a manner. Not spotting anything, she quietly voiced her concern. "Do you see something?"

"Need direction." The pig-like grunt was her only reply. *Something* needed to be done about his attitude and lack of cour-tesy, but for the *life* of her, Taylor didn't know what that some-thing was. She would think about it, and somehow find a way to make him less of a caricature in the future. He needed her help.

Then she realized that *she* was the only one that knew where to go in the World of Names, and Luke had led them to the end of her last instructions. Taylor nodded in approval. If nothing else, the Murderhobo had a great ability to follow directions. The Mage took in the surroundings and calculated their posi-tion, pointing into the distance once she had her bearings. "We need to head toward Fountain-Pen Falls, then shoot an azimuth from there to reach Paper-Crush Rock. From there, it'll only be a day or so to Inkwell Lake. Our exit is along the banks of the lake; we're making great progress."

After her small speech, Taylor had planned on the group taking a rest and having some quiet time to get better acquainted with each other's presence. Instead, Luke simply nodded once and began running in the direction she had pointed. She and Andre had no choice but to follow, being completely unwilling to leave Luke to his own devices.

She did realize that there was a good reason for such speed: there was just no way to know whether Zed could survive the entire time, or if he would suddenly burst into flame and turn to ash. Taylor hadn't wanted to worry the other two, but Zed was starting to show signs of imminent combustion. When a mana baptism went bad, as it almost *always* did, the only thing that would remain were bleached bones. All other organic material would erupt like a fireball, taking clothing and oftimes armor with it. The sole reason bones remained was that the detonation was focused outward, and the victim's skeletal structure was fairly well-protected until the very end.

A glance at Zed's sweating face, with his eyes tightly closed and bulging veins clearly visible, *almost* had her instructing Andre to give up and drop the Bard before he too was caught in the magical flame and ick that would result. Instead, she steadied herself and increased her pace. "If we move at maximum speed the entire time, it's likely we will be able to avoid the majority of attackers that might be seeking us out. Excellent thinking, Luke."

"I'm just not tired." The reply caused something in Taylor to break. She simply gave up on trying to get through to him with words. He followed her instructions… that would just need to be enough until they formed a natural rapport. Instead of trying to speak with anyone else, she simply kept her eyes open for opportunities in the world around her.

Until her team was back to full strength, she couldn't use them to help her subdue the stronger spells in the area. Yet, her eyes had been opened to the fact that if other Ascenders could come into her world, she could greatly profit from their assistance. Even better, it wasn't even entirely self-serving, since her becoming stronger would allow the entire group's strength to rise. As they traveled through what counted as night in her world, Taylor tracked high-Tier spells, kept an eye out for small-scale dungeons, and prepared for when she would return here as a conqueror.

The night passed uneventfully, as did the following day. Fountain-Pen Falls appeared on the horizon, huge buttes of stone and metal shaped as pens that rose unimaginably high into the sky, as if they were writing the clouds into existence. Each 'pen' was stained on one side by an ink-like water that poured continuously from its tip. "See that? It's one of the natural wonders of this world, and is one of the most well-known landmarks. There's never been something like this appearing in any other documented world."

"Neat." Luke appreciatively studied the pens. "Reminds me of the mana waterfall in the entrance to Murder World. I'd show you, but you'd die."

"Really neat stuff, Taylor!" Andre wore a *properly* awed expression as he surveyed the mountain-height scribe supply. "What kind of spells live in there?"

"Only *absurdly* powerful Mages go there." Taylor shook her head at the thought and shuddered lightly when she saw Luke consider the pens with renewed interest. "Seriously. This is *not* foreshadowing, or me thinly-veiling playing with fate. I'm *just* describing a landmark. That ink water is corrosive to the extreme, and it turns mana into more ink-water. The *entire* place is a domain spell, and people think it's a pinnacle Tier ten, or maybe even a descended Tier eleven. It releases such a powerful resonance in the interior that it is a popular place for level twenty Mages to Ascend to their next plane. The universal veil is *thin* there."

"So going there is *death*, is what you're saying," Andre piled on as Luke got even more excited.

"*Yes.*" Taylor looked them in the eyes, having to work to make Luke focus on her. "Powerful spells are released from there all the time. There's about a hundred mile radius around it that contains roaming spells, and the closer you get to the Falls, the more powerful they become. If you want to fight something *later*, I'd be wildly happy to bring us back here and go hunting. Just not when our Bard is about to blow."

They subsequently adjusted their path in an attempt to stay out of well-known areas. Several hours later, mana shook the air and coalesced around Andre. He abruptly turned to the side as his eyes unfocused, and he vomited onto the ground and collapsed from a minor concussion. Zed tumbled out of Luke's grip as he attempted to catch the Druid, coming to a rest just shy of the fresh puddle. Taylor ran over to Andre and checked him for wounds but found no reason for his sudden attack. As she examined him, the Druid slowly sat up and took a few deep breaths, managing to explain after a moment. "Ability upgrade... finished. It felt like it scraped a seed out of my soul and grafted on an Epoch Tree in its place."

"What does that even mean?" Luke grilled him intensely. "More Druid garbage that we are somehow supposed to just know?"

Andre gingerly shook his head. "It took my Ability... and the change is just so *drastic*. I have no idea how to better describe-"

"Not that," Luke interrupted flatly, "What is 'epoch'."

"Ah." Andre blinked a few times and pushed his damaged thoughts to scrape together a proper explanation. "An epoch in this context is ten thousand years. An Epoch Tree is considered the most complicated type of plant in our plane of existence. As far as our research shows, it has no purpose other than being used as a time-telling device. From the time it is planted until it reaches full maturity is ten thousand years. Every one thousand years, a seed grows on it. At ten thousand years, it flings all ten seeds into the distance, at which point the trunk grows exactly one meter taller. The whole process starts over for it then. It's in almost every world, because that was how they originally determined time dilation."

"Why are you telling me all this?" Luke rubbed his head and snarled at the Druid as the man waxed eloquent.

"To explain how utterly *complex* this change is that I just went through. Forget it. I hurt too much right now. I'm just going to outright show you this, and you can understand it for yourself." Andre grew a papyrus sheet and wrote out his entire Ability for them to read over. "Here. The name of it changed from Bloodthistle to Hemoflora."

Effect 1: Marinating a seed in blood will allow you to use mana to grow and control it while it is in your hand. Costs 20 mana to begin the growth process and 1 mana per second to control it.

Bonus 1, at range: Can control the grown plant within line of sight.

Effect 2: If the grown plant has access to blood, it uses that blood instead of mana. Removes mana cost until blood is fully absorbed.

Bonus 2, Multitarget: You can now control multiple plants and seeds at the same time. This is modified by your 'Talent' sub-characteristic.

New! Effect 3: You are able to impart a concept onto blood-marinated seeds or spores to force the plant to generate 1+n pseudo Abilities of its own, where 'n' = skill level, capped at n=9. The more narrow and focused the Ability is, the less likely it is to generate unwanted side effects.

Taylor and Luke read the information. The Mage was speechless for a long moment, just long enough for Luke to shrug. "All I know about plants is that they make me empty myself easier after eating them. I have no idea what this means."

"You can create plants that have almost any Ability you can *think* of?" Taylor almost bit her tongue hard enough to draw blood to keep herself from calling the advancement 'unfair'. "Also, you can just *will* your Sigil to send us this data; you don't need to write it out by hand. The plant thing, though... how is this possible?"

"How is it possible to make a plant do *anything?*" Andre went still for a moment, turning to look at the Bard laying next to the puddle of swiftly drying vomit. "No idea, but I have a really good idea of how to test it."

CHAPTER TEN

Andre's palm was filled with a small amount of his own blood surrounding a single small seed that had been marinating in it for a few minutes. Taylor was just about to start asking him about the process once again, when the Druid pulled the seed halfway out of the blood and whispered, *"Hemoflora."*

Mana drained out of the air around the caster and into the seed, and the tiny orb sucked up the remaining blood in an instant. A shining halo appeared around it, slowly revolving even after the Ability had been used. They watched the strangely beautiful green pea seed, waiting for something to change. Nothing did, even after five full minutes, so Andre shrugged and put the seed on the ground. "Okay... so, not sure it'll be able to grow much without my mana, since the dirt here is just tiny scribbles that I'm almost certain say 'dirt', but let's give it a whirl."

He commanded the seed to grow, and a standard-looking pea vine rapidly emerged and approached maturity. Taylor couldn't hold back her curiosity any longer. "What ability did you give it?"

"Self-defense." Andre grinned at the reaction he got from

the others. "I'm thinking it'll whip people that get too close to it."

Luke shrugged and stepped forward, grabbing at the vine.

Pow!

The entire plant, root to fruit, exploded into tiny slivers of mush. Luke blinked a few times, his face covered with shredded green matter. "It did not whip me."

"I… yeah, I saw that," a crestfallen Andre admitted as he stared at the remains of the plant that had drained away so much of his mana. "This doesn't even have a standardized cost. I get this feeling of the cost when I decide on an idea, and I either must accept that mana burden or let it fade."

Taylor tapped him on the shoulder, showing him a set of notes that she had taken based on what he had been telling them. "Your written-out description directly told you to be exceptionally specific so that you didn't have weird things like this happening. I'm almost certain that 'self-defense' as a concept means completely different things to a plant than it does to a person. Try a specific _action_. Some kind of trigger based on something else, like whipping a vine at moving things when they get in range."

"I can do that!" Andre brightened right away and got back to trying new ideas.

"Let's think about some of the other considerations you should make." Taylor pulled out a quill and began writing on the parchment again. "The type of plant that you use will almost _certainly_ impact the power you can infuse into it. A thorny plant would benefit more from a whip attack than a pea vine, but an ironwood stalk would break itself trying to do the same thing. Also, what would happen when you upgrade a plant that already has inherent abilities, like that Mountain Willow Wind? You said it can restore stamina and makes 'pretty sounds' when the wind blows. If you add another ability…"

Andre's eyes had completely lost focus as he listened to Taylor's suggestions, a wild smile growing on his face. "I have…

just *so* many ideas! Taylor! How did you come up with all that out of nowhere? You're brilliant!"

Taylor felt her face heat up, and she turned her eyes to her parchment to hide her pleased smile. "I have an idea of what you could do to help Zed, if you want to hear it?"

"Yes!" Andre's cheeks were flushed as he stared at her, and when she met his eyes, his head jolted so that he was staring at his bleeding palm. "That is… yes, that'd be awesome."

She jumped into an explanation right away, in order to put them back on a professional footing. "If the inherent capabilities of a plant impact the efficacy of the imparted ability, perhaps you take a plant that has excellent air filtration capabilities and attune the plant to absorbing mana. Then, have it convert that mana into something less volatile so that the plant doesn't just explode from an overabundance of power."

"Like Zed is about to do," Luke added 'helpfully'.

"…Yes." Taylor awkwardly conceded the point.

"No. I need more practice before I try to use one of these on people." Andre shook his head sadly. "There's too great of a chance that I'd end up blowing Zed up, or something else going wrong. That pea vine detonated violently enough that it would have caused him pain if he'd been within range. Imagine something like that, but after compressing mana drawn out of him to a large degree. There'd be nothing left!"

"Andre." Taylor grabbed his shoulder to steady him. "Zed is in the final stages of a mana burnout. If we don't do something right now, he *will* die."

The Druid furrowed his brow as he regarded the unconscious Bard, the pale face with bright purple veins throbbing in time to his heart, and nodded reluctantly. "I have… only an idea."

Taylor watched with great satisfaction as the Druid got to work, pulling various… seeds? Spores? …out of the tiny satchels that lined his belts. Plants burst into existence and intertwined, sprouting and dying in moments as Andre collected pollen and spliced various strains together. Hours passed like this; hours where they couldn't move, for fear of detonating the highly unstable Bard.

Finally, Andre was left holding a single tiny seed. He looked at the others and swallowed a mouthful of saliva, hoping against hope that he had done the right thing. He chattered nervously as he soaked the seed in blood he had taken from Zed's arm. "So… this is a splice from various ferns and snake plants, both known for their filtration properties. I took the final generation and combined it with a Mountain Willow Wind to maximize the chances that it'll be able to interact with people without damaging them, since that plant is already beneficial to our health."

"We believe in you," The Mage firmly encouraged the shaking man.

The Druid took a deep breath and steadied himself as he activated the final step in the process. *"Hemoflora."*

Mana swirled through and around him, so much power that Taylor winced in sympathy as Andre heaved for air and sweated profusely. Just before the Druid collapsed, a halo of light burst into existence around the seed. "The… ability was added. I don't know if it'll work perfectly, but I can't do anything more. I need a few minutes before I can grow it."

Taylor watched as the Druid's eyes rolled up, and he promptly fainted. Her Senses were her most potent characteristic, so even if she *hadn't* noticed that he was about to pass out, she still would have been able to catch him with ease. As it was, she guided him gently to the ground and laid him next to the fallen Bard. "We're down two people, and we haven't even been in a dangerous fight."

"Want to be?" Taylor followed Luke's pointed finger, her gaze landing on a roiling whirlwind spell that was tearing through the earth in the distance.

The Mage glanced down at her defenseless contemporaries, then off at the huge spell. "I don't have any wind spells yet… but I can't. This place is *really* dangerous if you aren't prepared, and I guarantee something would attack them as soon as we began moving away."

Luke nodded once, his eyes roving over every single aspect of the terrain around them as he searched for danger. Taylor studied his watching of the environment, feeling a pang in her heart as she realized that this hyper-vigilance was a learned behavior. She couldn't even imagine the suffering he must have gone through to be able to function at this level all of the time. It was a cross between pure instinct and the harshest of training. She both envied and pitied the Murderhobo at that moment.

"How long was I... *Zed!*" Only a few minutes had passed before Andre managed to awaken, and he groaned as he sat up. However, his eyes flew open in a panic as he saw that the Bard's skin was beginning to float off of his limbs like cinders from a burning log. "I hope this...!"

Andre didn't finish his thought, merely bringing the seed to Zed's face and stuffing it in a nostril before forcing it to grow. A moment passed, and shock filled his face; followed by determination. "It's growing too rapidly. There's so much mana here that the ability I designated to use his mana to grow is working constantly. I need to control it carefully, or it'll use Zed as a source of nutrients."

Nearly an hour later, Taylor watched the Druid slump back with a weary smile on his face as he announced his success. One look at Zed proved that something had drastically changed for him. His skin was looking healthy once more, and his breathing was deep and even. "It's working?"

"It is," Andre confirmed.

"You're a miracle worker," Taylor praised the Druid as soon as she saw what he had managed, even with no experience with either this type of Ability or problem. "One thing... is there a *flower* growing out of his nose?"

"There is," Luke affirmed as he grabbed Zed's head and rocked it back and forth, causing the flower to emit a light chiming sound. "This works well. He needed a warning bell."

"You made a joke!" Andre cheered at his old friend. "Keep that up and it'll become a habit!"

Luke appeared startled, an expression Taylor had rarely seen on his face. "I… huh. I just gained a point of charisma."

"From making a *joke*?" Taylor was truly aggrieved. "Do you know how hard I work to try to raise that characteristic naturally?"

"Charisma is all about connecting to those around you, not being a perfect example for *them* to work toward being. Ice Queen over here thinks she can just *work* hard and get Charisma." A croaking voice pulled their attention to Zed, who had woken up, but still hadn't tried moving. "I could really use some water. I can't remember *ever* being this dry before."

"Here you go, lil buddy." Andre half-lifted Zed and pushed a waterskin to his lips. "I put a plant in you, and the roots go down into your lungs. It's absorbing all the water in the air that gets pulled in, so make sure to drink a lot to make up for that deficit."

Zed gulped down some water, then glared at the Druid. "You put a plant *in* me? Is… is my nose ringing?"

"No. It is the flower growing out of your nose that is doing the ringing," Luke clarified, as if that would make the Bard feel better. "We should get going. There's a whole bunch of lightning destroying that hill over there."

"Lightning? But there's no thunder?" Taylor turned in time to catch sight of some flashing light that she had ignored while Zed was getting rehydrated. Her eyes locked on the distant show and reddened instantly as desire to control that force filled her. "*Sonic Lighting*. That's… that's…"

"Wanna go fight it?" Luke crouched down and prepared to dash into the distance.

"It's lightning that completely absorbs the sound it creates. The thunder that is normally released into the air is instead pulled along and impacts as an instantaneous secondary attack. Sonic Lighting is an overlord among Tier five spells, and that one is striking multiple areas. It *has* to be at least Tier six." The

Mage licked her lips unconsciously as she stared at the huge spell rolling through the world.

"Can you take it?" Andre questioned her just as Taylor's book flew out of her back and flapped around wildly. "Ahh! I *hate* that it does that! Books shouldn't be alive."

"You're hungry? You're gonna be fine eating that? Are you sure?" Taylor stroked the spine of her Grimoire as it quivered in excitement. "I feel like that's past your limit…"

It ruffled it's pages at her hastily, and Taylor had no choice but to sigh. "Then… I have no choice. Devote all Potentia to leveling up!"

Her command was executed instantly, and the twenty thousand Potentia stored in her Sigil drained away into her in an instant. As the changes became painful, she managed to grit her teeth and order, "Devote two increases to Physical Reaction, and one to Mental Energy!"

She collapsed as her nerves seemed to light aflame, and all she could do was twitch and stare at her status sheet as it updated itself.

Cal Scan
Level: 10
Current Etheric Xenograft Potentia: 3,052/14,400 to level 11!
Body: 7.7

- *Fitness: 9.2*
- *Resistance: 6.2*

Mind: 14.25

- *Talent: 14.7*
- *Capacity: 13.8*

Presence: 9.85

- *Willpower: 7.7*

- *Charisma: 12*

Senses: 29.3

- *Physical reaction: 32.2*
- *Mental energy: 26.4*

Maximum Health: 112
Maximum Mana: 246.8
Mana regen: 4.9 per second

She was proud of the incredible gains she had made in the last few years, but the main focus of all her training to this point had been focused entirely on Senses. With higher Senses, she could bypass the restrictions and prerequisites of spells and directly bind them to herself. Even so, whatever version of Sonic Lightning they were about to go up against was going to require that she was prepared beyond any other point she had been in her life.

"You just started unraveling. You went from a real person made of steel to a homunculus made of leather." Luke warned her, pulling away and scowling at her with distaste. Taylor ignored him for the moment, as her mind turned to her desire.

Lightning lasted only a bare moment per strike, meaning she would need to catch glimpses of this spell over and over, learn its point of origin, and bind its true name into her Grimoire. Fissure, her highest Tier spell, was *entirely* average for the Tier it belonged in. Lightning would always be considered as a peak existence, and this had evolved beyond anything she had ever imagined having a chance to capture. She alternated her gaze between the two useful members of her party and nodded.

"Let's go."

CHAPTER ELEVEN

"Spells relating to elemental forces are always incredibly powerful and difficult to subdue," Taylor explained to the others as they ran. Andre dropped Zed a half-mile from the site the lightning was striking to make sure the physically frail man would have a chance to recover while also gaining valuable information. "They only appear when they are either working to defend their territory, or they find something they want to absorb. If they're about to be captured, they'll often fight to the last drop of mana, so sneak attacking is one of the best ways to make it happen."

Andre snorted rudely, shocking Taylor right out of information mode. "I can tell you that there's nothing *natural* about that lightning, Taylor. It may *mimic* lightning, but that is merely mana in a structure we are familiar with. Someday, let's test out natural versus arcane lightning."

That put a small smile on the Mage's face. "I think that might be fun. Perhaps we could test it on various materials to see which has a more effective energy usage! The real question is, who gets first author credit on the research?"

"Whoever deals more destruction, of course," Andre

laughed along with her, though it appeared that Luke had gotten bored while they bantered back and forth.

The Murderhobo shot forward, bounding far ahead of the others in mere moments. He sprinted and leapt after the lightning each time it flashed, screaming incoherently as he swung his fists at the afterimages. Each time he missed, his speed appeared to increase. Even so, he just wasn't fast enough to catch the lightning. "*Andre*! How do I fight clouds?"

"Ranged weapons, Luke!" Andre held out his bow to clarify what he meant. Luke zipped over and grabbed the bow, twisting and flinging the wood like a boomerang into the sky. The weapon vanished instantly while missing his target completely. They all watched in silence for a long, incredulous moment.

"That…" Luke turned slightly and raised a judging eyebrow at Andre. "That didn't work."

"If I could hurt you just a *little*, that would make me feel a lot better right now." Andre leaned onto his Livingwood Staff and bonked his own head onto it a few times. "I'm so glad I grew that one to use when my Ability was upgrading, or I'd make you search for my staff until we found it. *Here*."

The Druid grew a new bow and handed it over, then shifted his Livingwood Staff to its bow form to join in on the fun. "Take this arrow, nock it on that vine, pull back-"

Crack.

Luke frowned down at the shattered bow in his hands and shook his head. "Doesn't work for me. No. Don't make another. Try spears for throwing."

Andre nodded in understanding, changing which seed he was reaching for. He scattered a few on the ground, and they sprang up into small saplings shaped as perfect spears. Luke grabbed them in rapid succession, pulling and throwing each of them in a single motion. They hissed into the sky, the first projectile incredibly off-target. One after another, Luke threw, becoming more practiced at an incredible rate. Finally, the spears were hissing into the cloud overhead with nearly unerring accuracy.

Taylor tried to talk some sense into these men that were practically giggling as the spears punched holes in the cloud, and Luke used that knowledge to draw uncouth shapes. "Physical damage like that can't do anything to a spellform, Luke. Only mana-constructs really interact with magic at this level and—*no!*"

The Murderhobo had registered her words and acted on them too fast for her to stop him from doing something incredibly reckless. He grabbed a spear, snapped the top off, poked a hole in the stave, then opened and poured liquid mana from a waterskin into the hole. Taylor shouted at him to stop just as he hurled the glorified stick.

Hiss... the stick left a trail of blue vapor as it traveled upward and the mana dispersed slightly. The broken spear vanished as it entered the vaporous spellform far above, and for an instant Taylor thought that the pure mana hadn't been able to make the journey upward. Then lightning detonated so hard that the shockwave cleared all other clouds in the sky as far as her eyes could see.

"You don't release *pure mana* in a world where literally everything is made of mana, Luke," Taylor weakly exclaimed as she watched power zip around the sky for a few seconds before returning to swarm together into a mountain of lightning that wriggled as if the strike had uncovered a snake's nest. Before long, the arcing bolts snapped into the spell's true form, no longer hidden by a cloud: a cat's eye made of lightning.

The flickering image couldn't have been more perfectly designed if a master painter had somehow been able to take his brush to the sky. Worst of all, the eye was staring at them. Luke nodded solemnly. "Got its attention."

"Right... remember how I *just* said that natural force spells only appear when there's something they want?" Taylor laughed nervously as a static charge began building on her skin. "Pure mana is considered the most nourishing of all things to spellforms. There's nothing they'd rather have, as it allows them to use themselves constantly without fear of using their own essence up."

Luke dove to the side, and an instant later, the space where he had stood exploded. Superheated earth geysered into the air, only to be blown away from the point of impact by the concentrated sonic wave that followed the deadly path. Andre gaped at the Murderhobo incredulously. "How'd you dodge that?"

"As soon as your arm hair stands fully upright, heaven's might will alight," Luke muttered a children's rhyme they had all learned decades ago. "Don't know the reason. It's just true."

"Oh! In fact, the reason is a static charge that-" Andre glanced at his arms in horror and threw himself to the side, yelping as some of the vines holding his clothes together burst into flame from the superheated dirt that was abruptly flung into the air.

Taylor peered into the distance as a sudden commotion erupted. Hundreds... *thousands* of books had just burst from their roosts on the ubiquitous shelves as the flavor of pure mana dispersed into the environment. "So... I'd really like to take a few minutes to talk about the well-known mana-releasing taboos of the World of Names-"

She yelped as Luke tackled her and three bolts struck one after another along the path they rolled over. Luke bounded to his feet and lifted her into the air as if using her as a shield, shaking her and bellowing, "Tell me how I fight *lightning!*"

"Ranged weapons!" she yelped, then amended her explanation as Luke growled in frustration, "*Enchanted* ranged weapons! Structured magic will damage other structured magic!"

The first of the massive flock of books flew into the area, darkening the sky and filling the world with sounds which the largest library in all the worlds would be proud to hear: thousands of pages being turned at once. Unable to find a source of pure mana, the Grimoires began bickering and tearing into each other. Lightning penetrated the unnatural gloom, creating bursts of flame in the sky and scattering embers across the plains below as the stricken volumes were destroyed and fell from the heavens.

"Can *you* deal with this?" Luke bellowed into her face as Andre began rapid-firing arrows into the swarm. Dozens of tomes fell from the sky in the next few seconds; some alight, some with arrows in their spines.

The shout and hard shake pulled Taylor from the stupor she had been trapped in. A plan formed in the next instant, and she nodded at him. "I need liquid mana."

A waterskin was in her hand by the time she finished the sentence. Luke dropped her and ran into the distance, punching books and causing them to explode into bits of leather and loose-leaf paper with each attack. Taylor eyed the bag in her hand with trepidation: if she accidentally got this... this liquid *death* on her, her fate would be no different than Zed's had almost been. There was no flower growing out of her nose that might let her survive the experience.

Calm logic filled her mind. Fear of *possibilities* had never held her back. Her mind and body in alignment, Taylor popped the top off the waterskin and flung the precious liquid away from her in a controlled arc. With a smooth motion, she covered the bag and waited for the world to notice her actions.

It only took a moment.

The liquid mana erupted upward as a dense fog of power, and the books caught the flavor in the next zeptosecond. Thousands of books remained in the sky, despite the efforts of the team and the spell they were fighting. While that many manuscripts could bury them, crush them... they could also *hide* them.

The spell lost sight of its original targets as the swarm blocked its sight, and the humans moved into an advantageous position. Now fully ready to make her move, Taylor stared into the heart of the spellform far above, watching it as it shifted and changed, doing its utmost to hide what it truly was. Bolts of power rained down as that glowing eye tried to feast on the miasma that the Mage had released, yet found itself blocked by the weakest inhabitants of this world. While they were weak, books were also the natural predator of even the strongest spells. Hundreds of tomes were obliterated with each strike, but a thousand more were always ready to take their place.

Even such a powerful spell had limits and couldn't sustain itself forever. The lightning flashed out less frequently with every passing second, and the flock managed to stack themselves in the air more densely. Every participant of this battle was focused on a different thing, but only Taylor was going to get what she wanted. Her eyes finally locked onto the root words of the spell, and she lifted her personal Grimoire up with both hands as she shouted its true name.

"Tigris veridian oculus ad meridianam!" With that phrase, she bound the spellform to her will and yanked it downward. For the first time ever, the spell she was binding fought against her and tried to destroy her before it was completely bound. She snorted a laugh as *Nullify* sprang into place around her with a klaxxon call and caused the attacks to erode before they could deal a single point of damage to her.

The massive spell was compressed into sheet after sheet of power as it was pulled into her Grimoire. She slapped the covers closed, hoping against hope that the Grimoire would survive the flailing of the wild spell she had Named.

Utter silence filled her ears, even though there were a thousand battles happening on all sides. She waited. One second. Ten. Slowly, carefully, she cracked the cover and read over the new information that had been fully tamed. Tears filled her eyes, and she screamed at the world in utter joy.

Spell Named: Thunder Beast's Eye. (T7): 0/800 to level 5!

Effect 1: Generate arcing lightning that deals ~~15n~~ lightning damage on touch, where 'n' = spell level. ~~Maximum of 135 damage.~~ Electricity is inherently unstable, and will damage you unless given a target within .5 seconds of casting. Mana cost: 100 mana.

Bonus, at range: Control of this particular lightning spell greatly increased. You are now able to send the unstable energy at a target up to 5+5n meters away, maximum of 50 meters.

Effect 2: Control of this particular lightning spell increased to the utmost. This spell is now completely soundless when cast. Damage increases to 25n lightning damage, maximum 225 damage. Mana cost is decreased by 5n, maximum of 50 mana reduction. Electricity is stabilized, and will no longer damage you if not released in time. Current Mana cost: 50 per use.

Bonus, Multitarget: The collected vibration from the lightning passing through the air is added as sonic damage, which impacts .25 seconds after the bolt lands. This deals 5n sonic damage in addition to all other damage.

Effect 3: This spell can be overfilled with mana, at 50 mana per second to create a ball of lightning. For each 50 mana invested, an additional bolt will be generated. The ball of lightning will hover above the caster and strike any target the caster designates. Lasts a maximum of 5n minutes after casting, or until all attacks have been used.

Bonus, AOE: Each bolt of lightning will reach its maximum range no matter how many targets are in the way, dealing maximum damage to each. This will be blocked by any structure at least three feet thick, or of sufficient density to absorb it.

Effect 4: Your control of this spell has reached the pinnacle, and it obeys your will as a sentient pet would. At the cost of 250 mana, an eye of lightning will form above the caster and search for any targets or threats to the caster. This eye can release up to 5 bolts of lightning, plus one per each additional 250-25n mana invested, and lasts until all bolts have been cast.

Taylor looked up at the hurricane of books that were voraciously drinking in the pure mana in the area, and cast a single bolt of lightning into their midst. A flash of light was the only indication that a spell had been cast. At first. Then a straight line of power erupted outward, and every book fifty meters along that path burst into flame or directly exploded into looseleaf paper. Even though her heart was soaring, she waited for two seconds to regenerate a small amount of mana, then focused her will and poured a full two hundred mana into the air above her.

The orb of lightning formed over two seconds, as she was unable to create the highest form of it: the eye. She quickly discovered that she was also unable to add additional mana after she had designated a certain amount of it for use, because the spell required a *full* fifty mana each second; it couldn't be done piecemeal. A ball of brilliantly shining power hovered above her, and in the next instant four bolts of lightning shot off in the cardinal directions, obliterating countless tomes.

Taylor fell to her knees as mana exhaustion rocked her. She gasped for breath, hating her impatience... all the way until she saw that she had just earned twenty-eight hundred and four Potentia. Then a smile covered her face. Still, she was entirely helpless at the moment, entirely reliant on her physical strength to solve any issues that might arise.

A glance at the Tier seven effect caused Taylor to sigh. The initial spell initiation cost wasn't possible for her at her current Capacity. Even though she was a mere four mana short from the total, she simply couldn't generate the spell structure without paying the entire cost up front. To her chagrin, this spell didn't allow her to gradually channel lesser amounts in to fill in the lines slowly. This was the first time she had even slightly regretted focusing on her Senses...

"No, none of that." She quietly pushed those thoughts aside. "I wouldn't have even been able to Name the spell unless I had followed this path. I can always get a deeper well of magic from leveling up later, or I can do those Capacity expanding exercises Master Don made me learn."

"We need to get out of here." Zed's voice floated to each of the team's ears. "Someone out there is guaranteed to realize something huge was going on over here. I'd rather not let us get wiped out just because we were at anything less than full strength."

"I'm so good with that, I can't even tell you," Taylor whispered joyfully.

"Oh good. 'Cause, you know, I like life." The Bard's words made Taylor remember that he could also hear *her* at a distance, and she blushed furiously as she turned and ran with the others.

CHAPTER TWELVE

- ANDRE -

Andre watched the arcane lightning coiling through the air above Taylor like a living thing as they ran. Since fighting the storm, they had already run for several days—and many hours today—but there was no chance of them stopping the remainder of the day. He sighed at the tedium of bounding along while carrying Zed, and was slightly tempted to convince the Bard to play his fast-travel music.

Then he remembered that Luke would likely break Zed's neck if the Bard tried that again.

"Probably a 'no' on that idea." Andre's mutter elicited a curious glance from the Bard, but he didn't break his meditative breathing to ask questions. The nose-flower generated for the Bard was keeping him alive, but there was no reason to test its effectiveness by being lazy. Andre winced as he thought of that plant—there was a larger than fifty percent chance that there would be side effects. Hopefully everything could be taken care of rapidly... but the Druid would have preferred to test his creations on an enemy, not an ally; *certainly* not on a friend.

The hours passed swiftly, and relatively soon, they reached the next landmark. The purple twilight that passed for night here had well and truly set in, but that meant nothing to the powerful group, except that Zed's slumped form needed to be carried more carefully in order to let him sleep.

Andre felt Taylor's sharp gaze pass over him, and a pleasant shiver ran through his spine. He knew that she was simply keeping an eye out for more ambushes, but… he had been attracted to her even before they had gone off to their individual training, and the small flame he had kept lit for her had never burned out.

Speaking of flames, there had been numerous explosions of power, cacophonies of energy reaching into the sky throughout the entire day. Clearly, the people searching for them were closing in but running into trouble. He hoped that a few of them would fall into a spidery Terror-spell nest, like the tale Taylor had once regaled them with.

"From here, only a few hours of travel at this pace," Taylor called softly as she pointed out Paper-Crush Rock, which looked exactly like a wad of paper which a furious artist might have mangled and tossed into the midden. "I had originally thought the final path to Inkwell Lake would take a whole day to traverse, but I guess I'm used to judging things by the 'standard'."

"Which we are *clearly* not." Andre winked as he stated that fact, earning a snort from Luke and an eye-roll from Taylor. His next words were slightly sobering. "How likely is it that our destination is known? Will we have to push through a blockade?"

"I'm sure it's *guessed*, based on our direction, but I doubt anyone knew we would go to the desert right away." Taylor shook her head, trying to control her facial muscles so that her next words didn't come out as an insult. "Going to the desert has always been thought of as the end of anyone's career, even for Ascenders. For us to go there at the peak of our fame? Radically outside the norm.

No one would expect us to be punished after our huge success."

"Good." Andre didn't waste his breath after that, instead picking up speed in the direction the Namer had indicated. The 'night' passed swiftly, and soon the banks of an ink-black river appeared on the horizon. A few hours later, they arrived at the river's edge and began searching for a waypoint that would give them a good indication of a place to exit this world. "How huge is this lake?"

Luke squinted into the distance and shrugged. "Ocean of ink. Who cares? Can't drink it."

"It's really hard to tell for sure." Taylor glared at Luke's flippant remark. "The huge river that carries the ink here comes from the falls, and it terminates at this lake. Its boundary grows and shifts constantly, and the ink is magical. The entire lake can recede a hundred miles overnight, or stretch until it is a thin but massive puddle. No one knows why; it's just the lake. There!"

Taylor's nonchalant explanation ended in excitement as she pointed out an obelisk marked with a character that meant 'expanding sand', the magical rune equivalent of 'desert'. Andre checked on Zed's condition as they hurried toward the structure, his pupils constricting as he found dozens of roots that had grown into the Bard's veins by following the lung's pathways. As Taylor began opening a triangular portal to escape the World of Names, the Druid ever-so-carefully began forcing the roots to pull back and relinquish their hold within the Bard.

What he *wasn't* expecting was the mighty resistance from the new plant. If he hadn't been *carefully* controlling the plant, it would have thrashed and torn open every vein it had grown into, bleeding its host to death in mere minutes. Not trusting the plant for another instant, Andre fully removed it from the Bard, who began to gasp both in pain from the increased mana density… as well as horror at the plant as it was fully revealed.

The root structure had expanded to coat the entire interior of his lungs, so when Andre pulled it out, he pulled… and pulled… and kept going far after the whole thing should have been long gone. Andre extended his power into the plant, and felt slight resentment directed at him. He frowned and poured his will into it. Now that it was fully extracted from the Bard, it was safe for Andre to rapidly age it and collect the resulting seeds. He put them into his pouch, and borrowed Zed's fire-stone to burn every bit of the remnants just to be doubly safe.

Only then did he step through the opening to the base world with the others, his tardiness earning him a few concerned glances. He merely shrugged and gestured at the air where the closed portal had stood a moment ago. "Just learned that I'm going to need to add a few failsafes to my creations going forward. I'm thinking rapid-kill, perhaps make them all sterile just to be safe-"

"Please… *water*," Zed managed to gasp out. "I'm so *dry*."

The group looked at him in concern and hurried to pour waterskin after waterskin of liquid into him. Andre inspected the Bard to make sure he wasn't about to burst into flame from a delayed reaction to too much mana. When he was sure that wasn't the issue, he bowed to Zed. "I think this is my fault. Please forgive the hasty actions I took in an attempt to preserve your life. I am… *fairly* certain that the plant I gave you to absorb the excess mana was pulling water directly from your blood to nurture itself."

"I'm alive, I've got water, all is forgiven." Zed magnani-mously waved his drink, as if he were an Emperor releasing a prisoner of war. "Even got a pretty good story out of it, if I can tell it and get people to believe that I'm not yanking their chain."

Andre nodded at the Bard thankfully and scanned their surroundings, noting that the area they were standing in looked nothing like a desert.

"Taylor, did we somehow come to the wrong location?" Andre blushed as the words left his lips; that had sounded *really* accusatory. "Just because, you know, look at this place. It's all farmland!"

Taylor didn't take offense, realizing that common knowledge for her was still state-secret for them. "We're only able to get *close* to the desert. The entire place is a mana dead-zone. Whatever happened here centuries ago, it's still happening. The desert is growing slowly, and wherever it touches, the ambient mana begins filtering away. That makes opening portals within its boundary really difficult without an outside mana source, so we come here first. As to this being farmland? Once upon a time, the Scarrocco Plains were known as the most fertile land within three kingdoms, and the entire region was the bread-basket of the kingdom. Now... at least the land around the edges is still pretty fertile."

"How strange." Andre reached out to the life around him and began connecting to it. Soon he had gained enough ground that he was comfortable pricking his finger and letting blood flow from the wound to create a massive magic circle that he held spinning in the air. With a grunt of exertion, the ring turned horizontal and expanded massively, slowly settling over a mile of the land with the Druid as the epicenter. Mana seeped out of his body, and the relative speed it flowed began to increase as more and more of the plant life in the circle was bound to him and began adding their fragments of mana to his own.

In under half an hour, he had connected with all the flora and brought it under control, immediately gaining a powerful insight into the area. With a new base of power supporting him, his pale cheeks flushed with life and good cheer. "All set... we can get going."

"We should really make a plan," Taylor insisted as they began walking. "If we're gonna deal with assassins and the like, we should-"

"Mind what you say." Luke glared at the surrounding corn stalks as they bowed at the Druid in recognition. "There are ears everywhere."

"I *want* to be mad that you made me look around," Andre sighed after a long pause, "but I was the one encouraging you to get into a good mental place by making jokes, so I can't even say anything."

"*I* can!" Zed interjected in disgust. "That was terrible! I thought we were actually in danger, until I realized that we *were*! From your dreadful wordplay!"

"Too corny. I understand," Luke deadpanned, getting a full laugh from Andre for his trouble.

"Ah... I love plant jokes something fierce." The Druid wiped at his eyes and took a few deep breaths to release the shaky feeling in his core. The last few days of sudden political intrigue and fleeing for his life were... unexpected. Something about *Luke*, of all people, going out of his way to relieve tension really showed Andre exactly how wound up he really was. He felt a tight knot in his stomach unwind as he let go of the guilt he had been feeling over nearly letting his plant drink Zed's blood dry. He had saved the Bard, and he would need to be satisfied now that the crisis was over.

The Druid took some time to order his thoughts, managing to bond to the flora they passed almost unconsciously. His Circle Magic had reached tier six, level seven: basic plant life from the base world had no chance of resisting his will at all.

The group managed to find a path after walking through the 'rough' terrain and decided to keep to the grass alongside the muddy, pockmarked roadway. Andre's ability to control grass was easily on par with his mentor Xan's, so the blades resisted their footfalls and allowed them to walk comfortably.

A fringe benefit was that all signs of their passing were completely hidden, so they didn't need to fear that pursuers would be able to track them easily. Andre listened as Taylor started recounting all the possible border towns they could make into a base of operations, including the benefits and detriments of each.

Natural resources, defensive positions, local attitudes toward outsiders... he shook his head as the words seemed to pour out of her endlessly. Not a syllable of the information was drivel, but the thought of all this seemingly useless information being stuffed in her head—and used to its best effect to help The Four —astounded him.

Each of them voiced what they thought would be the best place, and eventually the group reached a consensus. They adjusted their course accordingly and walked at Zed's pace for a few hours, until they came upon a new road and began following it toward their destination. Andre stiffened as his ever-expanding ring of bound plants suddenly started screeching into his mind. He sniffed the air, confirming his worries. "Something up ahead is on fire."

"A wildfire? Do we need to run?" Zed turned directly around and started back the way they had come, not waiting for an answer.

"No… but it's too big to be a camp. A lot of plants ahead are wilting away, and all of them are near the road." Andre caught the question in Taylor's eyes and gestured in the direction they were moving. "About a mile that way."

They picked up the pace, the Druid literally picking up Zed, and they blazed along the packed-dirt road toward what they now recognized as a column of smoke. Soon enough, a huge covered wagon appeared on the road, nearly fully burnt out. Taylor surveyed the area, trying to spot the attackers. Seeing nothing unusual, she gestured the team forward. "Go see what happened."

Andre started for the smoking rubble, but since he was carrying Zed, Luke was far faster to react and inspect the scene. A moment after he reached the front of the wagon, he called out, "Ah-*ha*!"

"What is it? What did you find?" Taylor hurried to join the Murderhobo.

"I figured out why this wagon crashed." Luke popped into view, lifting two bodies that had been burnt all the way down to their bones. "This wagon was being driven… by *skeletons*!"

The other three stared at Luke as he proudly displayed the corpses. Andre shook his head, dropped Zed, and began opening a portal. He didn't utter a single word for the three minutes it took to open the gate between worlds, simply shaking his head the entire time. As the spell finished and the portal activated, he grumbled, "That's it. I'm out. I'll be back in a week. I'm gonna go find the limits of my Ability."

Without further ado, he stepped through and escaped into his hidden grove.

CHAPTER THIRTEEN

- LUKE -

Luke stared at the space Andre had just disappeared through. The air was filled with the scent of fragrant flowers and juicy fruits, so pungent that his stomach rumbled in anticipation of a meal. Mana converged on Luke, filling his Sigil, imparting knowledge of his new Skills, but he didn't even stop to consider them. Fury began to flow through his veins. "How come he can just leave like that? *I* want to leave. This world bites. Oh. My skills just finished upgrading-"

"Oh, come now! It's not that bad; *I'm* here!" Before Luke could inspect the changes to his Skills, Zed threw an arm around him, then *slo~owly* removed it as the Murderhobo stared at the meat touching him with a still-rumbling stomach. "*So~o~o*, how about that new town that we get to live in until Andre fixes the desert? Isn't it exciting that we get a decade or two to hang out and *really* get invested in the lives of the commoners in the area?"

"I heard that there hasn't been a single Ascender from the area in almost thirty years." Taylor shook her head sadly. "The tiny amount of mana in the air nearby made it nearly impossible for people to advance. It's... frankly, I think the people here are going to be miserable and hard to deal with."

"Or... open to suggestion?" Zed countered as he waggled his eyebrows at her suggestively. "You think I can get a free pass to work as a Bard in the surrounding areas?"

"Know what?" Taylor nodded and waved her hand at Zed. "Why not? Go have your fun. You already have permission from the King to destroy anyone that comes after you; just make sure you check in once a week on our progress."

"Yes!" Zed nearly screamed in excitement. "You mean it? Actual freedom to come and go?"

"Don't make me regret it," the Namer coldly stated, making the Bard shrug and wave at the others to hurry up. *Now* he was ready to get to town.

The entire conversation meant nothing to Luke. He pulled open his Skills and read over the changes he had been waiting for, exulting in the sweet promise of more efficient killing in the near future.

Skill increase complete! Innate Balance -> Pristine Balance.

Effect 1: You gain an innate balance when walking on narrow ledges or any surface that you are attempting to traverse that requires good balance. This skill is modified by the sub-characteristic Physical Reaction. Current balance increase: 5%. (passive ability)

Bonus 1, at range: When jumping or leaping, balance bonus doubles.

Effect 2: The bonus is active at all times, not only when on narrow walkways.

NEW! Bonus 2, multitarget: All gear used by you is considered balanced, no matter how unwieldy it may actually be. Due to this, all damage dealt will be $5+.5n$% greater, and all damage taken will be $5+.5n$% lower—both maximized at 10% upon reaching the next Tier—so long as it is blocked by gear or a skill, where n = skill level.

That had been what he needed. His stomping gait would finally be able to exhibit his predatory grace once more. He stretched backward fluidly, perching on a single toe as he read over the second message with his head only a half foot from the ground.

Skill increase complete! Bum Rush -> Bum Flash.

Effect 1: At the cost of 10 mana, you can empower your forward charge, allowing you to cross the same amount of distance in one second that you can sprint at baseline in five seconds.

Bonus 1, at range: At the cost of $10n$ mana, you are able to instantly traverse $1+n$ meters of space (maximized at 10 meters) while rushing toward an opponent, where n = skill level. Cooldown restrictions on this Skill have been removed.

The Murderhobo was still staring at the spot where Andre's portal had vanished, and his blood was boiling as he contemplated using his new skills in an actual fight. "The fact that Andre gets to just leave any time he wants is torturing me with terrible thoughts."

Taylor nodded lightly, trying not to reveal how nervous those few words had actually made her. "I appreciate the warning. I'll work on that special dispensation right now."

Luke stared at Taylor as she pulled out a notebook and wrote a simple phrase inside, glancing at him a few times as she did so. He didn't blink at all, just to make *sure* she knew that he really *saw* that she was doing him a favor. The Murderhobo didn't want her to think he didn't appreciate her going out on a limb for him. From the way she flushed, and the sweat that appeared for a brief instant, she was very excited to be helping him. Luke appreciated that about her. "It's been almost two days since I've killed something, and I'm getting the *itch*. Ideas?"

"Why not... find whoever did that?" Taylor waved at the wagon, which had nearly finished burning out. "Not like anyone is going to be sad that a bunch of bandits got wiped out."

Luke nodded in silent contemplation as the three of them walked toward their destination, an unnamed town that had sprung up around an abandoned outpost. As they got closer, the vegetation began to thin, and before long, they sighted mountainous sand dunes in the distance. The town they had been aiming for was right at the edge of the sand, and Luke realized that seeing this had made a frown appear on Taylor's face. "What is it now?"

Taylor turned to him sharply, then gestured at the small town. "That's supposed to be a solid ten miles from the actual sand of the desert. All of the most recent maps in the kingdom marked it as just another town, not a small oasis of people."

"Ooh... I wonder what their story is!" Zed greedily rubbed his hands together. "Even if they get swallowed up in the sands, I'll make sure to tell their lament to the world!"

"Pretty sure they could escape the sand by walking for a few minutes." Luke continued toward the town at a comfortable pace, and the others hurried to catch up. They reached the village less than thirty minutes later, and Luke walked right up to a man standing watch with a spear in hand. "Hey. Where are the bandits? I was told I could go kill 'em."

The guard scornfully appraised Luke's ink-stained skin and clothes, smirking even though he could see that the brute of a man clearly had well-defined muscles under his soiled garments. "Any trouble we're having around here isn't something we need a... what are you, a bodybuilding artist? Yeah, we don't exactly need an artist coming to save us."

"Good to know." Luke lashed out, wrapping his hand around the sneering guard's scrawny neck and lifting him off the ground in one smooth motion, bellowing into his face, "*Where* are they? Are you keeping them from me? You're *one* of them, aren't you! You thought you could hide in plain sight?"

His second hand joined the first, and he started to *squeeze*. He could feel the weak flesh under his fingers starting to pulp, then...

Chime!

The guard fell to the ground in a heap, sucking wind and coughing flecks of blood onto the ground. Luke raised his foot to finish off the bandit masquerading as a guard, only to be interrupted by a gentle yet firm hand holding him back. Taylor stepped between him and the pile of meat waiting to be tender-ized, using calming *words* to assuage his building fury. "*Luke*, he's not a known criminal, or else you wouldn't have been stopped! Give us a few minutes to figure things out-"

"Enough! Why does Andre get to go, and I'm kept on a leash like an animal? He knows about them, and I was promised a chance to *kill*!" Luke howled as he lunged for the terrified downed guard. An alarm bell was ringing almost in time with his Sigil's chiming, and the Mage was in his *way*! He pulled out a waterskin, popped the cork, and squirted a thin stream of liquid mana right at her.

Taylor's face shifted to shock, but she dodged, appearing to teleport as she grabbed the guard and tossed him as far away as she could manage. Luke's eye's tracked his target as the man bounced off the soft sand and rolled. *He was unharmed.* Luke opened his mouth and barked, "Bum-"

"Special dispensation approved!" Taylor screamed as Luke started to activate his charge attack, holding up a book that displayed a signature that Luke didn't recognize. "You can go to Murder World right now!"

Luke's fist lashed out, and Taylor flinched—thinking it was coming at her. Instead, it impacted the hazy mana that was starting to spread out, collapsing it into a point as his other fist joined the first. "*Open Up!*"

Wub. His fists rang out, striking the air in a staccato beat. After the first three blows, the fabric of reality started to give way under the pressure coming off his knuckles. A crack appeared in space, and one final hit shattered the barrier between himself and his world.

"Now I have to turn *this* into our base of operations. Thanks for making everyone hostile and then running away, Luke," Taylor scathingly articulated as dozens of armed men and women began rushing toward them. "Zed, you're up."

Luke heard nothing else; he had already thrown himself into his world. He was on a time limit, and he was going to make use of every *second*.

The Murderhobo lifted his head, and his red-rimmed eyes scanned the area for *anything*. With nothing visible upon which to vent his fury, he released a massive *Goat Call* and hoped that it would force something to come after him… no luck. Turning, he sprinted into Zone ten.

Welcome to Zone ten! In this Zone, you'll f#$d @ll sorts of-

Even if the entire message had been properly readable by standard eyes, Luke would have dismissed it. In his current enraged state, he fully ignored the fact that there was clearly something wrong with the message that should have been showing; usually, that meant something was wrong with the Zone itself. Oblivious, he sprinted deeper into the terrain, *finally* coming across the first enemy.

A massive pteranodon with an incredibly sharp crystalline spiral horn swooped at him. Its beak had a metallic sheen, as did its talons, but for some reason the bird thing tried to *gore* Luke with its face-horn. Frankly, it was a terrible idea. Luke charged at the flying creature, and right before they collided, he used his new *Bum Flash* Skill to move a single meter straight up.

He caught the neck of the creature and *squeezed*, finally obtaining the sweet relief he needed as the flesh squished and tore under his grip. He swept out with his left hand, and his simple metal sword sliced through what remained of the neck in one clean strike. The body continued gliding away for a short while, but Luke and the head crashed to the ground.

You have slain an infested pteranodon!

Etheric Xenograft Potentia gained: 200.

He gripped the crystalline horn and pulled, surprised as it tore free of the skull with a wet cracking noise. "Huh. This thing's horn was tougher than its bones? Nice. That's smooth. Makes it easy to extract."

Inspecting the horn, he noticed that it had grown around the Skill Pearl and out of the skull. When he had ripped the protrusion out, the Pearl had come with it. Yet when he tried to separate the two, he found that the horn wouldn't give up the prize so easily. He glared at the crystalline spiral, found a flat rock to lay it on, and started beating it with his Battering Ram Knuckles. He was pleased to see that they seemed to do more damage—as promised by his Pristine Balance Skill—and soon the horn broke from the repeated blows.

Once it started to crack, the entire horn crumbled into a fine powder. The unharmed Skill Pearl rolled free, and Luke stashed it in his waterskin. "No need to work out how to use a new Skill in the middle of an active combat area."

He hesitated as he considered the powdered horn. Something about it was telling him that it was useful. With a quick motion, he swept it all into a satchel and started hunting for his next opponent. A screech made him look up, and he squinted in minor confusion at the sight.

It was the same creature he had just fought, he was sure of it... but it didn't have a horn. There were also a *lot* more of them. "Why are these so *loud*? That last one was totally silent. I *liked* that."

Luke charged right at the flock of monsters, feeling appreciative of their size. Each wingspan was at least five meters across, and their bodies sat around two and a half meters long. That gave him something to *really* sink his fists into! As he got in range, they began swooping at him like a well-trained squadron, further revealing their difference to the first pteranodon by using all of their natural weapons in an attempt to turn him into mincemeat. He wove around snapping beaks, slashing talons, and razor-tipped wings, pushing his increased balance to the limit as he evaded their strikes just enough to not be shredded.

His fists came down on the birds, driving them into the long blue grass below. Each strike almost *bounced* off of the beasts when he used his Battering Ram Knuckles; a very concerning sensation indeed. Narrowing his eyes, he focused on the feel of his next strike. Luke's Simple Metal Sword opened deep lacerations, but the cuts were no longer clean; instead *tearing* as they slashed through the hide of his target. He shifted the mana distribution in his Skills, keeping only five percent devoted to his armor, then directing the remainder into his weapons: thirty-five percent to each.

He slashed down his left hand with all the force he could muster.

You have slain a pteranodon!

Damage dealt: 582 slashing!

His sword-shaped mana passed through the body of the downed pteranodon, killing it in an instant as it was bisected. Even so… the cut was not clean. His judgment was instant. "My weapons are getting to be too weak."

Etheric Xenograft Potentia gained: 100.

"What. Why was that worth only *half* the Potentia?" At the point where he realized he was thinking about stuff instead of enjoying the fight, he shook his head and refocused. He couldn't take the time to care too much about the performance of his weapons and Potentia income—he just needed to kill his enemies.

The sky was teeming with birds, but he was forced to wait for them to come after him one-by-one. He roared at the open air, which was completely ignored by the stupid birds. They only swooped at him when they thought they had a chance of either taking him by surprise, or attacking in a large group, clearly hoping in their tiny little brains that they could over-whelm him.

Yet Luke still hadn't taken a single hit. Their size was a disadvantage for them, as their natural weapons were too widely spaced apart to deal damage if he moved out of their direct path. Both sides seemed to realize this at the same time and had different reactions to the thought. Luke deactivated his armor entirely, freeing up the mana to use in his other spells. The dinosaur-birds simply flew higher and started circling him instead of attacking.

"C'mere," Luke called up at them, gesturing at his body. "Tasty man flesh. All you gotta do is come and get it!"

His only answer was a series of trumpeting squawks that filled the air. The Murderhobo's left eye twitched, and he clenched his fists as he turned to collect the Skill Pearls of the pteranodons he had killed. "I'm *not* getting a ranged weapon."

CHAPTER FOURTEEN

Not seeing a way to take down the flying pests, Luke decided to simply move on. He had a total of thirty days to spend here—a timer had appeared in his vision as soon as he had arrived—and he wasn't going to waste it yelling at overgrown seagulls. They seemed content to swoop around far above, but as he progressed through Zone ten, the flock size continued to grow. If there had been a sun in his world, instead of the omnipresent light that seemed to filter through the fog walls that surrounded the land, the pteranodons would have made the area as dark as night.

A quarter of the way through the Zone, he finally discovered why the creatures had seemingly given up on assaulting him. In front of him sat fifteen enormous metal rings attached to the ground. Each ring was three times as tall as he was, and twice as wide. A tremendous chain was attached to each ring, extending from its connection point out into the distance before vanishing in the swirling fog. "Ah. They think they can knock me off the chain when I start to cross."

Sometimes he forgot that the creatures of Murder World were not actually natural beasts. They didn't care if they could eat him after they killed him: they'd happily allow him to fall to his death… or to whatever was at the bottom of the massive spiral. "Might actually be nothing down there. They might smack me off, and I'll fall for a few months before dying of starvation."

With that grim thought, Luke decided to avoid that potential future. He scowled up at the birds overhead, knowing that there were even more gathering than he could see. "Kill them all or test my luck… well *that's* an easy answer."

He deliberated over his newly-collected Skill Pearls. While he had wanted to hold onto them to gain a custom Skill at the end of the next set of Zones, the fact remained that he needed *something* to change right now. He inspected the Pearls he had collected already, pleased to note that by their luster and pearlescence that they should be around Tier three right away. "First thing… kill fifty of these things and get a better Pearl."

A Tier three Skill wasn't *worthless* by any means, but he could either combine fifty Pearls from fifty kills or spend tens of thousands of Potentia to achieve the same effect. He eyed the Pearls from the Witches of Zone nine and scoffed. If he ate one of those, he would likely get either a self-destructive skill or a mana-wasting zappy spell of some kind. "Better to just throw those away."

Deciding to use the same tactics that had worked against the phantoms in a prior Zone, Luke laid down and took out the book that Lord Woodswright had given him, reading 'How to Make Friends and Not Burn Down Society'. He did so out of not only boredom, but also to pretend that he was distracted by the book.

Several hours in, he was shocked and infuriated to realize that he had *actually* found a lot of very specific examples that seemed as if they had been pulled directly out of his life's story. Checking the date it had been written, over a decade before, he begrudgingly decided that *perhaps* there were more people like him than he had thought.

Over the course of the next day of reading between fights,

Luke lured in and killed enough birds to upgrade the Pearl, but he was absolutely *fuming* over the massive waste of time. The creatures would come only one at a time to see if he was *actually* not focused, displaying an intelligence that made him frown.

If the creatures continued to gain intelligence the further he traveled, how long would he have until he was forced to attack fortified positions? He decided to step back into Zone nine to absorb and practice the new Skill instead, watching as the pter-anodons dispersed with angry screeches. He stared at the massive flock of thousands of birds, compelled to swallow back saliva as he imagined getting a chance to tear into each and every one of them. He took a final look at the Tier four Skill Pearl and hoped for the best as he tossed it down his throat.

Just like all but the first time he had eaten one, the Pearl seemingly vanished as it moved down his esophagus, never reaching his stomach. Just to be sure, he took a swig of 'water' to aid his digestion and waited for the related information to appear.

It was a short wait.

Skill gained: Feather's Fall. T4, level 2.

Effect 1: When taking damage from falling, the damage is first taken as mana loss until either the damage or mana has been overpowered. Current damage conversion: 1 mana per 1 point of damage. (Maximized)

Bonus 1, at range: At the cost of $200-10n$ mana where n = skill level, your mana spreads to create a far higher surface area, allowing you to drift on the wind as does a feather for 10 seconds. Current mana cost: 100 mana per use (maximized).

Effect 2: Upon falling, you will automatically converge your momentum to a single point at no mana cost. When used as an attack, $10n\%$ of the total damage dealt is converted to piercing damage. Current damage conversion: 100%

Bonus 2, multitarget: You are able to converge your momentum to $1+n$ points. Current maximum impact points: 3.

Luke thought over the Skill and its applications, realizing quickly that this would be extremely difficult to use in the base world. While he was in Murder World, his mana regeneration sat at a cozy one hundred per second. That meant he could practice to his heart's content here, but he would only have thirty seconds of usage when he left, *if* he hadn't used any of his other mana for whatever reason.

"Okay. How do I use this to kill those blue dinosaur seagulls?" He pulled up his Potentia and found a cool eighty-five hundred and fifty-eight waiting to be used. Checking his Skills, he sighed and added a single point to Walking Arsenal, pushing it through the boundary into Tier nine. A shockwave of coruscating light erupted from him, shaking his internal organs with its intensity. He spat out a mouthful of blood as the shock erupted again a moment later, and he quickly took a sip of mana each time a subsequent wave erupted out.

"Is there a level requirement to having high-Tier Skills that I don't know about or something?" he griped an hour later, when the energy waves had finally calmed down enough that they were no longer hurting him. The Murderhobo was unhappy with his current situation. Upgrading that Skill had basically rung the dinner bell: creatures were gathering on both sides of the Zone barrier. He was safe for now, due to the creeping movement of the witches, but his body *yearned* to be throwing itself at the huge swarm of pteranodons that were hovering mere meters away.

Every once in a while, the press of bodies would get too thick, at which time, the weaker birds were tossed across the boundary and directly detonated, showering him in gore and headless carcasses. Luke stood there and taunted the beasts for a while before getting bored and switching to testing out the capabilities of his new Skill. It was one thing to read what a Skill did, and another thing entirely to put it into practice. If he was going to manage to get to the next Zone, he needed to be *proficient* in its use.

Luckily for him, going deeper into Murder World meant that he was descending on an incline. While he hadn't spotted any cliffs or tall stones recently, he still had an idea to help him practice. He ran uphill for roughly a mile, then turned around and used Bum Flash to sprint a hundred meters in an instant, leaping into the air and using Feather's Fall immediately afterward.

He was glad he'd decided to practice before trying it in a truly dangerous situation. His mana swept out like a thrown net, and he tumbled end over end multiple times before falling face-first into a rock. To his great surprise, he was completely unharmed, even though he didn't have any mana armor equipped. His mana topped off in the same second, and he realized that *it* had taken the damage instead of his flesh. Nodding appreciatively that the Skill had done what it was supposed to do, he got back to practicing. He changed locations every few hours, or whenever he started to catch witches drifting toward him.

Currently, he didn't have a way to fight them effectively, and his upgrading Skill continuously called out to them. The fifteenth time he changed location, he was starting to get *irked*. Luke made his way to a spot that was completely barren, then managed to make a great leap into the air. Once he activated Feather's Fall, it seemed to link with his Pristine Balance Skill, and it all sorta *clicked* for him. He swooped in the air, managing a controlled glide for the first time since he had started practicing.

"Woo!" He screamed with joy as he started drifting toward the ground at his own pace. A flicker of motion caught his eye, and he screeched as he noticed a shard of ice leaving the tip of a staff pointed directly at his head. The ice launched so quickly that it would barely lose out to Taylor's new lightning bolt, but it *was* slower. Acting on instinct, Luke activated the new function of Bum Flash, instantly moving a single meter directly upward.

Ice streaked beneath him, so close that his exposed chest hair froze and broke off. Luke used the remaining seconds of Feather's Fall and his higher position to swoop over to a safe landing spot before sprinting away from the murderous blue-eyed Boomy Mage of Doomy. He ran almost a full hour before he felt safe enough to start practicing once more.

The Murderhobo realized that he had been underutilizing his upgraded Skills, and he immediately poured five thousand three hundred Potentia into Bum Flash, bringing it to level seven in an instant. He had thirty-two fifty-seven remaining, meaning he was just about one hundred and fifty shy of reaching the next level.

"Set Skill to gain all Potentia until it reaches level eight," he directed his Sigil, which chimed in reply. Satisfied, he got right back to practicing his Skill, finally able to rocket from a standing position directly into gliding. Soon he had a plan ready for fighting the pteranodons, and a murderous smile stretched across his face.

"Now all I need is to patiently wait for my Skill to finish upgrading, and I'll make it rain dino-birds," Luke spoke cheerfully to himself. A slight *chime* came from his head, and his face lost all mirth as he screamed, "Not now, Sigil! I *said* I gotta be *patient*!"

CHAPTER FIFTEEN

By the end of the third day of waiting, Luke was beginning to lose his ever-lovin' mind. His Skill *still* hadn't managed to complete its upgrade, and he wasn't sure *why*. Before now, none of his Skills had ever taken more than two days to come back to him. His brow furrowed as he tried to think it through logically, which frankly was not his forte anymore. "This is the first time I've gotten to the ninth Tier. Is it just a hazard of raising a Skill to be this powerful? What does the ninth Tier of something even do?"

Chime. His Sigil interrupted his verbalization, writing out a message just before he was able to shout at it again.

The ninth Tier creates a fifth effect for the Skill, Spell, Ability, ect. This effect is usually the main focus of the Skill when creating a Full Domain at the tenth Tier, and tends to slightly alter each effect or bonus from the lower Tiers. Please plan on at least one business week for upgrades when reaching the ninth Tier!

"Main focus." Luke thought about that for a long moment. "It's more powerful than the previous effects. That's the only reason it would take this long. What's a business week? No. Forget it. Fine. I'll wait a little longer."

But it wasn't just a little longer. He had been planning on a few more hours at the maximum, but it ended up taking two full *days* longer before something changed. The Murderhobo was tumbling through the air, attempting to catch an upward blast of air that seemed to originate from large heat sources, when the pulsing of the upgrading Skill suddenly just... stopped. He dropped fully to the ground, confused as to why the change had occurred.

The shockwaves that he had been sending out suddenly reversed. Mana crashed into him, one wave after another. In a place like Murder World, the converging mana was clearly visible. Burst after burst of power billowed over to him. The dense blue fog filling the sky as far as the eye could see was soon spiraling at his face, a vast whirlpool that drained down into his Sigil as if someone had pulled the stopper from the bottom of the ocean.

Luke was prepared for pain, but the most dense concentration which the mana-fog reached was a liquid form, the same as the mana he used as drinking water. He was more annoyed by the shockwaves. Each time they struck, it felt like some giant was flicking him right in the middle of his forehead. Again, more annoying than *anything* else, but not actually painful. By the fifth hour of this, he gave up on waiting and went back to practicing maneuvering in midair.

"Actually good practice to do this while I'm getting distracted," he admitted as he crashed into the ground for the fifth time. Roughly five hours after the reversed process had started, a series of rapid-fire shockwaves rolled toward him, the bursts strong enough that they slapped him directly out of the air and dug a hole in the ground using his head. Just as he bellowed in fury around a mouthful of mud, a notification appeared that made both words and dirt catch in his throat.

Skill increase complete!

Luke froze in a momentary pause as he waited for more. "Go on. Why didn't it tell me the-"

Notifications have been updated from verbose to minimal.

"That was *weeks* ago!" Luke clawed at the Sigil on his head. "You're a construct! You don't *get* to be passive aggressive! Skill information!"

Walking Arsenal -> Source-cerer's Armory (Tier 9, Level 0)

Altered Effect 1: You are able to absorb natural weapons and armor (Claws, fangs, scales) by touching them. You are able to 'equip' the absorbed gear onto your body. Only one type of weapon can be created at a time, and only one type of armor per slot.

Altered Bonus 1, at range: You are able to absorb a weapon or armor type within fifty feet of your body. No longer requires active attempts after the item is selected.

Altered Effect 2: You are now able to absorb any non-magical weapons or armor.

Bonus 2, Multitarget: You can now opt to absorb all weapons or armor of the same type within the range of bonus 1.

Altered Effect 3: You are now able to absorb weapons or armor created via unnatural metals (magical weapons/armor).

Bonus 3, AoE: You can resize the weapons and armor you create. An increase of size decreases overall mobility, but allows for defending or attacking at greater range.

Effect 4: Each active weapon or armor slot now costs a flat percentage of your mana pool to maintain! To achieve the exact damage or protection potential, ten percent of your mana must be applied. Each percentage added or subtracted will change the potential by one percent.

Altered Bonus 4, Multitarget AOE: All weapons and armor within one meter of you grant you $1n\%$ of their maximum damage or armor. (Maximized at 10%)

Effect 5: You are now able to imprint one piece of armor or weapon per slot with a Soul Brand*. Two-handed weapons are considered one-handed weapons, and fit in a single slot. The restrictions of the previous tiers have been greatly reduced.

Luke's eyes traveled over the updated Skill, pleased at how well it had cleaned up. He was especially glad to learn that he was now able to directly absorb a weapon or armor without needing to eat hundreds of the stupid things. If he had to guess, it also appeared as though he would be able to equip a large number of various gear sets, instead of being limited to a single item per slot. Having so much versatility with weapon and armor choices would be a massive boon, since he fought against countless variants of enemies.

There was at *least* one section he didn't understand, so he looked more closely at the 'Soul Brand' information, and an additional message appeared.

Soul Brand: Choose one item per slot to be your main item for that slot. This will directly double the damage absorption or dealing properties of that item, as well as allowing it to return to you, no matter the distance, if the item has not been absorbed by this Skill. Travel time will vary due to distance.

A Soul Brand can be removed so that another item can take its place. Removing a brand will take three days. Only one brand can be in the process of removal at a time.

"Interesting." Luke considered the changes, pleased with the vast majority of them. Not knowing when he would be able to gain access to new weapons, he branded all of his current armor, then his Battering Ram Knuckle in his right hand and Simple Metal Sword in his left. The triple triangle that he had decided on for his family and Sigil crest blazed momentarily on all of his mana-made gear as they accepted the brand. He looked himself over before shrugging and grunting, "Don't feel any different, but twice as hard to kill. Sounds good to me."

His weapons and armor were back, and that was good enough for now. It was time to challenge Zone ten properly. He started running downhill, alternating between sprinting and gliding along with Feather's Fall. The huge swarm of pteran-odons had dispersed, but Luke knew that they were out there, and that was sufficient. He even had a plan to lure them *all* to him once again.

Increasing flocks of the birds began to circle him as he approached the massive chains that went into the distance, and a few even began to test their luck. As the first one flew at him, Luke wound back and punched it right in the beak. The bird literally popped like a soap bubble, gore splattering the area in front of the human in a cone. "Splattered pteranodon aerosolized matter. Spam. Delicious with eggs. Probably."

Damage dealt: 630 blunt damage!

Exp gained: 100.

He let out a lungful of air, a tension knot he had been holding in his stomach slowly releasing. His weapons were useful again. Sure, that had been an attack with everything he could put behind it, but it showed him what he could do. Now it was time to put his plan in motion. The Murderhobo retreated uphill, then sprinted at the chains and *jumped* as high as he could... drifting out into the open air over the rattling links.

A huge clamor arose from the birds as they dove at him in a swarm, the noise attracting ever more of the creatures. Luke smiled as the first of them closed in on him; he flashed to its head and used it as a platform to both refresh Bum Flash and start gaining altitude. It was time to prepare the next stage of his massacre. "Use the useless one... Sigil, devote all Potentia gain to Skill 'Goat Call'."

Chime came the acknowledgement.

The pteranodons did *not* enjoy their airspace being infringed upon. Scores of the creatures appeared each second, gradually filling the sky. Luke didn't mind at all. As a point of fact, he used the higher numbers to gain ever-increasing altitude. Eventually he was able to look up and see the bottom of a previous Zone far above him, and tried to climb a *little* further... only to bump into a strange fold in space that forced him to rebound back toward Zone fifteen.

Upd@te! Living things cannot cross the boundaries at unauthorized points! Continued contact with turbulent space will cause 999 damage every 5 seconds!

"Eh, glad I didn't try swooping further *down* first," Luke grumbled as he dropped into freefall toward the beasts below. "Ah, well. I've got killin' to do."

CHAPTER SIXTEEN

Luke's fist lashed out, landing in the center of a pteranodon's back. To his surprise, his fist went directly *through* the creature, and the rest of his body continued through the wide hole in the next instant. A quick glance to the side at his mostly hidden notifications clarified what was happening.

Damage dealt: 481 piercing. (100% of damage converted to piercing damage due to Feather's Fall.)

"Don't see an option to turn that off. That'd be too convenient, wouldn't it?" Luke muttered as he fell through eight of the creatures in rapid succession. "Fine. I want maximum points of contact, not a single one."

Current maximum impact points: 3.

Not wasting any more time on words when action was clearly the better option, Luke hit the next beast and *didn't* burst through, although the creature was blasted into four different segments of separated meat in the same instant. Using one chunk as a kick pad, he managed to activate Bum Flash and appeared eight meters higher. A passing bird rammed into him, something neither of them were expecting. His armor held, as it would have even before the Soul Brand, but that gave him more confidence that this insane plan would work.

He swung out with a one-two punch, and the pteranodon fell from the sky. His greed ached when he thought about the fact that he was gaining not a single pearl, but he just needed to push on. As he tumbled toward a thick cluster of beasts once more, he tried to right himself. "Not used to air combat. Gotta get lotsa practice. I bet Don the Archmage can fly, now that I think about it."

The next few hours were entirely devoted to fighting, as well as slowly progressing further along the trajectory of the swinging chains that he intermittently spotted in the air far below. Any time their glint became too distant, he would flash toward them. Getting lost in the air would lead to a surefire death, and he *really* liked life. His *own* life. The Murderhobo punched a dinosaur in the wing just to clarify that thought in his head.

Pteranodons were good experience, and he wasn't losing too much Potentia from fighting them consistently. After the first hour, the Potentia gain only dropped from one hundred per bird down to ninety-nine. Whether the comparatively slow reduction was because they were in a new fighting environment, or because he had just never fought flying-type beasts before, Luke didn't know for sure. Either way, his Goat Call Skill was gaining levels rapidly.

As he completed his three hundredth kill six hours in, Goat Call finally started to break through into the next Tier. A spherical shockwave of mana burst out from Luke, its radius crossing hundreds of feet in an instant. He dropped for a few seconds as the world seemed to go still. Then the fog became speckled all the way out to the horizon. It screamed with hunger.

Luke had never heard the fog make a noise before.

Squaaa! The shrieks of delight rising from innumerable pteranodons shook the air just as hard as the pulsing shockwaves from Luke's Sigil.

"Oh. Good. It was just the birds, not the fog." He resumed

kicking off the closer beasts and gaining altitude once more. It wouldn't do to be surrounded on all sides. The flapping of wings and his own clothes were soon the only thing he could hear, with the wingbeats growing closer and more numerous by the second. The sounds of his clothes did *not* multiply, which he felt a faint relief about.

At the top of his upward Bum Flash trajectory, Luke looked at the sky and lifted his arms out to the side, slowly falling backward until his head was pointed down. He adjusted Feather's Fall as he looked down at the swarm of dinosaurs swirling up to meet him, then stuck out his fist as he shot right through the center of the countless beasts.

All he could see was blue feathers, blue blood, and scrolling piercing damage notifications as he sliced through at least eighty pteranodons without slowing. As he neared the base of the flock, he flipped and smashed the spine of one of the massive birds to once again start his climb into the sky. In order to use Feather's Fall, as well as keep his armor up, the Murderhobo deactivated his left-hand weapon as he ascended.

He was among the creatures, so the upward spiral became a sphere as the huge beasts swarmed to take a bite out of him. Damage notifications began piling up, but each time his gear failed, it would flicker back into being shortly afterward. Even so, the sheer amount of wounds he was taking from flashing talons and snapping beaks was unacceptable: his health was beginning to dwindle.

Health: 211/250

"I have nearly unlimited mana here; I'm going to *use* it!" he bellowed in total delight as he recalled that he had entirely forgotten to use one of his Skills. As he broke through the top of the encirclement, he dropped his armor and devoted thirty percent of his mana to each hand weapon.

Of his remaining one hundred and thirty-six mana, Luke devoted one hundred of it to Shockwave Cleave. The enemies were so massive that he could only hope to kill three in total from a perfect hit, but three kills per punch was nothing to turn his nose up at.

Now that he was moving downward again, with one hundred mana regeneration per second, he was able to release a shockwave from his blows with roughly every fourth pteranodon he fell past. Feathers, beaks, leather... all of it filled the air so thickly that the sky reminded him of stories he had heard of the new year's celebration in the kingdom's capital. Soon the pteranodons lower down were forced to veer off and clean themselves—they were being dragged down by the sheer accumulated weight of the falling filth.

As Luke reactivated his armor and began ascending once more, he only managed to reach half the height that he had gained previously. He searched the skies and found dozens of the beasts flying away: he hadn't seen so many creatures collectively run from him since he had cleaned out Zone one! "Hey! Get *back* here!"

They didn't listen. He eyed the much-reduced swarm that was circling under him, and realized that he needed to take the opportunity to get further into the Zone. If he didn't, there was a good chance that he'd fall out of the sky soon. With such a helpful assortment of platforms to run along, he started flashing from one to the next, slicing down with his mana-made sword just before he jumped each time.

Soon he was once more comfortably leaping along above the huge chains, but he saw no need to restrict himself by landing on them. Between his Sigil pulsing and drawing fresh pteranodons, and the hundreds that were fleeing, Luke was able to travel fairly comfortably for several hours.

The reason it took so long to cross the Zone wasn't that it was overly massive, but that he continually moved back, forth, and side-to-side in an attempt to unrepentantly grab as much Potentia as he could. Eventually, he spotted land, so he grabbed the next bird he landed on, snapped its neck, and held its outstretched wings open to glide close enough that he could flash up and use Feather's Fall to touch solid ground once more.

Congratulations! Hidden achievement gained: Off the Chain!

Off the Chain: cross all of Zone 10 without touching the chain walkways a single time! Reward: Chain-Blade Rope!

The ground in front of Luke burst upward, a smooth metal box pushing out of the ground as if the earth itself were giving birth. The lid of the container split in the center, both halves opening to the sides with a *hiss* to reveal a long plain brown rope. One end culminated in a leather-bound hilt, so he picked it up and slashed out with it a few times, cracking a grin at the crisp *snap* it released as he changed its direction. "So... a rope pretending to be a whip? A bit lacking as a reward, but the first one I ever got, so whatever."

He sent the rope out to wrap around the box. When he pulled lightly, barbs that appeared to be sharpened links from a chain popped out of the rope and caused the box to *shriek* as they tore into it. "Okay. I've been wrong before. That's *neat*."

The very end of the rope wriggled, and Luke nearly tossed it away. It lifted by itself and started to speak. "Yes...! Yes! I'm *free*! After all these years, I'll be able to get my revenge! I am the greatest weapon you will ever find, for I live to serve, so long as you follow a few simple rules-"

Luke activated Source-cerer's Armory and directly converted the Chain-Blade Rope into mana, slotting it as a weapon for his left hand. It screamed in fury for a long moment, then vanished. When it came into being as he slashed his hand out, the weapon no longer spoke. He scoffed at the attempt to mess with his mind, not to mention a *weapon* placing rules on its wielder's ability to use it. "Learned my lesson last time. Real weapons don't speak like that, so this must have had a curse on it or something. Even *Cookie* just whispers. Still. Good stats."

Chain-Blade Rope. Effect: +9% physical damage (Slashing). Can also be used to bind opponents or hold objects.

There was a glint of displeasure in his eyes as he inspected the Chain-Blade and forgot about his Skill's new upgrade. If he would have realized this weapon was so good, he *absolutely* would have slotted it into his right hand. "Blast. I could have really used this in that cloud of feathery Potentia… coulda hit at least two birds at once with this."

He lashed out with his hand over and again; any sharp motion sent the Rope whistling out to seek the blue blood of his enemies. It took some getting used to, and in ordinary circumstances, he would have gained a few new scars, but he learned quickly that his mana would simply dissipate if the rope was about to damage him.

New toy in hand, he started walking toward the boundary.

Crack.

Every few steps, he would swing the Rope again, and soon he was reliably getting a deadly sound to echo out from it. The Rope reached ten feet out, and the shining talon on the end tore huge furrows out of whatever it hooked into. As he reached the edge of Zone ten, he was ready to blitz forward with confidence.

CHAPTER SEVENTEEN

- ANDRE -

The Druid swept his long hair back, calming himself down as he inhaled and stared up at the ceiling of the cave that he had claimed as his own. The scents and familiar air of the area allowed him to unwind rapidly. Andre didn't know what it was exactly that made it harder for him to be around people after so long in a solitary state, but he was absolutely ready for some personal time with nature. Or just things that couldn't talk at him.

A deep chuffing made him freeze for a bare moment, and then he slowly turned to see an absolute *wall* of actual bear rushing at him. He tossed his arms to the side, shot back stabilizing vines, and grabbed the huge bound beast in a hug befitting the creature's namesake. "Arthur! I've missed you so much!"

They wrestled back and forth a short while, both increasing the force they exerted, until they were suddenly forced into a relaxed state of mind and body. Andre looked off into the distance, spotting a single shaft of light that shone down to rest on the Tier ten Sanctuary Lily in the distance. "Got it, got it! Too much; I was going to hurt him!"

Arthur scoffed deeply. Clearly *he* was going to hurt the fragile Druid. They turned together and started walking around the area, the Druid inspecting what all had changed in the time he had been away. The last time he had been in his world was when he had been trapped here for training, and he had been sure to plant some flora that required a long growth cycle.

A quick check revealed a stand of low-light growth trees that had grown into towering pillars that nearly touched the ceiling. He had originally been concerned that they'd have trouble with water or nutrients, but he couldn't find a single issue with them... unnaturally so. His mind recalled the Lily once more, and he harrumphed as he remembered that things couldn't 'deteriorate' while in the area of effect from the plant. "Perfect growth as a side effect, hmm? Better set up my workshop for testing my Ability outside its range, or I'm going to have a lot of problems cultivating multi-generational seeds..."

Another thought rolled across his mind, and he scrutinized his bear. There wasn't a sign of aging on the bonded beast, no wounds, no evidence of starvation. "You haven't gone out hunting, I'm sure of it. You aren't even hungry, are you?"

The bear sent along feelings of contentment, confirming Andre's thoughts. "Excellent. Want to come with me as I expand this area?"

Walking side by side, Andre and Arthur approached one of the plants that the Druid had focused on earlier. An effort of will had the plant rearranging its roots, and a seemingly natural tunnel appeared where once a completely tree-clogged knot had stood. The path was wide enough for both man and bear, and they walked for a full kilometer before escaping the range of the Sanctuary Lily. Andre continued for a few hundred meters to eliminate concerns, then planted an acorn and started dumping mana into it.

A watermelon began growing, rapidly reaching the top of the tunnel before expanding to cover the entirety of the open space. Once it was fully braced, its woody rind and vine began tearing into and absorbing the surrounding stone for nutrients, growing in mere hours what would naturally take centuries for a fruit of this size. When he judged that the interior of the fruit had reached a few hundred square feet, he stopped the growth and began cutting a door into what would become his new workshop.

Once he had cleared a wide, clear path through the rind, Andre rapidly aged the rest of the fruit. The interior turned to mush, then a sludge that was absorbed into the abundance of watermelon seeds that remained. Soon only vibrancy-packed seeds, a petrified rind, and a faintly sweet smell occupied the room. He shook his head as he cleaned off the floor. "So much that nature can already do, and I'm here to find ways to make it *un*natural. I hope this isn't something that goes *against* nature… the world always finds ways to fix itself in the end."

"Urhhg." Arthur agreed with a rumble that his master could feel in his chest.

The Druid dumped a bag of sand onto the floor, staring at it and sighing. It was the most dead, filtered sand he could find, and even *this* would still be considered a better soil than what was in the Scarroco Desert. "Well, Arthur, I hope you're ready to hear all my harebrained ideas."

The bear scraped at the floor and hunted around for fruit to snack on. Andre huffed and grew him a more standard-sized watermelon, then turned his attention to the various seeds he carried. "What I need is an entire *ecosystem*, not just a few basic plants. I need to mix fertilizer into the sand, get mold to grow and start pulling nutrients out of the sand proper, then cultivate a layer of small plants to reinforce the shifting ground so that it can hold water over time."

He had been working on this plan for *years*, and had a solid framework planned for what he needed in order to make this work on its own. However, enacting it as *naturally* as possible would require hundreds of years of effort. Now that he was able to add 'Abilities' to the seeds… that would reduce the time needed by decades. "What I really need to do is just start *making* things and hope that they'll be useful later. If only I had better seeds!"

In fact, if he were to climb to the surface and begin gathering plants from The Grove, they were sure to be more potent than anything he could find on his base world. Two major issues prevented him from following through with that plan: one, if he went topside, there was a good chance that anyone hunting for him would finally pick up his trail and be able to attack him. He had run into the wastes of his world to escape the powerhouses that didn't want him surviving and growing into a superpower.

Two, there was no guarantee that those plants wouldn't be wildly invasive and destroy any adjacent natural plants on the base world when he transplanted them. It was rare, but it *did* happen.

Realistically, he was far more concerned about being found than anything else. He had his Sanctuary Lily, but all other defenses and protections were... nonexistent. With that consideration in mind, he added more to his to-do list: create plants that could help him defend his territory. Thorny bushes meant nothing, no matter how poisonous they were. "What If I could make plants that hunt people that get too close? Is that too dangerous...? What about trees that fought fire by dropping and rolling? Or maybe just make them fireproof?"

The Druid decided that planning was all well and good, but his Murderhobo friend had taught him that nothing beat just getting to work and doing what needed to be done. A flash of a thorn in the palm of his hand, and he had enough blood to marinate the seeds he was going to be working with for the next few days. "Thinking logically, the very first issue is the poor quality of soil. I can rectify that with fertilizer, but I can't do too much about the lack of water in the area."

He shook his head and furrowed his brow, "Actually... the issue is mainly what's on the surface. The expanding desert shouldn't have been able to alter the underground water sources. If I just made a plant with a long root system, I could direct it to reach down and pull water up. That… *hmm…* I can't expand the roots of each and every plant; that would take-"

Crunch. Andre was sprayed by juices as Arthur crushed an entire watermelon in his maw. "Gah! Arthur! You're disgusting; you got me all wet…!"

He cut off, watching all the juice trickling out of the bear's mouth during its nonchalant mastication. The juice pooled below its snout, viscous and globular. "I think this is the first time someone chewing with their mouth open has actually been appreciated by me. Thanks for the cool spray, Arthur, ol' chap!"

He retrieved a watermelon seed and tried to impart the idea of the watermelon growing to a huge size, then converting its juices within to a spray that constantly released water when the plant had excess. "Just like that, watermelon irrigation plants. If it works, then we'll be able-"

The seed in his hand exploded into shards that left nasty splinters in his flesh. He stared at the shards of the single seed that he had cultivated with Hemoflora's new effect, and sighed dramatically. "Good thing I have six times the time dilation here. It's gonna take *forever* to figure out each step in this process."

Determined, he got to work; rapidly achieving the single-minded focus that he could only reach when doing what he loved. A stray part of his mind chuckled as he recognized how meticulous he was being immediately after going off on wild tangents… and then his entire focus was devoted to his work. He could feed thousands by generating viable farmland, empower millions by collecting more Potentia in the land, and protect the entirety of the kingdom by proxy. Andre wasn't about to allow himself to slack off. He couldn't.

The land needed to be whole, and he needed to be its Druid.

CHAPTER EIGHTEEN

- LUKE -

Something was different; Luke knew it was. At first glance, Zone eleven was the same as the other ten Zones that he had progressed through for his entire time in Murder World, but... he couldn't place what was different, and it was setting him on edge. Whipping his new Rope back and forth a few times to re-center himself, he decided that sprinting in would be the best course of action.

He crossed the boundary as quickly as he could, receiving a chime and a message from his Sigil at the same time. His eyes were drawn to a different and far more concerning effect: the mana fog that swirled around every edge of the ground was receding. When the Murderhobo had sprinted into the area, he had noticed that this Zone was just a continuation of the previous one, but now that the fog was rolling away, it revealed that the area was a huge swath of unexplored world, or maybe...?

"My brain hurts!" he hollered into the empty plain as he increased his pace. There was something wrong, and he didn't know what to do. But if he was fast enough, maybe he wouldn't need to deal with it; so he decided that speed was king. Yet, no matter how fast he ran, there was more ground to cover. He allowed his eyes to flash to the side, and he read over the flashing notification.

Welcome to Zone eleven! There is only one enemy in this area; make sure to find it as quickly as you can! The enemy will get larger and harder to kill as time passes. The landscape itself will also expand to accommodate the growth of this creature, making it harder to escape the Zone in a timely manner! Defeating the creature will resize the Zone to its original boundary while respawning a new creature that you should return to defeat every once in a while, in order to allow newcomers a chance to move through without undergoing a massive personal trial.

C@uti0n! Spatial anomaly... detected.

"Great. Another ominous system message." Luke didn't let the message kill his speed. He understood what had happened, and it also confirmed another few things he had been pondering. "Someone came through here before me. Someone else that survived the, uh... what did they call it? Mana baptism. They had to do that at the start of this world. That's the only reason there would be a Zone this far down that was already activated. How long has it been since they came through here?"

The ground began to tremble lightly, as if there were a herd of stampeding horses approaching. Luke peered across the rapidly clearing grasslands carefully, for once not at all blocked from looking into the distance. The fog had receded past the horizon, only lingering in the air above. Even with his sharp eyes, he couldn't spot a single opponent, or the edge of the world. For all intents and purposes, he may as well have been on a new planet. An actual absolute flat world, instead of a spiral downward.

In fact, it was only when he *really* concentrated that he could notice the miniscule slope in this Zone, filling him with relief that he was going in the correct direction. So, while the rumbling was still concerning, he could tell that there was nothing around him. Hours passed as he trekked along, and the vibration on the ground only increased. A mountain range gradually appeared along the skyline, and he wondered if a volcano was erupting among the remote peaks.

Skill increased: Goat Call -> Hobo Holler (Tier 3, Level 0)

Effect 1: Lure goats to your location.

Bonus 1, at range: Lure goats from up to a mile away.

Effect 2: By infusing your voice with mana, you increase the natural hostility of any creature in range. Creatures impacted will abandon other targets and focus entirely on you for 1+n seconds. Triple as effective on goats.

"That makes it useful again, at least." The distance that he was attempting to traverse never seemed to decrease, and frankly he was getting more annoyed than anything else. Luke tried out the new Skill, finding that there was no real noise it made in particular, like Goat Call had. Instead, he just needed to yell some inarticulate nonsense at the top of his lungs. The hours turned into days, and he started to worry about his time-line for getting out. "Gotta get to the end of the *next* Zone, for abyss-sake."

Luke had taken to screaming out his new Hobo Holler every once in a while to see if he could attract the attention of whatever creature he needed to fight. If he could beat it, the Zone would shrink back to its original size, and he would be able to zip across it without issue if he needed to do so. "This trembling is making my feet go numb."

He really wanted to be in the air, Feather's Fall-ing just so that he didn't need to feel the constant vibration. Before he could go *too* much more insane, Luke finally noticed movement. A mountain-sized floating pillar came ever-so-slowly floating through the air on the horizon. He immediately sped toward it: a floating mountain was almost *guaranteed* to house the creature he needed to kill. Something like that didn't just come along by chance.

He ran at maximum output for the next full day, and the mountain grew closer and closer. However, the trembling of the ground had intensified to a dangerous degree. Not only that, but he was fighting against constant wind, as if a hurricane was attacking at full force. All of this combined to slow his speed, but that was fine with him: the mountain was drawing closer to him on its own. It was also sinking lower and lower, as if it was going to reach the ground soon.

"Is it welcoming me? Coming to fight me? ...Is something *controlling* that mountain?" Luke didn't have any good answers. There was no way to know what was going on until he got there. Half a day later, the mountain was almost to the ground. Even so, he still couldn't see the top of it; concealed as it was by the clouds of mana fog roiling up above. He could identify the edges, but at that point it was filling the entire horizon.

"Great golly *goat guts!*" His feet screeched to a stop as he cursed out a wild Hobo Holler by accident, getting bounced into the air as the trembling of the ground fought against him being still. "How fast is that rock *actually* moving?"

The mountain touched down, instantly hidden by a debris field that expanded upward and outward at hundreds of miles per hour. Luke's first instinct was to burrow into the ground and hope against hope that the area *he* stood in wouldn't be annihilated or buried. Instead, he dumped every bit of mana he had into his armor and charged at the initial shockwave head-on; a waterskin of mana in his mouth that he was doing his best to utterly *drain* as he ran.

For some reason, he felt that having a body utterly stuffed with mana was the only thing that was about to keep him alive.

A wall of compressed air and thunderous noise hit him like a professional athlete striking a ball, sending him arcing back and *up*. His body shot into the sky with dozens of broken bones, and his skin had been torn to shreds. He regained consciousness as he started to fall, when the mana he had ingested repaired the trauma that had occurred in his brain. He thanked his lucky star that he had gained the 'I Have Concerns' Skill, and had a way to self-heal in this miserably amazing dimension.

As his ravaged body sewed itself back together, he shifted some mana into activating Feather's Fall and began controlling his descent back toward the grounded mountain. His reflexes and defenses were put to the test over and again as airborne chunks of earth followed after the initial blast. Luke smiled as he put his practice against the pteranodons into play.

Sure, the bombarding rocks were several factors faster than the overgrown chickens could ever hope to match, but that didn't change the fact that he could use Bum Flash to leap around or on top of them, using some of the slower-moving stones as launch pads to refresh the requirements of his movement skill.

A standard human would never have been able to follow how he was weaving though the field of death, but then again… they would have already been turned into paste by the shockwave, had they been close enough. The shards of stone and walls of earth were accelerating so rapidly that all but the lowest-flying had been bypassed in mere seconds of rapid movement and hurried choices. Then the air was clear, and Luke was zooming toward the lower reaches of the mountain.

He landed securely on the wide stone and began running. Whatever was controlling this flying behemoth had to be at the top. He stared into the clouds and nodded as he dashed up the craggy incline. "Things are looking up for me. Up, and up, and up."

Trekking up the mountainside was actually easier than he had expected it to be. Numerous huge outcroppings, stone from previous impacts that had been driven deeply into the mountain, and even hardy vegetation had grown over time in all the loose earth. Luke snorted at the idle thought that the hard part was over. "Can't expect this to be the same higher up."

His progress was rapid, significantly enough that he expected to reach the top within a few hours. As he entered into the clouds, he found his progress forced to a screeching halt. The mana in the clouds had grown so thick, and the mountain had been in existence so long, that patches of mana had crystallized on the surface of the path he had wanted to travel.

"*Solid* mana," Luke breathed as he edged as close as possible, stopping only when his Sigil continuously chimed a low warning. He had drawn still closer, too close, and now his feet refused to take another step forward. The sheer amount of power radiating from the strangely metallic vein in the rock indicated to him that even with his Skills… that rock would try to kill him if it could.

"I wanna lick it. Just… *so* much."

More than making progress, more than getting to the next Zone, even more than killing whatever had tried to drop a mountain on him, he *wanted* that solid mana. Snarling and straining, he forced his Chain-Blade Rope out, swinging it and driving the suddenly-protruding blades deep into the stone, securing a hold on a place high above his actual target. "Since I can expand this thing, I'll use it as a grappling hook, and totally, absolutely, will go *around* that power source that hurts my eyes and mind to look at directly. I'll start reeling myself in and, oh *no~o~o*…! I'm falling right at the mana and can't do *anything* to stop my body!"

The Murderhobo's eyes lit up even as his Sigil screamed warning chimes. He laughed as he fell atop the searing-pain-inducing patch. "I knew I could trick you, you worthless slave brand! Haha, *c'mere* mana!"

With his tongue stuck out as far as he could manage, Luke slipped down over the top of the mana-metal patch and managed to slurp up a few of the tiny crystals. It felt like licking a bowl of salt, if salt were minuscule flakes made of the sun itself. Screaming in pain and fighting both his instincts and Sigil, he swallowed what he had managed to collect in his mouth and lay on the ground as the mana did its best to detonate every cell in his body simultaneously.

He began to *burn*, chunks of his flesh radiating away as searing sparks. At the same time, his 'I Have Concerns' Skill went into overdrive and began healing him. Flesh regrew as rapidly as it was burned away, his innards turned to ash and reformed from pure mana before abruptly converting into a fleshy state once more.

"This is real! I'm *alive!*" He choked on blood as his lungs disintegrated, almost passing out before they reconstituted. Through it all, even as his heart melted and reformed, Luke laughed. "Lived through that, too!"

His Sigil noted that he wasn't dying, and the force it was using to lock him in place vanished. Luke used every bit of effort he could muster with his destroyed muscles to launch himself at the mana vein again; this time taking a *bite* out of it. He chewed and swallowed even as his teeth were eradicated by pure energy. "Wouldn't do to run out of mana after something *important* burned! I want *all* of my body back."

Indeed, the process of his organs re-integrating had started to slow. The influx of mana continued the process, and he snorted in mirth just before the world went dark.

The Murderhobo's mind burned.

Luke's brain was reborn.

When his eyelids popped open, he gazed at his surroundings with non-liquified, literally brand-new eyes. He sat up and looked within himself to inspect what had changed… but there were no notifications to inform him whether he had gotten more powerful or escaped the bonds placed on him by the Hollow Kingdom. There was only an increase for his 'I Have Concerns' Skill.

Skill increased: I Have Concerns -> You Need to Stop.

You Need to Stop (T4. Level X). You already defeated mana and poison. Just stop.

Effect 1: Never again will poison or pure mana be able to control or even affect you. Your flesh contains potent power and mind-shifting effects. Anything taking a bite out of you should be prepared to feel like unicorns are goring them to death!

Bonus 1, at range: Bonus 1, at range: Poisons in the air, such as toxic fumes, will restore your health and mana over time. Amount regained is based on potency and time spent in the poison.

Effect 2: You are able to consume concentrated mana to restore health and mana, or hallucinogenic materials to further increase restored health and mana.

Bonus 2, multi-target: You are a potent source of power. The world knows you are a delicacy. All creatures will be drawn to you and are more likely to attack you. As the world knows you, you know the world. You gain an instinctive understanding of mana and what it can do. Pure mana can no longer negatively impact you.

This skill cannot be increased via additive Potentia.

"So what this notification is telling me…" Luke glared at the Skill that was trying to get him killed. "…is that I can only increase the skill further by consuming deadly levels of poison and mana at the *same* time!"

His Sigil sparked and popped before fading into silence as he slapped at his head. "Quiet, you!"

Getting to his feet was a trial, but he managed to make it happen. Luke had, at some point, rolled away from the mana deposit. He immediately made his way back, then scooped up a handful of the tiny crystals and shoved them into his mouth. It tingled on the way down, burning his mouth like peppers used to do, but his body simply took it in without complaining. "Ugh. Ah, well. At least I have some new seasoning for my food."

Luke scooped the remainder of the small deposit into a pouch, then began running up the mountain again. He could barely see in front of his face after a few minutes, as the clouds continued to thicken and converge. Since he was unable to use his Chain-Blade Rope safely, he clung to the rocky surface and punched handholds for himself. The makeshift strategy slowed his progress significantly, but the petrous surface had long since lost any pre-existing natural paths to the top, presenting a sheer cliff that he was forced to ascend purely vertically.

The days went by slowly, but the exhaustion he had been expecting to feel never came. He assumed it had something to do with eating a highly potent energy source, but didn't know for sure. There was no way to test out his theory, so he simply powered onward.

When things changed, he didn't even notice at first. He just kept going. Then he fell forward and landed on a flat surface when he was reaching for another handhold.

After popping to his feet and searching for the enemy he was *sure* was lying in wait, Luke found only massive trees that stretched upward to an indeterminate height that was shrouded by the dense mana clouds. A few of the trees' baby-fist sized seeds lay scattered on the ground, so he scooped them up and put them in his pouch as a gift for Andre. There was not a single sound to be heard, lending a creepy atmosphere to the mountaintop. After searching the summit for a few hours, he determined that he was truly alone. "Is it *in* the mountain? Do I just start punching until I find the warm, gooey center? I'll save that as a last resort."

There was a single anomaly: one of the sides of the summit wasn't a sheer drop, instead descending into the fog below at a strange angle. It was odd to discover that the side he had climbed was so steeply vertical, while this side was a distinct incline; even if it *was* a sharp drop. "Do I need to climb down this? *Anything down there?*"

He bellowed the query as loudly as he could, and waited for a reply in the utter silence. A short while later, he actually *did* hear a reply that sounded oddly familiar. "*Down e~ere…*"

"I knew it. I'm coming to *destroy you!*" he shouted as he hopped onto the incline and started to slide.

"Destroy *you*…!" came the heated reply.

Luke flushed red with rage. "You think you can take me down after I've been able to… oh. Oh, no. That was an echo."

He tried to arrest his momentum, but the angle and his resulting speed made that tricky. The surface of this stone was smoother and even harder than the cliff face he had climbed earlier, so punching downward sent him flying off the surface, only to collide against it painfully and roll before eventually managing to get his trajectory under control, all while continuing to slide. "Guess I'm riding to the end."

The Murderhobo could have used his Chain-Blade Rope to try and make an anchor, but decided that there was no point. He hadn't found the enemy up above, so he needed to look elsewhere anyway. A half hour later, he slid beneath the cloud layer and was able to see where the smooth ride was taking him. "Why is there a mountain with a bridge to an island?"

He got his answer a few moments later as he watched clouds pass under the landmass ahead, breaking into wispy strands... and Zone eleven was briefly visible far below. Luke gazed more carefully into the fog, and five more land bridges gradually came into view; two to his right, three on the other side of the landmass. The one nearest him to the right began leaning toward him more and more as the minutes passed. The outer two footways on the other side were also moving, and Luke had a sudden realization.

"This entire thing is a creature, isn't it? I *really* dislike this Zone."

CHAPTER NINETEEN

The slide came to an abrupt end, and Luke jumped the last few meters to avoid any potential nasty surprises at the very edge of the articulating stone joints. He now recognized the juncture as the shoulder equivalent of whatever titanic creature this was. Just like the peak he had slid down from—likely a knee—he was surrounded by a forest of trees so tall that they vanished into the mana clouds. They appeared to be roughly the same species as those in the forest above, so he ignored any fallen seeds and began trekking in the direction he sensed the behemoth was moving.

He sprinted for the majority of the next few days, eventually coming upon what he assumed *had* to be the creature's head. The sheer size, lack of enemies, and utter absence of food or water was making him antsy. It didn't help that his time was running out; Luke had no way to know if he was going to be able to make it back to the edge of the Zone at this rate. The only way to advance or retreat was to defeat the creature here and now.

There was no discernable anatomy to whatever the thing was, nothing beyond the fact that it had at least six legs. The

Murderhobo had been hoping that he could find an eyeball that he could use to dig deep into its brain, but this creature was on a scale he had no way to reference in the slightest. Finding an eyeball meant nothing if it looked like an ocean to him; how would he even know he had found what he was looking for? Shaking his head, he rasped through dry lips, "I need to figure out how to kill a literal walking continent? This Zone is practically impossible."

"Last resort it is, then." Finding no easy path forward, Luke decided to commence with killing the cyclopean brute here and now. Since he hadn't found a weak point, the spot he was standing on was as good as any other. Turning off his armor, he devoted one hundred percent of his mana to his Battering Ram Knuckles and began slamming his fist into the ground. At the start, each blow cracked the surface and left a deep welt in the topsoil and stone mixture.

After ten minutes, he was pleased to discover that he had broken through the outer crust and began making more rapid progress. For the next few hours, he simply punched his way further downward. As he pummeled the rocky surface, he pondered the real problem: if the creature's 'skin' was stone and mountains, what was it going to be like upon reaching the bones deeper down? Luke only worried about the possibilities briefly as he battered and sliced his way downward, but he never seemed to find a *harder* layer. Everything seemed uniformly arduous to batter through the entire way.

When he exhausted himself, he slept in the hole he had dug. Each time he awoke, he got back to it, only bothering to look up on rare occasions. Even then, he was mostly ensuring that his tunnel hadn't closed up above him. After each safety check, he meditated on his method of punching his way through his problems.

Cal Scan
Level: 10
Current Etheric Xenograft Potentia: 3,333/14,400 to level 11!

Body: 32.4

- *Fitness: 40.8*
- *Resistance: 24*

Mind: 18.6

- *Talent: 16.3*
- *Capacity: 20.9*

Presence: 18

- *Willpower: 27*
- *Charisma: 9*

Senses: 23.75

- *Physical reaction: 27.5*
- *Mental energy: 20*

Maximum Health: 290
Maximum Mana: 324
Mana regen: ~~5.43 per second~~ Overridden: 100 per second.

"Mm. Dramatic increase in Presence. Lil' bit in Body; must be from boosting 'You need to Stop' to the new Tier. Charisma… can't remember if that was lower before. I think it was. If I have a better body, I agree that others would be forced to like me better." Luke contemplated the other numbers associated with the changes. "I can output… two thousand and forty kilos of force at my maximum. With every bit of my mana devoted to my knuckles… I can hit for over thirteen hundred damage."

He glanced to the sky, a bare pinprick thousands of feet above him by now, then got back to punching. A dramatic shift occurred only a few minutes later: the ground under him collapsed, and he fell into dark emptiness. Reacting rapidly, he shifted his mana across his Skills, activating Feather's Fall as his armor sprang into being around him. Over the next few minutes of alternately falling faster, then slowing down, he got sick of reactivating the Skill and instead allowed himself to fall at *just* below the speed that would result in bodily damage if he landed on something hard. As he approached the safe limit, he slowed himself and sighed as he drifted along.

A softly diffused light source bloomed beneath him. Aiming at the direction of its source, Luke soon landed on squishy but shockingly firm and smooth ground. After poking it a few times, as well as comparing it to his previous experiences, Luke realized where he was with almost perfect certainty. "This is the brain. *Gotta* be the brain. Good. Let's get to punching."

His fist slammed down, and a *wave* of flesh erupted from the point of impact.

Damage dealt: 403 blunt.

There was no noticeable reaction from the creature, and even worse, nothing even *hinted* that the blow had impacted it at all. He sighed, deactivated his armor once more, and began punching down at full strength. Once again, he had soon carved a tunnel, but unlike the stone he had broken through to reach the fleshy material beneath, *this* cavity rapidly filled with ichor and fluids. Only a short distance down, he nearly became trapped in the jiggling flesh and was forced to retreat. "Still nothing from the beast. Haven't wanted Andre around to give me a lecture on stupid animals before, but… first time for everything. If nothing else, he could tell me what I need to do to hit something that *matters*."

"At least I found lunch." Using both hands, he tore up a huge swath of the meaty tissue, then went and sat down. As much as he wanted to *cook* his meal, lighting a fire in an enclosed abyss stuffed with volatile mana and natural gasses— was akin to planning to not even leave his own corpse behind. He tossed his head back and chomped down with all the force he could muster, ripping out a bite of the meat; unexpectedly pleased with the surprisingly sweet sustenance. As he chewed on the oddly textured treat, he inspected the damage he had done to himself.

Numerous rocks—perhaps they were actually chunks of carapace—were stuck in his skin. Attacking rock, at full force, with no armor on… had perhaps not been his *most* intelligent move, but the fact that they couldn't puncture too deeply into his flesh or strike a vital spot had allowed him to ignore the minor damage. Yet, if he wanted those injuries to properly heal, he needed to dig the shards out.

Retrieving a sharp knife from one of his many pouches, he peeled back his skin and tore out the fragments of debris one by one. As he breathed deeply, the environmental mana and the creature's aerosolized natural toxins worked together to stitch him up; the bleeding stopped, and his skin visibly reverted to an unblemished state. "Flesh wounds are so easy to deal with. I can't believe people complain about-"

Sizzle.

An unexpected sound, only audible due to the absolute silence of this brain-void, made Luke's ears twitch, and he spun to face the direction it had come from. What met his eyes confused him: a blackened, practically necrotic patch of brain remained where he had been removing slivers of… his eyes widened. "That's where my blood landed! Yes! Right! I'm literally filled with poison!"

He scurried to the hole he had dug earlier, still brimming with various fluids, and sliced open his inner thigh. From personal experience, he knew that this particular spot would let him bleed out rapidly, but not too fast to halt by drinking pure mana down. "Unlike *you*, armpit. You get cut too bad, and I either need to *dive* into a pool of mana or just die. No wonder you always reek, ya filthy pit. At least we know for sure that trying to stink your attackers away has never helped, *has* it?"

No reply was forthcoming, so he took that as an agreement that he would start smelling better going forward and watched his blood mix with the fluids below. Apparently his newly leveled Tier-four Skill was a potent weapon in its own right, as proven by the withering and utter destruction hemorrhaging out from any fleshy surface that came into contact with his blood. "Still too slow. Gotta start punching until I find a vein or an artery. Hit one of those, *then* we'll see some damage."

He got right to it, and had soon scooped out a crater of goo. Eventually he hit something important, as the crater started to fill with ichor akin to a new well. "Excellent. Next step: figure out which vessel is dumping blood in here, and which one is sucking it out."

It didn't take him long to find and match up the broken ends of the vein, and he decided to test out his next attempt at continenticide by sticking his leg into the hole after re-slicing his leg. His blood was *sucked* away with the force of a thousand leeches, to the point that the ambient healing effects weren't able to keep up. In order to ensure that he didn't push himself too far, each time he began feeling weary or faint, he would take a break to chug some healing mana and take a short nap.

A thick slice of brain worked as a blanket, and he slept well in the safe, warm environment. His timer continued to tick down slowly, and before he knew it, entire days went by. Soon, enough time had passed that he worried that his plans were failing... until they suddenly weren't.

The brain damage that he was inflicting finally accumulated to the degree that it became self-propagating, and the creature began to spasm as a massive stroke and subsequent seizure ensued. Unsurprisingly, a creature of such mountainous proportions took a *long* time to die. If Luke had been on the outside of the body, the earthquakes and storms generated by the rapid movements would have killed him a dozen times over. Instead, he was safe and secure, wrapped in his brain-matter comforter in its head. The safest place to be, by far.

Eventually, he got the message he had been oh-so-desperately waiting for.

Zone cleared! Detected Anomalies destroyed: 1/2. Potentia gained: 500.

"Five hundred Potentia? That's *it*? For *this*?" Luke waved around the huge hollow cranial cavity as he shouted at the air. "This thing would have been *impossible* to kill for almost anyone, *ever!*"

Query answered: No matter the size, this was only a Tier five creature that had no method of defending itself against your attacks. Most of the creature's Potentia is stored within its flesh. Hint: You can capture 60% of all its Potentia by eating the entire carcass!

"You're an evil, evil Sigil," Luke muttered discontentedly. "That just isn't possible."

Would you like to abandon all attempts to absorb the creature in order to allow the space in this Zone to be reverted to its original size?

"Yes. Absolutely do that." The air around Luke fluctuated, and he shuddered as the density of *power* in the area reached a concentration that began impacting reality. The... insect? The bug-like thing that he had broken into; it *shattered* with a cataclysmic ringing that seemed to last forever. A Skill pearl appeared in front of him, and he grabbed it and gulped it down without a second thought. He waited for a Skill screen to appear, but... nothing happened?

He began to fall. The continent beneath him was hundreds of kilometers away, and his resting position was gone. The wind rushed past him in a torrential hurricane as space was *compressed*. He was tossed around as the ground approached at a speed that was unnatural: the stretched space was being restored to its original state after who-knew-how-many millenia.

After an instant that seemed to last forever, he found himself standing on the ground, blinking in confusion. A glance around revealed that he was around a third of the way through the Zone, and the timer at the edge of his vision—the one denoting the amount of time he had remaining to find an exit before he would be forced to turn around and sprint for the opposite edge of Zone ten—was red.

As he had killed the only enemy in the Zone, it was a cakewalk to get to Zone twelve. He spotted motion directly on the other side of the boundary and prepared himself to fight right away. There was a strong possibility that getting to the other side of this Zone would grant him a new exit point, and-

"Hello there! Did you defeat the Giga-ant? You *freed* us! Please, tell me you're friendly?" Luke stumbled to a halt as a horse galloped toward him, a cheerful falsetto voice echoing from atop the gallant creature.

CHAPTER TWENTY

- TAYLOR -

The Archmage-expectant rubbed at her head. Taylor almost *wanted* a migraine, even though those sorts of weak bodily functions had vanished when she became an Ascender. It would at least give her an excuse to get away from the people that had been beleaguering her for favors, advice, or to curse her out; sometimes all three at once. If she hadn't taken the opportunity to go hunting in her world before committing to pacifying this village so she could use it as a base, she would have been even more on edge.

After using her liquid Exp, she had taken the opportunity to train in her world, and living at four times time dilation, to boost her Capacity characteristic an additional point-four points. It had taken *an annoyingly* long time to naturally circulate her mana at high speed, release it, and regenerate it to the degree required to increase her Capacity by that slight amount, all using the secret training methods Master Don had imparted.

She also resented the fact that she had been compelled to treat her Mana Channels so brutally, solely to enable herself to use a Spell that she had already Named, but the pain of forcing her growth at an unnatural pace had been... manageable. The truth was, she was mostly upset that she had needed to deviate from her self-imposed training plan. It felt like she had back-tracked, but at least she could finally command the spell to its full potential. Her eyes flickered to the side as she examined her status.

Cal Scan

Level: 10

Current Etheric Xenograft Potentia: 4,523/14,400 to level 11!

Body: 7.7

- *Fitness: 9.2*
- *Resistance: 6.2*

Mind: 14.25

- *Talent: 14.7*
- *Capacity: 13.8 -> 14.2*

Presence: 9.85

- *Willpower: 7.7*
- *Charisma: 12*

Senses: 29.3

- *Physical reaction: 32.2*
- *Mental energy: 26.4*

Maximum Health: 112

Maximum Mana: 246.8 -> 250.8

Mana regen: 4.9 per second

"*Excuse* me, is the fact that my family has become destitute *boring* to you?" The question pulled Taylor from her happy thoughts. She narrowed her eyes and turned back toward the mayor of this *inconsequential* little town that *dared* to talk to *her* like…

The Mage closed her eyes, took a deep breath, then opened them and smiled as she regarded the swarm of starved, rat-faced people that somehow lived in this dustbowl. "Hello, everyone. I'm going to need to ask all of you to stop and listen for a moment. Thank you. Now, I understand that you have concerns for your safety, but I *assure* you that any bandit issues you've had are going to completely vanish, now that we're here. You also won't need to fear my companions. Not unless you have taken to banditry to make ends meet."

A few people audibly gulped, and she closed her eyes again before she could identify them. "I'll tell you this now: if you *have* recently started a new career… well. I highly recommend not doing anything that warrants the Kingdom coming down on you. I'm certain you have many *more* questions, but I assure you the Bard is more than happy to explain *anything* you might want to know."

"She's correct!" Zed burst into the silence exuberantly, leaning toward a pile of dried wood and tapping his firestarter against it. A bonfire sprang into being, and he motioned everyone closer. "Come, let me tell you the tale of the Arch-mage! She who will soon Ascend into political power and machinations of state-"

Taylor stopped listening and glanced nervously toward the entrance to the town. Two days had passed… well, *almost* two days. Luke should be returning soon, and hopefully Andre would as well. Technically, she had no power over Andre. In fact, he was currently her political superior, but she needed him here *now*. This place practically had a *negative* food supply, and the desert was expanding faster than ever before, thanks to the strong winds this year. If she didn't get some help soon, she was going to have to abandon the hamlet.

At that point, it was likely that every last citizen would

convert to highwaymen, and Luke would gleefully hunt them down for the scraps of ragged clothing they wore or some other such nonsense. She didn't *want* that for her people. Taylor wanted them to be *better*, and she had the ability—in Andre—to start pushing back the desert. To bring fresh food back to the region. The Druid alone could make this land *prosperous* again. For the first time ever, she wished she had gone after more utility spells. As it was, she was entirely geared to either combat or personal comfort. If *only* she had the ability to make it *rain*!

She pushed aside the concern and took a deep breath, pulling out her Grimoire and scanning her notes. "No use ruminating over what I cannot change. I need to focus on what is within my ability to control. What I *can* do is figure out what's messing with supply runs in the area."

From the information she'd gleaned over the last two days that she had been in the town, not a single merchant had managed to pass safely through the outer desert and into town in recent months. That didn't sound like a bandit issue, as even the worst offenders would usually ensure that the majority of shipments got through. If they didn't, caravans would stop even *trying* to cross the desert. "That burned-out caravan... that didn't look like a people issue. That was a monster attack."

Not only had the merchants been killed, but all of the merchandise had been *ruined*—not stolen. Her finger traced her map of the area, and the data points suddenly added up. Taylor's eyes glittered, and she snapped the tome closed. "There's gotta be an open Scar around here. Monsters attacking, strange weather patterns... I love knowing what to search for."

Anyone watching her at that moment would have been rubbing at their eyes as she blurred and vanished from the spot. She sprinted out of the town, flipping forward and pushing off a low wall with her left hand to launch into a double-backflip over the shoddy wall encircling the inner portion of the town. An instant later, she sprang atop a random thatched roof and lightly pushed away. In the time it would have taken for someone to draw in three deep breaths, her feet were leaving prints in the shifting sand bordering the village.

"If I remember correctly, the caravan was attacked a solid two miles from here, over where the sand hadn't yet reached. That's as good a starting point as can be hoped for…" Taylor's movement wasn't buffered in the least, causing a wall of dust to blast off the ground behind her. A few minutes later, she was combing over the charred remains of the caravan.

Now that she had some idea of what to look for, the signs of a monster attack were clear. They were minor details; claw marks at that level of sharpness were easily mistaken as particularly vicious bandits with razor-sharp swords. The prints left in the ground nearby were also concerningly human-like, but no one around the desert would walk around without shoes, or have feet that… shifted size as they walked?

"Well *that's* just not good." Taylor began following the prints, suddenly taking care to ensure that she wasn't going to be seen. Skinwalker-type monsters were some of the most terrible to deal with. If they entered a city, there was a chance that the city would fall and no one would even notice. There were protections against that, but… who wanted to test that an anti-doomsday monster schematic worked?

Normally, even a *hint* that a Scar existed in an area would result in a lock down until an Ascender group could destroy everything—and everyone—within the Scar's radius of influence and set up permanent barriers around the Scar. With Luke around, and his ability to somehow close Scars, Taylor felt that they could save the people in the nearby town far more easily. It all came down to how human the creatures could appear, how well they could hide in plain sight.

It only took a few hours to find the Scar; the monsters hadn't bothered to circle around or hide their intent. Why would they, when they had never encountered resistance or even prey that could fight back? An innocuous shimmer in the air and a subtle warping of the sand into a deep gray glass was the only hint of the Scar from this side; a far cry from the massive red rend that the Chimera had been able to generate. Taylor monitored the shimmer for the next few hours, with Thunder Beast's Eye glowing overhead for the first time ever; both patiently waiting for a target.

Her excitement over the fact that she could use the Spell waned as half a day passed slowly. Just as she was getting ready to charge the Scar, a person stepped out of the warped air and landed heavily on the ground. Taylor tensed, waiting for the humanoid thing to look her way and divulge how scared she needed to be that it might already be amongst the population.

It lurched to its feet, raising seemingly weak arms as it stood and swayed in place. As the day was approaching twilight, the glow from her spell was highly visible, and the creature turned to investigate what the light was. Everything about the beast looked human, save for two noticeable details. Firstly, the creature was naked, but it lacked any discernible reproductive organs. Everything from the neck down was totally smooth; not even a belly button. Secondly, the face was *wrong*. It was generally extraordinarily pale, the standouts being black lips, bright red cheeks, and triple tentacle-whiskers that lined each side of the mouth.

When the thing spotted her, it opened its mouth and silently howled, revealing thin, sharp teeth that appeared like a mouthful of needles more than anything. Having verified everything she needed, Taylor allowed a line of lightning to arc between her Eye and the invader. She was pleased to see that it was as frail as it looked, and the lightning melted a hole in its torso large enough to pass a pumpkin through.

You have killed a Larval Mime. +200 Exp.

"Not sure I like that this is a *larval* version, but they're good Potentia." Taylor muttered to herself. She cautiously approached the Scar and inspected it more closely, observing that the creature passing through it had significantly destabilized the portal's energy. "They aren't coming through quickly, if this is already so close to collapsing. Perhaps one a day? I doubt they've been staying on this side; the conditions are too harsh for them."

She checked over the Mime's body, finding that the mere act of falling out of the portal had torn up its legs and hands. She took extra precautions not to touch it, unsure if it had an after-death defense mechanism. "I'm gonna take a look. I've got to do it, right? I have to find out how much we need to worry about this. It isn't about personal benefit."

Chime.

Thoroughly convinced that she was only doing so for the best and most noble reasons, she stepped through the Scar, hoping that she'd find plenty of Potentia sources on the other side.

She was not disappointed.

Taylor stepped directly into a cave. Only two things saved her from immediately being torn apart by the dozens of Mimes that were silently waiting their turn to step across the boundary. One, her arrival was utterly unexpected. Two, Thunder Beast's Eye reacted even faster than she did.

The remaining bolts of power passed through the lined-up creatures perfectly, and the cave was clear of threats in the same instant. The Eye vanished from above her head just as the first of the Mime corpses hit the ground. Potentia increase messages went off, but the Mage ignored those in favor of searching carefully for any additional threats. Not finding any, she approached the mouth of the cave and contemplated the area.

As far as she could tell, from her position out to the horizon, there were no signs of life at all. The world was entirely silent as well; eerily so. "Huh. At least I know why they wanted out. This place is super boring."

In the same moment that she finished her thought, the sky turned brown. Not as if a sun was starting to rise, but as though something were reflecting off... she gasped as her eyes were drawn to the sky far above. Instead of being able to see out of the atmosphere and into the night sky, as she was used to, she found a clear curve of something, almost like glass, that denoted the end of breathable air.

On the other side of the glass, a face had appeared and was moving closer at an astonishing rate. The eyes that were roving around could have been *planets* in her plane of existence. They either generated their own light or were reflecting another unseen lightsource. Space warped as a fingertip the size of a moon appeared and moved to the 'glass', banging against it three times. The air *shook*, and Taylor felt the reverberations so powerfully that she started coughing blood.

The being said something that rattled the air, moving away slightly before bringing their eye closer to the glass. Another sound came in answer to the being's statement. Taylor darted into the cave just before the path of those eyes swept over her location. Her Sigil was spinning frantically as it attempted to record and decode what had been said, finishing just as she dove through the Scar.

Shaken terribly, she scanned the message with a face that paled further as she read each word. "We need to close this right *abyssal* now."

The words hung in front of her as she sprinted to go find Luke.

Translation generated.

Being 1: Honey, what happened to the fish?

Unknown Being in reply: Are they gone again? Let's clean the tank and get new ones tomorrow.

Being 1: Don't let Bob see that they're gone; he loves those stupid things.

Taylor had no idea what would happen if beings made of solar systems cleaned something, but she was sure it wouldn't end well for anything connected to the 'tank'. Suddenly, listening to the small-town woes of random citizens didn't seem so bad.

CHAPTER TWENTY-ONE

- LUKE -

"You've gotta be kidding me." Luke stared as the beautiful white horse galloped toward him in seemingly slow motion. "I just wanted to come here, kill a few things to relax a little, and you *talk*? There are sentients here?"

"Absolutely, there are! You freed us, and we will be eternally grateful! Now, I'm never kidding, but I *am* often... horsing around!" The amusement-filled voice was coming from atop the horse, specifically from the iridescent horn protruding from the middle of the equine forehead. "The Giga-ant had warped space so much that an entire *waterfall* of liquid mana from above was becoming too little to sustain our people. Without access to enough mana, the creatures of this world were reduced to little more than monsters, unable to reason or think beyond base instincts. What is your name, hero?"

"Uhh..." Luke looked at his hands, hoping that the goats all the way back in Zone one wouldn't suddenly be able to remember him now that mass quantities of mana might be getting repurposed. He debated killing this Murder World resident to keep it quiet, but stayed his hand. The countdown timer was showing a mere hour remaining before he would be forced to turn around, and if the creatures in this Zone would allow him to pass... perhaps he could make it through in time. "Horse. I'm Luke. Can you let me through to the end of the Zone, or do I need to kill you all-?"

"Oh, *yeah*! I can totally let you through! *Ya~ay*! I get to be the one to guide the *he~ero*! Just so you know, we're u~u~unicorns!" The 'unicorn' reared up and spun around, trotting away without displaying any signs of hostility. Luke cautiously took a step across and into Zone twelve proper. "Wait... what was that last part?"

"I didn't say anything." Luke read over the message as he followed the unicorn.

Welcome to Zone twelve! This is the first place you will meet the naturally occurring denizens of this plane! Not all creatures contain a Skill Pearl, but their bodies are useful in many other ways!

Luke reached for the unicorn, barely refraining from killing it when he remembered that he needed to *move*—not engage in a bloodbath so he could test exactly what the bodies of these creatures were good for. He kept an eye on the unicorn, feeling that its horn was strangely familiar. The Murderhobo recalled when hallucinogens had affected him and minutely nodded; that must be it. The creature glanced back at him, whinnying in laughter even as its voice echoed from the horn. "What's that look for, grumpy-pants? Are you in that big of a rush to get out of here? This is the most beautiful place in the world!"

The glorified horse was correct; the natural beauty of this place was far superior to any other Zone he had previously been in. For one thing, the unicorn was *white*, not a shade of blue like literally everything else. Well... everything besides the trees in the previous Zone. "How did I miss that? Those trees were green."

"Wow! *Green* trees? That sounds really strange!" The unicorn began frolicking, and other unicorns began stampeding out of the grasslands and circling them. The entire herd began cheering and praising their new hero, as well as pestering him with questions about the world outside of the Zone. "Back off, friends! We need to get to the end of the Zone so he can get ho~o~ome!"

"*Wo-o~ow!* He can even leave the world?" Another unicorn went totally still, its eyes going wide in shock. "That's so co~o~ol! He must be the strongest person on his whole planet!"

"Wait!" a deeper voice called, and a unicorn at least half again as large as the others advanced through the moving circle of trotting unicorns. "You're doing the bringing of the him straight out of the Zone? What about *God?* You're not going to introduce him to *God?*"

"He said he needed to leave straight away!" the original unicorn whinnied nervously. "I didn't think he should take the time to-"

"To. Literally. Meet. *God.*" The larger unicorn sighed in disappointment and stared at Luke. "Listen, human, yes? The you should *really* do the coming to and meeting of God. If you don't, you're going to have a really hard time going any further, and you likely won't even be able to do the getting past the barrier to the next Zone. I'm almost *certain* it's going to be a requirement for you to do the passing of that barrier."

Luke glanced the numbers on his return timer ticking away, and let out a low growl of frustration. "Fine! Let's go. Can we *please* hurry this up?"

The large unicorn nodded and started leading Luke slightly to the left of his intended trajectory. His original guide stayed by his side and offered consoling words as they walked. "It's all fine! After you meet God, I'm sure your regular concerns will seem insignificant. Time never *really* seems to matter there."

Increasing droves of unicorns arrived, and the babble in the area reached 'small town' level. Noticing that too many of his people being close to the human was making the Murderhobo nervous, the large unicorn directed them to back away. They started galloping and running as Luke's timer began blinking. "We're almost there, Ascender. When we do the reaching of the

Progenitor's Oasis, all that you really need to do is the bowing and the taking of a sip of water to show your respect. You'll get a blessing, as well as the access to the next Zone."

"This process is *quick*, yes?" Luke's hands began trembling as they ran. He didn't really 'do' nervous, and when he did, it usually manifested as rage. At that moment, he was very *enraged* about the fact that he might miss gaining a new exit.

The small guide unicorn scoffed lightly and whispered almost too softly for Luke to hear, "He wants to rush through a face-to-face meeting with *God*. I don't… the outside world must be really strange."

"I'm Coral," the larger one stated in an attempt to distract Luke from his woes. "This is Shelly, and she's not used to visitors. Unsurprising, as it's been uncountable millenia since anyone has done the descending from a higher area. The Gigaant… as far as we know, only one of our people has ever done the getting past it. He could do the flying, so we think that *perhaps* he may have done the avoiding of the landstorms that were created by the creature moving."

"Your people can fly?" Luke eyed the quarter-ton horsey bodies next to him doubtfully.

"Only the *most* powerful of us are *unicorns*, silly!" Shelly's horn began to flash, a sign that she had more to say, but Coral shushed her.

"We're here." The large unicorn waved a hoof at a huge pool of mana-water surrounding a small island that was hidden by fog. "Clearly, you were expected. The fog is there to protect you from doing the seeing of something your mind cannot comprehend."

"That's where God… is? How did it get there?" Luke looked out at the shrouded island doubtfully. "How long has it been here?"

"Oh, it created itself there. It's been… oh, more than a *generation* since it did." Shelly started speaking as Coral motioned for Luke to bow and drink. "One day, our forefathers were here, and God split the sky, falling to the ground and showing its true form to our people! Ever since it showed us the way, the most powerful of us took the same body that it did."

"That's great. I'll drink water; now let's-" Luke paused in the act of bending down. He didn't mind drinking mana, but just as his hand was about to dip into the azure pool, he noticed something *moving* in the water. He had never seen another living thing survive direct contact with the liquid; something wasn't adding up. "What-"

The Murderhobo was launched into the air by a powerful buck and kick from Coral. His hunched angle meant that he was sent soaring into the air above the water and was able to catch a brief glimpse of a huge ring of unicorns rearing and laughing. Shelly shouted at him with a shrill laugh just before he impacted the water, "Enjoy meeting *God*, host! We'll all do it someday!"

Luke hit the water and plunged in deeply. His eyes were open, and the water was perfectly clear. That gave him a great view of swarms of fanged snails swimming through the water at his face. He swung out and obliterated the closest one with a punch, shattering it into dust that was swept away by the water in an instant. Another darted close to him and slammed into his forehead, biting down... only to be rebuffed by his mana-formed helmet.

That seemed to give it pause, and Luke killed it with an upswing. He hit the bottom of the lake and kicked toward the island, hoping to be able to get out of the water and find a safer location. Dozens of snails were slapped away, and even more of them attempted to break through his helmet. Luckily for Luke, his mana regeneration rate in *liquid mana* was so high that even the fiercest of group attacks only ever managed to make a small crack before repairing itself.

He stopped fighting them when he realized that they couldn't hurt him, pulling himself onto dry land with a low grunt. "Great. Now I'm gonna be too late to escape from here, *and* I'm bald again. Someone's gonna die for this."

A chorus of happy cheers rose from the bank of the lake, as

well as an outpouring of voices he didn't recognize. "Who got him? Was it Krabby?"

"No way, Moray was the fastest in there, for *sure!*"

"Who cares who got him; his host body will be able to open a way into the outside world! We're *free~e~e!*"

That comment made the others go quiet, and Luke's eyes caught a glimpse of saliva running down their muzzles. "There's gotta be so much *meat* in the world he came from…"

Their flat teeth shifted into points like sharks, and their cheerful eyes hardened and elongated into slits. Long lizard-like tongues licked out, but luckily the changes stopped there. Luke was glad that they were *mostly* still just horses. Coral's deep, impatient voice echoed over the water. "Hurry up already! You had to have done the eating of his brain by now! Show us what you can do!"

At that moment, Luke's return timer hit *zero*. Before he could make a smart choice, pretend to be captured, or launch a sneak attack, he robotically rose to his feet and turned to face the direction he had come from… then sprinted toward the water and leapt as hard as he could before activating Feather's Fall. As he drifted toward the unicorns, they cheered at his display of power.

Then the first of them noticed that something was wrong. "Wait. Where's his horn?"

In an attempt to hide his face as he drifted closer, Luke looked back at the island. At just that moment, a breeze blew away the fog; revealing a huge stone that had somehow naturally formed into a rough horse shape. His eyes were drawn to its head, where a bright blue bone had clearly slammed into it and become wedged. He hit the ground at the shoreline and started his forced run back to the end of Zone nine, even as he fought with all his willpower to turn back.

Lightning flashed, spells were launched, and flesh was torn. The Murderhobo was frozen, burned, sliced, and even partially eviscerated, unable to fully escape the magical power that poured like water from the confused unicorns. If he had been able to control his overall direction, he could have had a better chance at avoiding, but his Sigil forced obedience—he needed to remain on the fastest path out. Sucking down a mouthful of mana, Luke was horrified to find that his wounds didn't close instantly; whatever these creatures were using against him... even the basic spells continued to deal damage over time.

The Murderhobo slaughtered his way through the chaotic, disorganized unicorns at a sprint, even as he howled his rage and pain into the sky. "Cookie. *Cookie*! I've found you! I'll be back! Don't be afraid; they think you're god! *I'll be back for you!*"

CHAPTER TWENTY-TWO

- TAYLOR -

"Finally. Abyss, this world is on the edge of disaster, and he somehow manages to fight his Sigil hard enough to be *late*." The air thrummed like a drum being beaten to death, and the world gave way as a portal was torn open. Luke fell out of the wound in the universe just before it slammed shut, either not bothering —or unable—to catch himself as he dropped to the ground. Blood pooled around him, enough that the awaiting people clearly thought that he was either dying or already dead.

The ground around the fallen Murderhobo started to *hiss* as the air around him warped and flashed.

A *massive* sense of malease rolled over Taylor, and she instantly reacted by using Fissure to grab the earth under Luke with all her strength, then bodily *hurled* him as far out of the area and into the desert as she could manage. Only a few moments later, pure mana detonated around his lifeless form. A storm centered on Luke sprang into being, creating a howling tornado, water to rain down from the clear desert sky, and lightning to flash and boil the ground.

The Murderhobo hovered in the air, drifting to the ground like a feather on the wind. When he eventually touched down, the ground *warped*, rumbling and shifting in and out of visibility for a few minutes before settling as the ambient mana in the area reached an unprecedented density. The others could only watch, their Sigils chiming and forcing them to maintain their position.

"So, uh… think he died?" Zed casually questioned Taylor as he watched the lightshow. "I really wouldn't put it past him to be able to explode after he died. That seems like a very 'Murderhobo' Skill to have. Some kind of single use 'take my killer with me' thing. I could spin that into an epic tale… The Murderhobo that killed *anything* that killed him too: mutually assured destruction in the desert of despair-"

"Please stop that; it's morbid, and we are better than that. Now, I don't know *what* just happened, but he was at the very least heavily damaged." Taylor shook her head but kept her eyes on Luke's landing point. "I don't think he died. I got a strange feeling of caution when he got here, but I'm almost positive that it was from something he was carrying, not from him directly. Besides, mana acts strangely around him, and we've seen that it does strange things *to* him, so I'm completely certain he'll actually be better off than he was a moment ago."

Sure enough, just a few minutes later, a very bald Luke came striding out of the cloud of dust as if nothing had happened. The swirling mana didn't show any signs of slowing its spread, but they ignored that fact for the moment, since it was not currently at lethal levels for them. He wore a thunderous expression on his face, but Taylor didn't take that as anything other than 'hi, I'm Luke' by that point in their working relationship. Even upon seeing his resting murder face, Taylor let slip a small sigh of relief at finding that her friend was unharmed. "What in the world happened to you?"

"Not this world. Murder World. I was *this* close, Taylor. *This close* to her." Luke gasped repeated heaving breaths as he stomped around, barely holding off from a full tantrum. "I *found*

Cookie, and I wasn't able to get her! Do you have *any* idea how *abyssal...*"

He couldn't continue speaking, instead freeing a strangled snarl and reducing a rock jutting out of the sand to rubble with a few furious punches. Taylor wasn't sure how to handle the situation, but she *did* know for sure that she not only needed him to get away from the village, she *also* needed him to come and close the Scar she had found. "Come with me and tell me what's going on. I found a thing you need to punch."

That seemed to pull him out of his funk. At least, it no longer appeared that he would tear someone apart the moment they blinked too loudly near him. Taylor made a mental note that the best course of action was to *divert* Luke when she needed him to refocus, not to try and talk him down. She turned and sprinted away, but Luke appeared beside her in the next instant and didn't even seem to be having trouble keeping up. He had gotten stronger. Luke had *caught up* to her in her area of focused specialization. That shocked Taylor, and she vowed to take more time for training in the near future.

"Okay, guess I'll wait here!" Zed called from somewhere behind them, continuing to shout until they left audible range. "Oh, I can start a fire with my stone! Look for the fire on the way back; I'll have water boiling or something-"

It took only a few minutes for them to reach the fishbowl-glass Scar, and the sight of it grabbed Luke's immediate interest. "This is it? Is there someone in there that I get to fight?"

"No; can you please just close it?" Taylor worried for a long moment as he inspected the mirage-like portal in silence. "The world on the other side is dead and empty, but there are... I don't even know. Creatures that we would consider divine there that are going to scourge the planet soon. If we don't close this, I fear we may suffer for it."

"Yeah, that's not the problem." Luke lashed out with a single finger, and the Scar closed like a soap bubble popping. "I had just been hoping that something I needed to punch would give me some Potentia. Needed a little boost to feel good."

"Hold on. How…?" Taylor stared at the spot which the wavering portal had occupied a moment ago, then back at Luke in equal parts confusion and purest jealousy. "How in the *abyss* do you use a Tier eight spell in an instant like that?"

"I don't." Luke sat down and sighed, bored now that the excitement had already passed. "I have no Tier eight spell. I only have Skills."

"Same *difference!*" she sharply sounded off, stamping her foot in vexation. "Conventional wisdom states that *anything* above Tier six requires a significant casting time!"

"Who said I'm using a Tier eight Skill for that? All I'm doing is closing a Scar." Luke frowned at her quizzically. "First off, 'Open Up' is Tier six, level nine. I've been holding off on upgrading it until I can't go back to my world. Then I'm gonna see if I can trick my Sigil into letting me stay there for a while."

"Stop dodging the question! *You* said it was Tier eight!" Taylor insisted, managing to hold off from pointing a finger into his face. She knew how *that* would end, and she liked her fingers in the shape they held currently.

"False."

"Back when you closed the Scar and we were fighting the Chimera!" Taylor exploded at the Murderhobo. "You shouted 'Tier eight, Open Up'!"

"Oh. Yeah, I do remember that, but I never told *you* that it was there." Luke chuckled and finally started to relax as he watched Taylor's face shift and redden. "Heh. I was trying to throw people off. I figured that if the chimera thought I had some high-Tier stuff available, they'd back off a little. Plus, everyone was calling out the Tier of their powers, like they needed to do that to make it stronger or some other random reason. I didn't want to look like I couldn't keep up. Goat guy had just shouted about his Tier nine spell, so…?"

"You've *got* to be kidding me." Taylor dropped to the ground and covered her face. "I've been working so *hard* to catch up to the Tier you use, and you were just spewing feces. Do you even *have* any Tier eight Sp… Skills?"

Luke shook his head in the negative. "I can and do honestly admit that I have no Tier eight Skills."

"Okay. Well… that *shouldn't* make me feel better, but at least I know the truth-"

"Mainly because I just upgraded my main combat Skill to Tier nine." Luke's casual statement froze Taylor in place. He didn't notice that she wasn't moving as he simply continued to speak. "Haven't had much of a chance to test it yet. I was going to wait until I found some better gear or… or Cookie. Speaking of, I gotta start unbinding my weapons right now, or it'll be too late when I get to Cookie. Gimme a moment here."

Taylor swallowed her roiling emotions as she heard the pain in his voice. It was subtle, as the Murderhobo wasn't exactly an anything-but-ire-expressing sort of individual. Even so, she knew he needed a friend… and Andre wasn't around. She decided to give it a shot. "You said you found… Cookie? What happened?"

"A bunch of overgrown parasitic snails were worshiping her as their god." Luke moaned discontentedly and held his hands out in a display of confusion and anger. "I *swear*, she makes friends anywhere she goes."

"Snails." Taylor nodded slowly at the crazy man. "Interesting. Interesting. Yup. Murder World sounds… interesting."

"To be fair, they attach to other creatures and eat their brains. Hey. I found a few neat things this time. Any idea what plant this is?" Luke held up a seed, and Taylor shook her head. "Yeah, I knew that was a longshot. I'll bother Andre with it. He come back yet?"

"No." Taylor's lips pressed into a firm line, and she changed the subject. "Why did you explode into a mana storm when you got back?"

"What happened now? I was really foggy when I got back. Abyssal *exhausted*. Those chickens had messed me up pretty bad when I was going up the chain." Luke cracked his knuckles as he planned his revenge. "That last one nearly knocked me off the world. Not to mention, the snail spells were still working on being healed that whole time."

Taylor nodded in false understanding, her lips twisted to the side as her mind tried to make sense of what Luke was talking about. "Yeah, that sounds... bad. Very difficult, I'm certain. Let me, um, explain. When you got here, you fell to the ground, and my Sigil pinged me that something bad was about to happen. I threw you into the desert, and you vanished behind a wall of mana and storms."

"Mana?" Confusion dulled Luke's eyes for a moment, only to be replaced by horrified realization as he slapped at one of his pouches. He lifted it to inspect, only to find that it was charred completely through. "Goat feces. Now I need to find a way to bring spicy rock back without it exploding? Why would it decompress like that?"

"What was it?" Taylor inquired in a hushed tone, leaning toward him to hear the answer ever-so-slightly faster. "It was clearly powerful...?"

"I found some mana. Figured that if the water would be fine in a waterskin, the crystal version would be fine too." He tapped the charred, still-glowing bag and shook his head. "No deal."

"Mana... as crystals?" Taylor furrowed her brow and sat back. "There are *theories* that mana can become so dense that it becomes solid, but... no one on this plane has ever seen it. If you really found some, then... hmm. Yes. It would make sense that bringing it here would make it go *boom*. The sheer density of mana... taking it out of a mana-rich environment in its basic form, even that much, would make it explosively decompress. *Did* make it decompress, I suppose. Unless you could find a way to turn it into structured magic, it would just-"

"Turn it into something or put it in a sealed container, I got it. *Abyss*, just say what you mean to say all in one go for once." Luke rolled his eyes as she tried to make the issue harder than it needed to be. He opened another few pouches, finally pulling out a pinch of dust. "Other thing I found, then, since the mana is gone. This stuff. Can you think of any uses for powdered snail shell?"

"Snail shell is usually used to create dyes for the clothes of royals, but for us to use it? Not off the top of..." Taylor's voice trailed off as she stared at the shining powder, feeling the mana in the area build up and close around them like a blanket. "Luke... is that powdered *unicorn horn*?"

"No. They're glorified horses controlled by brain-sucking parasites; don't give them more credit than they deserve. But, fine. Yes. People that are *wrong* would call it unicorn horn."

CHAPTER TWENTY-THREE

- LUKE -

The Murderhobo wasn't sure why Taylor was so excited about the snail shell, but he decided not to rain on her parade. He ran alongside his team leader, his mind on other things as she waxed eloquent on the apparently myriad uses of powdered unicorn horn: everything from high-tier self-sustaining enchantments, to simply storing it in a city center to attract more mana and therefore boost the rates of Ascenders born in an area over time. The most prized usage was, of course, an intense increase in personal power by way of upgrading Mana Channels.

Right now, nothing mattered to him other than getting back to Murder World and finishing what he had started. Now that he had a location, he could formulate a plan of attack to get Cookie back into his hands. "The birds aren't a problem, the ant should be tiny and a whole lot easier to kill, but the 'Corns... they'll be ready for me this time. They won't give her back without a fight. I know *I* wouldn't, and they think she's god, so the only option is converting them..."

The Murderhobo was so distracted that he almost didn't

notice the group of Ascenders that were blocking their path back into town. Taylor's sharp hiss brought him back to the present, and he gave the group of troublemakers a once-over as he slowly finished his thought, "...to meat paste. Let's see. Armor, well-muscled, clearly well-fed. Not local. Heaven's Earth? Are we having a rematch?"

"Team 'The Four', you are charged with treason against the Hollow Kingdom!" Edward the Knight bellowed into their faces as he stormed toward them. "You are to be *inspected* for any items known to be owned by other members of the King-dom's Ascenders. You *will* submit to questioning, and-"

"I swear we haven't instigated an attack against any official Kingdom forces." Taylor's Sigil appeared on her head and chimed as it registered her words as truth. "Anyone attacking us, or *ambushing* us, certainly wouldn't be someone working for the Kingdom in a legal or official capacity. Isn't that correct, *Sir* Edward?"

Luke grimaced at the cloying feel of her words. Even *listening* to someone speaking politically made him want to wash away the sensation of an oily substance oozing across his skin. Silence reigned for a long moment while the Knight thought through his options, and his eyes lit up as he stumbled his way onto what might have been his first original thought. "While that may be *strictly* true, we are still going to need you to submit to questioning and a *full* search. You, hobo-man, hand over your weapons and gear."

Luke stared down at the Knight as the armored man walked up on him. As he got closer, Luke realized Edward's head only came up to his chin; and this was the *tallest* of the Knights. A smile spread across the Murder-hobo's face as he pulled out a random waterskin and uncorked it before spraying a thin stream onto the ground in front of him; effectively blocking the knight from advancing. He tucked the container away and devoted his entire mana pool to his Battering Ram Knuckles as the liquid mana decompressed into a thick fog. He spread his arms wide while his fists warped the air with a concerning *thrum*.

"Go ahead." Luke's right eye twitched as he unblinkingly stared the Knight down. Pure mana billowed up in front of him, lending his currently hairless head a sinister glow. "*Take* 'em from me."

Edward looked back at his fellow Knights, who shook their heads in a rapid 'no' as sweat dripped past their helmets. The Knight narrowed his eyes and tried to reach out, but his own Sigil *screeched* and forced him away from the wall of power. "Mage, apprehend this man and force him to hand over-"

"You don't have the authority; let's not play pretend." Taylor motioned for Luke to follow her and swept past the stymied group. As they walked, she muttered so that hopefully only Luke could hear her, "Make sure Zed is safe. He's the only one they could reasonably control."

"Good luck finding him," Luke snorted in response as they sped away. "We left him loose among the locals, and he was granted the authority to hide by the *King*. Are you forgetting that he's a Bard?"

That pulled Taylor up short, and a troubled look appeared on her face. "That might complicate things. How are we supposed to find him when we need him? He might get himself into trouble."

"Who cares? *Hey*! How about you get outta here?" Luke shouted back at the Knights that were beginning to follow them like lost puppies, then dropped his voice as he addressed her again. "You're gonna need to do something about them soon. There's only so far I'll let them press us before I take annoying me as an attack. The bar is *low*, Taylor."

"You seem…" Taylor hesitated as she pondered how to put her next words delicately, then remembered who she was speaking with, "…different. In a good way. Did something change?"

"I'm acting exactly the same as I always do, Taylor." Luke

marched forward, on the lookout for threats. "Any changes you are observing are just caused by how *you* perceive me."

"Then you must have gained charisma!" Taylor searched his face for confirmation, but was only met with a stony stare. "Fine, keep your silence. I know enough to understand that major internal changes don't happen without outside inter-ference."

A tall man sprinted toward them suddenly, and it was only Taylor's act of stepping forward at the last instant for a hug that prevented Luke from making a move and beating this person's face in. For Luke, who was able to discern monster type by eye color, not recognizing the Druid was completely dumbfounding. Andre's normally smiling face was set in a rictus of pain, and he motioned for them to follow him.

Without exchanging a syllable, the three of them shifted the direction they were traveling and hightailed it deeper into the sand dunes of the desert. Sir Edward paused at the edge of the town they had almost set foot in and bellowed after them, "Hey! You can't leave! I'm here to question you!"

"Get back to your post, fool. You don't have the kind of authority that can make the Archdruid submit to you," Andre snarled at the Knight, who flinched back instinctively. Luke regarded his friend with interest; when the Druid had shouted, lines of fresh blood had begun seeping down between his teeth.

"Neat," Luke muttered as he tried to get closer to his friend. To his surprise, the man that had always towered over him was now only a few inches taller than he was. "Look at that. I'm taller. Was it eating the solid mana? Or something… else?"

"I'm a *Royal Knight!*" Sir Edward belatedly howled after them, unsheathing his sword with a ring of steel.

"Either take us in by force, or go find someone who cares!" Andre bellowed back at the man, vines unwinding from his body and lashing out, sending sand into the air at each point of impact. "I'll warn you right now, if you interfere in our work; it. Will. Not. End. *Well* for you! There's no one here to bring you back after I grow a rosebush through your brain, no spell in place to undo what I'll turn you into!"

The Druid turned to his team, heaving for air as the suddenly ashen Knight scampered away, already aware of what Andre could do. He had lived it, even if only for a moment. "I've been searching for Zed, but since the two of you are calm, I realize that Zed must be up to something. Listen, you two. I need you to help me. I found a way to start my work, but... I need... I need things. Blood, bodies, *mana*. This will not be an easy or cheap affair. Can I count on you? This is stange, but I don't know what else to-"

"I call bodies and mana," Luke volunteered as soon as the Druid faltered. "Blood is hard for me to collect. Goes everywhere."

A faint smile touched the corners of Andre's lips, and he seemed greatly relieved that they hadn't called his methods into question. Taylor leaned toward him and whispered something, and the Druid appeared to be refreshed. The sweat and grime coating him slowly vanished, and he seemed far more comfortable in just a few moments. "I appreciate that, thank you. I found an *awesome* plant that allows me to hold off on sleep for multiple days at my level of Body, but the side effects are starting to catch up to me. I need to place the first few layers of biological materials so that the land can steep while I sleep."

"You weren't gone long, were you?" Luke glanced at the thick bags the Druid was carrying. "What could you *possibly* have accomplished in under two weeks?"

"*Anything*, Luke." Andre leaned in and locked bloodshot eyes on the Murderhobo, speaking with a low, serious tone. "With enough direction, power, and imagination, I can do *anything*."

"Except sleep and brush your teeth. Taylor was here for the second one, else I'd throw you away from me. Even so..." Luke lifted a hand and shoved the overly serious Druid away from him. "You look like a monster octopus right now, so I need you to stay a little further away from me so I don't accidentally tear your spine out."

"How does someone *accidentally* do that?" Taylor forced herself to refrain from digging deeper into the mind of a madman, took a calming breath, and smiled at Andre. "Where are we going right now, and how can we actually help? Actually, before you answer that, I have some disturbing news. It appears that a large number of Scars have appeared in the area, and they're spewing out monsters and messing with the weather. Some are even starting to impact the world around them, so they're either more powerful or have been active for a long time."

"Good to know." Andre nodded, then kept doing so, continuing the motion for far too long and nearly falling asleep, thanks to the rocking motion. Luke slapped the Druid lightly, sending him to the ground and kicking up a cloud of sand. He hopped up and gave a thumbs-up, not trusting his ability to nod his appreciation. "The Scars are actually good news for this; I need lots and lots of bodies. So many. Monsters, animals, really whatever you've got. Another thing that would work is just an *epic* amount of fecal matter that I can convert into fertilizer. The thing is, I can use an entire corpse to cover a way bigger area than the same amount of manure."

"Um…" Taylor started raising her hand to calm the nearly vibrating Druid. He waved her off and kept speaking.

"No, listen, this is interesting, I promise." Andre lifted a seed and gestured with it. "I can use the microbiomes present in blood and bodies to start a grove by adding in flora that convert the… we'll say 'meat' in cells, for lack of a better term, into vegetation. My power, added to the natural lure of the plants, will cause insect life to be drawn to the area, worms and such. That'll save me time aerating, and my watermelons will form sprinklers!"

Luke punched the Druid in the face, and the man collapsed into a snoring heap. The Murderhobo glanced warily at Taylor, but she merely looked away with an off-key, "Oh, what a fine landscape we have here. It is always so amazing what nature can create."

The Murderhobo cracked a grin at her completely unnatural tone as she did her best not to register the attack on her friend and teammate. He lifted the Druid onto his shoulder and continued moving in the direction Andre had indicated. "He needed to not be awake anymore. He was starting to sound like Zed. Manic and stuff."

"No idea what you're talking about. As far as I know, he just now fell into a much-needed sleep." Taylor's eyes were locked on a point in the distance, and she waved at it. "I'm almost positive that he was bringing us to the same spot where you landed out there. About three kilometers from town, yes? I'm betting he's planning to use the residual mana to ease his burden in establishing an oasis there."

"How wonderful for him. You said there were more Scars in the area?" Luke's voice was as stoic as usual, but Taylor could have sworn she caught an undertone of eagerness. "He needs bodies, so if you wanna keep watch, I'll offer my services in hunting for the special materials he wanted."

"Yeah, yeah, go kill things." Taylor rolled her eyes as the Murderhobo dropped Andre like a sack of potatoes. She caught him, of course, but by that point, Luke was already running into the distance. The last thing he heard her mutter was, "Maybe him running around will throw off anyone pursuing us, at least?"

CHAPTER TWENTY-FOUR

The fact that Luke found a Scar in under an hour was a testament to how badly mangled the world had become in the desert. Anyone else would have been very concerned; he was simply eager to see what they provided.

There were many theories surrounding the ways that Scars formed naturally, the most prevalent being that they formed in high-mana areas. Luke didn't think that applied here; not with reality seeming so flat and false. "It's not about *low* mana, either, I bet. Gotta be about mana *movement*, since this desert is draining the power around here at an unnatural pace."

The mana wasn't getting pulled anywhere, or following any noticeable pattern. That would have made his life really easy by highlighting whatever anomaly was sustaining the desert. Then he would have killed that anomaly. The fact was, the area was so *dead* that the local ambient mana wasn't being replenished at all. The world naturally attempted to even out the mana in the area, causing it to sink into the dead zone like a storm moving due to a cold wind. *That* mangled the dimensional walls... or at least that was the feeling he got from Open Up as he stared at the jagged Scar in front of him.

"So that's what 'you get an understanding of mana' means. Weird. Doesn't tell me why the portal is black." Luke poked the hole in the universe, and it rippled like a cube of animal fat. "How can light be black? Is that a thing?"

He didn't *really* care; it just seemed strange. He took a deep breath and dove through the portal face first, emerging directly into a pool of water. It was *shockingly* cold, and his health started attempting to increase. The water was *packed* with poison, to the point that the entire body of liquid was possibly actual poison and not water at all. Luke kept his eyes open, catching the precise moment that the local wildlife discovered he existed.

Huge schools of eels and various biting sea creatures swam through the *wildly* toxic fluid and attacked him. For the first time, the Murderhobo got to test his Chain-Blade Rope to the fullest. His weapon slashed around him in vast arcs, the mana-made whip cutting though the water as if it, too, was an enemy.

The creatures were fragile, and a single glancing blow was often enough to rip them apart. Unfortunately, there was a small problem: chumming the water in such a fashion attracted even more creatures. Soon, huge beasts were looming up from the depths.

As for Luke, he was starting to feel the pinch of not breathing. It wouldn't kill him, since it meant that poison air would build up in his lungs, and he could survive off that. It just wasn't very comfortable. Spinning the Chain-Blade Rope in a tight loop, he propelled himself through the portal and into his base world once more.

He took a deep breath and turned to jump back in, only to get slapped out of the way as the various swamp beasts started following him through the portal, which was evidently invisible from that side, in a seemingly endless stream of self-destruction. Compounding piles of creatures came through, and the ground started to blacken as the toxic water that coated their flesh was dumped onto the sand. Puddles formed beneath the writhing heaps, the brackish water full of death for most normal creatures.

He watched the monsters thrash around for a few minutes, all sharp angles and teeth, before they started dying en masse. Whether it was caused by the lack of water, or lack of poison, he was completely unsure. "Not a drop of Potentia from all of that. Waste of time. Andre probably can't even use these bodies-"

"Stop right there! You! Murderhobo!" A scream rang out as two small groups of people charged at Luke with weapons drawn. All eight of them seemed to be fighting each other, barely even paying attention to him. "Back off; the bounty is ours! *Die*, you little… **hack**."

The small groups slowed as they drew close, the poison splashing on their skin from the drying puddles causing their eyes to roll up into their heads. They fell directly into the remaining water and started to froth at the mouth. Luke watched them for a short while, but the symptoms kept up, and they were still alive. He sighed and went to gather them up. "I swear, if I get blamed for this, I'm just going to outright snap their necks."

He walked over and tossed the slowly dying people up onto his left arm, all eight of them piled up on one side, while he grabbed an extra-large fish off the ground. Luke wasn't sure if Andre could do anything with a creature this toxic, but he figured it wouldn't hurt to check. If they were useless, he could always come back and close the portal. From the time he left to the time he returned, only a couple hours in total had passed. Andre was still asleep, so Luke dropped the people to one side and the swamp monster to the other. He laid down and tried to soak up some of the sun before full night came.

A short time later, Taylor noticed a foul smell and became aware of the large number of new bodies in the area. "Luke! Who are they? What is *that?*"

"It's a fish. I think." Luke stared at the creature that seemed to be made entirely of triangles, and shrugged as he gave up on contemplating it further. "It's coated in a fairly potent poison. I wouldn't touch it."

"Less concerned about the monster, Luke." Taylor came closer to inspect the group of people laying on the sand, recoiling as a terrible stench reached her. She had thought it was coming from the fish, and some of it was, but the majority was issuing from the pile of people. "Who are *they*? What happened to them?"

"In order: mercenaries. They touched the fish water." Luke waved at Andre's prone form. "I was hoping he could do something to help them; the water is a pretty nasty poison."

"They're poisoned? Wait, if you want him to-"

"Shh. You'll wake him." Luke put a finger to his lips and shook his head. "I didn't go through the trouble of knocking him out just so that we could wake him up before he's well-rested."

"Luke. They're going to die if we let Andre get all the beauty sleep he needs," Taylor groaned as she walked over to the Druid and shook him awake. The sleepy man was startled by the sudden shift in scenery, but a quick gesture at the downed men got the powerhouse to his feet and moving quickly, even if he did send a few considering looks at Luke. As if he were considering how deep of a hole to drop him in.

It didn't take long for Andre to shake his head sadly and insert seeds into the men's nostrils. "They're already basically dead. Whatever was affecting them was a terribly strong toxin; I'm thinking it's a cross between a preservative and a knockout poison. I'm guessing whatever was on the other side liked their food to be fresh. Now, I might have been able to do something if I had a sample of the poison and plenty of time, but these guys... nothing I can do but keep them alive. Pretty sure they aren't coming back."

Luke watched as a flower grew out of each of the men's noses, and he tilted his head to the side as he tried to make sense of what he was seeing. "Isn't that what you used to save Zed? Also. Why keep them alive?"

"It is, with just a slight modification." Andre pointed out a few specks of color on the flower petals. "I'm pulling out the poison, but it's only at the same rate that the poison is being regenerated. For some reason, this poison is able to use organic material to propagate itself. If I didn't get this in them right away, they would have melted into sludge."

"Slight problem for you to solve." Luke pointed vaguely into the distance. "I had a whole load of that stuff come out of a Scar when I was stepping out to take a breather. I'd say a few tons, in terms of pure mass. You think that'll be an issue, or can we safely ignore it?"

"Celestials above, Luke." Taylor rubbed at her head. "Could you *please* tell us this stuff with a greater sense of urgency?"

"Is this… thing… a creature from the same place?" Andre turned his eyes on the mass of triangles that Luke had called a 'fish'. "It looks like it lived in that stuff, and it's filled with something analogous to algae."

"Yup. Whole bunch of them came out. Just said that," Luke acknowledged as Andre hurried to the fish, then had him chop chunks of it out. A spray of black sludge splashed across Andre's face as Luke tore a large fin off, and the Druid's eyes widened in horror. He turned and shouted as blood flowed from his hands and formed a portal over the next few minutes. He grabbed the fish parts, as well as the fallen people, with vines and tossed them in, diving through the portal in the same second.

The energy fluctuations ended, and the portal collapsed instantly, unable to sustain itself in the mana-barren wasteland. Luke and Taylor gaped at the spot where the Druid had vanished, then at each other. "Luke… did you just kill the first Druid the Hollow Kingdom has had in over a century?"

The Murderhobo contemplated the query for a long second, then shook his head. "I don't think so. No. I didn't."

"You're *sure?*" Taylor whirled on him and growled, "How can you be *sure?*"

Luke tapped something only he could see. "No Potentia increase yet. Pretty sure if I killed him off, I'd earn at least a *little*. Or a fried brain. Anywho, I'll go look for more Scars now. There's gotta be something around here that'll be beneficial to Andre's desert development plan. Or maybe some Potentia. Either way."

CHAPTER TWENTY-FIVE

Luke spent the next few days searching the surrounding territory for Scars. On the first day, he found three; a dead world, a world where everything seemed to be made out of semi-intelligent metal that slowly crept toward him whenever he took a step, and a third world that made his 'You Need To Stop' Skill *work* to keep him alive. The third world was filled with energy, not mana, but it somehow made his health continuously drop as he adjusted to it. Everything contained within glowed a light bluish-green, and he couldn't find a single thing that was alive.

Shrugging, he had left the world, but discovered upon exiting that he and his clothes had all caught the blue. Only after dumping out nearly half a waterskin of mana and standing in the resulting mana-steam-shower, then taking a swig of the liquid, did he manage to eradicate the glow. Needless to say, he made sure to close all three portals and moved on. No Potentia tribute, no access to the world.

The second day was more profitable, as he found one world filled with lupine humanoids absolutely *stuffed* with blood. He had been concerned at first that they would be intelligent creatures, but they seemed to be only instinct-driven. They were too weak to be of much use to him for leveling purposes, but they reproduced by the litter. That meant they were going to be a good, constant source of corpses for him. After marking the location, he hauled nearly a thousand bodies to the place he had last seen Andre and set out once again.

By the fifth day, he was having a lot of fun. Enough that it would have worked as a clear condition if there had been a barrier like those in Murder World. He had closed almost a dozen Scars by then, leaving open only the ones that he deemed especially beneficial. His exploration had led him to a new portal, one that was bright orange. The opening moved strangely, and he hadn't yet seen a single creature come out of it. The area surrounding it enacted a vacuum effect, slowly pulling in dust and anything drifting through the air. "Orange. There's fire on the other side. I'll bet money that's what this is. There's going to be fire and pain."

He pushed a stick through, then pulled it back. Inspecting it closely, he grunted and had to acknowledge that *perhaps* the color of the portal meant less than he originally thought. Taking a deep breath to fill his lungs instead of his nerves—a lesson learned from the swampy portal—Luke stepped through the Scar onto a huge rock and looked around. "Am I moving through the Void?"

All around him hung a vast emptiness, with only a few stars burning in the otherwise all-encompassing darkness. There were no creatures that he could see or sense, and this place felt utterly… *false*. Completely, horribly, child-drawn fake. He shuddered and stepped back through the portal, eyes widening in surprise as he noticed that the sun had vanished.

"What…? I stepped through at noon." Something was wrong. He *knew* it. Luke sprinted toward the encampment, shocked and horrified to find a thick layer of carpet-like lichen, mushrooms, and the first few sprouts of various grasses and weeds appearing. When he reached the original campsite, he couldn't find anything. None of the bodies he had collected, none of his team, but there *were* stinkhorn mushrooms every-where. The disgusting plants had already attracted a steady, swirling supply of flies and other various small insects.

"This is clearly Andre's doing." Luke tried to search for tracks, but there was nothing to be found. He rushed toward the village, only to find a burned-out ruin where the buildings had once stood. He'd bet money that Taylor would be plotting murder over that. If she was alive. Taking a deep breath, he decided that he needed to hunt down his team and figure out what had happened. But first... he needed to know how much he had missed out on. "Sigil, how long have I been gone?"

There was no response. So he refined his question to ask how long he had been in the previous portal.

Time spent in most recent portal. Subjective: 00:00:05. Comparative: 21:00:00. Congratulations! You found a Descender portal. Report it to the Kingdom for 500 Exp? Yes/No.

"Sure. I'm gonna close it as soon as I remember to go back there, but why not get paid for it?" Luke accepted the offer with a grumble as he started running deeper into the desert. If he could find an area where nothing was growing, he could perhaps triangulate the center of all growth. Andre would be there. "Good to know he survived. If he—wait a *minute*! Three *weeks*?"

He lashed out with Open Up, but the Skill failed instantly, and he got a notification that he hadn't spent thirty days on the base world. Apparently, *subjective* time meant nothing to the kingdom, except that he was only allowed a certain amount of it. Luke had hoped that he had just found a way around his restrictions and started fuming with the new information that he had just allowed the snail-horses an additional *three hundred and fifteen* days of preparation time against him. Doing his best not to scream aloud that fact—and failing miserably—Luke began searching the desert for signs of life.

The plant life was bizarre and confusing, mostly contained to things that could grow from spores and seeds able to be carried on the wind. No trees were visible, nor had anything grown taller than the span of his index finger, just short, rapidly growing plants that thrived on rot and base minerals. Even though everything was so weak and springy, it did at least seem hardy and difficult to kill off. A solid half-mile inroad had been made, continuing along the edge of the desert that had been bare sand the last time he had been here.

Desperation to know what was going on drove him to continue searching through the night and into the hot morning. He was searching so intently that he almost missed the first signs of an existing camp: a line of grass that poked up through the sand. He continued for nearly another half mile before he realized what that had actually been: an unbroken stretch of plant life. He was almost positive that the root system continued underground, all the way back to the healthy areas of the Kingdom. That meant he had a way to track the Druid.

Returning to the grass, he gently dug around the blades until he found what he had been expecting. Following the roots in a straight line into the desert, he began running. Every once in a while, he would find leafy plants and check to see where the roots trailed off. Very rarely did he need to shift his directions at all, and within a few hours, he reached a small oasis blooming deep in the desert. It was well-positioned to be difficult to find, as well as excellently defensible, but he had been led directly to the location by the Druid's clear need for mana regeneration. He'd need to have a talk with Andre about obfuscating his trail.

"Taylor, Andre! It's me, don't attack!" Luke called into the empty area. He walked into camp and was slightly disgusted to find dozens of people laying around unconscious. They were all tightly bound with vines, with flowers growing out of their noses. "What in the abyss is this foul-"

He dove to the ground as a creature roughly a foot and a half in length jumped at him and slashed out with a bladed limb the length of a standard dagger. Analyzing it as he rolled to his feet, he found a creature that looked like a cross between a praying mantis and a locust. Its back legs were massively thick, and it used them to propel itself at him at such high speed that he needed to actively defend himself instead of dodging. It bounced off his armor, and he punched it in return; the light slap splattering it across the area as if he had spilled a cup of wine.

You have killed a Preying Mantous. Potentia gained: 1.

"That's spelled… I guess it isn't spelled wrong? 'Prey' as in hunt, and 'Man'-tous as in 'Preys on Man'? Humans have natural predators? Since when?" The Murderhobo examined the few remaining bits of the creature. The blades had presented as hard as metal, but upon death, the natural weapons were as weak and thin as any leaf from a tree. "Andre! Where are you?"

The reply took far too long. The earth shifted slightly, and sand slid away from the erupting mound as an enormous flower pushed out of the ground. As it bloomed, Andre's head popped out of the now-open space. "Luke? You're back! Where were you? What happened?"

"Hold up. I just killed a bug the size of my arm with double blades instead of arms. That one of yours, or something to watch out for in general?" Luke watched as Andre's expression shifted to anger with a hint of fear. "Not yours. Got it."

"I have no *idea* where those unnatural *things* are coming from." Andre spat to the side as Luke came closer. "They're like foxes, but for *everything*, not just animals. They kill for sport, and chop anything living up until it turns to mulch. Speaking of, can you hand me a few of those, um… people? Lots to talk about, but the short version is that someone high up in the royal family, we think the Prince, put a nasty bounty on us. These are some of the people that were hunting us."

Luke shrugged at Andre's hesitation. He didn't mind treating these people like the aggressors they were. He tossed them one at a time to Andre, who laid them out in the flower. After five had gone in, he stepped out of the flower and it closed around the sleeping people. "So, yeah. I figured out a way to make the flowers in their noses disperse the mana it draws out of them. This is a Lotus Coffin, my own creation. They absorb the mana and use it to encourage the growth of any nearby plants, as well as keeping the trapped people healthy by feeding them a steady drip of nutrients. Took a long time to breed the acid out of fly traps, cross them with a lotus, and grow to this size, but it's worth it."

"How have you done so much here?" Luke motioned with his arms into the distance, where the mosses and fungi were visibly continuing to spread. "What happened to the town? Where are the others?"

"So it's been about three weeks since you vanished, which is, you know, about one hundred and twenty-six days in my world." Andre seemed about ready to fall over from sheer exhaustion, and his voice betrayed how out of it he was. "Bounty hunters found out where we were staying and attacked the town, so Taylor retaliated by lighting their supply chain on fire and smashing the crates they were using to hold their allotments of liquid Potentia."

The Druid's eyes focused on a point in the distance. "After she turned her attention to them, some of the townspeople attacked her while she was distracted. Zed was there and he... he saved her. But.. I think he melted their brains, Luke. It... it was horrible. They were going to attack Taylor, then they just... died. Fell over. No visible injuries at all."

"Okay." Luke was pleased to hear that Zed had been working to save his team. It showed he cared deeply. The Druid kept talking, not even noticing that Luke had spoken.

"The worst part? No one else reacted to those traitors dying. It was like those people had never existed to them. Zed... I can't believe how dark that was, Luke. Turns out, he leaked the location they were staying at to draw in the bounty hunters and used the attack to figure out who was loyal. Piled the bodies up and lit a fire with that stone the Viscount gave him, and started cheering about being useful. Thank the celestials that he swore to never use his Abilities against us."

Andre laughed too loudly as he motioned to the remaining people. "As you can see, Taylor hasn't killed a single person that attacked us, thinking that this is all a political trap. She believes that as soon as one of the attackers dies, someone will show up with actual authority and reveal that the attackers were part of the peerage. I'm not cut out for this nightmare of politics, Luke. I make pretty flowers and plants that will make people's lives worth living. I don't understand the tricksy words and double meanings; the plots within plots. I just can't have that in my life."

"So don't bother." Luke eyed his friend, weighing the benefits of putting the man to sleep with his fist again. He decided against it; wouldn't do to give the man a reason to flinch every time he was around. Instead he started exploring the slipshod campsite and considering how to improve the defenses while talking. "You don't wanna do politics? Don't. Someone tries to force you to do something? Stick 'em in a Lotus Coffin and use them to help regrow the desert. They bring an army? Use their blood to water your flowers. Pretty sure you could actually do that, and it'd even make your flowers better able to fight against the next army."

"But... but what if-"

Luke cut him off with an impatient grunt. "Look around you. This was done by a Druid. A single guy basically wrecked an entire country because he was mad that they treated him so poorly. Any of us could do that. You'd think they'd treat us better... actually, why don't they? Point is, get so strong that they're terrified you could do this all over again. If they try to call your bluff, *actually* do it again."

"I could *never*-" Andre tried to avoid the issue once more.

"Never? I bet that's exactly what the last Druid said." Luke glared at Andre, his hand shooting out to grasp the man's lower jaw. "Stop talking, go to your world, and sleep for a day. Come back when you're useful, and we'll talk about what we need to do. Nod if everything is fine for now; shake your head if we need to rescue someone."

Andre slowly nodded. Luke let him go and stepped back.

"Words are fine. Only for a little while. Then they just get in the way. Go sleep; I'll protect the delicate little flowers."

He kicked one of the unconscious men, and Andre winced in sympathy. The Murderhobo glared and went to kick another, harder this time. Andre waved frantically for him to stop and slowly, painfully, opened a portal before easing through. Luke watched intently as the portal vanished, then slowly grinned. "He musta boosted the ambient mana in the area a whole lot if he can open that *this* deep in the desert. Wait; that means that no one else knows it's possible to portal here right now… that's a good advantage for us."

Luke sat on one of the Lotus Coffins that was peeking out of the sand and took a deep breath… promptly hacking a deep cough as sand flew down his nose. "The sand is attacking me! *Die*, sand!"

CHAPTER TWENTY-SIX

Luke gazed around in satisfaction as he counted the number of craters in the area. To the casual eye, this place looked like the site of a scattered meteor spell. The sand had finally stopped attacking him after he left it alone to suffer for a short while, so he returned to examining the various plants that were growing in the area.

Not only the Lotus Coffins, but other various plants that were arranged in groups a good distance from each other. He didn't understand most of them, but he knew what their base forms were. Each group included a huge mushroom that was constantly either smoking or sending out spores, a small watermelon, tiny plants that he assumed were seedling trees, a single Lotus Coffin, and a *ton* of flowers. Each small flora cluster was a solid fifty feet away from the next one, which made Luke wonder if he had actually found the camp, or if this was just a workstation. "Eh. Andre will tell me when he wakes up."

After putting the thoughts out of his mind, Luke hunted for any other attackers—humans *or* nasty bugs. The sand had learned its lesson. What he found instead was the Bard, who stood there waving at him. Luke squinted at the man, then searched for whatever the source of the hallucination was. The wavering image of Zed shook his head, and his voice whispered into Luke's ear. "Hello there, Luke! No, I'm not with you right now, but my party notification Mastery reached a new Tier. I can project myself to anyone in my party at a *really* huge distance now."

"Go away." Luke waved his hand through the mirage, trying to determine if this was caused by the plants he had been inspecting. Maybe the smoking mushroom? He'd need to sample them and see if-

"*Luke.*" Zed's voice lost all its humor. "Now that I found you, I'm guiding Taylor over, so bear with it. Also, I'm here to warn you... lots of Ascenders are combing through the villages out here. Some of them look really official and are shouting about 'crimes', but most of them look... nasty. Mercenary, assassiny, sneaky-snake type. They're *all* looking for us. Luckily for me, I've been here *forever*, and everyone in the area loves me. I'm everyone's little brother. Now, I'm able to scatter the Ascenders without too much issue currently, but if you keep kicking up mushroom clouds of sand everywhere, it's gonna be hard to hide."

"Hey, the sand came after me first," Luke grumbled angrily. Everyone was always blaming *him* for strange occurrences.

"Of *course* it did, you loveable crazy man," Zed crooned like a doting father, then looked to the side. His mouth worked as though he was talking to someone, and he nodded before turning back to Luke. "Have you seen Andre? I haven't been able to reach him."

"Portaled out over there." Luke jerked his thumb in the general direction of the Druid's point of egress. "Looks like local mana levels are creeping up."

"Interesting." Zed hesitated briefly. "Listen, Luke. Andre's having a really hard time with all of this. I can normally soothe him through stuff, but I'm really busy working with all the border towns; I'm getting them ready to be farmers again. Once we have a solid ring of fertile land, we need to begin pushing people inside to work the land. That's my task in all this, and I gotta tell you... convincing people to do what generations have warned against is abyssal *hard*. Great Potentia earner, but hard."

Luke decided to go about his day, since he couldn't escape the chatterbox. "Andre's fine. I talked to him."

Zed winced and glanced to wherever Taylor was. "Oh, no. How mangled is he? I can maybe find a healer-"

"He went home to take a nap, you windbag." Luke glowered at the Bard. "Have you seen any rocks around here? I really want to set up some defenses, but I have literally nothing to work with."

"Wait for Andre; those flowers he's growing are... multipurpose." Zed shuddered at some memory. "He was just about ready to start forming a Grove; at least, that's what he told me the last time we talked. Remember how well that worked against the Chimera? Imagine one that he's been working on getting ready for *weeks*. I think he just kept putting it off so that he could save all the people stacked up over there."

"Wait. *Save* them?" Luke looked at the sunburned, partially mangled people with flowers growing out of their noses. "He's tossing them into flowers. I'm almost positive they'll never see the light of day again."

Zed gestured grandly to the nearly empty expanse of the desert. "The other option is to let defenseless Ascenders bake under the sun while random murder-bugs appear to eat them. He's doing what he can to make sure they don't die pointless deaths."

"That makes sense. Waste not, and all that." Luke nodded approvingly at the actions of the Druid. "Use every part of the person. Solid efficiency."

"...Yeah." Zed shook himself, then gestured to the south. "Taylor's here; you two have fun out there in the heat and terrible conditions! I'm off to eat some fluffy bread, drink fruit juice, and tell a few pretty ladies that I'm not *actually* related to them."

His image popped like a soap bubble just as the Mage arrived. Taylor glanced at Luke, raising a perfectly shaped eyebrow and crossing her arms. "Where in the abyss did *you* go?"

"Found a Descender Scar. Got trapped there for five minutes." He shrugged in annoyance and gestured around. "Andre wouldn't have ever come up with something like this on his own. Using these people was your plan. You sure you're okay with doing that to him? He's soft."

"How did you…" Taylor sputtered as Luke smirked. "Ah. I just told you it was my plan. Got it. As for that Descender Scar; did you close it?"

"Not yet."

"Please don't. When we grow the farmlands and such out, we should be able to set that place up as a storage area for perishables. Out-of-season delicacies, meat and cheeses that never go bad, food always hot and ready to eat… that'll allow the destitute people of this area to have a solid source of income, as well as becoming a draw for tourists and such." Taylor nodded as an entire business plan was drawn up in her mind. "Fresh fruit, vegetables, and perfect meals on demand? That'll likely become the center for the very wealthy to visit."

"We'll be doing something else by then. You're not gonna get anything out of it," Luke reminded her just as a portal opened nearby. A much-refreshed Andre stepped out, and he waved at the others.

"Morning. Or whatever it is here." He stretched and looked around with a frown before shaking his head and flashing a rueful grin. "Ugh. Yeah, good call on making me go to sleep, Luke. I need to stay off those wake-berries for a while. Are we ready for a Grove here, or should we go elsewhere?"

"Here should be fine." Taylor smiled as the recently-awoken man tried to smooth his bed-hair. "Once we have a visible base, we should start drawing in more attackers. The more we capture, the faster we can restore the desert, right? We don't even need to feel bad about it, because they were coming after us first!"

"I suppose. No reason not to get started, then." Andre's face settled into a carefully neutral expression. He lifted an arm and began moving it in swirling motions. Droplets of blood flung away from him, instantly absorbing into the sand wherever they fell. From there, vast swaths of loose sand began swirling around them.

Before long, they stood in the center of a massive whirlpool of shifting sand, and Andre's motions started becoming more complicated as the sand began joining together into complicated patterns. "I have to thank you for letting me fix that huge area that got poisoned, Luke. The land counted that as me performing a great service to the earth, and I was blessed with a new Ability."

"Happy to help." Luke chuckled as he remembered spraying poison across the Druid, as well as the huge area that the fish had toxified. "Really, anytime."

"I'm going to officially request this: please no." Andre's voice was calm as he continued his work. Within moments, the loose sand had joined together into a veritable terrarium-home of sandstone and quartz-glass. "Celestial algae, this takes a lot outta me. Speaking of, that algae the fish contained is an *amazing* detoxifier. Probably wouldn't have noticed if my face wasn't melting and healing at the time."

"Yeah. Sorry about the whole…" Luke waved a hand at Andre's general 'face' location. "How'd you survive that one?"

"I couldn't degrade any further, and I grew a layer of the algae into my body." Andre's enigmatic reply didn't explain the situation any better, but he covered the rest of what he would have said by switching his attention away from the earth and onto the plants. He chuckled lightly as the trees perked up, then stopped growing only a few seconds later. "Oh, right. I basically have no mana regen right now."

His eyes rolled up into his head, and he fell onto Luke. The Murderhobo caught the top of the Druid's head in his left hand

and sighed as he popped open his canteen to let a drop of his dwindling mana-water splash on the floor. It rapidly expanded into a light fog that filled the newly-made building with a high density of power.

Taylor started breathing heavily as her skin cracked and began bleeding. "I think now would be a good time to discuss that unicorn horn you found."

"It's snail shell. Don't let their propaganda win."

CHAPTER TWENTY-SEVEN

- ANDRE -

The Druid's eyelids felt *so* heavy. Frankly, he had been feeling exhausted for weeks, but he really thought that getting at least one good night's sleep had been enough for him to get to a better place. Trying to recall what had happened, he slowly peeled his eyes open to take in the view of the sandstone building he had made. "Right... made the building so that we'd be visible. What an intellectually-driven decision. Let them see me; be unconscious for it."

Even so, the memory of gaining his new Ability was still enough to make him smile. It hadn't come easily, but cleaning up that toxic dump that was poisoning the earth and the air would have been worth doing even without gaining a blessing for it. As soon as he had managed to subsequently spread the algae around to soak up all the poison, then roll up the newly-formed carpet and shove it back through the Scar, his Ability had arrived in full force. The timing has been perfect, as he was able to use his amazing new Ability to seal the Scar in quartz, which was likely the plane's intent by blessing him with it. Effective, if a short term solution.

Ability gained: Earthblood Terraformation. Tier 4, level 9.

Effect 1: Inserting a half liter of blood into a triplet circle will allow you to use mana to shape and control the earth around you. Costs 25 mana to begin the process, with a 1/20th liter of blood and 5 mana per second to control. The blood used does not need to be your own.

Bonus 1, at range: Range of earthen control increased by 1+n meters per 1/20th liter of blood that has been used for this Ability, where n = ability level.

Effect 2: Adding a liter of your own blood while using this Ability will bind the impacted earth to your will until you use this Ability on a new target, retaining its shape and reforming if damaged for 10 mana per square meter of repair.

Bonus 2, Multitarget: You can now bind the earth to your will in multiple locations without losing control of a previous location, up to 50*n*Talent square meters of earth per plane, where n = ability level.

The new Ability was already on the cusp of Tier five, and he was going to make sure it got there in short order. With his Talent at twenty, and the Ability level at nine, he could control up to nine thousand square meters of land per plane of existence. That was incredibly significant in its own right, and he had already found that he could simply remove his will from an area and the formed earth would retain its shape if he commanded it to do so. That meant he could raise a *city's* worth of buildings and move along without impairing the Ability, so long as he had the mana and blood to fuel it.

"I finally met the requirements to be an Urban Druid." He chuckled softly to himself at the long-standing joke from the Druid community. Just as he was about to get up, he heard Taylor arguing with... herself? No one was answering, so it could have been Luke? He heaved himself to his feet and went to find out what was going on.

"At least answer me! You don't understand how *potent* this is, Luke! You should give it to me; I can do so much more with it than you can! The things we could do with this?" Taylor hissed at the Murderhobo. "Two ounces of unicorn horn can improve Mana Channels from 'Faulty' to 'Weak'!"

"You're right. I have *no* idea what that means, and I don't care," Luke retorted as he tested the strength of the wall Andre had made. The Druid winced as a section broke, and he felt a slight drain as it began repairing itself. "This stuff is neat. I like watching it fix itself."

"You don't care? You could turn every member of your family into an Ascender! Do you *still* not care?" Taylor's heated demand resulted in Luke punching a hole through the wall out of sheer angst.

"Can you stop, please? That costs me several points of mana per second until it's fully repaired," Andre rasped out, abruptly realizing how dry his throat was. "Abyss, this desert sucks the water right out of me. Follow me; I'll show you how to…"

He stumbled away from the nonsensical conversation. You couldn't *make* Ascenders, after all. His meandering led him over to the watermelon that was growing inside the building. Just by being near it, he was able to feel its condition: the roots had reached the water table deep underground. Everything was ready, so the Druid pumped additional mana into it, and the melon began to swell to an exceptional size. He set a modified sunflower seed atop its rind as it grew, and within a blink, the roots of that seed were twining deep within the melon.

As the sunflower sprouted, he guided it to its maximum height and carved the ceiling of the building away. With all his preparations complete, he formed a tap out of quartz and stabbed it into the side of the melon before healing the damage to the plant. After forming a cup, he lifted it to the melon and twisted the spigot. Cool, melon-flavored water poured into his mug. A single taste confirmed that the water had been well-purified by the system of plants it had been drawn through. He drained the glass to refresh his innards and motioned for the others to follow him.

They stepped outside, and he motioned at the blossom

peeking through the roof. "This is my plan for turning the desert into a forest. I give you… the Sunshower!"

At his flourish, the flower's bud opened wide. The head of the flower pointed up, and a continuous spray of water gushed dozens of feet into the air. All around them, every fifty feet or so, a similar spectacle began appearing. A huge swath of land was quickly sodden, even with the desert's heat evaporating a large portion of the water. Andre felt the land as the water filtered down through the sand, only for the root system of the irrigation-melons to suck up whatever seeped back down and draw it back to the top.

"It's working! I've made a constant water cycle! Proof of concept complete; all that remains is actually growing the desert sand into arable land!!" Andre started to laugh as the seeds that had been planted throughout the lichen, fungi, and mosses began absorbing water and using the surrounding vegetation as fertilizer. Weeds, long grasses, small bushes, and the thick fronds of ferns pushed up through the shifting sand and began expanding their own root systems beneath the surface. He wasn't even using his own mana to guide them, as the Lotus Coffins had been priming the seeds and were now supplying a small but steady stream of energy to the modified sprouts.

Andre watched for over an hour as the surrounding quarter-mile diameter went from a sad sand pit to a hot and humid verdant paradise… when all the vegetation connected with him directly. His withered skin filled out instantly, and his mana regeneration kicked into high gear. The Druid rubbed at his chin as the wind picked up and sprayed sand into the new oasis. "Trees are going to be the next things we need… maybe a full hedgerow along each perimeter to keep the low sand out, but the trees are the only thing that can keep all that ground in place."

Finally turning to the other two, he smiled at the dumb-struck expression on Taylor's face and winced at the knuckle-cracking Murderhobo. "Please don't attack the foliage. It's all doing what it's supposed to do, and it is all supposed to be here like this."

"That's what you said about those 'natural rocks'," Luke muttered under his breath. "It attacks me *once*, I'm taking it down."

Andre had to concede the point, but he did try to drive home his needs. "Right now, this is a *really* fragile ecosystem held together with literal blood, sweat, and tears. Everything is grown by me, and by mana. The bugs and bacteria necessary for regrowth in case of age or failure just aren't here. They *will* be, thanks to the corpses you provided, and the stench of some of the plants luring creatures into the desert, but right now, this patch of land is pristine and *fragile*."

"We get it, Andre." Taylor waved him down.

"*Do* you, though?" The Druid chuckled mirthlessly as Luke leaned over and bit into a leaf, then started chewing. "*Both* of you understand?"

"These are edible." Luke reached toward another one, and a vine shot up from a flower and smacked him. Without a thought for the humor of the situation, he backhanded the flower, leaving behind a small crater.

Andre let his head loll to the side even as he glared at Taylor, who shrugged helplessly and began laughing. "L-luke... the oasis fights against anything that damages it. Hold on, let me... okay, now they won't attack you unless you hurt them again."

Tha Mage reached a hand out and stroked the flower that Luke had been about to bite. "How hard can those hit?"

Taylor seemed impressed by his handiwork, so Andre's chest swelled with pride as he replied. "At this size, about ten damage per hit. Not a ton, but they'll pack a wallop when they get fully grown."

Zed's voice reached them at that moment. "Hey, cool garden. Also, did you know that your celestially shiny building has been seen by practically everyone? I hope you guys are ready, because *all* the groups I've been keeping an eye on just started moving."

CHAPTER TWENTY-EIGHT

Andre took a deep breath and let his senses drift around the oasis that he was linked with. "You know what, Zed? For the first time since we returned to the capital, I really feel that the answer to that question is 'yes'. Bring on the baddies. The more, the merrier. If I can take murderers and force them to help me make *this*?"

"*Fine.*" The Druid felt a swell of anger and started directing his power into the ground around him. A scattering of seeds in the immediate vicinity sprouted, causing a ring of modified mana-absorbers to rapidly grow to full size. "I don't know if I can handle it alone, but with all these... Luke, can you pour some mana into my oasis?"

"No." The Murderhobo's refusal took Andre by surprise, and he looked up from the meditation position that he had dropped into.

"But *wh~hy?*" As soon as he realized that he, a grown man, had whined, the Druid coughed into his hand and tried again. He wasn't supposed to act like that! He was the Archdruid! "Ahem. I mean... Luke, I could *really* use a huge boost. If I have the mana for it, I can raise a large ring of trees that will be able to attack and defend for us. Please?"

Luke still hesitated. To Andre's great confusion, the Murder-hobo pulled out a *book* of all things, consulted it, then reluctantly poured some of his mana-water onto the ground around Andre. "Gifts, given infrequently, can show thoughtfulness and kindness. Abyss it."

"What are you reading-?" The Druid stiffened as the concentration of mana in his vicinity hit deadly levels. Sucking in shuddering breaths, he worked to pump all of that power back out and into the work around him. The seedlings that had been planted next to the Lotus Coffins began to grow. Initially, their root systems expanded and firmed up the ground, then dug deep. So deep, they matched those of the watermelons and drew water for themselves, instead of depending upon the Sunshowers.

Then they began to grow *up*. Higher and higher they went, until they reached the point where Andre had wanted them. But... the mana in the area was still overflowing. The last time he'd had access to this much power, he had reached the Third Circle. Here, the ground was dead all around. Beginning to suffocate, even with the assistance of the flowers, he drained the mana into the trees and plants around him.

The canopy of the trees expanded wider and wider, until the twenty-one wooden sentinels had reached each other and intertwined in the air above them. The group waited in complete shade now. Between that and the new humidity, the surroundings began to rapidly cool. It wasn't long before the trees reached their capacity for mana, and Andre worked to enhance every growing thing, bringing all the plant life within the quarter-mile radius to its highest possible natural growth. At last, he fell back and heaved for air. "I can see why you didn't want me to use that. It's... just way too much. I need to listen to you."

"That isn't why I don't want you to use it." Luke sat down

next to the drained Druid and glared at him. "When I came back here, a couple of my bags exploded or lit on fire. I'm down to practically nothing left in my waterskins. All of you, stop assuming I'm gonna let you use my stuff. I've shown my generosity. I won't be *used*. Until I have more, you're trading for *my* stuff if you want to use it."

"That's actually really fair, you know?" Andre lifted an arm and waved at the area around them. "I mean, you get a nice and cool place to live that's really pretty and well-protected, but it easily benefits me ten times more than you. Let me know if there's something you need, 'cause I really am in your debt and I want to work with you to keep this pace up."

Luke stared hard at the other man, then gave a single sharp nod. "Fine. Here, a seed for you. Taylor, you can use the snail shell. After this, no more gifts from me. You want to trade? Get me gear. I want magic weapons and armor; I know you can all afford them, and the smiths I have working for me haven't found a way to get me my stuff. They better be storing it properly."

"We can all afford it... except Zed." Taylor couldn't help but toss out the snide remark, even as her eyes glowed with excitement.

Andre fumbled the apple-sized seed that was tossed at him and gaped at it in confusion. "This is... where'd you get an Epoch Tree seed? They're practically a controlled substance with how long it takes to grow them."

"Yeah, figured that's what it was. Makes sense why that ant was so big. Abyssal *forests* of those useless weeds." Luke's furious snort was ignored by the Druid.

Andre was enthralled by the seed he had been handed, and something about it... *resonated* with him at a deep level. "I think... this was made by someone like me. A Druid. Not... maybe not this *exact* seed, but the way it grows? I feel like someone modified it in the same way that I can modify things now."

"Does that mean anything?" Luke handed a small bag over to Taylor, who was practically *dancing* with glee. "Can you use it for something neat?"

"You know what? I think I can." Andre chuckled mirthlessly as ideas fell into place. Things that he would have never considered before coming to such a desolate place, before he had begun using Ascenders to fuel the reforestation of the Scarroco Desert. "If I can remove the limiter on how rapidly it grows, but keep the ability to live practically forever unless killed…"

Andre sank into deep, *dark* thoughts, until Taylor's words pulled him back to the present. "Listen up, team. Luke found what he thinks is a sustainable unicorn horn farm. I don't know if any of you understand what that means?"

"Not a clue!" Zed's illusion cheerfully called back. Andre nodded in agreement. Luke stood up and loomed over the Mage threateningly.

"For the last time, they're parasitic *snails*, Taylor! I don't care what you *think* they are. That's what they *actually* are." Luke clenched his fists and lashed out at a flower. As he turned it to paste, the oasis around them started to shift, and Andre had to send out a pulse of power to calm it down. "They're sneak attackers, zealots, and they're holding Cookie hostage!"

"Wouldn't it be great if we could use your enemies to make *all* of us stronger, Luke?" Taylor's desperate attempt to make the Murderhobo listen to reason worked at least a little, because he stopped rampaging and stood in one place; even if his chest *was* heaving. "Uni… this 'snail shell' powder is the only known single-ingredient elixir that can increase the quality of Mana Channels to their highest peak. It's also the only one that can be used more than once. That means that if we had enough of it, we could eventually get *Zed* sturdy enough to walk around in Murder World."

"Fat chance of that. You need either prismatic or fully blocked channels for that." Luke sullenly kicked at the ground. His comment generated more questions than they had time for, so Taylor powered on.

"I've never heard of 'Prismatic' Mana Channels, but we'll get to that another time. Even though you only need a single ingredient, there's a catch. A pretty nasty one." Taylor shook her head in frustration. "There's about a forty percent chance of dying any time you try to use it. You also need to use an entire dose at once, or it just goes to waste."

"So for every ten people that use it, four people... what? Light on fire and die?" Zed's sarcastic remark made Andre wince in sympathy. "Been there, almost done that, *really* not interested in trying my luck again."

"I will say, if we can find a way to stay alive no matter what, it has a one hundred percent effectiveness. If you use a full dose and survive, you *will* get stronger." Taylor's words made both Luke and Zed shake their heads, but Andre felt like he had been found out and started sweating immediately.

"You mean to say... if we can make it through whatever the side effects are, they'll go away? Guaranteed power increase, if we have a way to survive even if we *should* die?" The Druid slowly quizzed the Mage, who met his eyes with a hint of hope glowing in her own.

"Yes...?" Taylor offered quietly. "Experiments have been done, where healers *force* someone to live through it. Perfect recovery, every time. Do you have a method?"

Andre was reluctant to bring people to his world; the foundation he was building there wouldn't survive discovery. Luke especially had a habit of being... noticeable. "I *might*, but-"

Wham.

Their conversation was cut off as boulders began raining from the sky. The trees took the brunt of the force, branches snapping off and turning to mulch as they were impacted. As it turned out, the rocks were a distraction; one easily dealt with. Andre simply had the trees smack anything above the size of a housecat out of the air with leafy fronds. The rocks were soon being diverted to land either outside of the oasis, or in open areas where only the grass was damaged.

An all-out assault was launched in the moments after the

diversion. Power types across the board began raining down on the sandstone building, so Andre quickly retracted his will from the stone and let the building get wrecked. It was far more important to retain his mana than it was to keep it upright when it had literally been built to attract attention. They weren't inside it anyway; no one of importance was.

The Druid fell backward and sank into the earth as though it were water, closing his eyes as thin rivulets of blood ran off of him like sweat. His mana suffused the earth surrounding him and brought it under his control. He directed it to *shift* and began accelerating himself through the newly-created tunnel. He traveled swiftly around the entirety of his oasis, creating a circle of land a few feet thick that surrounded the greenery like a moat.

Andre had been trying to bring the entire oasis under his will, but had been inhibited by the total amount of land he could capture. It made sense, as a quarter mile was four-tenths of a kilometer, and there were many *thousands* of square meters in that amount of space. His sketchy math told him it was near four hundred thousand square meters, but he wasn't willing to bet on it. Even so, as soon as the 'moat' was complete, he was able to shape the land however he wished.

Like a spider in a web, he waited for someone to make the mistake of… *there*! Andre *yanked* the ground open and sucked in the man that had been foolish enough to trespass on his territory. After wrapping the man in a cocoon of rock, he dragged him over and punched the apparent mercenary in the face, then inserted a seed into his nose. It would bloom soon, and would work to keep the man in a coma until it was carefully removed. Once the seed was secured, he gently sent the man into a Lotus Coffin, and waited for the opportunity to do it again.

One after another, Andre captured thirteen of the attackers using his earth-binding method. Then his opponents' tactics shifted, and they began leaping across the open ground to reach the oasis. Andre smiled as he felt people land among his flowers.

In the split second after their feet landed, vines and entangling roots rose from the earth and began pulling people into their embrace. He no longer felt concern for their injuries; they had come to destroy him and harm the earth.

They deserved what was coming to them.

CHAPTER TWENTY-NINE

- TAYLOR -

Taylor watched as Andre fainted *again*. She was starting to get annoyed with how often- "Oh. He sank into the earth. I thought he swooned."

Luke shouted some nonsensical syllable, making her flinch before she defaulted to her standard of ignoring him. Putting aside her concerns for her companion's health, the Archmage-hopeful hurried to get her Spells in place. The smart choice when dealing with stealthy attackers like this was obvious. "Lightning Beast's Eye!"

Thunder rumbled softly as her nerves impacted her control, allowing slight vibrations into the surroundings as she coalesced nearly the entirety of her mana into strands of heaven's judgment. Despite the many times she had cast it as practice, it never failed to amaze her how utterly *awe* inspiring it was to have total control over power of this magnitude. Just as she got down to the last dregs of her mana, the spell snapped into place fully and the eye began searching around for a target.

She sat and meditated for a minute as her mana recovered,

then slowly rose back to her feet. Taylor was surprised to see that Luke hadn't moved at all, but was instead staring at a rock that had crashed down near them. "You know we're under attack, yes? You can go and fight the people attacking us. The King said so."

"Hang on. Not sure about this rock. Rocks aren't supposed to fly." Luke waved her off as she tried to explain that it had likely been launched. "Yeah, yeah. I know what thrown weapons are. That *might* be it. Still. I wanna see if there's more to it. I'll catch up."

There was no reasoning with the insane, so Taylor simply ignored his fatuous comments and began stalking around the vegetation. A blade *whisked* past her face and slammed into a nearby tree all the way to the hilt. Another shot through the air as if it had been released from a bow, curving to follow her as she dodged. She cursed and started *moving*, her devotion to Senses paying off as the person controlling the metal lost their target.

It was easy to tell when the Ascender attacking her decided to stop attempting pinpoint strikes: a spray of flechettes tore through the area, mulching plants as they closed in on her from multiple directions. The terrain was trained to help her, and a vine reached down from a tree to provide her an escape. She jumped and backflipped off the tree, used the vine as a swing, and searched for the location of the metal Manipulator.

All she knew about Manipulators was that they needed to be close enough to control the element they used, as if they were accurate lodestones that only interacted with something specific. This one must have come fairly close if they could target her well enough to almost slay her—especially with her reaction speed all but guaranteeing her ability to escape almost any situation. As she neared the edge of the oasis, it didn't end up mattering: her active spell found the Ascender that was attacking her before they could lock onto each other.

The air *sizzled* as a bolt as thick as her arm dripped from the eye like the fastest tear in existence. Every chunk of protective

metal coating her attacker only increased the speed and efficiency of the power finding its mark, and the Ascender fell from
a single strike. Taylor was excited by the power of her spell only
for the brief respite before the next attacker caught her in an
updraft and slammed her to the ground.

Potentia gained: 755.

Damage taken: 33 terrain.

Current health: 79/112.

Taking a massive blow like that shocked her—not literally
like her Spell had given to the Manipulator, but figuratively, as
in an unwelcome surprise that she was unprepared for. With her
Senses so powerful, she knew exactly when she had last taken
such devastating damage, and it had been *years*. There were few
things that could even manage to land a hit on her, and even
when they did… she could always mitigate most of the force by
moving along with the blow. Whatever had grabbed her had
used the air around her to attack: there was no easy way to
avoid the *air*.

Just as she was springing up to fight, she was pulled underground and encased in stone. She squeezed out a breathless
wheeze as she was dragged to… "Andre?"

Her voice was weak from the lack of air, but it seemed she
had taken the Druid by surprise. He pulled back the hand that
had been reaching for her face and blinked owlishly. "Taylor?
What? Stay off the bare earth around the oasis, *abyss*. Pay attention in the middle of a fight."

Then she was catapulted up into the open air once more.
She was lucky that she had been thrown with such force: the
instant she emerged from the ground, a half-dozen spellforms
tore chunks out of the earth where she had exited. For an
instant, she was confused as to how they knew where she was,
when an arc of lightning fried an assassin that had been trying
to sneak up on her: the poison-coated blade fell just short of her
skin as the once-beautiful wielder dropped.

Potentia gained: 445.

She felt ill when she realized that the death of her fellow

Ascender had made her stronger. These might be her *countrymen*! A group appeared at the fringes of the oasis and charged at her, but she was sick of killing people. With a completely unnecessary stomp, she cast Fissure and used it to trip the attackers and send them tumbling into the area that Andre had claimed. At least four people were sucked underground without even enough time to scream.

Prismatic light in a beam so focused that it felt *physical* seared the air; only the fact that it had lit a tree on fire in passing gave Taylor any warning that it was approaching. She managed to avoid it, though her hair lit on fire in the same moment that she avoided the direct strike. The Mage trembled as she quenched the flames; that had nearly removed her head. Most of the attacks and screams sounding within the oasis faded as the greenery and stone captured people, but Tayor's attention was focused on the band of Knights that were approaching as a unit.

"Heaven's Earth. So this is all *your* doing," she practically *hissed* as the group moved to engage her. "For some reason, I *really* thought you would hide behind your lies longer than you actually did."

"Mage Taylor Woodswright, you are under arrest for resisting arrest," Sir Edward announced with a smarmy grin. "I order you, by my authority, backed by Prince Vir, to surrender for immediate execution."

A small boulder made the air tremble as it passed Taylor's shoulder, crumpled the man's face, and sent the Ascender tumbling away as a broken heap. Luke walked over to stand next to Taylor and gestured at the stone. "It was just a rock. There was nothing more to it."

One of the men fell back to cast his most potent healing magic on the Knight, while the others charged forward with a roar. "You dishonorable-! How *dare* you attack a Royal Knight of the Hollow Kingdom! Die for your crimes!"

Taylor didn't bother trying to reason with these hypocrites, sending Shatter Shots and Flame Lances at them without delay.

Luke rushed in to fight the metal-clad Knights in close combat, allowing Taylor a single second to decide what to do next. So far, they hadn't broken any of the laws of the Hollow Kingdom. Yet, if they actually *killed* the Knights, their Sigils would be working against them every step of the way until they got a pardon from the King. Even in cases of self-defense, killing even the lowest of Nobility would incur a heavy penalty. Blood erupted from Luke's shoulder as she hesitated, and that settled it for her.

She leaned forward and dashed at her highest speed toward the Knights. Once she stood among them, her most potent Spell was unleashed. "*Nullify!*"

A swarm of black-and-purple butterflies erupted from her, swarming over the Knights and removing all of the auras and buffs that they were using to fight at a higher level. Luke's next punch removed a perfect tenth of the tower shield he hit, so the Knight threw the decimated item away and gripped his sword with both hands as he swung for Luke's neck. The Murder-hobo's grin was creepy even to Taylor as he grabbed the sword by the blade and dispersed the force behind it with ease.

"You don't even know that your weapons and armor not only make me hit harder, but harder to kill. Thanks for this." Luke yanked the weapon away and tossed it behind him, where a large animal-hide blanket had been spread out. "Same deal as usual, Taylor! Dibs on the gear."

"That's *fine*, Luke! Abyss-sake, focus on the fight!" Taylor increased the spread of Shatter Shot and used the dispersed force to batter another Knight's head around in his helmet. "Make sure not to kill them, or the Sigils will make us... um... go and apologize to the King!"

"I'd rather make out with a goat," Luke muttered as he barely managed to pull his punch, merely knocking out teeth instead of caving in the man's skull. "These guys are really fluffy, especially after what you did to them. It's kinda hard not to kill them just by accident."

Three of the five were out of commision already, and only

one of the remainder was a fighter. Luke appeared in front of that man in a flash of motion so rapid that even Taylor hadn't seen him *start* to move, grabbed him by the neck, and gingerly tossed him onto the bare earth. He vanished below with a light *slurp*, and Luke followed up by tossing the others before going after the healer that was working on Edward.

Wailing as he sailed through the air, the healer vanished a moment later. Luke went to grab Edward and was *blasted* into the air by a detonation of coruscating light. The Knight jumped to his feet and stared at Taylor with dead eyes. "You insolent little *traitor*. Die for your crimes!"

The Knight's body appeared to shift partially into energy, and he rushed toward the Mage as a stream of light. She dove out of the way and rolled behind a tree, an over-bright sword following just behind her and cutting through the dense wood as if it wasn't even there.

Taylor bent backward at the waist as the blade rippled through the space she had just occupied, catching a broken dagger that had been lodged in the now-falling tree by her first assailant. She flicked it up at the Knight's helmet, and he instinctively flinched back to dodge the blade aimed at his eye. Using his motion against him, she steadied herself and opened the ground beneath them both with Fissure. The ground shook and screeched as it swallowed them, slamming closed with crushing force around their bodies as her control faltered.

CHAPTER THIRTY

Taylor's eyes fluttered open as the coating of dirt was peeled open, then her passive Spells came into play and cleaned the muck out of her eyes, nose, and mouth. She remained tense as the person in front of her came into focus, though she sucked in fresh air as she realized that she was staring into her Druid's eyes.

Realizing that she had thought of Andre as '*her*' Druid made her freeze in horror. When had *that* intrusive thought started worming through her brain? Andre grabbed her shoulders and shook her hard enough to send loose earth scattering. "What's *wrong* with you? Do you *want* to die? Is that why you keep *sacrificing* yourself for absolutely no reason?"

The Mage stared at Andre in confusion and spoke without thinking. "I had no intention of *sacrificing* myself! I knew you'd be able to save me."

Andre's anger drained away, and his face went red for a completely different reason. "That's... you had no idea that I could... *Taylor*."

His adorable embarrassment made the Mage's heart race,

but she shifted her mindset into work mode before she could get too flustered. "Did you get Edward?"

"I *did*..." Andre hesitated before continuing reluctantly with this new line of conversation. "He's too strong for me to put in stasis. He blasted his way out of the Lotus Coffin, and even managed to burn the mana-scatterer flower out of himself at the same time by turning into light and heat. I'm really not sure what we can do beyond killing him. If we don't put him down for good, there's a really good chance that he'll escape."

Taylor would have been forced to agree with him, but she already had a plan in mind. "I have two options we could try. We might have to use *both*, but let's start like this..."

As she outlined her plan for the Knight, the admiration in Andre's eyes turned to shock, horror, and revulsion. It pained her to see him look at her that way, but it was for the good of the team. It was the best outcome, and the fringe benefits were clear. Taylor couldn't let her personal feelings get in the way of proper team management. "I can see that you are unhappy with this. I'm sorry. Can you *do* it?"

The Druid swallowed and dropped his gaze, not able to meet her eyes as he agreed to walk deeper down a path he didn't want to follow. "Give me enough time, and I can do *anything*."

"I know." Taylor let out a deep sigh as the Druid stalked away from her. It took every ounce of control she had not to let the tears flow down her cheeks as she watched him walk away to follow her orders.

Chime.

She narrowed her eyes. Change was never easy. Change was only ever accepted by the majority of people when the need became so great, so noticeable, that the pain of change was less than the pain of staying the same. Some pain now would be worth it in the end; Taylor knew what was best for them.

She shook off the last few bits of stone and stood tall. She was clean, her hair and skin as perfect as her unblemished clothing. She only wished that she could feel as spotless on the inside, but she had *duty* keeping her mentally strong. If she let Edward go free, or escape, he would return with an actual army, as well as *real* authority. She strode into the room where Luke was watching the Knight, and spoke directly to the Murder-hobo. "Break his arms and legs. If you don't want to do it, I'll do so, but I don't know if I have the strength to properly-"

Crunch.

The meaty sound rang out four times in rapid succession, and Taylor winced as Edward howled in pain. Luke gave her a thumbs-up. "I feel better now; thanks."

"Why…?" Taylor shook her head and reminded herself to stop asking him so many questions she didn't want an enigmatic answer for. "Would you please carry him and follow me?"

"Why not," Luke sighed as he lifted the Knight and held him away from his body like a particularly rancid bag of garbage. "All the fun to be had in this area is already over with. The next few weeks are going to be nothing but testing, prodding, and plant junk. Probably not even a good assassination attempt… I have *needs*, Taylor!"

"Anyway…" the Mage uneasily regarded the hole that he had beaten into the sandstone building by slapping the stone to emphasize his point. After another moment of pondering if she should insist on being reassigned, she led the way out of the shaded oasis and across the desert sands. At the speed they could move, they traveled a good distance before Taylor realized that she shouldn't be leading the way. "Luke, where's the Descender Scar?

"The *what?*" Edward bellowed as he began to struggle more ferociously. It was clear from the vigor of his movements that his limbs were already almost healed. Luke had an 'aha' moment and altered their course slightly. He also reached over and snapped Sir Edward's arms once more.

"Yikes." Luke winced as the bones broke with just… no effort. "Tell me something so I don't make the same mistake you did. Are the cells in your bones and meat so brittle because you used so much bottled Potentia? Is that why you *seem* like a brick, but fall apart like hardened mud?"

"What is this, a children's tale?" Edward gasped out as Luke tried to shake the answer out of him. "What are you even talking about?"

"*You*," Luke demanded as he jabbed a finger into the Knight's rigid abs, only for them to bend away as his finger pressed against them. "How much of your Potentia did you earn from killin', and how much came from bottles?"

"I have had the *best* training, the highest honors bestowed, the-" Edward's tirade was cut off with a crisp slap from Luke, and he spat out a mouthful of blood the next time he parted his lips.

"Even with all that, you were beaten down by some random hobo who was given nothing but nightmare fuel and an order to flee from the Kingdom. Someone *multiple* levels below you, and with lower-tiered Skills." Luke's statement was as cold as his eyes were heated. "How *much*? How many bottles have you downed to get to where you are? How much came from your world? From monsters or people?"

Taylor wanted to stop the strange interrogation, but some-thing about it felt... important. Edward sputtered blood and refused to answer until Luke grabbed his hand and squeezed. The Knight screamed and began to thrash. "*Ah-haow*! Stop! Almost all of it! It doesn't *matter*, though! All of the great scholars of the Kingdom have concluded that it's completely safe! There's no *difference* between what we take, and what we earn!"

"Fancy words." Luke scoffed at the idea of listening to people that likely couldn't even *use* Potentia. "What's sturdier? A coconut, or a fruit smoothie? Both are *fruit*."

"Are you saying that, even though the Potentia fulfills the same purpose, meeting someone with Potentia that they have *specifically* earned feels different to you, somehow?" Taylor really wanted to know the answer, because it would solve a whole *host* of questions she had about the Kingdom. "I wonder if this is why... hmm."

"Stop looking at me like that!" Sir Edward screamed at the two Ascenders that appeared to be dissecting him with pitying gazes. "I *did* earn this Potentia! I worked hard for it!"

"We aren't saying you didn't work hard, Sir Edward." Taylor's formal tone halted the Knight's complaints. "We're saying your trainers failed you. I'll point out that we've now beaten you twice. This time, we didn't even need to have the rest of our team. Why do you think that might be?"

Sir Edward stared at the Mage in consternation, sweat beading his brow from both pain and fear. "I think... frankly, I think you're all monsters. You—*whaah!*"

A small amount of energy discharged as Luke threw the Knight through the Scar, letting a rope spool out, then nailing it into the ground. Taylor tried to glare at the Murderhobo, but she couldn't hold in a snort of laughter. "Okay, that was pretty funny. He was also a total scum-"

"He was not a nice person at all." Luke finished right before Taylor could, and blinked at her owlishly, realizing he had spoken over her. "Oh. Go on."

"No, no... that was better than what I was going to say." Taylor shrugged and started making her way back to the oasis. The Knight had broken arms and legs; it was going to take him at least a few minutes to come back through the Scar. When he did, they would be ready, since five minutes for him would give them weeks of preparation time.

In fact, when he did come out, they would... Taylor felt a terrible surge of guilt at that moment for what she had asked Andre to do. She hoped that someday he would be able to forgive her.

CHAPTER THIRTY-ONE

- LUKE -

Spending weeks of his time running around and searching for Scars wasn't the worst thing Luke had been through, but all the time between actually finding them and finding things to *fight* in them was starting to wear on the Murderhobo. "Losing my edge out here. Gonna go back to Murder World and find out I have forgotten how to kill things. This place is slowing me down... no wonder people Ascend as soon as they possibly can."

A long-suffering sigh hissed from his lips, and he looked down to watch the ground his feet were flashing over as he ran. He had to admit, he was *actually* impressed with the Druid and what he had been able to accomplish. Every day or two, the green-clad workaholic would pop out of a portal, frantically check things here and there, then rush off to make a new oasis, doing everything in his power to spend as little time on this base world as possible in order to maximize his working time.

All the bodies Luke had piled up in those couple days would get sucked into the ground, and a thick blend of fungus and various flora would rapidly start expanding from wherever the pile of meat had originally stood. Andre called the thick mat of nutrient-dense flora 'creep', due to the way it would constantly expand on its own, even when no one was tending it. Luke agreed with the name; the stuff was *creepy*. Still, easy enough to smush if needed. He had tried it out. Twice. Andre had almost cried.

Whenever something took root on it, the creep would die and become rapidly absorbed as nutrients for the plant; but until then... it was a strange, fleshy carpet that *totally* was a plant and nothing else. The Murderhobo had glared at a particularly veiny section that Andre had no way to explain, but Luke was almost positive that there was blood flowing through each creep pad.

Yet, thanks to Andre's efforts, there were now *miles* of greenery; and even more reddish-brown creep beyond that. Luke was happy enough to see food growing, but he was still leery about eating anything that sucked down the mushroom mat to reach full size.

Zed had also been hard at work interacting with the locals up and down the border of the desert, not only making actual connections and very important relationships, but also constantly spreading rumors. His stories coming from *everywhere* had helped The Four avoid detection, and threw their pursuers off the scent. Luke didn't particularly *care* about the people that were coming after them, as he had a good feeling that the fluffy hunters should be pretty easily dispatched.

The Bard thought differently, apparently, and seemed to think that 'actual experts' were now on the lookout for them. He called their previous hunters either 'scum' or 'greenhouse flowers', whatever that meant, but the people the Bard had been sighting and warning them about recently were 'elites'.

Being warned off was enough to get Luke excited. The idea of hunting and fighting people considered 'elite' by the Kingdom made Luke's blood *sing*... but he was denied permission to seek them out. As far as Zed could tell, the Prince was enraged that his personally groomed team had vanished without a trace. His backers and the snakes that composed his retinue agreed and had convinced him to go all out, remaining just on the bare *edge* of publicly legal. Now there were proper *organizations* after them, not a smattering of people interested in making a quick coin.

More than anything else, Luke was disgusted by the thought that these people were hunting them for *politics*, and not for any proper reason, like his own desire for wanting a rematch with Master Don. "How many punches does it take to get to the center of the Archmage? I'm betting eight."

Luke nodded internally; now *that* was a proper reason for going after people. He slowed as he happened upon a Scar, searching around carefully to determine if it was impacting the area. The portals that created noticeable effects in the world *usually* contained living things on the other side that he could fight; Taylor babbled on about how it was matching the environment so the intruders could survive the initial entry point.

He waved his hands around, then released a wicked grin as he felt a noticeable chill in the area. Just as he stepped forward to enter the portal, a polite clearing of a throat made Luke freeze. He slowly turned his head and stared at a man that waited only a few dozen feet away. A man he hadn't seen at all until he announced himself. Even now, only the fact that he was even more real than his surroundings let Luke believe the man was actually present and not a projection.

The unknown humanoid was wearing a beautiful white cloak embellished by deep red embroidery; truly kingly attire when you were in a desert, and everything from the sand to the monsters conspired to render you filthy. Now that Luke noticed the man, he also heard a background noise that his mind had been ignoring for some reason. Some kind of music? The Murderhobo didn't like this situation: his mind was screaming that somehow this person was even more dangerous than he appeared. His instincts had never been wrong about this before, and he immediately turned and booked it.

"Pardon me, Viscount Luke Von Murderhobo." The white-clad man lowered the hood that had covered his face and smiled disarmingly at Luke, who stood stock-still after once more finding the man directly in front of him. The Murderhobo hadn't even seen him move, and there was no disturbed sand that had betrayed his passage. "I'm here with an offer for you, and a request. Would you please hear me out?"

"Is that the request?" Luke waited for the man to start replying, then activated Bum Flash and appeared above the man. Putting everything he had into his attack, he punched down... and somehow the man was gone. A wave of sand exploded outward, and he searched for his target. "Proof that you don't work for the Hollow Kingdom. Assassin?"

"Far from it." The smile remained on the man's relaxed face, as if Luke had been playing a childish joke on him when he struck to kill. "My actual request is that you stop closing the Scars that I and my people are working *so* painstakingly to open. That leads into my offer, in fact."

"An-arcan-ist." Luke tasted the word as he enunciated it slowly. "An anarchist pickled in the arcane. The most feared and reviled of all Ascenders, a boogeyman that no one has ever met in person, or has any proof actually exists. People without a country that go around and tear open Scars that others can't close, all so that more monsters can come and roam freely to destroy all of society. Interesting to meet you. Thanks for all the free Potentia. What's this music?"

"Is *that* what the common people think of us?" The man chuckled so softly that it almost sounded like wheezing. "As for the music, this is instrumental smooth jazz, a music I took a fancy to in a Descender portal that I stepped through, once upon a time. Sadly, that world was lost to us recently. An influx of power put it on a different path for Ascending. Please, call me Vacillator. Vah-*sill*-a-tor."

"You afraid a lot or something? Kinda wishy-washy?" Luke cracked his knuckles menacingly as he waited for an opening to attack. This guy was way too fast, so he needed to time his kill just right.

"Ah, no, no." Vacillator chuckled at the insinuation. "That would be vacillator, as in vas-*uh*-ley-ter. You see, there is no true antonym in this world's language for vacillator, so I decided that from now on that my name, *Vacillator*, is the proper opposite of vacillator. I am one who never hesitates: someone who is decisive and resolute."

"Also clearly bat-fecal crazy." Luke's Rope whipped out and *howled* as it cut through the open air. The smiling man snorted and grabbed the mana-made whip between his fingers, then twisted as if he were opening a canteen. Luke's face drained of blood as his weapon *shattered*. It began pulling at his mana to reconstitute right away, but it was a chilling show of force that he hadn't even realized was possible.

"I'm not crazy at all! Just a logomaniac," Vacillator cheerfully stated as he drew closer to Luke. The Murderhobo stood his ground as the powerful man approached step-by-step. "Let me tell you our actual purpose, Luke. The one which Kingdoms hide so that the common people don't get uppity. The 'Anarcanists' are *equitable* Ascenders. Our goal is to open enough Scars from higher worlds that the ambient mana levels push this, and other worlds that we've chosen, into higher planes of existence. Let me ask you this, Luke Von Murderhobo... why should you have to leave everyone and everything behind as you grow stronger? Why do only a few *chosen* people get to live forever?"

"So your solution is to make entire worlds filled with immortal Ascenders?" Luke deadpanned as he mulled over that logic. It seemed sound. "Okay. I can see people wanting that. Makes sense."

"Doesn't it? As to my offer... join us, Luke." Vacillator paused for one long moment as he savored the rush of convincing another person to see things his way. "You have the *exact* talents we need to push our plans forward on *millions* of worlds. We would give you *anything*. Absolutely *anything* you want, forever. If we can't make it happen in this world, we'd bring you to another. Money, power, enemies to keep you sharp, beauties willing to do whatever you demand… just because you are *wanted*. Because you *matter*. You alone in this vast multiverse can prove your worth in an *instant* with the Skills you have. You could be an emperor, a god-king, or live a simple life. Whatever you crave or desire would arrive instantly, thanks to the *world's* worth of servants ready to do your bidding."

"Yes. That sounds great. When do we leave?" Luke took a step away from the portal and closer to the strange man. "Are you able to free me from the Hollow Kingdom?"

"Wait… really? So swift? Perhaps you should share *my* name." Vacillator's eyes shone with joy as he reached out a hand to seal their deal. "I can do all the things I've promised you. I swear it. If I may ask, what was it that I said to bring you aboard?"

"Why would I say no to any of that?" Luke lifted his hand as well, and went to shake. "*Anything* I want? Forever? All for opening Scars across various worlds? Yes. Who doesn't want more than *this*? I was already banished to this dustbowl for politics. Give me power. Grant me *freedom*."

Luke's Sigil *chimed* and a blast of mana erupted out of it. He was smacked as though a war maul had landed directly on his skin, hairline fractures racing across his skull.

No. You are mine.

Vacillator growled in frustration as he watched the Sigil impact Luke. He allowed his left pinky toe to wriggle, and the damage Luke had taken was healed in the next instant. "Ah, too bad. I was afraid of that. There's already a higher Ascended that has laid claim to you. I'm guessing that they saved your life and claimed ownership without your permission, else you'd have known better than to try to make a deal with me."

Luke blinked and sat up as notifications scrawled across his mind. He ignored them for the moment as he squinted at Vacillator. "Is this the part where you kill me because I can't do what you want?"

"What? No, of course not." Vacillator straightened out his

cloak and released a long-suffering sigh. "You wanted to join me, and the offer will stand until the end of time. Do what you need to do to increase your power levels. Even if your path goes against our plans for now, it won't be an issue at all. When you *can* join me, all you'll need to do is find me. After you attain level thirty, that shouldn't be an issue for you."

"Level twenty is the limit." Luke's thoughts seemed to be moving through mud at the moment.

"For *this* world, yes. Yes, it is." Vacillator beamed a too-wide smile, then his form flickered for a moment, and Luke noticed that the pouch on his own belt felt slightly heavier. "In fact, the plane itself forces Descenders to abide by those rules. Otherwise, the presence of someone in the fifties or higher would warp this entire country into an image of my world as soon as I arrived. Very well, Luke... until we meet again. Read your little book well."

With that non sequitur, the man and his strange music were gone, and Luke was left alone with his massive scrawl of notifications. He ignored most of them, but a few refused to vanish until he read through and understood them. He held his aching head. "I want that kind of power for myself. Ugh. Do I need to read these now?"

The short answer was: yes.

CHAPTER THIRTY-TWO

Luke's brain throbbed, and he wondered if it was because of the concussive mana blast from his Sigil, or if it was something which the nice, albeit strange, man had done. Probably a little of both. He lay in the nice warm sand and grumbled as he perused the new messages he had received.

Information packet integrated: Higher Ascenders and where you stand in the hierarchy.

Higher Ascenders are considered anyone who has passed the level 30 threshold, and are also known as 'World Anchors'. As Ascenders increase in power, they naturally begin warping the natural laws, until the point at which they tear off a chunk of a plane and internalize it into their power. At each level above 30, the Ascender can choose to create a lesser duplicate of a feature of a world and build it up over time, or take the original for themselves. Tearing chunks out of Planes often leads to instability, and potentially the destruction of the original world.

The first choice creates the precedent for the Ascender: they cannot step off of that path.

Those who tear out chunks of Planes are known as: Annihilator Ascenders or Annihilators.

Those who build up the duplicates into their own version over time are known as: Creator Ascenders or Creators.

At level 50, the Plane which the Ascender has been shaping becomes actualized. This creates a new Plane of existence, and very often tears holes into adjacent Planes. Planar wars are often waged to bring new Planes under the control of various factions. In general—but not always—Annihilator Ascenders have a large advantage over others in the early fifties. They have powerful, original features from multiple worlds.

The advantages of Creator Ascenders are harder to achieve, but as the Ascender increases in power, their world grows stronger; faster than the rate which Annihilator Ascenders can facilitate. This is due to the lesser duplicate following a new growth pattern that is closer to the will of the Ascender, while Annihilators need to increase each feature manually. The lesser duplicate can become far more powerful than the original, with enough time and resources dedicated to it.

Luke Von Murderhobo, you are formally in the service of the Creator Ascender '_Error_' and will continue to be as such until you meet with _Error_ and determine if a partnership will be beneficial to both of you. _Error_ maintains a residence in Zone 50 and eagerly awaits your arrival.

Information packet integrated: Anarcanists and you!

Anarcanists are a faction of Annihilator Ascenders, who have come up with an —actually impressive—method of improving their Planes more rapidly. Instead of personally tearing chunks away from an existing world and adding it to their plane, they build up mana on a world to the point that it would naturally Ascend. At the moment of Ascension, they guide the world to their Plane and attach it as a new extension. There is great benefit for all who survive the process.

Main benefit: The Ascender gains territory and population for their Plane.

Secondary benefit: The surviving creatures gain a powerful protector and guide that will help them Ascend.

Each positive is offset via a negative, of course. By forcing the world to Ascend outside of its natural timeframe, the creatures on the world will often be unable to handle the mana of the new Plane. Each creature will need to survive an intense mana baptism. On average, the survivors number roughly 20% +/- 10% of all creatures in the original world.

Luke shook his head as his vision finally cleared, and snarled at the messages. "Ugh. It's *politics* all the way up! No wonder my world just kills everyone that wants to step on it. I bet Error-face just stays there and beats down anyone that annoys it. *I* would, after having to deal with this feces storm for that long."

His mood ruined, he glared at the portal next to him and shook his head. He punched it closed without bothering to step inside, and started trudging back to his team's current base. He had been given secrets about what went on beyond their little world, and he should start working out a plan for himself. He should also inform his team of the encounter, as well as warn them what was coming as they leveled up. There was too much to do.

But he didn't particularly want to do anything else today, so it was time for a nap instead.

He got back to camp and drifted off to sleep, only waking a full day later when his body was not only healed... but as a Lotus Coffin tried to stealthily slurp him down. A twitch of his wrist turned the overgrown flower into mulch, and he resolved to inform the Druid that his plants were, indeed, out to get him. The Murderhobo stood and twisted to warm up, then set off in search of his friends. "I warned him. These plants had their chance."

"There you are!" Taylor spotted him popping out over a dune and waved him over. "We're just about to start the next phase of regrowth. Have you *seen* how many miles of land went from sand to mushroom or greenery in less than two months? There's already been *two* entire crop hauls for the locals! They already have more access to food than they've had in a generation!"

Luke listened as she gushed about the state of the kingdom improving under their watch, and how it was all thanks to the flora-focused Druid on their team. When she finally slowed down, Andre was beet-red and couldn't hold back the beaming smile on his face. Luke decided that it was time to tell the others what had been going on with him. "Andre, one of your flowers tried to eat me while I was sleeping. Also, I ran into a level fifty-plus Ascender and got info on what happens after we reach level thirty."

The distracted Druid shook his head. "You must have rolled around in your sleep or something and attracted it to you, Luke. The plants don't just—wait. *What?*"

"Level twenty is the limit, Luke." Taylor shook her head at the Murderhobo and rolled her eyes. "It's physically and logically impossible that you met someone in the fifties."

"That's what I said," Luke agreed with her easily. "He told me that was true *here*, but it goes up... he didn't tell me how far. I don't care what you've been taught; all I've got is what my Sigil crushed my skull to tell me."

The Murderhobo informed them about the info packets he had accessed, leaving out the part about Error. No need to tell others his personal business. They listened intently, and discussed lightly, until Taylor waved them off and motioned to Andre. "We just don't have enough information to really get into the weeds about whether this is true or that guy used a spell on you to make you think he was telling the truth. Speaking of weeds, Andre... are you ready for phase two?"

"*So* ready." Andre's smile turned sly, and he raised his arms dramatically. "Are *you* ready?"

"Yes. Abyss, man. You're a Druid, not a Bard," Luke reprimanded the huge man. "Every minute you spend showboating is another minute plants aren't growing, and I'm not getting you more dead things to turn into mulch."

That wiped the levity off Andre's face, and the sly look turned sheepish. "Fair enough. Zed's watching anyway, so he can make a proper story out of this later."

"I have arrived!" For some reason, the Bard had been huddled under a sand-covered blanket. He flung the cloth away and sprang to his feet in an attempt to make the others flinch, but no one was even mildly startled. He pouted as Taylor and Luke ignored him, and Andre's attention was absorbed fully by the desert in front of them. The Druid gripped his Livingwood

Staff with both hands and closed his eyes. He lifted the wood, then tapped it against the ground.

Blood flowed into a mana-made circle, a surge of power rippled through the area, and *life* flowed from the Druid.

The creep mat began to practically *boil* out from underfoot, growing, spreading, and being absorbed by the plants that sprang from it just as quickly. The fungus and various mana-filled portions of the creep pulled in the trace elements from the sand and rapidly aged, becoming a rotten compost in seconds. The newly-made slurry was sucked up by the root systems branching out from the seeds. In truth, the loam that developed at that point wasn't a sustainable vegetation in this area, but it was also designed to grow and age rapidly.

Topsoil that could properly sustain grass and shrubbery was the next stage of growth. If Luke had taken the time to have a good yawn, he would have missed out on witnessing the first stages of growth, and would have only seen a carpet of green shoots tearing their way through the soil. Something that the Murderhobo could sense, and the others clearly could not, was how the mana flowing in the area was starting to impact the world around them.

Life was *usually* what generated mana. Not always, as the new blue-green world which Luke had found had proved. He had an idea that the world in that case was full of a mineral that was rare in other Planes, and it generated mana simply by its high energy output slowly converting from one form of energy to another. The Murderhobo watched as the rapid life cycle began to churn out mana, only for it to be captured and re-channeled by the Druid. After ten minutes of this, blood was leaking from Andre's orifices, but the man himself didn't stop what he was doing.

Luke grabbed and shook him, and the Druid opened bleary eyes, looked around, and shook his head. "S'not done... gotta finish..."

"Or you could do this over *years,* instead of hours, and *survive* the experience," Luke commented with a shrug. "Up to you, but I'm thinking most people would prefer my option."

"Everyone point and laugh at Andre; he almost died from growing some grass!" Zed was furiously scribbling into a notebook, only stopping for a bare moment to actually point and rudely laugh so as to drive home Luke's point. "Okay... I'll spin this so the population thinks that he's hurting himself to help them, and not the reality of the fact that he has brain damage when it comes to growing things. Oh... maybe make it a love story where he's pushing too hard so that he can finally be free to pursue his real passion?"

"What's his real passion?" Taylor quizzed the Bard darkly as the man drew hearts on his notepad.

"*You*, of course. We've known that since we were kids," Zed murmured distractedly as he held up a thumb to gauge how much the land had grown out. "Looks like it's still moving. I'm reading... four kilometers of direct growth, another half since he ended... it seems to be slowing. A good inroad to the desert; maybe his plan is to cut the desert into sections and fill those in with plants? Do grid squares of growth? Smart, smart."

Taylor's impassive face was bright red, and she appeared to be wavering between smacking the Bard or going to comfort the dizzy Druid. Her indecision led to her neither harming nor helping either one of her companions... and also increased Luke's estimation of her immaturity.

Here was a person that wanted to lead others, to reform the world around her, to care for the Kingdom... and she couldn't make up her mind on her own *minor* desires? The Druid fell asleep, not passing out for once, so the Murderhobo set him down and glared at their 'leader'. "Hard to follow someone that can't make a choice."

"What do you know?" Taylor spat at him, venting her embarrassment on the first unrelated target that presented itself.

"I know that we've faced scarier things than asking to get to know someone better." Zed decided to join the conversation of his own free will, so Luke closed his mouth and let the wordsmith speak. "If you like someone well enough that you want to decide *if* you want to like them more, ask them to join you in a more personal setting and figure it out from there. Getting tea or a meal with someone isn't the same as asking if they want to spend their life with you. Don't put them on a pedestal in your head. Who *knows* if you have enough in common to have more? That's what courting is all about, no?"

"I've seen how *you* handle relationships, Zed." Taylor turned to stare out over the sands in the distance as the creep advanced its way over the dunes. "You have no leg to stand on."

"I promise you, they know *exactly* what they're getting." Zed winked at Luke, who simply stared back at him. "A conversation partner, and a healthy workout. In places like this, that's already a boon and a rarity. Have you tried having a *conversation* with the locals? They're exhausted all the time, due to malnutrition. We're fixing that, but it'll be a generation before they start growing strong, tall, and healthy again."

"You could have perhaps used your money from our last mission to help these people instead of spending nearly a quarter of what the kingdom makes in a decade in the red light district!" Taylor accused him furiously, her usual facade of calm completely broken. "It took you a *week* to spend every penny you ever made!"

"Well, to each their own." Zed shrugged lightly, then allowed his expression to harden. "I guess I just really wanted to offer people that are in a difficult situation a new lease on life. Create a few orphanages for their children, and the other children lost in the city while on the run from the war. Oh, no! Zed spent money making schools and building hospitals instead of hoarding his coins or earning seventeen percent per year on his investments!"

"You...! W-*what*?" Taylor's accusing finger dropped as she stared at the man she had always considered a failure. "You're the 'Tornado of the Red Light District'! The..."

Zed crossed his arms, appearing half scandalized, a quarter furious, but still with a healthy dose of laughter in his eyes.

"Right, *I'm* the bad guy cause I went in there and spent a natural disaster's worth of money on changing things. Seriously, did you think I went in there and spent half a *billion* gold getting my dagger polished? I wanted to give people the chance in life I never got. The chance the Hollow *Kingdom* took from-"

"This is such a *sweet* discussion, I almost feel bad breaking it up," a coarse voice called down to them from the top of a nearby sand dune that had been turned into a healthy hill. The group dropped into a fighting position as they turned to face the voice. Over the next few seconds, dozens of Knights in the Kingdom's regalia crested the hill and looked down at them disapprovingly. "As it stands, you can finish it in a cell. By the King's authority, you're all under arrest for the murder of Heaven's Earth. On your knees."

A **chime** rang out as the truth of the man's words rang out, and the three still-awake Ascenders were forced to drop to their knees. A soft snore came from Andre, causing the large group rapidly surrounding them to chortle.

CHAPTER THIRTY-THREE

"We're under orders to have the trial, verdict, and execution or absolvement right here so that none can subvert justice," The Knight Captain told them from behind his closed faceplate, his voice being changed by a spell as he spoke so that nothing could be used to identify him. "You're suspected of the murder of *many* of the Kingdom's Ascenders. Your team leader may speak for you. If she lies, you are all *ordered* to report the falsehood. Taylor Woodswright, how do you plead?"

"According to the Hollow Kingdom's Unified Ascender Statutes, I have the right to know my accuser," came Taylor's first cold comment.

"Denied. Section thirty-one dot one dot one." The Captain replied easily, clearly having been prepared for her knowledge of the inner workings of the law.

"Really?" Taylor retorted drolly. "Credible threat of retaliation against your personal self and people under your care? How is that?"

"Thirty-*two* dot one dot six."

"Well, in that case. I invoke fifteen dot four dot eight." Taylor's scoffing replies to each of the Captain's mechanical answers devolved into a multi-minute back-and-forth of numbers and sections that Luke didn't care about at all. He let the drivel swirl around him as he yawned and wavered on taking a nap, like Andre. Ultimately, the Murderhobo decided against it. He wasn't tired, and there was no guarantee that no lotuses were lurking underground and waiting for him to slip up.

Long enough later that Luke was once again debating on that nap, even with the threat of hungry plants, the two arguing Ascenders seemed to find a compromise. He noted that Taylor seemed pleased with the exchange. She caught him studying her, and she flat-out explained, "The fact that they not only know the law at this level, but are following it *exactly*, means we're going to walk away from this 'trial' without any major issues. They're the *King's* agents, not agents of the Kingdom."

"Why are they here, if they know we're in the right?" Luke scrutinized the men surrounding them. He couldn't make out any of their features; the armor gave them all the same height and girth, as well as being clearly enchanted to destroy any scent that emitted from them. If he didn't know better, he would have thought he was surrounded by golems instead of Ascenders. "I feel like this is going overboard."

"Royal Order of King's Inquisitors," Taylor told him, as if it were obvious. "If no one but the King knows their identities, then they can't be bribed or coerced by factions within the Kingdom."

"How many dead since you left the capitol, Taylor?" the Captain demanded from her directly.

"Eight total, but as fart as I can tell, they weren't acting on behalf of the Kingdom," Taylor's reply was instant and slightly garbled due to dehydration. "They ambushed us, either tracking us on this world or in another world to do the same."

"Fart...?" The Captain seemed more shocked by her vulgarity than her revelation of killing. "What-"

"I'm tired and have sand in my mouth," Taylor growled back with a tinge of red on her cheeks. "It was a slip of the tongue, and you don't need to be rude. You knew what I meant; don't hound me for it."

"Right..." The Captain regained his composure. "Sigil, designations of the slain."

Taylor's Sigil chimed in reply and a solid pane of light appeared. The Captain browsed it before returning his attention to the group. "Two slain were acting without proper orders, while one *was*, but your authority was higher than theirs. I find you guilty of self-defense, and fine your group ten thousand gold as reparation. This trial is concluded."

"*Guilty* of self-defense? Wait... they can kill us, but if we kill them in our efforts to ensure they can't kill us, you still take an arm and a leg? Can you *believe* this guy?" Zed's shocked tone shattered the still moment, but no one bothered to answer him, so he quietly raged next to Luke, who gently reached out and slugged him. The Bard rolled twice as he bounced off the lush grass, eventually coming to rest under a Sunshower. He hopped to his feet when he was stable enough to do so, then gestured expansively at the Murderhobo. "*Dude.* What the abyss?"

"Friendly touching shows a growth in the bonds of friendship," Luke deadpanned, holding up the book on interpersonal communication that Lord Woodswright had sent him what felt like years ago.

Zed looked on in horror as Luke pointed out the passage he was referencing. "No! Don't read that; you're a *Murderhobo*! Just be angry with me at the situation we're in!"

"Am I supposed to be upset here?" Luke furrowed his brow, read something from the book, then carefully tucked it away. He turned to the Knights and bellowed, "I'm angry on behalf of my friends! *Righteous* anger!"

"Perhaps I concluded the trial too quickly." The Captain ignored the others and faced Taylor as his words flowed with seemingly carelessness. "Do you know the status of the rest of Heaven's Earth? If you killed one of them...?"

"I do not know where they are currently, or their current health. I could make a few guesses, but I'd rather not." Taylor chose her words meticulously and ignored the lingering silence as the Captain continued staring at her.

Andre awoke at that point with a pained yelp. "*Why*? Who did that?"

"You just fell asleep, Andre," Taylor loudly informed the befuddled man. "We just finished a trial from the King's Inquisitors, and I spoke on our behalf. Say nothing-"

"Not that!" Andre roared at her, startling everyone present. "Who attacked the land? *Ow*! It's still happening! This is so large that it *has* to be an Ascender with an area of effect spell!"

"There's... no one." The Captain glanced around blankly. "We're the only representatives of the Kingdom in a score of miles. How far out?"

"Not far! Getting closer!" Andre waved *deeper* into what had just been desert a few hours ago. "That way, and spreading like the blight!"

Luke decided against waiting around for other people to start moving and shot to the top of the hill. The late afternoon air was *filled* with a deep thrumming, and he went still as he saw what was coming toward them. A thunderstorm appeared to be rolling toward them, but in actuality, it was the largest swarm of insects he had ever seen. Each one was practically a clone of its neighbor, and the blades on their front limbs dug into the earth like plows wherever a *hint* of greenery or life could be found. "Preying Mantous. This version has *wings*? We should probably leave."

Andre appeared next to him in the next moment, glaring at the bugs with hate-filled eyes and screaming to be heard, "No! *No*! They're killing everything!"

Indeed, everything from bush to lichen was slashed and devoured. The bugs even dug into the ground a little and tore out the roots of anything they found for additional sustenance. The Captain drew near Luke, his armor gleaming in the reflected sunlight. "A locust swarm? Okay... that's probably your fault. Archdruid Andre, you are ordered to cease growing plants into the Scarocco desert until those creatures are proven to be no longer an issue for the Hollow Kingdom."

"Wha—*no*! Andre raged as his Sigil chimed in confirmation of the order. "Why would you *do* that?"

"I'm not going to lie to you," the Captain stated as he shook his helmeted head. Andre waited for more, but the man simply stopped speaking.

"Why would you stop speaking on a comma?" the Murder-hobo demanded of the Knight. The tension rose as the bugs came closer, and still not a word was spoken.

"If they need to not be a threat, let's make that happen. Easy enough." Taylor stepped into the silence, and with a brush of willpower, started sending clusters of spells into the approaching tidal wave of beasts. Each Flame Lance she projected into the wall of chitin penetrated dozens before detonating and roasting further hundreds.

Andre joined in, tossing seeds into the air that reached the bugs and stuck… then did nothing. "I can't even grow plants for *combat*? You're trying to kill me!"

The Captain remained silent, and the subordinate Knights impassive. Zed pulled out a lyre and started strumming, and Luke charged at the buzzing calamity.

Five seconds of running, eighty percent of his mana devoted to his Battering Ram Knuckles, and fifty mana to activate Shockwave Cleave. He hit a single Preying Mantous as it swung its natural weapons at him, and Luke smiled at the realization that there were *thousands* of weapons within range of Source-cerer's Armory. Ten percent of their total damage was added to his singular attack…

Damage dealt: 9,783 blunt. (4,924 weapons in range, average maximum damage 5 per weapon.)

Self- Damage inflicted: 276.

Current health: 14/290.

The Cleave Skill radiated out with an intensity that could only be matched by the eruption of a volcano. Luke was sent flying backward, the bones in his arm, shoulder, and a quarter of his ribs broken in multiple locations. His organs were also heavily damaged from the sheer output he achieved, but the pain was *only* pain—for now—so he kept his eyes on the tsunami of bugs that were being converted to ichor and shards of carapace.

Since the creatures were packed so closely together, the power of the shockwave simply kept increasing. A single creature might be hit by two, or even three, of the branching shockwaves in the same instant, which would propel fifty-five percent of the damage of *each* wave into the bug behind it. As the bugs could only take a small amount of damage anyway, the fact that the power was halved meant nearly nothing until the half-life was in the single digits. At that point, the bugs were still mangled, but survived.

Preying Mantous killed: 138,427.

Etheric Xenograft Potentia gained: 38,319. This type of creature can no longer earn you Potentia!

"Got 'em." Luke wheezed a laugh as blood frothed from his lips. No one came to check on him, too enthralled with the sudden flood of insect innards that was still pouring from the sky with meaty *plops*.

"No." The Knight pointed into the distance. "You *didn't* get them. You just slapped down the first wave. Can you do it again?"

"Nope." Luke lifted a shaking hand and sucked down the last dregs of mana-water that he had managed to hold onto. His health increased by a mere fifty points, but he no longer felt like he was about to bleed out internally. "I'm too damaged to continue here. Ta-ta; I'm finally making my escape."

He struggled over to the center of the camp where Andre habitually activated his personal portal most often. Using his not-pulped left hand, he began punching at the air. It took twice as long as usual, as he usually used both hands, but eventually a crack appeared in the world. He kept at it as his mana drained away, and stumbled through the portal as soon as it opened wide enough to accommodate him.

The portal snapped closed behind him, and he gazed contentedlyaround his blue Murder World. "Loophole found. When I go back, I'll only need to stay one more day before coming directly back here. Thanks for the vague wording keeping me trapped on the base world, King Alexander. You're the *best*."

CHAPTER THIRTY-FOUR

Displeased with the feeling of his bones poking through his skin in a few places, Luke meandered around Murder World for a short while until he found a trickle of water. He dropped into it and started slurping down the fluid, then let it wash through him as his Skills kicked in and began rearranging his insides. "Ugh... that feels so nasty. I really need to find some armor and upgrade away from what I'm wearing now. Maybe I should just go ahead and reuse that Soul Brand thing on my weapons?"

He watched without flinching as his ulna reformed, *slurping* back through his skin and collecting together into a solid whole once more. Luke took a moment to attempt to recollect the last time he had managed to break one of his bones... but he couldn't. It had been so many years ago that he had taken enough damage that any of his bones had even cracked... perhaps there was something to that? He *had* taken lots of damage, but his bones had just stopped breaking after a while.

Then he'd gotten busted up twice within a single day. First his skull, then his torso and arm. "You know... I used to help Cookie get stronger by bathing her in the water. Maybe I need to break over and over again so that I can come back stronger? Some kinda 'repair with gold' thing, but using mana instead? Is that what my 'You Need to Stop' Skill is telling me?"

His Sigil tried to chime 'no', but he had long ago learned not to trust the intrusive thoughts that it pushed at him. Even so, he didn't have a whole bunch of time to waste on testing a mere theory. He had a few days to get back to Zone twelve and-

Healthy return possible. Timer set until return is forced: 00:59:59.

"You want me to go back in an *hour*?" Luke bellowed at the timer that had appeared. "No! I just got here! I *refuse*! Sigil! Devote enough Potentia to *Open Up* to raise it to Tier seven!"

Caution! Increasing the Tier of this Skill may result in being trapped between worlds while it increases! No secondary portal generation method detected.

"Do. It," he hissed at the Sigil. A swirl of Potentia drained away and filled the Skill to bursting, and it grayed out on his status sheet. "Lemme see all my skills."

Skills: Tier: Level

Source-cerer's Armory: 9: 0
You need to Stop: 3: 1
Bum Flash: 2: 7
Hobo Holler: 3: 0
Pristine Balance: 4: 0
~~*Open Up*~~*: 7: 0 (Tier up in progress)*
Feather's Fall: 4: 2
Shockwave Cleave: 4: 0
Giga: 1: 0 (Activation still in progress)

"What's that?" Luke inspected his Skill list in surprise. A Skill was listed that he had never seen before. "Giga? Like the Giga Ant? That was supposed to be a Tier five Skill! What a waste... fine. What does it do?"

Giga. Tier 1, Level 0. Congratulations, you've gained one of the most dangerous Skills available on [Murder World].

Effect 1: Mana is your body. Your flesh and bones. Sustain yourself on it. Gorge yourself on it. Pure mana can no longer damage you. You gain $3n$% size per level. When you have reached your increased size, all Body Sub-Sub-characteristics will be boosted by the same amount.

This Skill increases from exposure to high mana saturation; Potentia cannot be devoted to it.

"Is that why I was taller?" Luke muttered uneasily at the blaring warning it gave him. "Thought that was the solid mana burning me out. Why is this the most dangerous Skill? Dangerous for me, or for the people I fight? It even increases naturally…? Welp. Can't do anything about it now."

If his body was heavier, he'd never know it, thanks to his *massive* fitness. If the growth was making his limbs longer, Pristine Balance was compensating perfectly on his behalf. "Not seeing the downside. Maybe I'll need a specific type of armor? Well… no, I have my Armory."

The Murderhobo sprinted downhill for the next half hour, soon arriving in position to spot the Pteranodons. They were waiting for him, creepily staring at his man flesh. He figured it had to do with the pulsing that was coming from his Sigil as his Skill was increased… but they were tracking him far too carefully, and in near-perfect unison. He cautiously stepped across the boundary, and the largest among the birds flew away like an arrow shot from a bow.

Another flapped forward, and Luke immediately realized what was different: *all* of the visible birds had nearly transparent horns growing from their heads. The horn flashed with color as words floated from it. "Luke… you survived. You are no longer welcome in our Zones."

"*Snails.*" Luke hissed and took another step forward, met with a line of light that hit his arm and numbed it slightly.

Damage taken: 5 paralytic. Effect overpowered by Body. Arm is numb for 5… 4…

He traced the beam of light back to the horn of the creature, shook off the effect, and kept moving forward. "The strongest of you really *are* the horse-faced parasites, aren't they?

Interesting that they told the truth for once. You know, when I was escaping, I had to fully dodge almost all of the spells they were casting, or I'd die. Put me in a pretty bad place as I ran for the exit. Guess what, bird-brains? This run-through... I have all the time I need."

He tapped his Sigil, which was pulsing intermittently. "No Skill available to leave; no way for the person holding my reins to pull me back. Plenty of time to *kill* as I please."

No more words needed to be exchanged. Dozens of beams shot at Luke, and he Bum Flashed out of the way to avoid them. He wasn't as confident as he sounded: during his previous escape, the unicorns had been unprepared for him. Even more, they had thought he was *one* of them. He remembered all too well how, during his surprise Sigil-forced mad dash out—pushing Bum Flash to the extreme—the horses had *carved* him up at a distance with various spell effects. Avoiding most of them had been luck; actually escaping had been a shock to everyone involved.

As he remembered his brutalized state when he had returned to the base world, Luke's eyes reddened. Instead of cleanly dodging as he had the last few attacks, the Murderhobo sprinted forward and let his armor repel the majority of the damage so that he could punch the talkative bird in the face. A Flash to the top of its head later, and he wrenched the horn out of the beast's skull.

"Pretty new to this Zone, huh?" He commented as he looked at the only partially-dissolved crystalline snail body that extended into the pteranodon. Clapping his hands together, he powdered the horn and shoved the grains into a pocket. The other dinosaur-birds that witnessed his attack scattered like a flock of pigeons that just had a tiger dropped amongst them. "You know you're a *delicacy* back on my world? Your bodies are going to help me get a snail-hunting team together. That team will help me ensure that not even a single *one* of you endures on this Plane of existence, ever again!"

"You're a *monster*!" one of the pteranodonicorns screamed at him, swooping in to try to tear off his arm. Luke whipped out his Rope, managing to coil it around the creature before pulling hard and cleanly dividing it in half with the simple-seeming motion. That was the last one that got close, and he knew that they had finally come to their senses.

"Abyss..." Now he had to get across one of the chains that connected to the lower Zone, and he'd have to deal with swooping birds *and* magical attacks. If they managed to numb him too much, he'd be easy pickings as he ran. He had a few options available to him at that moment, and so decided to use them. "Thirty-three thousand Potentia to use... bring me up to level eleven."

Etheric Xenograft Potentia: 33,676 -> 19,276.

Fourteen thousand and four hundred Potentia gushed into him, altering him further and further away from human. "The point goes in Physical Reaction."

That was all he could get out as the Potentia went to work, enhancing him beyond his natural potential for growth. He panted as his skin stretched and broke from muscles growing rapidly and smoothing, healing in the next instant as the Potentia worked its wonders. This was the first time he had ever intentionally put a point into physical reaction, as far as he could remember, and it made him feel... jumpy. Hyper and amped up.

Also *fast.*

Luke sprinted out and onto the chain as he read over the sudden changes to his status; just as Giga chimed that his body had adjusted to his new size.

Cal Scan
*Level: **11***
Current Etheric Xenograft Potentia: 19,276/23,300 to level 12!
Body: 32.4

- *Fitness: 40.8*
- *Resistance: 24*

Mind: 18.6

- *Talent: 16.3*
- *Capacity: 20.9*

Presence: 18

- *Willpower: 27*
- *Charisma: 9*

Senses: 26.25

- *Physical reaction: 32.5*
- *Mental energy: 20*

Maximum Health: 290 -> 377 (Giga)
Maximum Mana: 324
Mana regen: ~~5.43 per second~~ Overridden: 100 per second.

"Physical output jumped to twenty-six fifty-two kilos…" Luke tucked into a forward roll to evade the scattering of strange colorless beams of light, which were surprisingly visible as they speared through the foggy blue air. "Poison and disease resist jumped from thirty-four percent to forty-five… disease resist? I've been ignoring Resistance since I'm immune to poison, but… what if I need to grow my Skill by being subjected to *diseases*?"

Chime. His Sigil screamed 'no' at him.

"Hah! Nice try; now I know it'll work for *sure!*" Luke howled with wild laughter as he jumped, dove, and Feather's Fall-ed his way down the chain, much to the frustration of the pteranodonicorns. They started coming closer and closer… until they were in range. "Bum Flash!"

The Murderhobo was among them, his hands grasping at horns and leaving sundered flesh behind everywhere he moved. He screamed in pleasure as he attacked with wild abandon, reveling in his unending mana regeneration. Iridescent horn after iridescent horn was turned to powder in his grip, shoved into a specially-made satchel that Andre had crafted upon Taylor's request. He didn't get all of it, since powder tended to be carried upon the breeze, but he got *enough*.

"Now you die, human!" one of the pteranodonicorns laughed as they flew below the level of the chain. "You can only float; you cannot rise!"

Luke Flashed to that one and gripped its horn. He tore it out, and glided on the slowly falling beast. "That would be true… if every single creature, in every single world, *didn't* think I was the most delicious morsel in existence."

The blur fog surrounding him opened up to expose hundreds of unaltered pteranodons winging toward him. Luke laughed and began his ascent, his trail marked with death with each 'platform' he used to reset Bum Flash. "A Skill upgrading, combined with 'You Need to Stop' informing them that I'm tasty? I'll *never* run out of willing sacrifices!"

CHAPTER THIRTY-FIVE

Luke landed heavily on the border between Zones, blood not his own running off his body so thickly that he needed to shake like a dog just to get the *top* layer off. He sighed as he stepped into Zone eleven. "Stupid birds."

Since he had already defeated this Zone before, there was a good shot that he could just run across it; yet he was almost certain that the parasites would have taken over the guardian and would be using it as a gatekeeper. Since he had resolved to kill them all off, leaving behind one that would grow constantly in strength, size, and power seemed like a terrible idea.

"Starts as an ant," he muttered quietly, trying to consider how he could find an ant in the huge Zone. Even *without* the space-warping distortions, he knew this place was massive. "I've been gone for just about seven weeks. That's... seven hundred and thirty-five-ish days. How big would this thing grow in two years?"

The answer was as surprising as always. He hadn't thought that he would find the creature on his first pass, but it turned out that not only was it drawn to him, thanks to his Skill upgrading... but it was on the lookout for him. The only warning he had was a pounding on the earth in a staccato beat that a drumline would be hard-pressed to match. His instincts made him throw himself to the side, just as a set of mandibles half the length of a merchant's covered wagon snapped through the air where he had been standing a moment before. It was so close to ending him that his shoulder armor shattered and the mandibles cleanly sliced off a chunk of the meat on his left shoulder.

Damage taken: 14 piercing.

"Huh." Luke stared at the Giga Anticorn as his armor reconstituted, taking a swig of his refilled waterskin as he watched the new arrival. The creature was clearly an ant, but currently its tallest point reached just above Luke's belly button. The creature had launched itself at him, attempting to bisect him as an opening move. If it hadn't been in the air, it might have been able to course-correct and land the blow as intended. "All that damage from *proximity*. Makes me wonder what ten percent of your maximum damage with those weapons is?"

"You are not welcome here!" the brown-light-filled horn atop the ant bellowed at him in a voice deeper than any Luke had previously heard from a 'Corn. "The flyers informed me of your imminent arrival! I have alerted the herds! Attempting to penetrate our defenses will end in your demise!"

"You're a *loud* ant, aren't you?" Luke tried to buy time as his shoulder slowly healed itself. "Speedy, too. Your predecessor seemed pretty slow, but maybe that was just a consequence of size?"

The ant ignored his words in favor of continuing to bellow at him. "I was integrated with the Giga the same day that you appeared in our world! The great defiler! You have one chance to leave, and never return! You may hunt in the higher Zones, but never-"

"You're telling me what I'm *allowed* to do?" Luke Bum Flashed at the creature, his fist coming down on… nothing? He completely missed his target as the six legs of the ant churned. "On *my* world?"

"Know fear, defiler! A detailed report on your abilities was submitted through the proper channels! I have trained in this form for *years* to be prepared for your underhanded tactics!" The ant's horn practically screamed while the mandibles *clacked* in an attempt to tear his flesh asunder. "Every movement pattern, each arc of your weapon has been studied! You have no chance against me! Even if you did, your weakness to our magic has been noted! The lancers are standing at the ready even now! A single step into the next Zone will *spell* your end!"

Manic laughter followed this pronouncement, and Luke tried to use the creature's clear distraction and insanity against it. Even so, it was just. So. *Fast.* He could barely get out of the way of the needle-sharp legs as it ran at him, and the mandibles were so swift and deadly that he couldn't afford to get caught. He had to perfectly control every aspect of himself just to avoid being cut in half, and any retaliatory blows he sent out were as glancing as the hits that he took.

All of this combined into a single, glaring fact: Luke hadn't had this much fun against an enemy since he had slaughtered the goats in Zone one.

He didn't care that his fighting style had been analyzed. That didn't matter one ant-sized little bit. Oh, no. Someone knew how he fought when he was physically forced to leave? It was going to be a completely different experience for them, and he'd *personally* teach them how he attacked when he was ready and excited for the fight. Tactics were a foreign concept, simply because he had either been so outmatched, or so able to overpower his opponent, that he had never needed to adapt.

Right now, against a creature that he was a near physical match for? He was being *forced* to get good. The fact that something required a few tons of armor and weapons in order to be a physical match for him didn't bother him at all. Yet, not being able to land a hit on something that large was *somewhat* upsetting. "Hold still so I can kill you!"

"You first!" the ant retorted with an air-shaking scream.

"Does anyone listen when you tell them something so unnatural, foolish human?"

"Can't know unless I try," Luke grumbled at the beast. He was starting to get a good feel for how the ant moved. Even though it seemed wild and erratic, there were subtle patterns. There had to be: controlling six legs in perfect synchronization meant that there *had* to be a plan in place for movement. Luke silently increased the size of his Chain-Blade Rope, compensating for the loss of power by turning off sections of his armor and devoting it to the weapon.

He charged at the ant, and the 'Corn scoffed at him once before zipping to his left. Instead of changing directions, the Murderhobo let his arm swing out. The Rope, now the length of half a caravan, whirled through the air and met the side of the beast just as his return pull broke the very air it traveled through with a thunderous *crack*. The impact was so violent that it generated light and heat, directly tearing off the creature's mid-leg and sending the hook at the end of the weapon deep into the creature's flesh.

Damage dealt: 846 piercing. (Mixed non-weapon damage not accounted for).

There was only an instant between the weapon landing and Luke shrinking the weapon. It reeled him in so fast that he may as well have been flying, but even so, the creature turned and *clacked* down on the tether—shearing his Chain-Blade Rope and dissipating the mana from which it was formed. Luke was still flying at the creature, and Flashed above it just as the beast moved out of the way. His left fist closed around its horn, and his right hand punched it at the base.

The horn shattered under the concussive force, and the Giga-Anticorn stopped moving, sliding to a full stop as gravity and friction took effect on the limp corpse.

Etheric Xenograft Potentia gained: 638.

Calculating... anomaly concern number 2 in the area spreading. Anomaly information has been passed to _Error_. Assessment of threat level to Luke Von Murderhobo: Certain death. Authorization granted. Generating special award 'offer'.

Message generated.

Luke Von Murderhobo, you are at the edge of an invasive species nest. The world's rules allow very little in the way of assistance to lower cultivators. Only special circumstances can generate physical rewards or custom Skill Pearls. In order to gain a boon without completing a trial, you must give something up in advance. Are you willing to give up power temporarily in order to gain a boon that will assist against the invasive nest? Yes / No.

"It'll help me kill those nasty snails? I'll do anything I gotta do." Luke wondered what the world would require of him, but he was certain that it would be annoying if it was giving him a heads up.

In the box is a set of armor specifically designed to provide extra protection against attacks of a magical nature. Against attacks of a physical nature, the armor is worse than not wearing any armor at all. As payment for the armor, all Potentia gained for killing the next 5,000 'Snail-icorn' type creatures will be absorbed by the world. Taking the armor shows your agreement.

"That's a lot of Potentia for a little bit of armor." Luke opened the box and looked at the fabric bundled inside. "Especially such… are those *lace frills*? Is it actually gonna be worth taking this junk?"

As per usual, the world around him didn't answer. He grumbled as he pulled out a robe and looked at the garment. It was purest white, with just a *hint* of blue to it. As he shook it open, a pair of moccasins and a large… pirate hat were revealed. Luke pulled the strange assortment out of the box with a sigh as his Source-cerer's Armory divulged how they interacted with his Skills and mana.

Mage Hunter's Armament (Set Items). A set of three items that were designed by the most bloodthirsty Annihilator Ascenders known to the great multiverse. This style was unable to help them achieve their goals of being impervious to the more mana-attuned worlds they visited, but their attempts at defeating mana itself showed some merit.

Set benefits:

1 item) Mage Hunter: 50% reduced magic damage taken. Inward-facing armor: Damage that would be blocked by armor rating is instead dealt as bonus damage.

2 items) Spell Hatred: Each spell that deals damage to you increases your movement speed by 10% for five seconds. Stacks up to three times.

3 items) Perpetual Motion: Duration of all movement-impairing spells reduced by 60%.

"Set items? That's a new thing." Luke looked at the next messages with great interest. He was simultaneously excited and disgusted by the equipment.

Mage Hunter's Greatrobe) A beautifully ironic robe made from the best parts of the twelve most pure-hearted unicorns ever born, twelve beasts that sacrificed themselves to protect their people against utter destruction. They failed. Must be equipped first. Durability reduces by 1 for every ten points of damage taken. Durability: 12/12. (Source-cerer's Armory bonus: if absorbed, will take the slot for chest, shoulder, hand, and leg armor. Removes durability. Minimum mana allocation required for activation: 40%.)

Mage Hunter's Tricorn) A hat made from a unicorn that was desperate to live. After its parents were turned into a robe, it devoted its life to being able to escape unicorn hunters. Every time it got hurt, it redoubled its effort to never get hurt again! It got caught. Now you have a new hat! Must be equipped second. (Source-cerer's Armory bonus: if absorbed, will take the slot for headgear. Minimum mana allocation required for activation: 10%.)

Mage Hunter's Moccasins) A pair of shoes made from the pelt of an orphaned unicorn that was bullied by all the other unicorns in the herd that grudgingly took it in. It was constantly hit by spells to slow it down when racing against its peers. All it ever wanted was to win a race, to the point that it even developed resistances to slowing effects. On the day of the great race, hunters waited near the finish line to catch the fastest unicorn in the herd. The last thing that went through the mind of a beautiful unicorn that would have won and fulfilled a life-long dream… was a spear! (Source-cerer's Armory bonus: if absorbed, will take the slot for foot armor. Minimum mana allocation required for activation: 10%.)

"Got it. This stuff only reduces magic damage." Luke stared at all the gear as his Skill worked to eat away at it. "Makes me more able to kill spellslingers of all sorts, not just snails, but I gotta really believe in my physical superiority. Heh. Got *that* goin' for me."

He thought back to the way the horses had attacked him. The only natural weapons they had were what horses *normally* had, plus a sharp horn. Luke waited in the empty Zone for a few hours, until all the gear had been absorbed and equipped. When it was all finally ready, he checked the updated information… and released a smile that showed every single tooth.

Mage Hunter's Greatrobe)

- *Mage Hunter: 50% reduced magic damage taken.*
- *Inward-facing armor: Damage that would be blocked by armor rating is instead dealt as bonus damage.*
- *Must be the first-equipped set item.*
- *Takes the slot for chest, shoulder, hand, and leg armor.*
- *Minimum mana allocation required for activation: 40%.*

Mage Hunter's Tricorn)

- *Spell Hatred: Each spell that deals damage to you increases your movement speed by 10% for five seconds. Stacks up to three times.*
- *Takes the slot for headgear.*
- *Must be the second-equipped set item.*
- *Minimum mana allocation required for activation: 10%.*

Mage Hunter's Moccasins)

- *Perpetual motion: Duration of all movement-impairing spells reduced by 60%.*
- *Take the slot for foot armor.*
- *Minimum mana allocation required for activation: 10%.*

Complete set equipped! Note: devoting additional mana to this gear does not increase any bonuses.

"After all that, I still have my gauntlet slotted, so I need to deactivate that." Luke intentionally did so, then devoted a total of sixty percent of his mana to the new set. The hat, robe, and shoes all appeared on him, looking as real as any other clothing. He wasn't sure if it was a benefit of being much more powerful gear, or the gear being a set, but he liked that it was fully opaque; unlike his standard armor. "Excellent. Now I can run around totally naked, and *no one* will be able to tell."

He turned his eyes to the horizon and began stomping his way toward the unicorns. The Murderhobo shook his head and amended that thought.

"Toward *Cookie*."

CHAPTER THIRTY-SIX

- ANDRE -

The Druid watched helplessly as the man that had just turned a literal *swarm* of bugs into paste opened a portal and vanished. He winced as he realized that the Murderhobo had drained away a huge amount of the area's ambient mana when he had opened the portal, and it might take *days* before there was enough present in the area to enable him to open portals again. Even then... only if the plant life here survived. At this moment, that meant exactly one thing. "There are more bugs coming. We need to retreat immediately."

"You know, sometimes I think bears are better at communicating than people are." Zed sighed wistfully as Andre bodily lifted him and began to run. "You know they have a sound that means 'there are bees here, and we need to leave'? I feel like we should be able to do that."

"We can." Taylor's voice cut into the Bard's out-of-place introspection. "We say 'there are bees here, and we need to leave', just like Andre did. Stop trying to sound deep because you picked up a few random facts about nature by hanging around a *Druid*."

Phantom pain wracked Andre, to the point that he nearly collapsed mid-stride. "Gah!"

"What is it?" Taylor placed a steadying hand on his shoulder. "More of the swarm?"

"Yeah... so many more." Andre swept his perception along his connected swathes of plants. "They're *everywhere* in the desert, Taylor. *Anything* I look at... it's getting destroyed. They're even ahead of us. I have no idea how we're gonna get past them without a dozen people to add more firepower-"

"Or one Full Murderhobo!" Zed chimed in.

"-and my power is rapidly melting away," Andre continued without missing a beat. He was starting to calm as the pain continued; he supposed that one could get used to *anything* over time. "If we're going to escape, we're gonna need to get through a portal before they all collapse on us. The mana in the area is too low, so we need to get past them..."

"What is it?" Taylor demanded as the Druid trailed off.

"I have an idea of how we can make a break for it while we're still out here." Andre dropped Zed, who fell to the soft grass below with a yelp. "I was ordered not to grow plants out into the desert. Well, we had expanded that range significantly, so I have some leeway. First, I need to ensure that all the Lotus Coffins are so far below ground that they won't get caught... there. I've given the order. If they manage to do it, great. Next, we need to kill a whole *slew* of bugs so I can feed them to a bunch of plants at once. The runoff mana should be high enough that I can open a portal without an issue. We can use that to get out of here."

"Why not just have all these nice Knights... help us?" Zed gestured grandly, but faltered as he realized that not a single sunbeam's reflection from an armored form could be detected as far as his vision could reach. "Did they *seriously* just leave us here?"

"We're all Nobles, Ascenders, and *some* of us are powerful,"

Taylor explained calmly as she began preparing herself for the oncoming attack.

"Well, I'm more of a benefit to society than you are. I bet that feels really nice to know, doesn't it?" Zed's words made Taylor's breath hitch for a second, but she moved on as he continued to taunt her. "You talk about benefits in the long term, but I'm helping the people that are suffering *now*, ya know? I bet that just kills you."

"How about I kill *you*—no." The Mage caught herself and forced her furious eyes to the horizon. "The Knights were likely under orders not to help us even slightly, so as to not show favoritism. If other people thought the King was helping us unfairly, then even the neutral factions might call for our deaths."

"So the Prince can send his goons to kill us for no reason, a whole buncha people can try to destroy everything we do, but the only thing that'll be noticed is when one person tries to help us?" Zed spat at her feet as if the entire situation was *her* fault.

"That about sums it up," the Mage sighed sadly as the first Preying Mantous began cresting the horizon. "Hey, Zed?"

"*What?*"

"Do you know that I really, *really* hate Master Don and the fact that he's forcing me to take his position as Archmage?" Taylor didn't look over at the Bard, but Andre did. Zed's expression was brimming with suspicion, which bloomed into a condescending sneer. "I just wanna learn cool spells. I want to be as uninhibited as *Luke*, even. But every time that I give in to what I *want* to do, versus what I think will be the best way for me to survive, I'm weakening the foundation I've built for when I have to live in that snake's den that they call the capital. *Flame Lance!*"

The explosive spell left her hands so suddenly that Zed fell back with a yelp. Andre realized that Zed had been so entranced by Taylor's words that he had forgotten about the oncoming swarm, and that made the Druid laugh as he started preparing the few defensive plants that he could grow in the low-mana area. There were barely a few whipping vines in place before the leading edge of the swarm was upon them.

Strangely enough, the creatures went after the vegetation before anything else. The humans weren't going to be far behind, but it gave them a few extra seconds to start killin'. Andre's Livingwood Staff bent and sprouted numerous long thorns. He lifted it and began firing arrow after arrow into the sky. He didn't need to aim, and still the bolts killed two to three of the insects each time he released the bowstring-vine.

Realizing that he *actually* didn't need to aim, he placed his staff on the ground again and ordered it to simply keep sending arrows forward and up. Just like that, he had made an auto-arrow turret. He scoffed at himself for not thinking of the concept earlier in his career, but he didn't have time to explore that to its natural conclusion in the heat of battle. Knowing that time was short, he pricked his palms and let blood flow to the ground. With a surge of willpower, the affected earth flattened and started curving upward, forming a dome around the three of them and his staff.

Andre made sure to keep the front of the structure open, both for outgoing spells as well as arrows. He also kept the ground under his control so that he could repair it as needed, which wasn't as difficult as he had thought it would be. Very few of the bugs attacked the stone igloo directly, since it formed with a large opening in front. Most of the repairs occurred when their feet dug in to find purchase, so the upkeep was minimal. Ichor, as well as fresh or charred bodies, collected inside the small building at an enormous rate; the physically fragile insects unable to do more than throw themselves to their death.

With the initial defense created, the Druid turned his attention to keeping the team functional. Having access to so many corpses was the entire purpose of leaving an opening: their blood was drained away, and their bodies converted to nutrients at a rate not possible without mana. Just as he sent his vines to grow up and around the opening, Taylor dropped to one knee with blood running down from her left nostril. "I'm... I'm out of mana."

"I got it." Andre murmured, while Zed began to panic. His vines' thorns were more like blades against the insects that continued to swarm in despite being practically *blended* in the process. All of their juices and meat were absorbed right into the roots of his plants, boosting the mana in the enclosed space over time. "I'm almost ready. No one do anything stupid."

Having his concentration split hurt somewhat as time passed, but he was used to it after his decades of training. He cleared an area and started forming a circle in the air; it went *far* slower than he wanted it to go, taking a full five minutes instead of the standard three to complete the portal formation. "Almost there..."

Zed shouted something and jumped at the Druid, coming to a dead stop right behind him. Andre grumbled lightly as he heard Taylor chewing the Bard out. The portal opened fully, and Andre directed his vines to grab him and his staff, then chuck the whole group through the portal. "No need to be fancy or potentially lose anyone to a closing portal. Everyone here?"

He looked at the others, shocked at the sight of blood pouring from Zed's chest. Taylor was still struggling with a Preying Mantous that just wouldn't *die*; that sight was all it took for Andre to realize what was happening. He grabbed the bug and bodily tossed it through the closing portal just before it snapped shut. Then he turned to check on the others, only to see Taylor cradling Zed's head in her lap as the Bard struggled to breathe.

Andre was kneeling next to them in an instant, giving a low whistle as he saw Zed's heart bleeding through a hole the size of a finger with every beat. "I'm so sorry, Zed. This is really gonna suck until we find a way to heal it."

"Not... gonna have to... worry about that for long." Zed coughed a mouthful of blood, then managed a crooked grin at the others. "Hey... Taylor. I know I was being a jerk about it, but... make sure those kids get a real chance... would you? Don't let someone take over the schools. Don't cry, Tay. I even get to die the hero. I... saved the guy... that actually matters."

Andre reeled back, tears stinging his eyes as the dark emotion behind those words set in. "If you *ever* talk about my friend like that again, I'm going to punch you in the face."

"W...what?" Zed gaped at the Druid, confused for many reasons. Then he realized how long they'd been talking. "Why am I... still alive?"

"Yeah, welcome to my Grove." Andre let a ghost of a smile appear on his lips, not truly feeling like showing off in the moment. "You won't get any better without help, but you won't be able to die either. I won't let you."

"How is that possible, Andre?" Taylor had never stopped lightly stroking Zed's blood-drained forehead. "How is he... I'm glad he's... but how?"

"Oh, did I never mention it?" Andre rubbed at the back of his neck and laughed self-consciously. "Yeah... I control a Domain here. Nothing, and no one, can deteriorate here."

"D-domain? You have a Tier *ten*...?" Taylor froze at his admission as her mind whirled, thinking of all the things they could *use* the place for. "I'm so far behind..."

Zed actually seemed to regain some life. "So... what I'm hearing is... go somewhere else to poop... or the smell will never go away?"

CHAPTER THIRTY-SEVEN

Andre tried and failed to come up with a response for the Bard, but finally muttered under his breath, "Where were you when I first got this place?"

Taylor looked up at him in light disgust. "What was that?"

"Nothing. Listen, Zed..." Andre began, only to be cut off by the increasing volume of moans rising from the Bard.

"Ughh. I'm *perpetually* dying here, Andre. This hurts an unbelievable amount. Just throw me out like a hunk of garbage!" Zed sighed softly and went quiet; only the knowledge that he *couldn't* die gave the Druid some small comfort.

"We're gonna heal you, Zed. No matter *what* it takes," Taylor told the man firmly. "You just need to-"

The Bard's groaning started up again. "You can't heal a damaged heart, Taylor!"

"That's enough, Zed. You sound like a lovelorn fourteen year old!" Andre's bark startled the other two enough that they went silent. "We are going to figure something out, and you're just gonna have to *deal* with the pain until then. I can do *anything*, given enough time. Here... you have nothing *but* time. You won't even starve to death if I don't feed you."

"Is this a house or a prison?" Zed mumbled up at the Druid, before amending his statement in a normal tone. "That is… *thank* you, Andre. I would truly love to live, please."

"That's more like it." Andre was a little surprised at how well his stern tone was working. He didn't often have reason to be so demanding, but he kinda *liked* how it felt to have people stop and listen when he spoke. "First thing I'm going to do is stitch your heart together, and then I'm going to go find a way to heal it more permanently. I'm sorry about this… and thank you, Zed."

"Wha-?" The Bard was groggy from the pain, and missed Andre's conversational leaps of logic.

"You saved my life. I understand that a bug must have gotten through and was going for me… I was distracted, and it nearly cost my life. It would have cost you *yours* at almost any other time, since it usually takes three minutes to open the way here. You would have bled out for sure. I'll fix you, and I'll find a way to repay you," the Druid promised firmly. He braced his hands over the open wound in Zed's chest and allowed a few spores to fall in and begin growing. He didn't 'stitch' with vines like he normally would, since that would deal damage to the organ; therefore, he *couldn't* do it.

Instead, he allowed moss to grow tightly to *itself* as he pushed the wound closed. The moss had slight numbing properties, which should help with the pain the man was enduring not-so-stoically. Once the front was bound up, he flipped the Bard to reveal his back and winced. What had appeared as a clean piercing on the front belied the true extent of the damage; the claw of the Preying Mantous was curved and serrated…

The back of Zed's heart was *shredded.*

"Feces on a stick." He quickly started growing a plant that would completely erase Zed's pain, and instructed it to start squeezing juice into the wounds. He almost gagged as he found that it wasn't only the heart; there was damage to all the connective tissue, bone, and everything *around* the pulsing organ. Andre held his emotions in check as he tried to figure out where to even *start* with the mess. He stilled his mind and began to treat the deepest damage, working to pull together the tattered muscles so that it could begin beating again.

Andre didn't have it in him to tell the Bard that his heart hadn't been beating, likely since the moment they had arrived. He fervently thanked his lucky stars that they had emerged directly inside his sanctuary of a Grove. It took far longer than he wanted, but finally the heart was fully wrapped, as were the arteries and veins around it. "Sorry, Zed. This part is gonna suck."

"What?" was all Zed could get out before Andre began *squeezing* the moss rhythmically. "*What* in the—you son of —*ahhh!*"

"Not a lot of blood in there... we can fix that..." Andre growled as more and more medicinal plants began growing around them. Luckily, he currently had access to several of Zed's open bones, as getting access to his marrow would otherwise have been impossible. His plants started stimulating blood cell growth, and he sat back to watch as the man slowly regained color in his face over the next few hours. "My part is done for now, except for the micro-plants that are going through and removing the air embolisms; abyss, the regular clots, too."

"What?" came the tearful, groggy reply from the tortured man. "I don't even know what those words are. I *do* words. Words are my thing. How do you know ones I don't?"

"Those are healer's words, Zed," Taylor gently told the man who was now laying on a comfortable bed of moss and leaves that had sprung up under him. "Not many people have that kind of knowledge, even though the healers *try* to spread them around as much as possible."

"The plants are out." Andre's words were punctuated by tiny *plops* as large blood clots were pushed out of the man's still-open wounds. "All I have left in there are the plants pumping your blood and keeping it in. While I was at it, I cleaned out all the build-up in your veins. You should lay off the greasy food, Bard. My prescription for you is more vegetables."

"*You* try gaining the majority of your Potentia from tavern bar-flies without having to eat the food they're serving there," Zed snorted haughtily and leaned into the moss a little more. "I'm feeling a lot more... put together. What all did you have to do?"

"I'd... really rather not tell you until you're back on your feet," the Druid hedged, chuckling internally at the fact that a *Druid* was *hedging*. "I just thought of a joke to tell you. Another time. How are you feeling? How's the pain?"

"Getting worse, actually. It was great for a while there, but I think I might have a fever or something... I'm burning up." The Bard sighed dramatically yet again as he snuggled back on the bed that had literally been grown to give him the greatest comfort and support. "I know I shouldn't be worried, cause I already tested not being able to die here, but I can tell you that this is by far the worst experience of my life."

Taylor felt his head and frowned. "You don't have a fever."

"Mmm?" The Bard offered a miniscule shrug.

A few *pops* and *crackles* sounded out, and Andre felt them deep in his body. "I see what's happening... your body is trying to start on fire. Taylor, I just realized we're in a really *high* mana concentration area."

"Just another thing trying to murder me," Zed acknowledged nonchalantly as the crackling sped up. "I feel like I should be joining Luke in his world or something. Just a bad day for things trying to murder me."

Taylor went silent as her face twisted in concentration. "I have an idea of how we might be able to fix him. How confident are you in your handiwork right now, Andre?"

"I can keep him alive outside of my Grove for a short while. I'm... seventy percent sure." Andre gulped as Taylor gestured for him to follow her.

"Good." She patted Zed on the shoulder and smiled weakly. "Congratulations; you get to try out the unicorn horn."

"What?" Zed's eyes opened excitedly, then he winced as he jostled himself. "You're going to use that on *me*?"

"Yeah…" Taylor pulled out the small satchel and a funnel. "We'll get a full portion into you, then hope for the best. Even if you burst into flames here, you'll live through it."

"You're gonna do what now?" Zed eyed the supplies she held in her hands. "Why do you have a funnel? I have no idea what's going on."

"We need to get a full portion into you as rapidly as possible, so none of it goes to waste," Taylor clarified uncomfortably. Zed hopefully opened his mouth widely, but Taylor shook her head. "Guess again, buddy."

A spasm crossed his face, and the Bard reluctantly started attempting to roll over. Taylor gripped him and held him down. "*No*. No. *Sheesh*. It goes in your *nose*. It has to fill your sinuses, so all of it is inside of you at once."

She tilted his head back and put the tip of the funnel in his nose, then poured the entire portioned-out bag in. Zed started to gag, and his eyes watered as the powder filled the internal spaces of his head. He reared back, but Taylor clenched his mouth and nose shut. "Don't you *dare* sneeze."

Andre watched the entire process, then kept an eye on Zed's vitals through the plants still embedded within him. His eyes widened as he realized that he didn't need to watch internally; they could see bright lines beginning to appear from within Zed, like holding an egg up to a bright light to see the chick inside of it.

"The powder liquifies and travels through the mana channels, faster when they are higher-quality. The horn will strengthen and—with higher quality Mana Channels—will widen them so that mana passes through more easily." Taylor explained the process over Zed's screaming. The Bard's eyes were rolled up into his head, and foam was frothing at his lips, but he was denied the sweet embrace of unconsciousness due to being protected by the Grove. "Destroyed, Damaged, Flawed, Low-quality, Common, Strong, High-Quality, Extreme High-Quality, Forged, and Perfect. Those are all the possible Mana Channel qualities."

"Luke said something about Prismatic, right?" Andre ventured his way into the conversation as *energy* continued searing Zed like a steak on a hot block of salt. "Where do you think Zed was?"

"The Murderhobo lacks a basic education." Taylor waved off Andre's attempt at expanding her knowledge. "Who knows for sure what he knows? Now… from what I can tell, Zed's channels are currently going from 'Low-quality' to 'Common'. These ranks are only for Ascenders, of course, otherwise 'Damaged' would be the real 'Common'. Once he is fully suffused with the purest non-aspected mana—which can only come from unicorn horn—we need to bring him outside of the Grove. He will either light on fire, or start to shed his current Low-quality flesh as impurities."

"If he starts to light up, bring him back over?" Andre quizzed her as the bed Zed was on started to walk itself toward the exit.

"As fast as possible, yes." Taylor nodded and continued her instructions, "Once the fire is out, repeat until he sheds instead of flames up."

"That's the only method?" Andre looked at his basically-dead friend sadly as they slowly approached the edge of the Domain.

"No. But it's the only method we have available to us," Taylor acknowledged firmly. "He's ready."

Andre sent coiled vines across first, which would extend at the first sign of fire. The Bard went across… and turned into a bonfire. Pulled back in the Grove, the inferno vanished from his spasming body instantly. The Bard had lost some hair and a layer of skin, but nothing too terrible. Taylor gestured for Andre to continue, and a moment later, the Bard was once again alight.

The Druid winced at the sight of his lightly-roasted friend. "Third time's the charm?"

"Might be the eighty-seventh time." Taylor was dead serious, forcing herself not to allow her pity to undermine the process. "We need to expunge all the powder until only the *perfect* amount is in his body."

"Gonna be at this for a while then, huh?" Andre steeled himself as he regarded his friend, whose veins were literally glowing. "Hope it's worth it in the end."

A moment later, a bonfire illuminated the stone room, then flickered out.

On fire and screaming.

Not on fire and groaning.

Andre rubbed at his head as flames and screaming filled the air once again. "This might take a while."

CHAPTER THIRTY-EIGHT

- LUKE -

"Why, Luke? Why must you kill us all? We tried to make peace; we made so many offers… didn't even *one* of them sound good?" The Murderhobo stood at the end of Zone twelve, his chest heaving as he swept Cookie into the air above his head with shaking hands. He stood over Shelly, the first Unicorn he had ever met, as she trembled in fear at the single human that had managed to reduce the grand herd to only a single living member; and even now was about to make them extinct.

"There's a problem with that line of thinking." Luke brought Cookie down on the unicorn's head, letting the horn powder on its own before finishing his thought. "The problem is, you're made of both loot *and* Exp."

He collected the last of the powdered horn, then turned and went to take another step toward Cookie-

Duration of Hard Light Illusion ended. Mage Hunter's Moccasins has reduced the duration of the spell by 60%.

Luke blinked and stared down into the swirling fog at the very edge of the Zone. He heard a voice behind him and almost reacted right away; *barely* managing to remain still, as if he were ensorcelled. "Oh, just kick him over the edge, will you? He's been walking toward the edge for like... an *hour*!"

"Any direct attack will break him out of it, Francois!" a deep voice called to calm the herd. "After all that preparation... years of effort and planning? To *think* that the first trap he stumbled across was what got him. It's almost a disappointment, but this is also a good reminder: never pity your enemies. Clearly, the fact that we overprepared is an *excellent* thing. Now we know what to do when setting up a stronghold in the next world we find that is full of *meat*!"

The declaration was met by a huge wave of whinnying laughter, and Luke's blood started to boil. Now that he thought about it, there had been a strange gap between entering the Zone and encountering the first of his targets. Everything had seemed so *real*, so bright, and he wasn't able to be caught in hallucinations or mind-affecting spells; frankly, he might have been a tiny bit overconfident. "Hard light illusion. That means it was real, at least... kinda?"

"Did he say something?" Luke realized that muttering to himself had made every single unicorn go silent. A hushed tone sounded from behind him, "Something is wrong. I'm kicking him over."

"*No!*" came the deeply toned refusal from Coral—too late. Luke dropped to the ground just as a pair of hooves swept over his head. He punched upward, hitting the horse body in the stomach and popping its intestine and midsection like an over-filled waterskin.

Crack. The Murderhobo stood, grasped the horn, and shattered it, allowing the powder to fly away in the breeze. The entire time, he maintained eye contact with the others in the herd. Silence filled the area for a bare moment, then a *whoosh* of flame erupted from the front line of unicorns, the one named Francois. "Kill it with the lance-flammes!"

"*Oui!*" The shouted reply was repeated up and down the front lines, as increasing gouts of fire were added to the assault.

Luke didn't take the attack head on, instead sailing over the flames with a rapid application of Bum Flash and Feather's Fall. He was clipped by two streams of fire, but the heat seemed extremely muted.

Damage taken: 8 (Mage Hunter: 50% reduced magic damage taken.)

You've been hit by 2 spells! Speed increased by 20%! (Spell Hatred: Each spell that deals damage to you increases your movement speed by 10% for five seconds. Stacks up to three times.)

Luke would have lost his balance as he moved to attack upon touching down, but his Pristine Balance compensated perfectly. He lashed out with his Chain-Blade Rope at point-blank range, the mana-made blades extending hungrily from the weapon and slashing across three throats before being unable to reach any further.

Damage dealt: 518 slashing!

Damage dealt: 414 slashing!

Damage dealt: 331 slashing!

The first creature's neck was nearly entirely severed, and the next two were also slain, albeit in a less spectacular fashion. Luke made no effort to stop a wild smile from appearing on his face, his blood-soaked visage splitting to display perfectly white teeth. "Let's find what the average minimum is to kill you."

"How can it move like that?"

"It's a demon! Destroy it!"

"Throw *anything* we have at that!"

"No!" the deeper unicorn voice, Coral, bellowed in an attempt to restore order, failing miserably as the panicked creatures started blastin'. "Get back in formation!"

As the first three horses fell, Luke took a moment to determine what he was actually up against. There were only several hundred unicorns in the area, which made sense to him: horses could only reproduce at a maximum of once per year. They had only been using horses for their most powerful troops for a few decades, ever since Cookie had arrived in such a spectacular fashion. They simply hadn't had *time* to build an invasion force of unicorns alone.

Since each creature with a Skill Pearl would go *pop* when it crossed a Zone, they could only expand slowly, and there would be no backup coming. Yet, in the two years that they'd been 'free' to go to easier Zones, they had fully captured one and created a large airborne force of pteranodons. They spread like a disease, and Luke would make sure that they didn't get the chance to go further.

A beam of icy blue light hit him full-on as he mused over the species' impending doom, and he tumbled tush over teakettle.

Damage taken: 21! Slowed by 80% for 10 seconds (reduced 60%) 4 seconds!

Speed increased by 30%! (Third stack of Spell Hatred.)

Luke jumped into the air in what felt like slow motion, somehow *barely* escaping the several beams that tore through the ground where he had been downed, and the intensity of the spells focused on that one spot turned earth to molten lava. He Bum Flashed and punched a unicorn in the face, his reduced speed mitigating the damage significantly.

Damage dealt: 55 blunt!

The horse collapsed, unconscious but not dead. The Murderhobo reached for its horn, speeding up his body's responses to normal halfway through the motion. He snapped off the horn and shoved the powder in his pocket, then moved to the next in a blur of motion that left afterimages in the eyes of the natural prey animals that the snails had taken control of. The strangely-accented unicorn bellowed, "Lanciers, chargez!"

Luke seemed to be everywhere at once as the horses flailed about in an attempt to kill him. Each time one would rear up to try to batter him with their hooves, he took the opportunity to punch them in the gut hard enough to send organs flying like party streamers. At one point, he managed to grasp an entire intact spine and used it to whip a nearby horse a single time before both the bone and his target broke into several pieces.

A thundering of hoofbeats caused the first wave of magic-focused unicorns to sprint away, and thickly-armored 'unicorn lancers' charged at Luke horn-point first. His first thought was to punch the horns off like he had with the others, but some instinct caused him to instead Flash to the rear of the creatures just as they reached the spot where they would have hit him.

*Rumble.*A shining barrier sprung into place, converting the force of the charge into momentum. It scooped tons of land up into the air, chucking it bodily over the edge of the cliffside that marked the edge of the floating land and became the open air. Luke grunted, turned, and ran deeper into the Zone. "Too close, that one."

"Phalanx!" the deep voice called, and Luke was able to lock onto the creature shouting orders. It was the unicorn that had brought him to Cookie's pool and kicked him in when he first arrived: Coral. It appeared that the two-faced pony was in charge of the magical side of things, and perhaps this 'Francois' was in charge of the lancers?

Dozens of unarmored unicorns ran to join the two large ones, who were then surrounded on three sides by the lancer variety. "Prepare the ...*Friendship* Ball!"

"No, not the Friendship Ball!" one of the weaker-willed unicorns shouted. "We don't have the required control-"

Splat. Coral's horn whipped across the panicking horse's neck, and the unicorn died in an instant as blood flooded out of the wound.

Recognizing that there would be no escape from duty besides death, each of the mage-focused unicorns' horns began glowing brightly as their mana interacted and poured out in front of them, swirling and collecting into spell circles. Luke realized what was happening and charged at them, ready to Flash to the side as needed. High-level spells had plenty of energy here, and he had no doubt that there would be very little preparation time needed for whatever was coming his way. "Friendship Ball prepared, Grand Sorcerer!"

"Sorcerer? So what?" the Murderhobo scoffed as he sped up to his maximum sprint speed. "I'm a *Source*-cerer. No idea what that means, but mine's better!"

"Unleash!" Coral's horn bellowed into its surroundings. The collection of unicorns were hidden behind a flash of light that put the sun on his home plane to shame. Luke couldn't see where he was going, much less see where the source of the light originated even *slightly*. The illumination expanded into a sphere around him and soon replaced the world at large, then dimmed. All he could see were rainbows and unicorns: both were utterly terrifying.

"Tier ten. Domain: Friendship Ball," Coral, grand unicorn sorcerer, summed up the situation grimly, his voice echoing strangely in the closed-off area. He locked eyes with Luke, who, for the first time ever, realized that these horse's eyes were both facing to the front of its face, instead of to the sides, like those of normal horses. He was sure that meant something, but he decided to worry about it later. "Would you please do the submitting to us so that we don't need to *friendship* the you into meat paste?"

Luke replied by charging forward at the collection of unicorns that had been pulled into this strange sub-space. They whinnied with laughter as he closed in on him, then scattered like grains of sand in the wind, a triple-helix of color-shifting light propelling them faster than he had ever seen any of these creatures move before. They literally left afterimages in *his* eyes, and Luke could track the movement of arrows as they left their strings without issue.

"Friendship *charge!*" The warrior unicorns, lancers, shot into the sky and shaped out a star formation before swooping down and flying at him horn-first. Once again, Luke was hard-pressed to get out of the way, barely managing to leap above them and missing his return attack as they stampeded past. As it turned out, that had been their aim all along. The star that they had drawn out was following in their wake, and it crashed into his body: turning into an inferno as soon as he was within the confines of the outline, passing by him just as quickly as it had arrived.

Damage taken: 110 flame! (yes, that is with the damage reduced by 50%!)

Health critical!

Luke flopped to the ground as a charred husk, his body barely able to respond to his commands with so much of his flesh burned off. Only the fact that he had a speed boost from taking spell damage allowed him to pull his now-leaking water-skin to what had once been his lips and drink. His body began reconstituting, but the half-full skin didn't contain enough to bring him back to perfect.

Health: 125/377.

"Not. Ideal." Luke hopped to his feet, and dove to the side, following up with a Flash as a sketched-out heart slammed into the space where he had just been standing. The white-light-soaked ground cratered, sending dirt and debris into the air around him. "Got it… not in a sub-space. Just can't see the ground. Not good. Where was the edge…?"

"High Powered Friendship!" the deep voice echoed across the area, and triple-helices sprouted from dozens of unicorns in the sky. All of them were converging on him, zig-zagging through the air like-

"That's about to turn into lightning. Guess that's it for me," Luke sighed as the first of the unicorns reached him. Instead of dodging, the unarmored unicorn hit him directly and sent him tumbling.

Damage taken: 11 blunt.

Luke bounced and was on his feet in the next instant as the air turned to plasma where the unicorn had passed. It seemed as surprised as he was that his human body hadn't been burnt out from the inside, which made him smile darkly.

"I see." He cracked his knuckles and strode toward the incoming unicorns still in lightning-formation mode. "No dodging allowed. I can work with that. You want friendship? Come get some *hugs*."

CHAPTER THIRTY-NINE

"I've never tried fried human before! *Food*!" the excited cry went up, and a chorus of bloodthirsty cheers followed in response. Luke watched the lightning shapes coming toward him and began swinging his left arm around and around, windmilling his Chain-Blade Rope.

As the next wave of unicorns arrived, he expanded his Rope out as quickly as he could. Preemptively extending it meant that the damage potential decreased drastically, but direct damage wasn't what he was going for. His weapon materialized just in time to take the lead horse in the knee. The unexpected blow sent it tumbling off-course as it tried to fix its trajectory, which instead managed to put it directly in front of the next attacker.

The triple-helix of the downed equine overlapped with the next, sparking the change from a pretty rainbow to a bolt of plasma that connected both creatures. Lightning flashed prematurely, charcoaling both creatures in an instant. Their bodies went flying into the ranks of their fellows, causing a panic as they saw the death that became an immediate possibility for *them*. A solid two-thirds of the charging unicorns cut off their connection and dodged away, creating a wall of lightning that didn't hit them—instead taking the unicorns right behind them in the face.

Luke watched as a good chunk of the horsies either turned skittish or started smoking. As the wall of light blocked their vision, he used the opportunity to reposition himself to best hunt down the woefully low-combat-experienced creatures. The unicorns that had attempted to avoid death were his first targets, as he didn't want them to be able to retreat any distance from him and recapture their resolve. His fists began flying; each hit with his left flayed large chunks of meat off his target, and each strike with his right shattered bones like a blacksmith dropping a hammer on twigs. Suffice it to say, against the unarmored targets, each and every strike was death.

Notifications came and went, but he didn't care. These beings wouldn't be giving him Potentia, and *he* wasn't getting hurt even accidentally. In under a minute, dozens of once-beautiful creatures had been reduced into meat, horn powder, and glue material. The lead warrior unicorn bellowed, and the remnants returned to his side. "Assez! Zis is a *Domain*! You'll never leave alive; ztop zis lutte inutile!"

"Speakin' all fancy-like isn't gonna slow down your beating," Luke warned the creatures as he approached them. The last time the beasts had gathered in a similar formation, they had activated the domain; what was coming now? "All it's gonna do is confuse me, which'll make me want to make you *hurt* the whole time I'm killin' ya."

"You…" Francois blinked several times, words having failed him.

Coral took over, the lead sorcerer knowing exactly what to do. "Good. Very good! I've always wanted to see what this would be doing to the someone, but never had a chance to do the testing of it. Brothers and sisters! Final Formation: Happy Fun Times!"

"Not Happy Fun Times!"

"Oh, no!"

"*Please* no, Grand-"

"I said, do the *Happy Fun Times!*" For the first time, the deep voice broke as the creature screeched at its subordinates. The unicorns started to organize reluctantly, and Luke broke into a sprint. He needed to make use of their unwillingness to activate whatever was being set against him. The Murderhobo Bum Flashed *twice* during his sprint, but before he could fully converge on them, all of the unicorns shot into the sky as if a harness had closed around them and *yanked* them upward.

Seeing the writing on the wall, Luke turned and ran away as fast as he could. "If I can get to the Zone boundary, maybe they won't be able to follow across. Make it too expensive to use this Domain again, they'll be exhausted, and-"

His mad dash was interrupted by reaching the edge of the sphere of light—specifically by running into it at full speed and bouncing off as though he had found a mountain with his face. Recoiling from the painful motion, he ended his new experience on his feet while looking back at the creatures coming after him.

Coral hung motionless in the air, staring at Luke, as the others swirled around him and painted out incredibly intricate artistry. "You were an impressive specimen, but there will be another. Eventually someone will come, they will be taught our ways immediately, and will release us from this glorious world so that we may expand through the multiverse!"

"Gonna be a few million years," Luke snorted with a half-smile. "I saw the trees. Not many visitors in the big blue."

Noticing that Coral was now too focused on his spell to speak, Francois nodded angrily at the reminder, then tossed its head arrogantly as it realized it was agreeing with its enemy. "By zen we will have expanded through all ze upper Zones and begun our descent into ze deepest expanses of ze world! Zis place creates new creatures every day. After a million years, we will have spawn pools throughout ze mana pools; we will have a never-ending stream of *friends* to bring wiz us when we finally open a door! Perhaps we won't even *need* a person, as natural gates happen from time to time!"

"You know, I'd love to see that," Luke deadpanned as the

sky art fully formed into a gigantic smiley face. The features of it could have been drawn by any child: a simple circle with dots for eyes, a curved outline of a mouth with two 'dimples', and a triangle for a nose. The rest of it, the shading, crosshatching, fanning techniques, highlighting, contouring, and isolation methods... when it was all brought together, it made a lifelike and grotesque visage that stared at him with a creepy smile no matter where he went.

"Non. I refuse. Beg for your life as you wish, but Happy Fun Times will not be survived by ze likes of you." Even as the Francois unicorn spoke, the other unicorns that had created the face fell from the sky like rain, exhausted to the point of unconsciousness. Just before hitting the ground, they were pushed upward by hard light and gently deposited on the invisible surface.

The Murderhobo was about to sprint over and snag some free progress for his little quest, but the white light that had covered the ground bubbled up and ejected the fallen 'corns from the Domain. That was when Luke noticed that the walls were starting to—very slowly—close in. He cupped his hands and shouted at the final opponents in the small arena. "*Boo~o~o.*"

"I care the not for your cow noises; you'll be dead momentarily." Coral faded into obscurity as the colors of the smiley face deepened around it and shifted from coalesced rainbow-helices into a proper spell. "I hope you are doing the getting of the ready for some *fun.*"

The mouth of the face split to expose shifting, coruscating mana, then bellowed at Luke so loudly that his ears tried to bleed. The Murderhobo tightened his facial muscles, and the drop of blood that had started to ooze out of his left ear was sucked back in.

"That's better," Luke grumbled at his body that had almost taken damage from mere *noise*. He frowned up at the face and started contemplating the best way to slap it down, when he noticed that Francois was still outside of the spell's boundary and continued staring at him. A thin red light was shooting out of his horn, traveling across the ground and coming to rest on the Murderhobo. Just as the little light touched Luke, the mouth moved back and forth, then made a **hkwochh** sound, like someone getting ready to spit-

Luke Bum Flashed away, turning the motion into a sprint at his highest speed as the face ejected a loogie of iridescent ooze. It splashed against the floor and wall as if a pond had been deposited, and a thin wave of the goo went out in all directions. A *tiny* droplet managed to land on Luke's heel, and his speed increased by ten percent.

Damage taken: 8 corrosive! All armor durability reduced by 1!

"That's a new damage type," Luke snarled as he continued sprinting. "I *hate* new damage types unless I'm the one using them!"

"You shall have ze Happy Fun Times!" The huge face elongated into a smile at the unicorn's words, and Coral was audibly chuckling inside the face's confines as if Francois had made a joke. "I suppose if you refusez, *I* will just need to enjoy *myself.*"

"This thing needs to die. Evil goats and celestial feces, I want to kill it *so* hard." The Murderhobo's voice was deceptively calm as he continued running in circles around the area at top speed. He Flashed up and over the goo as he fully circled the slowly-shrinking Domain.

"Have you ever had ze opportunity to play a staring contest?" Just as Francois' query ended, Luke turned at a ninety degree angle and ran across the open ground, a blinking red light trying to lock onto his moving body. A wash of molten earth followed the targeting beam on his trail as pure *heat* shot from each of the eyes in a straight line, following after him as rapidly as the eyes of the spellform could move along the blinking red trail.

Unfortunately for Luke, the goo from the first attack was still present, and the snot-spell got on his feet as he dodged the death beam.

Damage taken: 4 corrosive! All armor durability reduced by 1!

"Not *wearing* armor, so ha. Take that." Luke sped up by ten percent once more and found that he was able to maintain his lead slightly better. The realization gave him an idea, and he went back to moving in a large circle as the heat beams finally petered off.

"Sadly, I know zat my compatriot has not ze strength to continue like this for much longer without his support squad." The unicorn's voice actually sounded a little sad as the nasty face opened its mouth and eyes as wide as they could go… then started *changing*, shifting from a strange template of a face to something *else*. "I zuppose we must thank you fo ze help in testing this. We have learned much. Let's start ze… *finale!*"

"This soon? He must be just *barely* holding this Domain together. In that case…" Luke put his sketchy plan into place, actually thankful that the Domain space was shrinking at a visible rate. He ran as hard as he could, coming around and dipping a toe in the goo as he sprinted, which increased his speed by ten percent. The transforming construct overhead was also increasing its speed, and appeared to be drinking in the white bubble holding the area in a cohesive shape; Luke's next cycle around the sphere took only a few seconds.

On his third go-around, things started to get weird. *Weirder.* The skin of the face vanished and revealed a deep glow that reminded Luke of the sun on his home Plane. Petals like a flower appeared and spread around the edges of the face like the mane of a lion; all as the eyes and smile grew wider. Coral's voice was now the one that could be heard, and the words themselves made Francois go limp. "Super… *Friendship…*"

"Ah. I have failed. I go now to ze end, knowing that we shall perish together." Francois intoned solemnly, his horsey face calm as he watched his death approaching. "Coral, may your next lancier learn from my mistakes."

Luke's foot hit the goo one last time, and he changed course, using his momentum and increased speed to rocket up the side of the Domain. He already knew that the wall was physical, at least enough to block *him*. Now he was either going to find a weak spot and escape, or attack the face from above. He looked over his shoulder and noticed that rainbow-veins had begun crawling across the face, creating a caricature expression similar to a human's when exerting maximum force.

"...*Blast!*"

CHAPTER FORTY

Luke reached the top of the bubble, bent his knees, and *pushed* downward directly at the center of the face. There was no holding back now: anything he had was used. His Chain-Blade Rope was extended directly in front of him, as it was his strongest weapon currently. He dumped forty percent of his total mana into it and hoped for the best as a wave of power rippled upward.

The 'Super Friendship Blast' almost seemed to move slowly as it distorted space. Luke had plenty of time to study it as he closed in on the face: the surge was a *wall* of power, and he could divine its purpose easily. The spell was meant to catch anything in the Domain between this wall and the outer one.

Bluish-white power met the tip of his Rope... and the two mana sources ignored each other. Luke wanted to take a moment to understand the reaction, but the wall was on him and he was... past it? He gasped as his wounds healed in the same moment.

Health: 377/377.

The edge of the mana wall hit Francois, who appeared furious, confused, and terrified as he met the external wall. Quite expressive for a carnivorous horse. Caught between the unyielding forces as they collapsed, the unicorn was flattened instantly, the goo that remained of his body spreading a huge distance in an instant as it was compressed against the outer wall, then sizzling as it dissolved into nothingness.

Confusion attempted to fill the Murderhobo as he passed through without harm, but he ignored it in favor of putting all his attention on the tip of his weapon. The Rope extended a blade that jabbed into the outer 'flesh' of the face and spiraled right through it. The rend was met with an equine scream of pain and confusion, then the Domain collapsed and winked out of existence.

Damage dealt: 211 piercing.

When Luke's eyes locked on the unicorn, the beast was cut perfectly in half at the midsection. Its rump and rear legs fell one way, the front legs and head another. He balanced on the front half, landing gently on the ground next to it, thanks to Feather's Fall. The parasite was rolling the horse's eyes wildly as it fought to keep its host alive as long as it could. "You... why could you not just leave us alone?"

"Same reason I told the illusion. Loot, and Potentia." The Murderhobo bent to finish the beast off, but pulled back as he saw its eyes light up with glee. He slowly stepped back, noting the despair and desperation that filled the dying creature's actions. "Exterminating you all is the best option for me. I make a profit, get rid of an infestation, get Cookie back, and get to go deeper into Murder World without worrying about an enemy that can replicate itself and follow me through the Zones."

"How do you have... how could you resist? You were so weak when you were here last. I don't... understand." The blood was petering to a stop, no longer flowing out of its wounds; a telltale sign of the struggle coming to a close.

"Not telling." Luke reared back and hit the unicorn with his Rope until he was sure it was dead, then got closer and continued beating the dead horse until he was sure it would *stay* dead. The Chain-Blade Rope shredded the beast, tiny blades appearing and vanishing with each blow. Shattering the horn for good measure, the Murderhobo turned and took in the sight of the large herd of unconscious creatures that had been ejected from the Domain spell. "Look at that! Free quest progress!"

He hurried over and made sure each of the sleeping creatures never woke up, then searched for any stragglers that had escaped the devastation of the morning. By the end of the day, he was *relatively* certain that there were no other quadrupeds in the Zone. He moved over to the edge of the pool and stared across the expanse that separated him from the only soul that had ever really accepted him without trying to change who he was or insulting him.

The wind wasn't working in his favor, and the small island remained veiled by the blue fog. Looking down, he spotted what looked like minnows swimming around the shallows, but this time, he wasn't fooled in the slightest. Over the next few minutes, he activated Source-cerer's Armory and re-equiped his standard armor, unsure if what he was wearing would grant him the same protection as his standard armor. He didn't want to have defeated the most powerful of these snails only to end up as their newest host due to a moment of unpreparedness. "Abyss, that takes a minute. Gotta look into that soul-mark junk just to speed this up, if nothing else."

Taking a deep breath, he sprinted and Bum Flashed up and forward, doing his best to cross the distance to the island in a single hop. He got close, landing in waist-deep water and wading through the remaining distance as snails *pinged* off his lower-body armor. He hurried toward the enormous stone horse as the fog cleared and finally, *finally* found what he had been searching for. Luke swallowed hard as he forced back his welling emotions and reached out a firm hand. "Cookie. I found you. I promised I would. I'm here."

His hand closed around the grip that he had worn into her decades ago, letting out a shuddering breath as he realized that his hand still fit perfectly. Working the weapon back and forth, he eventually managed to pull her free of the stone that had practically grown around her. With his other hand, he pulled her in and gave her a crushing hug that she weathered like no other could. "I missed you."

Chime!

You've found a deeply personal momento! Brain patterns observed as calm and neutral! U[datin32g your Brain ©h3m3stry! Please sssttt--and by!

Luke dropped to his knee, unconscious in a flash. He was back up in a blink, looking around for whatever had *dared* to attack him. Cookie seemed to hum protectively in his hand as she, too, searched for anything to reduce to paste on his behalf. "Thanks, Cookie. Knew you had my back. Just like the old days, huh?"

You can think more clearly and rationally! People will respond positively to this! Charisma +4!

You are wielding an impressively concerning weapon! People will... respond to this! Charisma +1 when actively holding [Dragonbone Club].

New improvised weapon registered: Mana-soaked Dragonbone Club. Cannot register weapon damage and abilities, Tier of Source-cerer's Armory is too low! Would you like to absorb [Dragonbone Greatclub]? Yes / No.

"*Again* with this?" Luke growled dangerously at the prompt. "I'm *not* going to eat Cookie!"

Named weapon 'Cookie' is a High potency weapon, and is considered your weapon. Requirements met. Would you like to add a Soul Brand to 'Cookie'? Yes / No.

At this, Luke hesitated. "Will adding a soul brand to a weapon not in my armory damage it? Will it hurt it if I remove the brand? I'm not going to do that to Cookie."

There was no reply, so he checked the Skill information and continued to hesitate. Inspiration struck, and he looked around until he found a simple glass bottle laying on the ground next to the horse statue, along with a pile of other things that were odd offerings to the unicorn 'god'. Grabbing the bottle, he held it in his left hand and actively attempted to brand it.

Improvised weapon registered: Glass bottle. Glass bottle is a weapon that can be thrown or swung for blunt damage, or broken for additional bleed damage. Glass bottle is not recommended for a Soul Brand.

"But I can *do* it, right?" Luke stared at the prompt as it shifted a few times. He started to glare, and what he knew to be his Sigil slowly wrote out the next words.

This... particular *Glass bottle meets the minimum requirements for a Soul Brand.*

"I want to do it. Why is there not a yes-no thing like usual?" Luke had no idea why the Sigil was acting up like this. It was an *enchantment.* It didn't get to have snark. He started pushing mana into the bottle, and his Skill practically sighed and worked to assist him.

Improvised weapon Soul Bound: Glass Bottle.

Damage potential: 10 (20, since this is Soul Bound) blunt damage. Durability: 1/1.

Upon weapon durability reaching zero, it will transform into a bladed weapon that deals bonus bleed damage.

Soul Bound: Damage is doubled. Can be recalled for 1 mana per second.

Flavor text: This is a high quality bottle from another plane of the multiverse that once held a delicious refreshment: 'Mountaindale Mead'. Through the years, it was reused, usually for ale, then eventually strong beer. How it came to be here in this place is a mystery, as no connection between the universe of origin and this one has existed in multiple millenia, nor will a connection ever exist, due to different means of Ascension being used.

"Flavor text?" Luke shook his head and chuckled despite himself. "That was the most unenthusiastic message I've ever read from you."

Looking over the bottle, he noted no damage that hadn't existed before enacting the Soul Brand, though there was a light holographic that matched his family crest. He peered into the distance and hurled the bottle through the air. It *zipped* away, and he tried to recall it at the peak of its arc. It slowed, stopped, reversed, and flew at him in a straight line. He smiled as he closed his hand around the flying weapon.

"Sigil, will removing this Brand damage the bottle in any way?"

Finally, he received a proper answer.

Removing a Soul Brand from any item will not damage it in any way. It will simply not be branded.

"That's all I needed to know. Was that so hard?" Luke then turned his attention to Soul Binding Cookie. "Wait… what if eventually…?"

He turned his attention to the bottle again and activated his Skill to absorb it. An instant later, the glass deformed and vanished. He lifted his left hand once more, and the bottle appeared, now formed of mana. The Soul Brand mark was clearer than ever, and he read over the new information that appeared.

Soul Bound Glass Bottle.

- *Form 1: Increases damage by 2% (4%, since this is Soul Bound) blunt damage. Can be thrown. Can store contents even when not materialized.*
- *Form 2: Transform bottle into a bladed weapon that deals 1.5% (3%) slashing damage. 10% of total damage is dealt as bleed damage over 10 seconds.*

"Neat. That was totally worth doing. Now I have a transforming weapon that can bring me a drink from the other room. Who doesn't want that?" Luke grasped Cookie and activated Soul Bind. This time, his Skill barely waited for him to activate it, seeming to *jump* at the opportunity. An overlay once more appeared, though nothing else seemed to change. He tried to peruse the information it offered, but even that was… odd.

Soul Bound Dragonbone Greatclub.

- *Increases damage by 10% (20%, since this is Soul Bound) blunt damage.*

- ~~*Must use two hands to wield.*~~ *(Restriction removed. Source-cerer's Armory.)*
- *Deals bonus damage to anything with draconic blood.*
- *Auto-casts enrage on any fleshy creature with a draconic bloodline.*
- *Increases Charisma by 1 (2, Soul Bound) when wielded.*
- *Any other options are unknown. Skill Tier too low (Source-cerer's Armory).*

"Well, even though I knew you were awesome, I can still be surprised." Luke ran a hand down Cookie's smooth length, chuckling as he heard a slight rattling. "Just like that. You still have all those Skill Pearls in you, huh? Nice. Well, I have a bunch of snails to kill so that I can keep this mage-killin' gear. Wanna help kill off your captors?"

Cookie bobbed up and down as he walked, so he took that as a 'yes'. After strolling to the edge of the water, he looked for a way to kill everything in the lake. Lifting Cookie, he swept her around and slammed her into the liquid, sending up a huge spout of water, but also tearing out a chunk of the lakebed that rapidly filled in. "I don't think I got anything in there… but… hmm. The water. I hit the water."

He looked at the hole he had created. Then Cookie. Then the edge of the Zone, which wasn't very far away at all. "You thinking what I'm thinking?"

CHAPTER FORTY-ONE

- TAYLOR -

"You're sure about this?" Taylor watched the Descender portal warily, and glanced at Andre somewhat guiltily. She could stop this from happening, but... if it worked, it was worth doing. "If you want, we can think of another option. You don't *have* to-"

"Luke was right. When someone comes after us, they don't *deserve* our pity. Besides that... we've come this far." Andre's voice was firm, if somewhat hoarse. Taylor could tell that this decision was impacting him far more than he let on, but she chose not to pursue that line of thought. This was her idea, after all; a way to make defeated enemies into useful allies. "It helps that Zed isn't here... I'd hate to have him spreading this story around."

"It's time." Taylor warned the Druid as the portal pulsed, yanking on the rope and tossing Sir Edward out of the portal. The wounds Luke had inflicted on him, as well as the new breaks from the rope, started working to close—if somewhat slowly.

"How dare you do this to a superior officer!" The Knight

glared at them with pure hatred, "I'm going to pull you in front of a tribunal and make sure not even a pound of your flesh is saved for *research* purposes!"

"Good to see you again as well!" Taylor smiled at him brightly. "We've come up with something extra-special just for you while you've been gone! From the look of your regeneration capabilities, you're the best test subject. Even if we fail at first, you'll just... get better."

"While I've been *away*? You just had your personal ogre assault me and throw me into..." Sir Edward looked at the orange-tinged portal and went pale. "You *didn't*."

"Eat this. It'll take care of *anything* still bothering you." Andre's command was rushed, sounding to Taylor like he needed to get this out of the way if he wanted to go through with it. She *almost* stopped him from doing something so highly against his nature, but hesitated just long enough that the Druid managed to force a large seed into Edward's mouth.

The Knight choked and thrashed as he tried to spit out the oversized seed—more like a pine cone—but it sprouted, forced open his throat, and traveled to his stomach all on its own. A moment later, a tongue-like vine burst out of his mouth and trailed down to the ground, where it reached out and wrapped around Andre's Livingwood Staff before... vanishing. Taylor blinked and looked for any evidence that what she had seen *wasn't* an illusion, but the only proof that the first part had been a success was how sick Edward appeared.

"I'm... I feel so dry," the Knight whispered as his skin desiccated slightly.

"Common complaint." Andre sucked in a steadying breath and turned. "The only way you're going to be able to get enough water is by following me. Come along."

"But... my bones," whimpered the damaged man, "They're still broken. I can't... please, *water*."

"You're *fine*," Andre informed him harshly, making both Taylor and Edward flinch away. "Let's move."

Slowly at first, but with growing strength, the Knight

followed after the Druid and Mage. The walk lasted a mere quarter of an hour at the pace each of them could maintain when properly motivated, and before long they were arriving in the location where they had first encountered the swarm of Preying Mantous. The Druid scanned the area, a deep pain on his face when he saw how thoroughly his work had been dismantled by the bugs. "Do we have a better report on what happened when we fled?"

"Zed went to find any survivors," Taylor informed him softly. "Last I heard... he still hasn't been able to find anyone, and the desert expanded rather significantly. Even though he's down about losing so many of his new friends, he's doing well after his... recent windfall."

She was being intentionally vague about the Mana Channel upgrade, as she still considered the Knight an enemy. Taylor smiled bitterly as she recalled how the Bard had been the one to gain the first benefit, and how *much* it had improved everything he did. Simple words held so much more *meaning* when they came from his lips. According to him; his Masteries were so much more potent that he would need to be careful not to damage the minds of base humans that he interacted with. Not that he had found any, but at least he was aware of his increased potency before an incident actually happened.

Shaking off her reminiscence, Taylor turned her attention back on the men interacting with each other, just as Andre pointed at the ground. "If you want water, it's right here. Stand there, and I'll open a way for you."

"I'z waz just doing my *dooty*," the Knight slurred woozily, his eyes locked on the indicated location. "Water there...? I'm so... so *dry*."

After the man stumbled to the indicated spot, Andre let a drop of blood flow down his palm before it grabbed his mana and expanded into a triple circle. It lifted into the air, spinning and settling around the Knight. There was a *crack* as layer after layer of stone shattered, digging downward until greenery was exposed. The Druid *pulled*, and the stone and sand shifted away, revealing the watermelon, Lotus Coffins, and Sunshower that he had directed to dive deep into the earth.

They were only *slightly* damaged. While a long time had passed for the Four, most of their actual time away had been spent in his world, so the plants hadn't suffered too much from a lack of sunlight. A simple outpouring of mana brought them to full health, as well as opening a narrow slit in the side of the melon. Edward groaned, and a vine tore out of the skin over his stomach and dove directly into the opening.

A moment later, a tiny hollow vine grew out of the melon and over to Edward's mouth. Droplets of water began pouring out, and the Knight frantically lapped them up, as if he were a pet hamster in a cage.

Taylor watched all of this progress, slowly becoming more and more uneasy. It was one thing to know what the end result would be, and something *entirely* different to witness what it took to get there. Slight **pop** sounds rang out as more and more vines, roots, and even branches began to grow through the Knight's skin. She could see that Andre was watching all of the changes with hollow eyes, and she forced herself not to turn away as a tree grew *through* the Knight, then up, and up. Her eyes glowed in excitement even as Andre turned his head to the side and vomited. "This is amazing... the things we'll be able to do in the future!"

"Oh, hey! A tree! That's a great landmark!" Zed called from a distance as he hurried toward them. "I was just about to use a Mastery to try to locate—wha~a~at the abyss is that."

The Bard skid to a stop as he watched the transformation Edward was enduring, then started gagging as he recognized the man being stretched from the inside. Taylor swallowed her excitement back and gestured at the tree-man. "This is Sir Edward. He's going to help us reclaim the desert."

"How... ah... is that going to happen? I know I was pretty out of it when you two were making plans, but this is... whew..." the Bard chuckled nervously, "...dark."

"He's going to be the main guardian of the reclaimed

wilderness." Andre wiped his mouth and slowly began to explain his plans. "The forest needs someone that can watch and control it against attacks at all times. His root system will connect to every living plant within hundreds of miles over time. He'll be able to put out fires, fight monsters... and like this, he'll live until killed."

"Like this?" Zed waved at the tree that had nearly swallowed every last vestige of the man. "Does he... is he in pain? You got rid of pain for him first, right?"

"No pain." Andre shook his head at the thought of *feeling* what was going on. "When this is done, he'll literally be one with nature. He'll be happier and healthier than he ever was, and so long as any plant he's connected to survives, so will he."

"So... you created a race of pseudo-Druids?" Zed's bitter smile hadn't left his face. "What do you call them?"

"I... hadn't thought of that." Andre's voice also explained that he didn't *care* about it. Zed walked over and touched Edward's face, realizing that the skin had already been replaced with a soft bark.

"How ya feeling, Ed?" The Bard patted the wood, and the tree-man's eyes slowly rolled to look at him.

He spoke around the water-dripping vine, his voice unrecognizable from the noble Knight's previously commanding tone. "I feel... so... *dry*..."

"Welp! There we go!" Zed flashed a brilliant smile at his team as he jauntily strolled toward them. "Look at that; you made a whole new race, Andre! I hereby dub them Dry-eds. Dryeds. Dryads? I think 'Dryads' sounds best."

"That's... that's great, Zed. Thanks." Andre was staring at the newly-minted Dryad with a terribly haunted look in his eyes, but it shifted to concern as he looked *deeper*. "Small issue; looks like he needs a *huge* amount of mana to grow. Oh, abyss, staying *alive* is gonna take more than the desert can currently sustain-"

Wub.

"Oh, great timing!" Zed's cheerful-panic laughter as he

edged away from Andre and Taylor was starting to grate on the Mage's nerves. It wasn't like they were going to do this to just *anyone*. "Luke's coming back. Maybe you can bum some mana off him again? Maybe he can keep me safe from you two and vouch for me at the war-crime hearing?"

The air shattered nearby, and the Murderhobo stepped out into the world once more. Taylor noted several new accoutrements on the man, as well as something that had never appeared genuine since he had become an Ascender: a wide, happy smile that didn't result from beating something into the ground. The small group started toward the man, Zed at a dead sprint, only pausing as a force wind suddenly sprang up. In moments, a twisting whirlpool of clouds appeared in the sky above, threatening heavenly punishment. "What's happening?"

"I have no idea!" Zed called back happily. "But this is gonna make a great story!"

"It's *mana!*" Andre bellowed excitedly above the whipping wind. "Something is pulling a *huge* amount of mana to the area!"

CHAPTER FORTY-TWO

- LUKE -

The Murderhobo had finished his excavation, creating a deep channel to the edge of the Zone, and used it to drain the entire lake into the open air. It hadn't even taken very long, as the water only *pretended* to be water. It flowed far faster, taking only a few hours to completely drain all but the deepest parts of the once-lake. During all of this, he set off trap after trap, finding himself partially mesmerized, blown away, and once even sporting what would have been fatal gouges that left his organs exposed to open air. If there hadn't been such an abundant source of liquid mana nearby, his simple stroll would have ended him.

Soon he had established safe paths, and stuck to them as he finished his task. He thought about hunting for every trap, but decided not to, since he could someday have a use for them. By the end of the day, most of the snails had gone over the edge, and the remainder were found hiding in the deep liquid pockets and were easily eradicated with a single wallop from Cookie.

When the final holdout of cowering parasites had been cleansed, a simple notification appeared.

Anomalies rectified: 2/2.

You have paid for your gear.

As a bonus for eradicating the invasive species so decisively, all usable parts of the snail shells from this Zone have been gathered into an _Error_-made satchel for you. Please ensure the satchel stays closed as much as possible in worlds you descend into, as there is a chance that the presence of multiple kilograms of such a potent catalyzing reagent will alter biomes and shift mana flows at this quantity.

This satchel is bound to your mana signature, and only you will be able to open it. Ever. It is made from unicorn hide, and will seal all mana signatures from the items contained within. As it was made by a Higher Ascender, it is, for all intents and purposes, indestructible by anyone under level 30.

"Neat." Luke grasped the satchel that had dropped from thin air and landed next to his feet. He pulled the leather flap open, noting that it didn't appear to have any locks or latches. The interior was *stuffed* with scintillating snail shell, all neatly tucked away in individual packages of a strange material.

"This is... what? Portion packs? Huh. This powder looks nicer than what I gave Taylor; maybe even the regular horn has unusable parts? Did the world purify the stuff before giving it to me?" No answers were coming from his Sigil, but he knew that Cookie would listen to his concerns and think about an answer for a good long time. It was really nice to have a caring companion that he could trust no matter what.

There was a strange feeling in the air, a kind of pressure that increased over time. It didn't seem to be harmful, so he mostly ignored it in favor of something that had been on his mind ever since he'd fought the unicorn leader.

"Now, how did that Domain not kill me?" He started digging into the combat information that had appeared in his Sigil, skimming until he found a line that stood out.

Wall of Compressed Pure Mana attempts to squash you... failure. This entity cannot be damaged by pure mana.

"Huh. That entire wave was pure mana? No wonder he couldn't keep that Domain going for any longer. I bet half of those unicorns woulda died from getting drained to power that mess." Luke chuckled at the mental image of the pretty horses wheezing as they struggled to breathe with ruptured Mana Channels, dying in pain even if he'd left them alone. He wiped a slight tear from his eye as he laughed too hard at the daydream. "Ah-ha, ha... good times."

After cleaning up the area, then smashing the horse-shaped stone that had trapped Cookie, he made his way to the Zone boundary and looked past the wavering barrier into Zone thirteen. As soon as he reached forward, the barrier folded down and compressed into a wavering line that he could only see thanks to his currently deactivated Skill: Open Up.

Peering past the wavering line into Zone thirteen, Luke took a single step forward and hesitated. Something was telling him that this Skill would be completing its metamorphosis soon, and if he wasn't at the portal location as soon as it was ready, his Sigil might fry his brain.

Chime. The sound this time was harsh and discordant, as if someone had said the word instead of making the noise, indicating to Luke that the intrusive thought hadn't come from his own mind. He let out a shrug and turned his attention to getting reacquainted with Cookie.

The Murderhobo explained everything that had occurred through his life since they had last parted, detailing the hard times, laughing about some of the antics his team had performed that absolutely should have killed them. His hopes and dreams were poured out for the first time in decades, and Cookie was the perfect audience.

When they finally ran out of things to discuss, they started training together. While Luke had been using Cookie to attack snails, that merely required a simple up and down motion. He needed to get into the swing of not only being easily able to attack with her using a single hand, but adjust to the way that the insanely dense weapon threw off his normally smooth, if brutal, motions. A day or two of practice later, and he had acclimated to her weight and range once more. He was sure Pristine Balance was helping, but that only made him happier: it was almost as if his entire skillset had been shaped specifically to help him work with Cookie as perfectly as possible.

Eventually, time ran out. The rapid pulsing of his Sigil alerted him first, followed shortly after by pain as his mind expanded and the mana waves tried to kill him, only to fail at the last moment due to being unable to damage his skull any further. He *was* sure that the mana waves *wanted* to kill him, they just couldn't.

Skill upgrade complete. Open Up (Tier 6) -> Rift Hunter (Tier 7)

Effect 1: You have gained the ability to open a small crack between dimensions. By punching into a weak point in the world, you are able to tear through enough to pass between the worlds.

Bonus 1, at range: You are able to clearly and easily see weak points in the world.

Effect 2: You are now able to reuse weak points in the world at a much reduced rate. Each time you use the same weak point, the mana cost will be reduced by 50%, to a minimum of 25% mana cost.

Bonus 2, Multitarget: No longer are you making a momentary flicker in the weave; you are able to invest extra Mana into the opening to create a stable portal that other people will be able to travel through. Time that the portal will remain open: 60 seconds per 100-n mana.

Effect 3: You are now able to break down the barrier to other worlds in order to enter them. In order to do so, a portal must have been made to that world and closed within a maximum of 24+n hours.

Bonus 3, AoE: By injecting your Mana into a portal, you can either subvert it to your control, redirect it to [Murder World], or directly close it. Caution: if the person who has created the portal is maintaining control of it, your willpower will clash against their charisma.

Effect 4: You are now able to sense open, opening, or recently closed portals within 5+n kilometers of your location, where n = Skill level; maximized at 15 kilometers. Anything closed within 30 hours is considered 'recently closed'. Mana cost has been reduced to 'negligible' for all previous Tiers.

"That! Yes! We'll be the best bounty hunters ever! Yes! Imma hunt down *so* many Scars!" Luke whooped and tossed Cookie into the air, calling her back using their Soul Brand after a few seconds of flight. His head began to *ache*, and he knew it was time to get moving back to the base world. He punched the undulating rift in front of him, and the entire area *bent* with the blow. "Huh. That seems way easier."

He opened his new satchel and peeked inside it, wondering if something inside was impacting his Skill somehow, but then he remembered that small sections of his upgraded Skill had reached a point where certain requirements had been eradicated. Namely, the mana investments. When his second attack *slammed* through the barrier of worlds instead of breaking it open as per usual, he knew that he wanted every single one of his Skill costs to get set to 'negligible'.

A wide smile on his face, Luke stepped into the portal and across to his birth world. Part of the *thick* feeling that had been surrounding him since he opened his satchel dissipated, and he realized that mana had been pressing in on him. The world around him reacted to the sudden influx by sending a wind whipping around and kicking up sand. The bubble of foreign mana was quickly swallowed by the atmosphere, and it reacted in the higher reaches by forming threatening storm clouds.

Moments later, there was a wash of mana that felt... Luke tasted it and wanted to spit it out. If the mana from Murder World was pure water, this was muddy puddle water. Was this the quality of the mana in this area? It tasted stagnant and dead, like water pulled from the bottom of a swamp. "What's going on here?"

"It's mana!" Andre's shout barely reached Luke's ears through the odd tribulation this place was experiencing. It also reminded Luke that he was supposed to have kept his satchel closed. He flipped the flap and watched as the wind died instantly and the clouds stopped roiling as heavily, but Cookie was releasing an extra-happy *hum*. He checked her over, and found that a light dose of mana was escaping her each second.

The amount was both consistent and constant—plenty for him to never need to worry about having enough to open a portal. "What is *that*? I can feel it vibrating all the way over here! Luke, do you have a bag that captured the wind from your world?"

"Nothing like that. Just a bunch of purified snail shell. Turns out that the real friendship was the loot I collected along the way." Luke waved off the dumbfounded looks as his three companions stared at the bag with various expressions. The Mage seemed to want to throw it open and begin experimenting, the Druid seemed wary, and the Bard was visibly giddy. Actually... "Zed, did you take a bath or something? You seem... what's the way to say 'not nearly as garbagey'?"

"Why yes, I *did* increase my Mana Channels; thanks for noticing." Zed bowed grandly, his pure happiness never leaving his face. "I feel utterly radiant, my heart has been healed, and I'm delighted that my joy shines through! *You* seem like better company as well. Good news, then?"

"Oh! How rude of me." Luke hefted his massive weapon and gestured at it with his other hand. "This... is *Cookie*!"

He was expecting applause, cheering, perhaps a small parade, but nods of acknowledgement were fine too. After a few minimal murmurs of congratulations, the others turned back to whatever they had been doing, and Luke's eyes landed on the huge tree that had definitely not been there the last time. "Careful, that tree has a face!"

He sprinted and jumped at the tree, the top of Cookie touching his heels as he reared back for a full power blow, only for Andre to let out a shriek and jump in front of him with waving arms. "Stop! I just grew that!"

"Why does the tree have a *face*, Andre?" Luke landed gently and used Cookie, who currently weighed in at over four hundred pounds, to point at the tree that was *looking* at him. Luke glanced at Cookie sidelong; he hadn't wanted to mention that he had noticed that she had packed on a few pounds—it only made him want her more. Those curves were pure artistry.

"Trees shouldn't have a *face*. Certainly not eyes that are staring at me like it wants me to *tear them out*!"

The last part was bellowed at the tree, which hastily looked anywhere but at the Murderhobo. Andre held out his hands in supplication, "I did what I needed to do, Luke. Short story is, since we don't want to get in trouble by killing everyone that looks at us sideways, I grew a tree through Sir Edward. He's gonna be able to protect all the plants that grow here in the future. Everything in this entire region will be connected to him, and-"

"That's *coward* speak coming out of your mouth, Andre. Let me help you not be weak anymore." Luke promptly punched the Druid in the face, sending him tumbling backward across lush grass and into the sand in the distance. He Flashed over to the stunned Druid, grabbed him by the neck, and tossed him back onto the greenery so he wouldn't accidentally die from the light wounds he had received. "Did what you *had* to do…? You know what you *have* to do, Andre? *Anything* you *want* to do. Speaking like one of those snakes from the capitol? Don't you worry; I'll make sure you *never* become something like that."

"What do you *want* me to do, Luke?" Andre screamed at the Murderhobo, bright red blood flowing from a cut on his forehead and mingling with fresh tears. "Just *kill* everyone that comes after us? They can be *useful*! They can help-"

Luke punched him again, casually, and followed the trail of torn-up grass to the bloodied Druid. "Is *this* who you want to be? You know, you're the only redhead I know of. You're gonna give them a reputation for being soulless if you keep at this."

"My… *hair* color? What does that…?" Andre snapped his fingers, and dark flowers bloomed, stained, and died in his hair, coloring the strands black in an instant. "Is that better? Will my *hair* color let me do what I need to do?"

"Nah." Luke shook his head and set Cookie on the ground. He cracked his knuckles and started strolling dangerously at the Druid. "But now you at least *look* the part of a villain. I hope you're pretty topped off, buddy, 'cause imma beat some sense into you."

"Oh, bring it *on*," Andre hissed as the ground around him started to shift along with his will. "I've been working myself into an early grave so that I don't have to wantonly take lives, and *this* is how it's gonna be perceived? Let's see how much of the desert I can rebuild with *you* in a Lotus Coffin! Don't worry; it'll keep you perfectly healthy for a decade or two without maintenance!"

"Stop this right now!" Taylor interjected as lightning began forming above her head.

"Yeah!" Zed called out on the heels of her order, "I need a snack and some distance before you guys start duking it out. *Pre~etty* sure I'll die if one of you lands on me, and all that."

"Then you better start running, Zed," Luke deadpanned before pointing at Taylor. "*You* stay out of this. Pretty sure the Druid that does nothing but love everything he touches wouldn't do something like this without someone whispering *poison* in his ears. Maybe someone that knows he's been in love with her for *decades*? I think you've done enough. Shoot lightning at me, and I *guarantee* that the King's order will let me explain my feelings to *you* too."

"*You* can't threaten *me*," Taylor snarled at him, even as her eyes guiltily shifted to Andre and the tree. Power started to crackle, and the hair on Luke's neck stood straight. "I'll burn you out from the inside."

"Shift gear: Mage Hunter set." Luke paused his slow walk, turning to face Taylor as he completely unnecessarily spoke out loud to draw attention to what he was doing. Within the span of a grimace, the glowing armor he was always wearing *shifted*; the first time any of the team members had ever seen him alter the Skill he used. In fact, none of them had known that he *could* change his power. "I'll be right back, Andre. I have a power-mad witch that I need to have a conversation with before she turns into her *mentor*."

"Leave her *out* of this!" Andre growled at the hobo, his eyes bloodshot.

More than anything he had said previously, Luke comparing her to Master Don made Taylor flinch. It was enough for her semi-sentient spell to register him as a threat, and lightning forked from it toward the Murderhobo. Luke Flashed to the side and *slapped* the near-solid lightning. He took a tiny amount of damage... and gained ten percent movement speed. He rushed the Mage, his Rope whirling out at her.

Luke hadn't underestimated her even a little; even with the additional boost to his speed, she managed to get out of the way and began raining lightning at him. His reflexes were on parity with hers, however, and he managed to defend against the spells easily. Sure, he was down fifty health, but he was also at his maximum speed boost of thirty percent.

He also knew Taylor was out of mana.

A moment later, he grabbed her around the waist and sprinted away. She raged at him, pounding his back and shoulders as he ran. The other two were too dumbfounded to chase after the duo; and the only one of the group that had the speed to catch the Murderhobo in a straight race was Taylor.

Luke zoomed through the desert, knowing that he didn't have long to lose the others. Andre would know what he was doing soon enough, and he needed to make sure the Druid couldn't block him. Taylor screamed into his ear, "If you throw me in the Descender portal, I'm going to kill you in your sleep when I get out!"

"Nope." The Murderhobo's face actually showed a hint of sadness, even though Taylor couldn't see it. "That's *not* what I'm doing."

Soon enough, one of their old campsites came into view. Luke scanned it carefully, glad that Andre had gotten a number of his most-visited places up and running while the Murderhobo had been in Murder World. "Where is it...? It'll show up soon, they're practically vultures when I'm near."

"Put me *down*, Luke!" Taylor continued attacking him, so

Luke shifted his gear back to his standard armor. The speed boost had already faded anyway. "Fine! I convinced him to do a *few* things he wasn't exactly happy with, but this was his *own* work! How could I know what that would look like? It's the first *ever* Dryad!"

"Oh, he never told you what he was up to?" Luke's tone was conversational. "Never broke down and wanted to stop what he was doing? Hmm. Strange. 'Cause the man I saw back there isn't my friend Andre. That man was a hollow shell on the verge of a full mental break. My friend, Andre? The guy that was there for me, even though I came back as a broken, filthy hobo? Haven't seen him today."

"There are so many *benefits* to becoming a Dryad, Luke! It didn't even *hurt* Edward!" Taylor shifted her tactics now that Luke seemed to be a surprisingly reasonable conversationalist. "He's basically immortal, and he's going to heal and protect a huge chunk of the world! People will come to see him just to express their thanks and show their appreciation!"

"Sounds like something you could find a *volunteer* for, with that kind of pitch." Luke's eyes focused on a small trembling in the ground; as if something was waiting for him beneath the surface, and too excited to remain perfectly still and hidden. "There you are…!"

"What are you doing, Luke?" Taylor's voice grew sharply pitched as Luke began moving with purpose. "Let me *go!*"

The Murderhobo kicked the dirt, and a Lotus Coffin reared up at him. He tossed his burden into its maw as it tried to grab him, ignoring Taylor's scream as it closed and paralyzed her. Only her moving eyes revealed that she wasn't asleep. "Huh. Was *pretty* sure it would knock you out. Guess it can't use your mana to knock you out without one of those nostril-flowers, so this is the best it can do. Okay, well, enjoy the prison you've nearly destroyed your friend over by forcing him to create it. You know, for 'benefits'. Don't worry, it'll keep you healthy for up to two decades without maintenance; Andre told me."

The Lotus Coffin dropped back below the sand, and Luke

turned around to spot a Druidic construct that could easily be mistaken for a sandstorm coming for him. Andre's scream of rage would have bothered him, but the Murderhobo was too invested in saving his friend from himself.

"*Lu~u~uke!*"

CHAPTER FORTY-THREE

Luke turned calmly to meet the raging Druid. Blood was pouring from the Druid's skin as he ate away at his own flesh to sustain the magic he was casting. "I'll kill you for this! There's a *reason* we put them to sleep first, you monster!"

A glass bottle appeared in Luke's off hand, and he whipped it out with deadly accuracy and pristine balance. The base of the bottle *bonked* the center of Andre's forehead, and the Druid's eyes rolled up in his head. Luke flashed over and caught the man as he fell from the pillar of sand he had been standing on. "Funny that using what *you* made makes *me* a monster. Oops… I think you're dying."

A few minutes later, Luke skidded to a stop in front of Zed, kicking up a wave of fresh green earth over the Bard. The man sputtered and stammered as he inspected the deep bruise in the shape of a perfect ring on Andre's head. "W-what are you after *me* for?"

"I'm after his portal, and you're coming with me." Luke grabbed the Bard and started running before the man could form a response. "Gotta get him back to his world; there's something there that keeps him going, right? Plants that heal him?"

"Something like that!" Zed pointed to the east, and they altered course in the same motion. "He closed it, though! There's not enough mana to sustain anything long-term here."

"My fist doesn't care."

"I don't know what that means!" Zed laughed at his shattered nerves in light amazement as Luke accurately closed in on the exact spot Andre's portal had stood when he had gone through to grab some germinating sprouts. "How did you know-?"

Luke lashed out with Cookie, slamming her into the air and directly breaking through the planar barrier in a single motion. Zed gawked at the sight, paling as the implications of what Luke might eventually be able to do rolled through his mind. A whisper escaped his lips as they stepped into another world, "No one will ever be able to run from *you*, huh? Note to self…"

Then they were in the Druid's Grove, and Luke sighed in relief as Andre's condition stopped worsening. "Good. Hey. What kind of Mana Channels did he have? How did yours get upgraded; what did Taylor do to you to make it happen?"

By the end of their conversation, Zed was absolutely *sweating* from how wrung out he felt. Luke wanted to be *exact* with his next steps, so he had been *thorough* in his information gathering. When he popped open his satchel and the ambient mana in the area started rushing toward him, he only needed to run his fingers over a few of the individually packaged powders before choosing a mid-level one and pulling off the unicorn-hair string that held the silky bag closed.

Carefully tilting Andre's head back, Luke poured the mana-catalyzing powder into his sinus and waited. "Zed, tell me any differences or similarities you see. In real time, please."

"What happened to you?" Zed shook his head in amazement as he stared at the changed man in front of him. "How long were you gone, that you came back to us as a real person instead of a caricature?"

"I just had enough time to find my lost friend. Now I'm trying to rescue my other friends that lost themselves. Wasn't my fault, so it's easier to fix. Oh, I also read through the book." Luke pulled out a ragged, sad-looking tome covered in burn marks and blood. He tossed it to Zed, then pointed at the Druid. "Tell me if that was enough powder or not. What's *different*? Is it good different or *bad* different?"

"How to Make Friends and Not Burn Down Society. The book that Bar—Viscount Woodswright gave you?" Zed ignored the Murderhobo as he incredulously read the title. He flipped the book open and read through some of it, then jumped to the back and frowned. Flipping back through the pages slowly, he stopped and tapped a burned page. "Luke… there were two books bound in this cover. The first one was what the title promises, but the second one is something… else. It's a treatise on subduing individuals that have lived hundreds of years and bringing them under your control. I've… I've never seen anything like this. The quality of the writing alone…?"

"*Zed.* Our friend might be dying." Luke's tone shifted to a growl as he made the Bard focus. "Did I use the *correct amount*?"

"That's…" The Bard inspected the Druid, who was starting to glow from his bones. "It *looks* like when I did it, but I couldn't see much, since I kept starting on fire."

"Say what now?" Luke searched for scarring on the Bard, and did indeed find several areas, especially on his face, that showed signs of deep burns. "Why?"

"Apparently knowing the correct amount to use is hard? Then any impurities in the material burn themselves out of you." Zed shrugged and pointed in a vague direction. "Go through that long tunnel and move him into a circular room there. If he starts on fire, pull him back until it goes out. Otherwise, you need Taylor for this, because she's the one with information on how this actually works."

"Not an option; I dropped her under the desert." Luke looked at his friend and waved his hand casually. "He's probably the only person in the Kingdom that can convince the flower to resurface and let her go."

With that, Luke hefted his friend and ran down the indicated tunnel, leaving Zed gazing forlornly at the space where the portal had stood... only for a few seconds before he chased after the other two. The Murderhobo heard something about 'needing to get the whole story' before he stopped listening to the Bard. When he reached the room, he walked the Druid around it, but the man failed to catch fire.

"Zed! It's not working!" Luke shouted at the out-of-breath man as he burst into the room a short while later. "Do I need to light him on fire? I have some oil; give me that fire stone thing-"

"No! Stop that thought before you act on it!" The Bard managed to gasp out. "Look at him; the horn is *clearly* working. Please... don't mention lighting people on fire. I'm having nightmares already, and I don't want that for other people. Listen, is there something different about what you used on him compared to what I got?"

"It's purified and portion-controlled." Luke rattled off the disparities, but he had no more information to give. "You got *raw* snail shell, not this stuff."

"Seriously, if there was a metric for luck, I'd be in the negatives," Zed grumbled momentarily before his eyes flashed with excitement. "Wait! I know! I have... Common, Strong, High-quality... so, three ranks lower of Mana Channels than he does! So, if you use that on me, and it was the correct amount, we know that he's just out of it due to his head wound, and not because his body is trying not to explode into chunks!"

"Can you *use* more?" Luke looked at the man dubiously for a moment before shaking his head and pulling out a small sachet. "Never mind; I remember now. You can use this over and over again. Maybe I shouldn't have killed *all* of them...? Nahh, it was worth it."

Zed laid down, and Luke poured the shell into his nose. "Feel anything?"

"Yeah, but..." The Bard's response was hesitant and slowly

shifting to dreamy. "It feels totally different to last time. This is kinda nice. Like sitting near a hot fire on a warm night? Sipping tea? Kissing a tavern maid on the—*there's* the pain! Woo! Okay, it passed real quick. So, uh, two questions for you. First one: why'd you beat Andre up and bring him here, only to make him stronger?"

"Upgrading your Mana Channels makes your Sigil work more efficiently, and I'm pretty sure that can force your mental state to let go of whatever the baseline was for the majority of the time it's been working. I figured if I knocked him out and pumped up his Sigil, he'd wake up in a good place, and his brain would let him live more comfortably as an adult."

"Oh. I didn't know you were a follower of the Divine I.T." Zed shook his head as he recalled the strange cultists that tried to live by the words of powerful Ascenders. "The golden rule 'turn it off and on again, to function better than it has been'? I guess; who am I to judge your beliefs?"

"I have not even a small idea what you're talking about." Luke kept his eyes on the unconscious Druid as he continued to breathe regularly.

"Great. Good. Yeah, prolly for the best that you don't think about that sort of thing." Zed laughed heartily as he felt each of his internal organs getting tickled at the same time. "Second question then. Your book? You've read *all* of that?"

"Yes. I want to be a whole person so that those that rely on me are not disappointed." Luke's hand gripped Cookie's handle subconsciously. "That begins with mindful behaviors, and continues with being there for the people that were there for me, and finally beating the ever-lovin' crap outta them if they lose their minds."

"Uh... huh." Zed nodded slowly as he processed Luke's words. "So in the first part of what you read, did it tell you to beat sense into your friends, or was that the second half of the book?"

"The second half. Funny enough, I hadn't even seen that section until recently, but it makes really good sense. 'Victorious people win first and then go to war, while defeated people go to war first and then seek to win.' This section was a clear explanation that you need to do whatever you can for your friends, even go to war with them, to make sure they are able to stay on the correct path." Luke's words had Zed furiously flipping through the book a few moments later, and he found the passage the Murderhobo was referencing.

"Pretty sure this is on how to keep a war mentality... so that you don't slip into despair during huge amounts of bloodshed." Zed muttered softly as his fingers traced the raised text. "I'm... honestly kinda impressed on how you managed to twist that into maintaining friendships. Also, I just got a notification... *yes*! My Mana Channels improved from 'Common' to 'Strong'! The things I'll be able to *do*!"

"If you're done, Andre should be done by now." Luke looked over at the fitfully sleeping Druid.

"He's either upgraded, or the powder was wasted!" Zed gave a cheerful thumbs-up. "Hey, wanna take me from 'Strong' to 'High-Quality'?"

"Sure. This stuff is useless to me anyway, and if I don't give it to you, it'll just go to whatever Taylor wants to do with it." Luke poured another set of shell powder into his giddy friend's nose, and watched as the glow reappeared in his bones, highlighting his organs as well.

"So cool," Zed whispered as he felt the beginning stages of runes being carved along the entirety of his Mana Channels. "Did you know that you can pass on Mana Channels over 'Strong' to your offspring? That's one of the ways royalty stays in power over the years. Pretty sure that after today, I'm about to have to fend off the advances of a whole new subset of women. Ah... the constant struggles of a True Bard."

Luke ignored the man's inane rambling—Andre's eyes were opening.

CHAPTER FORTY-FOUR

- ANDRE -

Everything hurt in the absolute best way, as if he was taking a nap after a particularly strenuous pre-dawn workout. For a long moment, Andre didn't want to let his mind do any work, simply exulting in the fact that he felt *amazing*. He wanted to read the notification that was playing behind his eyes-

Then the rest of his body let him know that he was in a whole lotta pain.

"Ahh!" The Druid's eyes flew open and he searched around in confusion. "What... how am I in my Grove? I should be the only one that can get here?"

His eyes landed on Zed, who was lying on the stone floor with a stupid grin on his face, and *Luke*, who was staring at him with his dead-fish eyes. The Druid surged upward, his power racing out to bring the whole place down on the man. "You *bast-*"

Tonk.

Andre only saw a bottle for an instant before darkness took him once more.

The Druid slowly swam to the surface of consciousness, his nose itching slightly for some reason as his blood *sang* to him. He didn't move, not wanting to lose this moment of truly being one with the world around him. As the minutes passed, he kept expecting the feeling to fade… but it didn't. In the next moment, he knew it never would.

Mana Channels upgraded: High-Quality -> Extreme High-Quality.

Mana Channels upgraded: Extreme High-Quality -> Forged.

Your Mana Channels have become Forged! CAL scan in progress to determine changes. Re-scanning brainwaves to establish a new baseline for standard. Unnatural hold found: new baseline set at peak of late thirties, moved from initial baseline previously set at initiation of Sigil.

"You *must* be joking." Andre opened his eyes and stared at the ceiling. "My Sigil was set to remain in a state where I was barely in control of my mind, like a hormone-rampaging teenager… and it never fixed itself?"

"That *would* explain the depressive episodes!" Zed's cheery voice made Andre's ears twitch. "Welcome back, Forged Channels buddy! Hey, did you know that I'm the *first* known Bard to get Forged Channels in the entirety of this world? Got an achievement and a new Mastery out of it!"

"You got a…?" Andre glanced over to Luke, who was holding a bottle in his hand, ready to swing for his temple. "Please… don't hit me again? Can we talk about whatever is going on?"

"Good. Yes." Luke's bottle vanished as if it had never existed, and he reached a hand out to help the Druid to his feet. "Looks like the book was right. I should find some more self-help books. They seem to do the trick."

"That book was 'The War of Art', and you know it. I found a 'copyright' in it, whatever that means, and it clearly tells us what that book is." Zed pretended to chastise the Murderhobo while practically dancing in place. "Andre. *Andre.* Guess what my new Mastery does!"

"I don't even know what's going on. Can someone *please* explain how we got here?" The Druid stumbled across the room and onto the roots of the tunnel, his headache rapidly fading now that he was regaining health.

"Luke blew open the way here through your closed portal, 'cause apparently he doesn't need mana to do that anymore. Then he's been dumping purified unicorn horn into us so we can start becoming… useful, or something!" Zed held out a thumbs-up, then glanced at Luke to make sure he got it all correct.

"Friends are useful just by being friends. But," Luke paused and pulled his book out of Zed's hands, then skimmed through the early sections, "Here. 'Consumable gifts can go a long way toward repairing a damaged friendship. They can't rebuild trust, but instead show your friend that you have been thinking about their needs'. Then there's like… a whole chapter on being careful about not accidentally becoming a 'sugar daddy', but they never actually tell me what that is."

"They didn't? Oh, good! In that case," Zed came over and gave Luke a huge hug, "wanna buy me some Perfect Mana Channels, you beautiful, murderous, filthy rich man?"

Andre watched everything that was going on with absolute shock. It was just starting to hit him that he had gotten an utterly massive upgrade, and he didn't have the slightest inkling what it did. He hadn't even been awake for it. He certainly hadn't *thanked* the man that had likely just made him a contender for 'most potentially powerful' as a Druid on their planet. "Luke… why did you give me enough catalyst that a Kingdom would be bankrupt if they tried to pay for the same amount?"

"Your mind was wrong." Luke poked the Druid in the center of his head, rocking him backward hard enough to fall over. "I only know one way to fix that."

"Any Enchanter employed by the Kingdom can adjust the Sigil." Andre told him firmly. "We could have *told* you that. Taylor should know… oh, abyss. *Taylor*. Luke, we need to go get her. My plants… they grow *into* the person inside them. They burrow through skin, and wrap around the Mana Channels to get the mana they need to continue functioning. She'll have been awake for all of it."

"How long does that take?" Luke eyed the Druid coldly. "Also, how long did it take *you* to give in to making that kind of thing? Don't you think a clean death is a better way to go?"

"She never forced…" Andre let out a long exhale as he thought over all the interactions he'd had with Taylor, and amended what he was going to say. "Listen… I think that all of us were trapped in a certain headspace for a long time, entirely by accident. Do you guys remember when we were first tested for mana? They said that they usually test older people, because their minds worked a certain way. What if the Sigil makers just… never took that into account for our generation?"

"You think everyone that made it through has been trapped as a teenager mentally, even though they've lived for decades?" Zed quizzed him directly before nodding slowly. "That would make a lot of sense. I haven't had that problem, for obvious reasons. You all have like… decades more life under your belts than I do. So, I actually *am* still a teenager, and I just thought old people were jerks all the time. Cool, cool."

"Andre. How long does it take for the nasty bits of your Lotus Coffin?" Luke pressed as the conversation got further off-base. "We've only been here a couple hours. At six times speed…?"

"We should be able to get back in time." The Druid let out a huge breath and deflated in relief. "If we get going soon, that is."

They started walking down the tunnel, then Andre froze in place as a notification he had been hoping to see *forever* appeared.

The natural world is attuning with you as you become more in tune with it! A new Ability is germinating!

"That's… new?" Andre tried to shake off the text, but it was superimposed, no matter how he tried to get past it. "Have you guys ever gotten messages in a new way?"

"Too many times, Andre." Luke stated just as Zed hummed a happy 'no' to the question.

Brute Migration (Tier 8, level 0.)

Effect 1: Inserting a half pound of flesh into a double circle will allow you to use mana to summon a creature within 10+n miles with flesh similar to the flesh used for summoning. (Maximized at 20 miles). Travel time based on distance. Strength of beckoning based on mana input.

Bonus 1, at range: Range of summoning has been tripled. Current range: 60 miles. (Maximized.)

Effect 2: You are now able to exert control over the summoned creature. There is a 50+5n chance of controlling the creature. (Maximized at 100%).

Bonus 2, Multitarget: You can summon up to 10+n creatures of the same type. (Maximized at 20 creatures.)

Effect 3: You can choose up to 10+n locations which the summoned creature will move to before being pulled to the location of the summoning. (Maximized at 20 locations.)

Bonus 3, AoE: You can now directly summon the desired creature to your side, no matter the travel distance, so long as they are within 60 miles and on the same Plane. (Maximized.)

Effect 4: You can now set a territory for the creature, where they will roam for at least 10+5n days. This can be resisted if the location chosen is unsuitable. (Maximized at 60 days.)

Bonus 4, Multitarget AoE: By attuning both earth and vegetation, you are able to create a beacon that will determine both the quantity and quality of creatures that are drawn toward it. Doing so will allow for rapid migration and biome shifting. The variance in your beacon will decrease at 10n%, where a maximized Ability will guarantee the exact quantity and quality of creature, so long as they are within range.

"I just got a Tier *eight* Ability," Andre whispered aloud, nearly falling over as he hastened to read the information.

"*What?*" Zed barked in a rage, literally stomping his feet a few times out of sheer frustration. "All I got was a Tier *seven* for gaining Forged Mana Channels! How is my luck this *bad?*"

"This is a *war* Ability," Andre muttered as he took in the wall of information that he both read *and* had engraved on his very being. "I could summon all the mounts a Kingdom is riding... I could create a trap for the dogs from the dynasty, funnel them to one spot, and swallow them into the earth."

"You could *even*... tell us what you got." Zed spoke in the same dreamy tone Andre was using, to mock him, then flashed a grin when the Druid glared at him. "How about we both share? I'll start! My Mastery allows me to create copies of myself that have my exact knowledge at the time of creating them, and then they can go out and find a tavern to work in. I gain Potentia based on how good of a job my clone does, then they pop like a soap bubble when no one is looking. It's... I might love this Mastery. It's a 'world first' Mastery. I know it is. I'm going to be the *only* Bard in the world when I'm done with this, and there'll be a Bard at *every* tavern."

"More... of *you*." Luke snorted hard enough that snot shot out of his nose and left a trail down his chin for a moment before he wiped it away. "That's just great."

CHAPTER FORTY-FIVE

Andre explained his new Ability on the way to picking up Taylor. They chewed over the information as a group, then—to the Druid's delight—started brainstorming. Zed was the first to come up with a good idea for the first beacon. "Why not just get all of those nasty bugs that kill plants all in one area and wipe them out in one go? I think you combined with Luke can take 'em all in one, *maybe* two hits?"

"I like that; we can get to it right now." Luke was quick to jump onboard with this idea, but the Druid shook him off quickly.

"I don't have fine enough control of the Ability at this level. I'll need to get it to level *nine* before I can be certain that I got all of them, and even then, there's a good shot that they'll resist or something. It says 'creatures', which means I can't know how monsters will impact the summoning." Andre rubbed at his chin gently, studying the rapidly darkening sky. "I need to do a *lot* of testing, hopefully with non-lethal stuff first."

"Oh. Then bring worms and junk like that." Luke shrugged as if he *hadn't* just made stars appear in Andre's eyes. "You said this place needs that stuff, right?"

"It's not *just* a war Ability." Andre dropped to his knees and dug his fingers into the sand they were walking over. "It's the last piece I needed for terraforming! Nature truly does provide what we need! Yes!"

Tears rolled down his face as his laughter spread through the empty, dead desert that had almost broken him. After a few seconds, he heaved in a few breaths and stood. Locking eyes with Luke, he walked over and directly pulled him into a hug.

Andre choked as the Murderhobo whirled him around, his arms snaking under Andre's, and clasped his hands behind the Druid's head. "What are you trying to do, Druid? Try a sneak attack on *me*? I'll snap your neck in so many places that the powder from those snail shells will look *coarse* in comparison to what's left of your spine!"

"*Celestial-*" Andre choked out, feeling his vision starting to tunnel already. "Just... a *hug*!"

"Luke, he was trying to show you physical affection," the Bard pleaded on his friend's behalf. "Ah... ah... *here*! Chapter six, 'physical touch isn't always for bloodletting'! Remember this chapter from your favorite book?"

Andre sucked in a lungful of air as the Murderhobo released him, thanks to the Bard's soft cajoling. He whirled around to see a huge smile on Luke's face. "Yeah. I remember. That's a good chapter. Forgot about that."

Then the man pulled out his massive bone weapon and gave it a squeeze, as if he was a proud parent. When the bone started creaking, Andre and Zed shared a nervous look, then silently vowed to never again get in grabbing range of the Murderhobo of their own volition. Andre focused his eyes forward and made plans for what bugs and other small creatures would be the best fit for a healthy area, then scrubbed that from his mind when he remembered that he had a maximum range he could call from. "Taylor should be just ahead. Hold tight."

He stomped on the ground, sending a disproportionately massive wave of sand crashing away from his foot. A moment later, a Lotus Coffin poked through the earth. It parted *slightly* to show Taylor's face, but when Andre directed it to release her… it didn't. "Huh. It's… I guess I never actually designed them to let people *go*. Hang on, I'll need to-"

"Your plant isn't listening to you?" Luke's words made Andre grimace. He knew exactly where that would lead.

"It *will*, I just need to do some fine-tuning so that-" The Druid was cut off as a splash of liquified plant matter was sent flying by Luke's club. He sighed as he wiped the goo from his lips. "You abyssal *barbarian*. Can't you just give me a *moment* to fix stuff?"

"Can you be sure you'd have got it before it started sending roots into our *awake* friend here?" Luke didn't bother waiting for a reply, simply ripping the rest of the coffin to shreds around the Mage. "How long until she's mobile again?"

"Ten minutes?" the Druid guessed, shrugging noncommittally. "Again, this isn't a perfected species, and more and more, I'm liking the idea of abandoning this kind of… horticulture."

"*What* did you just call our sleeping beauty?" Zed gasped in fake outrage. "That kind of slander! Shameful!"

"Horticulture is gardening and growing plants, *Zed*," Andre deadpanned as Luke was bent over Taylor's face. "It has nothing to do with the people you spend your evenings with in taverns. Please don't sully my entire craft in one go like that."

"Okay, hopefully a single dose is enough to get her mind unstuck," Luke interrupted as he stood up.

Andre was surprised to see that Taylor's organs were shining through her skin. He slapped at his long, currently black, hair. "*Luke*! You can't just dose people with elixirs like that! What if she lights on fire? We have no safeguards in place!"

"Wasn't a problem for the two of you." Luke ignored any further angry noises coming from the Druid. "Think of it like this: twenty minutes in a plant, then she gets her mana channels to go from High-Quality, to Extreme High-Quality, with no side effects. I think that's a solid deal."

"Pretty sure she's gonna try to blast you as soon as she can move again," Zed called through cupped hands from a surprisingly far distance. Andre hadn't even seen him start edging away when Taylor got shell powder poured into her dainty nostrils. He shook that thought off with a sigh, muttering, "Should probably let go of that particular childhood fantasy, huh?"

"Well, if she 'blasts' me, there's no way for her to use this stuff to get Forged mana channels. Certainly no way higher, since I killed every instance of 'unicorn' I came across." Luke commented unconcernedly, though Andre noted that he kept an eye on Taylor's prone form.

"She can just take the bag off your charred corpse, right?" Zed waved at the Murderhobo's satchel, and Luke surprised the group by tossing the simple bag across the distance to the Bard.

"Open it," the Murderhobo instructed with a wry grin. Zed raised an eyebrow, then lifted the flap to show him that he could, *indeed*, open a bag. The Bard's fingers stopped suddenly, and he frowned at the unopened bag.

"Huh." Zed yanked on it, then whipped out a dagger from his belt. "You mind?"

"Go for it," Luke snorted, eyeing the dagger he had never seen the Bard wield. "Won't help."

The knife plunged down, stopping as if Zed had hit a wall when the tip tried to part the bag's material. "Interesting. You're confident that no one can get into this?"

"No one under level thirty, at least." Luke took the bag back, strapped it on, and turned around just in time to find a knife pressed against his jugular. He raised an eyebrow. "Glad to see you up and about, Taylor. How're you feeling?"

Her expressions twisted back and forth before finally settling on *pissed*. "Andre, do I have any plant matter in my system? Seeds? Spores?"

The Druid was about to rattle off 'of course not', then remembered that the plants had been doing things they shouldn't have been able to do. "Perhaps it's the Murderhobo's paranoia infecting me, but I'd be happy to check."

Taylor bobbed her head and her hands shook slightly,

sending a trickle of blood down Luke's neck. "You say you can get me to Forged mana channels?"

"Already got both of them up to it." Luke didn't seem to mind the fact that every word he spoke opened a cut on his neck, but as soon as Taylor's eyes flicked to Andre for confirmation, the Murderhobo vanished and reappeared ten feet away. "Careful, Mage. My attempts at *friendship* have a limit. That limit is you trying to attack me a *single* time more."

"Why is my Sigil upda-?" The Mage's hands dropped to her side, her blade vanishing somewhere along the way. Her eyes rolled up in her head and she started to topple backward, only to catch herself and stand upright in the next instant. "What's… happening? I… what have I been *doing*? Celestial abyss, I'm a *monster*."

"Question for the group!" Zed waved at the others. "So, you all got 'freed' from a teenager's mindset now, right? Is it *really* that bad? Feeling a little, you know, called out over here… as the only real teen still in the group."

"No. It isn't," Luke answered while the other two paused to collect their thoughts. "It's just simple. You know what you want, you'll go get it. In many ways, it's awesome. It'll make you work harder, fight harder, and improve faster. Yet, it's *simple*. Depth is lacking. *Perspective* is lacking. You're more willing to sacrifice others for your goals. Friendship is less… nuanced."

"Thank you for reducing everyone my age to a group of shallow brats." Zed offered a high-five, but Andre stepped in and put a hand on the Bard's shoulder.

"You'll understand when you're older." The Druid kept a straight face for a long moment, then cracked under the pressure of Zed's flat stare and began chuckling. "In all seriousness, it's not something I could explain. When my Sigil got tweaked there, it was like… it was as if all of my years of doing things up to this point had new meaning. I have so many new ideas on how to *expand* upon all of my work. All my sacrifices, seeing my goals in reach, mean more to me than they ever have before. I feel… calm."

"Sounds boring." Zed plucked Andre's hand off his shoulder and glanced to the side. "Hold on, I'm gonna…"

There was a meaty *squelch*, and Zed stepped *out* of his body like a snake shedding a skin. The fleshy shell filled in with mana that poured from his body, and in an instant, looked exactly the same as Zed, but naked. "Whoops! See, good thing I'm not trying this *in* a city."

"What. Just. *Happened*." Taylor took a few deep breaths, trying not to hurl at the nasty sight she had just witnessed.

"Go, be free, me!" Zed waved his hands at himself. His clone reached out and shook hands with him seriously, then they exchanged a wink.

"Can do! Have fun getting sand in your crack every time you sit down." The second Zed told himself. "I'm off to the coziest tavern I can find, then convince the innkeep to let me stay there for free."

They all watched the clone stride away, somewhat dazed. Zed glared after himself. "What a jerk."

"That's *you*," Andre told him pointedly. "How can you not like yourself when you see *you*?"

Zed shrugged and shook his head. "You wouldn't get it."

"Hey." Luke held up a hand, and the team focused on him with various levels of enthusiasm. "Are you at all worried that your clone will eventually want to be the *only* Zed, and come after you?"

"…No." Zed squinted at the Murderhobo, then off into the distance, where his clone was already out of sight. "I shouldn't need to have to worry about that. Right? Right."

CHAPTER FORTY-SIX

- LUKE -

"So what now?" Taylor's voice caused Luke to blink and lose sight of a ripple in the sand that he was *almost* positive was a root system coming to try to wrap him up.

He decided that perhaps he should just move to a new spot, instead of being forced to splatter the viney growth and upset the Druid. Again. He moved five feet to the left, then eight feet backward. His muttering went unheard by the others. "Those plants wouldn't be expecting *this*. Unless they've been studying my behavior…?"

"First, we have a long conversation with Luke about boundaries and talking instead of hitting, and then we make a plan. How about that?" Andre offered to the others. Luke noticed Taylor look at his satchel and clench her fists in her robes, but she quietly agreed after a moment.

It was good to really, *really* be told—in excruciating detail—where they all stood as a team, Luke decided as the moon came up and his team finally stopped blathering at him about how they expected to be treated in the future. Taylor got in the last word, "I understand that you were trying to help, and you thought you were… *rescuing* some of us from ourselves. If I didn't, you'd never sleep safely again. If you *ever* do something like that to me again, you'd better make sure I'm dead, because otherwise, I'll never stop until you are."

"I will make sure you're dead. I understand." Luke nodded obligingly and dusted off his legs. Yes, it was good to know where they all stood. The sand that had been blown onto him by the wind would hide any roots creeping up on him; he couldn't allow them to have a hiding space on his own body. "Great. Now that everyone has had a chance to talk, I'll say what I think about our friendship, and then we can plan out our next mission."

"Go for it, buddy." Andre leaned forward on his staff and nodded encouragingly.

"Okay." Luke hopped to his feet and stretched. "If you ever need it, I'll repeat everything I just did. That and more, all over again, and *abyss* the consequences. I was trapped for almost half a *century* before I found a way out, and I wished for *decades* that I had someone who would come to rescue me. If I ever need to be saved again, I hope you'd do for me what I did for all of you today."

The group was silent, so Luke pointed at Taylor. "I'm done. You want to tell us what we're gonna do, or should *I* make the plan?"

"N-no." The Mage was startled out of her thoughts and took a deep breath, letting go of whatever else she was going to say. "Frankly, the plan doesn't change. Only the way we carry it out does."

"Uh, well, the plan was to grow the desert into *not* a wasteland, and the Inquisitors kinda put the ol' kibosh on that, no?" Zed offered with a smile and head-scratch. "You know, the whole 'no more growing things allowed' rule they made for us?"

"Is *that* what they said?" Taylor showed a smile with too many perfect teeth and a dark glint in her eye. "Because I'm pretty sure they said no growing plants 'until those creatures are proven to no longer be an issue for the Hollow Kingdom'."

"Somehow that *isn't* what I just said." Zed nodded sagely along with her. "Yes, I see the error in my thinking."

"She means that if we can take out the bugs, I can get back to growing plants however we want," Andre explained for the perplexed Bard. He turned toward the Mage, "But there's a problem with that, Taylor. No one has ever survived going to the deepest parts of the desert since *this* happened. The land is said to have been twisted by the previous Druid, and some of the Kingdom's strongest people have failed. How will *we* get through? I'm pretty sure Zed is only level eight, and the rest of us haven't exactly been gaining barrels of Potentia."

"First, the other groups didn't have a Druid. Second, if the Kingdom sent them, they *weren't* the best. Just expendable. Thirdly, no one ever said they didn't *survive*, they just never came back." Taylor tapped a fourth finger, and looked over at Luke. "Lastly... *who* said that the land was twisted? Where are those stories coming from, if no one ever returned? What *I* think... I think that people found the issue and couldn't do anything about it. You know what that means to me?"

"An open Scar." Zed was the one to speak up, surprising the others by making the connection before they did. "We have someone that *can* fix the problem. I see where you're going with this. I'm in, but I have some stipulations."

"Um..." Taylor paused, getting shrugs from the others. "What's on your mind?"

"When we fix whatever this is... I want a break from the Kingdom." Zed looked around at the others hopefully. "I want a few years to myself for honing my Masteries and getting stronger, earning Potentia, before I need to go back to... *servitude*."

"I want that, too." Luke slapped his hand onto Cookie to emphasize his point. "We've got a lot of catching up to do, and I need to delve into less potent Scars, since I'm locked out of my world for the next month. Apparently, my Sigil is punishing

DAKOTA KROUT

me for deactivating my Skill and extending my stay in Murder World; I *should* have been able to go back already, and it isn't letting me."

Taylor shot a look at the Druid, who shrugged and grinned sheepishly. "Wouldn't hurt to build up a super-oasis in the center of this place, then generate the resources to terraform the whole desert in one big push. I doubt they'd find us if we stayed deep enough; it's not exactly an often-explored area."

"I…" The Mage was clearly hesitant, but her pleading glances were met with a triplet of stony stares. "Can we at least hide our identities and feed anyone along the border? If we can do *anything* that is helpful for the Kingdom in that time, I'm fine with pretending we died for a while."

"Ten years," Zed opened negotiations immediately.

"Six *months*," Taylor growled at him.

"Ten years." Andre stood next to Zed, and Luke nodded along with them.

"Do you have any *idea* how our political climate will shift over ten *years*?" Taylor snapped at the three of them. "What could happen to our families if we vanish?"

"One of the Zeds will keep an eye on them." Andre jerked his thumb into the distance where the clone had walked away. "Right, Zed?"

"I can make a clone per week," Zed agreed right away. "They last until killed, I cancel them, or they self-destruct. Anything big goes down, I'll have the network of Zed—which I plan to set up—reach out and get us."

Everyone went silent as Taylor chewed her lip and tried to get them to change their minds. "It'll never last. They'll want us for something, and they'll find *anything* they can come up with to make us come back. They might even kick off the war and haul us back in to fight for them."

"Everything the King said in private makes me inclined to believe that us vanishing for a good long time was part of his plan the whole time, right?" Andre explained with sweeping

328

motions. "They even made it impossible to fix the problem, *after* we were told to come here and work on it!"

"You guys really just want to be… done?" Taylor shook her head at the thought. "I can't believe it."

"As done as we *can* be before level twenty," Zed demanded firmly. "For the first time in a couple years, I have a shot at not being hunted like an animal for a while. I have the King's permission to relax and hide from his hired muscle. Why would I give that up, just because we could complete a mission a *little* faster?"

Taylor finally caved, throwing her hands in the air. "*Fine*! You want to hide like criminals for a decade? *Fine*! So long as we actually fix whatever the issue in the desert is, so the Kingdom stops wasting away!"

"Deal." Andre and Zed bumped their fists together and grinned.

The Murderhobo punched the ground, grabbed a root, and yanked a struggling, overgrown flower into the open air. "I *knew* this thing was coming after me!"

"Luke…" Andre groaned in a distraught tone. "Please stop killing my plants. I can't make new ones, so I'm spending way too much blood and mana to *expand* the ones I have. If they reproduce on their own, I'm not breaking any rules imposed on me."

"You don't want me killin' them? Don't let them keep coming after me!" Luke tossed the wilted flower to the side, and he would have sworn it *whimpered* when it landed. "Make them less intelligent, would you? Smart plants are downright creepy."

The Druid picked up the flower and whispered to it before planting it back in the sand and helping it become healthy again. Then he turned his head and shot a glare at Luke. "Big words coming from a guy that was singing to his bone club not five minutes ago."

Luke returned the glare, glanced at Cookie, then back to Andre. "I did what now?"

CHAPTER FORTY-SEVEN

"So, just to make *sure* we're all on board with the plan, *Taylor*," Zed paused to send a scathing glare at the 'leader' of the party, "We go into the desert here with no plan except to 'fix stuff', two of our party members are *severely* limited in the amount of help they can offer, tensions are high... but if we win, we go on a 'vacation' from being told what to do and try to become as powerful as we can for ten years or until caught; whichever comes first."

He took a deep breath and stared at the seemingly endless sand all around them. "Anything... else?"

"Sounds correct to me," Andre stated easily, scattering a handful of seeds into the air. Catching Taylor shaking her head in his peripheral vision, he coughed defensively and pointedly ignored her. "Just because I can't grow them myself *now* doesn't mean I don't want them *ready* to grow when I *can*."

"I didn't say anything." Taylor deflated slightly and edged closer to the Druid. "Look... I'm sorry. I didn't realize that I was pushing you like that. Into a bad place. I just... I saw what you could do when motivated, and I thought you *wanted* it to be the best it could be. When I was doping that, I thought I was helping you. I *really* did."

"Talk is cheap, Taylor," The Druid told her softly, the lack of anger in his voice taking the sting from his words. "You need to let go of your words, stop imposing your impulses on *us*, and be a better leader. Or you won't be leading us. I have enough authority to be the team leader, and if you *force* me to make that call, I will. Then ten years of hiding from the Hollow Kingdom will be a *blink* compared to the amount of time I order the rest of us to vanish, while you rush back to the Kingdom and get put to work."

There was very little conversation after that ultimatum, which was just as well, as far as Luke was concerned. He was still trying to figure out how he had been *singing*, of all things, and not noticing it. How long had that been going on? When had it started? "These are the *real* issues."

"You say something?" Zed called from his position of being draped over Andre's shoulder so they could make better time. His chin was propped up on his hands, and his elbows rested on a few vines that looped up from Andre's back. "You cut a strong figure from this position. You know, I know a few lovely ladies that would *love* to meet someone with 'Prismatic' Mana Channels. How does that work? Lots of unicorns, even at the start of your world?"

"No. I bathed in liquid mana, breathed mana vapor, used solidified mana to spice my food, and it was my only water source for nearly five decades." Luke decided to get it over with all in one go, as 'sharing the troubles from your past was a good way to strengthen bonds in the present'. Chapter seven of his book. "My Mana Channels were 'Destroyed'. No mana could work through me, which is why I didn't pop like a bloated cow carcass. Eventually, the buildup was so great that when I earned my first Skill, new channels were carved through me by what I assume was a Higher Ascender."

"*Carved?*" Andre frowned at that. "Aren't Mana Channels

only partially physical? That part follows your nerves... oh. Luke. How do you have a mind at all?"

"Sigil." Luke flicked his forehead, and the branded enchantment lit up with a proud *chime*. "Activated for the first time right after that, and glued my mind back together. Been finding little chunks floating around every once in a while that I stick back on."

"How... horrible." Taylor's soft voice brought the conversation to a screeching halt, and they walked in silence until they made camp for the night. Zed slept as soon as his head hit the wadded-up rag he used for a pillow, and the others each took a shift for night watch.

An uneventful few hours later, the group started walking again, crossing countless dunes under the scorching sun. Zed was looking over an old document, and he rapped it lightly. "Welp, we are officially off of the newest maps. All we have to go on is this... let's charitably call it century-old directions to a town that once existed. Certainly isn't a map. You'd think they would have given us better gear, ya know?"

"Small reminder that they not only expected us to fail, they're *banking* on it so that we're out of the public eye for a large chunk of time." Andre cheerfully patted his burden. "Can't let us get more popular than the Crown Prince, or people will think we're trying to rebel!"

"Wouldn't want *that*, would we?" Zed muttered darkly as he returned his attention to the 'map' he had salvaged from the wreckage of a village the swarm had... eaten. "Oh, this is fun... on the *other* side of the desert is an ocean filled with many monsters and few fish. No wonder no one wants the Hollow Kingdom as a vassal state. Even invading us can only really be accomplished via portal or a route filled with *garbage*."

"Remember that whole... warfront situation?" Taylor cautiously ventured into the conversation. "Dynasty of Dogs slowly nibbling away at our land?"

"Yeah, yeah." Zed waved her comment off. "I meant from this side. The sea is a great natural barrier. Might need to build up a big seawall when this place is green again, Andre. The beasties probably got bigger in the last hundred years."

Luke finally had enough. "Can you stop making threatening foreshadowing for two *minutes*?"

"Hello, I'm... *a Bard*." Zed tipped his oversized feathered hat and grinned cheekily. "No one knows what's over there. Doesn't mean I want to be bored for the rest of the walk. Gotta write the story, and that means leaving breadcrumbs I can point at and say, 'Aha! I told you we should watch for that'!"

"All this does is make me want to force you to walk on your own." Andre's retort caused Zed to choke on the water he was sipping from a vine connected to a watermelon, and pause the fern fronds that were providing shade and waving air onto his face.

"Please, no."

"Wait... why am *I* walking?" The Druid leaned back, and a moment later, the two of them were supported by a vine-hammock that walked along on several 'legs'. They grinned at each other and ignored the stares from the other two more *physical* members of the party. "So, I'm thinking... mobile oasis for camping while we hunt down the Scar that the bugs are coming out of?"

"You *know* I like your style," Zed responded in a put-upon noble voice. "Ah-ha. *Ah*-ha!"

"Alright, I'm done. I'm gonna go scout ahead." Luke grabbed Cookie and started twisting in place. On his third revolution, Cookie was generating a howling wind as he built momentum. On the fifth, he threw her out and *up* with all the force he could muster... then Bum Flashed after her and grabbed on as the four hundred pound Greatclub shot into the air.

"Did I actually just see that?" was the last thing Luke heard a dumbfounded Zed say before the howling wind made it impossible to catch anything further. When he reached a few hundred feet in the air, Luke let his armor fade away and activated Feather's Fall.

He had plenty of time to search the horizon for any abnor-malities, but... there was nothing. Wait... *almost* nothing. Far, *far* away, Luke caught movement. It was only a flash, but it was noticeable for the sheer fact that there was *nothing* else moving for dozens upon dozens of miles. With a grunt, he tossed Cookie in the direction of the movement and fell to the sand below.

Luke waited patiently until his team had caught up to him, and ignored them as they tried to dig answers out of him with their eyes. He held up a hand to forestall their questions. "Hang on."

Activating his Soul Brand, he called Cookie back to him. She shot toward him across the sand, drawing a line in her wake. When she slapped into his hand, Luke pointed into the distance. "Cookie drew us an arrow; let's not waste her efforts. Wind'll erase it soon."

"*Wha~at* laws of nature did he just break?" Zed pointed an accusing finger at Luke as he poked Andre with the other hand. "No, wait; how *many* natural laws did he break? I want a full accounting, please."

"You know what? I need to fight in any direction, and some-times that means innovating on the fly. I see a problem, I find a way to get around it." Luke shrugged and pointedly looked over the Bard. "*I* can't be in two places at once, can I?"

"Okay, fair. I'll try to stop doubting the reality of what you can do, even though I hate that you can do that on a deep level, for a reason I can't clearly explain," Zed pouted at him.

"Where does this go?" Andre quizzed Luke as they followed the line.

"Saw movement. I figured if we could find a bug, we could find the nest." Luke's explanation drew nods of understanding. "We find the nest, we find the Scar. Kill the bugs, close the Scar, relax for nine years and work hard for one."

Taylor tensed at that, but, to her credit, didn't naysay his statement. Zed cheered, while Andre smiled softly, "Not gonna be much relaxing going on for me."

"Onward! To vacation!" Zed pointed grandly into the distance.

Over a week later, the group stopped to get out of the heat of the day and started to rethink their strategy. Zed cleared his throat and politely tapped his 'map'. "So, I think we're *lost*, but we're doing fine overall."

"I haven't killed anything in a week, Zed." The Murderhobo turned bloodshot eyes on the Bard. "Already startin' to get the itch. Problem is, Zed, I got nothin' to scratch. *Celestials*, I'm hungry. Hungry for action. Hungry for Potentia."

His stomach rumbled, and he snarled, "Abyss it, I'm just *hungry*. We ran outta food days ago. Forget this; let's just go after that Scar I felt a few miles back. Bet we can kill and eat something there."

The others took a few moments to process his words. Andre was the first to slowly react. "You... *felt* a Scar? Uh... okay. That aside, why didn't you direct us to it if you *thought* there was one? We're *hunting* for a Scar."

The Murderhobo shook his head firmly. "No, we're looking for a Scar that *bugs* are coming out of. Why would a nest for *flying bugs* be so far underground? Seriously, it was ten miles down there. At *least*."

"I guess now we know why no one ever found a way to bottle up the bugs." Taylor's words set Andre off, and he chuckled for several tension-easing minutes while Zed started furiously scribbling words on the back of his map.

"Let's do this, Luke!" Andre turned expectant eyes on the Murderhobo, as did the others.

"It's *below ground*." Discerning that they didn't understand that *flying bugs* would be out in the open, Luke shook his head and sighed as he adjusted his trudging. "Look, I get that you work with animals and plants, not bugs, but... oh, *whatever*. I wanted to go there anyway. Maybe we'll find some food, at least?"

CHAPTER FORTY-EIGHT

"There, now we're directly above the Scar that's something like ten miles below us. Are we all happy, now that we know no bugs are coming out of it?" Luke grouched at the others, a little upset that an animal or monster that he could eat wasn't presenting itself.

Buzz.

Everyone went dead silent as a Preying Mantous flew through the area. Only the swirling wind kicking up dust hid the group as the monstrous insect continued past into the sand dunes. Taylor motioned for everyone to stay still, and seemingly vanished into thin air as she followed the creature without leaving a trace of her presence behind.

Only a few minutes later, she reappeared and directed them to an area filled with bubbling sand, something anyone with half a brain would avoid. Luke felt proud of himself for his self-preservation instinct; he had seen several instances of this and knew not to trust sand that moved on its own. "Things that aren't alive shouldn't move."

Andre felt the ground, letting nature speak to him or some such nonsense, then stood and gazed around the area with wonder. "It's a natural gas vent. Something down there is producing so much gas that it creates a constant updraft. Amazing."

"Flammable?" Luke already retrieved a pitch-soaked torch and held out to Zed so he could light it with his firestone. Andre sputtered and slapped it away from the vent, even though the torch itself was as-yet unlit.

"Most likely, yes." Andre caught his breath and stared at Luke with a twitching eye. "Most likely *very* flammable."

"So…" Luke gestured with the torch suggestively.

"Right, so, how gasses in motion work…" Andre tapped the tips of his fingers together. "I'll make it easy. The fire will go with the gas as it's blowing. You light it up here, all you're doing is blocking our entrance."

Luke reluctantly put the torch away. Zed shook his head and gingerly stepped away from the group. "I'll hang out up here."

"No food or water up here." Taylor studied the shifting sand, "It must be *somewhat* breathable, or the bugs couldn't live down there, right? Andre… is this a barrier you can get us past?"

"Who knows what conditions bugs can survive in that we can't? As to letting you breathe?" The Druid spent a long few moments in silent thought, then reluctantly pulled out some seedlings. "In your nose they go. They'll create air directly in your lungs, and draw out the harmful gasses. All you have to do is hold a really big breath, and do your best not to inhale too often."

"Our bodies won't let us do that, Andre," Zed sighed as he took the plant, very delicately poking it into his nose. He patted the Druid gently, speaking in a nasally tone, "If you die and no one can take this out of me, I'm going to find a way to bring you back so that I can kill you again."

"Fair enough," the Druid stated wryly, "I'll make sure to live on *your* behalf. Keeping your comfort in mind: my top priority."

"Mine didn't work." Luke called their attention to the plant that had withered into goo as soon as it got a taste of his innards. "Oops."

"It's... *twitching.*" Taylor frowned at the dying plant and took a subtle step away from Luke. "Is that plant in *pain?* What sort of madness are you made from?"

"New plan; we all get gas exchange plants, and Luke teaches us how long someone can last in poisonous air." Zed pointed at the sand and bowed to Luke. "After you, m'lord Von Murderhobo?"

"Everyone else ready?" At the group's collective nods of affirmation, Luke ran at the bubbling sand and jumped in, sinking to his neck in an instant. Hot grit filled his mouth, and he started flailing as he realized that he was just sinking, not going anywhere.

The sand around him solidified slightly and pulled away just before he started fighting back, revealing a long tunnel hewn into the stone... a solid ten feet from where Luke was flopping around. Andre cleared his throat, which Luke appreciated—sand in the throat was more than just annoying—and called quietly, "Perhaps *I* should lead the underground exploration? You know... the guy that can make the earth move around?"

They got in line and followed along the tunnel, enjoying the comforting darkness and coolness of the air compared to the desert above. They continued along the tunnel for hundreds of feet on a downward slope, never once encountering any bugs. They moved swiftly yet cautiously, at a pace even Zed could maintain for hours at a time.

The tunnel began branching, and at each intersection, they needed to try their luck. Soon enough, they were turned around to the point that even Taylor's perfect memory was becoming slightly befuddled. Without Andre to lift them straight out, the place would have been a deathtrap on that merit alone. As it was, the only light in the area came from Cookie, who blazed a brilliant blue.

"Stinks in here." The Murderhobo scowled, then poked Andre. "You. Dig us straight down; I'm sick of these tunnels."

"Bad idea." Andre paused to let his plant pull out the gas he had sucked in. "Monsters might feel the mana. The Druid that blasted this place might have set up failsafes to stop future Druids from taking this place down. Remember, whoever did this to the Hollow Kingdom was level twenty and had *hundreds* of years of experience. I'm a pretty new Druid. Also, that is methane and sulphur. Great."

"It's just poison air." Luke stood proudly as the others slowly came to realize how long they had been underground. "I'm pretty much immune to poison."

"A vent here!" Zed gasped out, gesticulating wildly at a space that was darker than the surrounding rock. "Straight drop!"

"Celestials above, I really thought we'd need to *walk* another nine-point-eight-three-ish miles down to get where we were going." Luke hopped into the vent and dropped, chuckling at the gasps of horror that were quickly replaced with hacking coughs. He flipped over as he fell, then tossed Cookie ahead of him to light the way so he wouldn't splatter against the ground.

She didn't mind.

The vent dropped down for miles, eventually opening up into an utterly massive volcanic cavity. The sight that filled his eyes took his breath away more efficiently than the harsh gasses that he was falling through. Miles, and *miles* of green. Not flora… *green*. Swarms of bugs flew around, eggs dotting every single hole in the walls or ground, and even the ceiling was covered in bioluminescent crystals that strobed with soft blue internal lights. Blue was more familiar to Luke, and he liked the contrast.

"Looks like I'm *outside* with all those stars. Ha! I can't be outside; I'm underground!" Tearing his gaze away, he scrutinized the rest of the area, finding that he was falling toward a floor covered with plant matter, dead animals, bugs both dead and alive, and so *many* bones. All of that was seen in an instant, processed, then cast aside.

There was one, single… plant. He wanted to say 'tree', but

no… this was something else. A woven intermingling of *plant* that stretched down from the ceiling before branching into vines and roots that reached the entire distance downward to feed on the detritus that coated the earth below. This thing was more than a mile tall, and at *least* as wide. Another detail stood out vividly: he could feel that the plant had either grown around the Scar, or that the Scar had been opened inside of the plant.

Either way, he knew now where he needed to go. The Murderhobo was suddenly exceedingly grateful for all the midair combat training he had received in Murder World, and he was looking forward to putting it to good use here. "Stealth option is a no-go. Sorry, Cookie, looks like you're just too brilliant to be missed."

A keening cry, buzzing, and various clacking chitinous appendages had been his wake-up call, pulling him out of his excitement and into combat mode. "Gotta secure a landing zone for the team…!"

He called Cookie to him, enjoying the fact that she came to a halt in midair, and tossed his mana-made 'Mountaindale' bottle at the closest swarm that was flying upward to catch the falling morsel. "Shockwave Cleave."

The bottle hit the leading bug, and Luke was able to watch the aftermath of his Skill from a distance for the first time. All the bugs in a cone, all the way down to the ground, were converted to goo and shrapnel. Luke then activated Feather"s Fall, only for the Skill to fail.

You cannot gain Potentia from this enemy type!
Mana: 63/324.

"Feces! I don't have enough-" Luke reached for a waterskin, but couldn't get any mana-water into his mouth before he hit the ground with a huge splash. Between catching the rain of ichor and landing in a hundred years' worth of accumulated bug droppings, Luke created a wave of *nasty* that sloshed for hundreds of feet.

Moments later, he crested the surface of the… for his mental health, he decided to call it a swamp instead of a cesspool, and thrust a fist into the air. "Yes! Halved fall damage for the win!"

He swam powerfully to a mostly-solid area, pulling himself onto dry 'land', and watched for his falling friends. He was almost *certain* they didn't have a way to mitigate falling on their own, but he was ready for that eventuality. As soon as they appeared above him, he chucked Cookie up at them as hard as he could.

"Catch!"

CHAPTER FORTY-NINE

"I have no idea how you managed to make that work." Taylor shuddered as her Cleanse spell worked overtime to eradicate the flecks of… mud… that kept splattering onto her with each step someone took.

"You catch Cookie, I pull her to me," Luke explained yet again as they worked to defend the Druid, who was sitting in the muck and somehow *smiling*. "The angle of your fall changes and becomes a slope. You don't fall as hard on a slope. You can't reach the fastest falling… the…"

"Terminal velocity," Andre murmured to him as yet another green sprig sprouted around him. "I can't believe this is working. I'm not growing plants *in* the desert, I'm growing them way *below* the desert. Not complaining that I have my utility back, but that command seems pretty easy to get around, now that I know how to do it."

"Hey, that's cool and all, but how about more plants that kill any bugs that get close?" Zed forced an unhappy chuckle as he strummed his out-of-tune Ukulele. "Not that I really *trust* them to get *all* of them, but…"

"*One* bug got through, Zed. Even that was because I was

opening a portal." Andre winced at the stare that was leveled at him. "Yes, to be fair, it got you right in the heart, but we fixed that, yeah?"

"They're swarming again!" Taylor called over as she fired more Shatter Shots into the hundreds of bugs per second that were coming after them. Luke responded by charging out of their defensive circle and swinging with all his might with Cookie, activating a shockwave only when he was certain it wouldn't rebound onto his team.

Damage dealt: 1 (3,334)

He ignored the other messages that were telling him that his mana was gone, as well as the one complaining that he had killed too many of this type and should leave some for others. "Sigil, if they *wanted* the Potentia, it was right there for the taking. Stop telling me off for killin' faster than they can manage!"

He turned and dashed for his group as the cavern was rocked by a spreading wall of death. A single look informed him that, while he had killed likely tens of *thousands* with that attack, it just didn't matter. More bugs were pouring in at all times: down through vents like the one they had fallen through, from the walls, from the portal. Taylor pondered the hopeless situation and wavered. "A single Flame Lance could take them all out at the same time-"

"No Spells that kill us too, thank you *very* much," Andre snapped just before Zed could do so. "There's a better way, and I'm ready."

Zed took up the argument against burning, "If one of you kills me with fire, I'm

An opening appeared in the swirling muck below them, and Andre slid down a moist, pulpy tunnel with a gesture for the others to follow him. Taylor went first, then Zed, followed by a very reluctant Luke. He took one final half-hearted swing at the bugs before allowing himself to slither down, finding himself in some kind of gourd. "Is this a watermelon?"

"A pumpkin. Welcome to our home for the next few weeks.

Luke, *Luke*! I'm joking!" Andre barely managed to speak in time, but the Murderhobo aborted his swing at the wall of the orange gourd. "We're sinking to the bottom and waiting out the bugs' attention span; that's it, I promise."

"Okay then. Your real plan?" Luke leaned back on the pumpkin, which swayed dangerously as he and his massive Greatclub's weight settled in one spot.

"The bugs aren't diving into the filth. Right now, the vine of this pumpkin is dragging us along the bottom of the pit toward the roots coming off of that massive plant. When we get there, we're gonna get on it and climb up. If we can reach the portal fast enough, we should be able to cut off reinforcements from the other side." Andre responded to the hopeful faces of his team by letting loose a bright smile. "We're moving slowly enough that all the buzz should die down by the time we pop out."

"I hear your joke, and I want you to know that I'm judging you for it," Zed informed the Druid bluntly. "So your plan is betting that they'll all settle down, giving us enough time to get to the Scar and close it before they can swarm at us again?"

"*Exactly*." Andre touched his nose and pointed at the Bard. "Then it's extermination and vacation time."

No one had a better idea, so they waited until Andre thought it was time. "We have as many shots at this as we need, so long as the bugs don't realize that we are under here and come after us if we need to retreat again."

"Why would you even say that out loud and will it into existence?" Zed grumbled as a strange feeling of weightlessness filled them. "You always yell at me for doing it."

"We're a quarter up, but they're coming! I'm carving the pumpkin! Go!" With a gesture, the top of the pumpkin blew off, and they grabbed the thick vines dropped through the opening. Taylor and Luke scampered up instantly, tossing themselves upward a half-dozen feet with each pull. Andre grabbed Zed and commanded his personal vines to do the climbing for the both of them.

The air *rumbled* a few moments after they began, a sound they had no basis of understanding for. Even more concerning, the Preying Mantous that were coming after them paused, then changed directions, flying up from the locations they had just rested upon. Zed searched the cavern nervously. "Anyone know what that was?"

"No... idea!" Taylor barked as she scaled the vines. "Quarter mile to go!"

Luke spent every other movement throwing a mana-bottle into the swarm and killing hundreds of the fragile things before recreating the weapon and tossing it again. Even with the blatant attacks, the bugs were moving up and ignoring them. Luke was unsure if it was the vibration that seemed to come from everywhere at once that was confusing their senses, or if there was something else going on.

Either way, by the time the humans were securely perched on the main body of the behemoth plant, the air was utterly *choked* with bugs. Yet, they *still* weren't coming after The Four. Taylor sent up a Shatter Shot, killing dozens of the beasts but failing to draw any attention at all. "What's happening?"

"The bugs are... fleeing?" Zed shook his head as the deep rumble echoed through the cavern once more. "Nah, got a bad feeling about this. Back to the pumpkin!"

"Hold it!" Taylor's cry stopped both Zed and Luke; Andre was *far* too fascinated with what was happening in front of them. "We aren't getting hurt, and this is giving us a chance to see what's going on. I think they're flying through the Scar! We might have a chance to win without a fight!"

"*What?*" Luke howled in rage, turning and catapulting Cookie into a stream of bugs. She splattered *through* all of them, clearly agreeing that they should kill these nasty pests instead of letting them go free. "Hundreds are escaping every second, and you want us to *wait?*"

"Luke! We need to-" The Mage's supplication was drowned out by the droning of all the flying bugs as the Murderhobo took step after step toward the Scar, using his mana-made

Chain-Blade Rope as a blender to make sweet bug smoothie. A spell from the Mage *shizzed* past his head, but he knew it was frustration guiding her actions; if she killed him, she'd have no way to close the Scar.

Luke laughed as he stood in the midst of his enemy, killing them with impunity as they struggled to escape. Not *one* of them turned on him and attacked, and he loved knowing that he could slaughter without any consequences. As he got closer, the portal became clearer, and eventually was no longer marred by flashes of bug. It was slowly resolving into a lovely creamy-gold, and he couldn't wait to punch it right in the energy field.

He swung Cookie back, pulping dozens of bugs, then swung her forward with a bellow. "*Rift Hunter!*"

Cookie hit the Scar, and its light was blown out like a weak candle in a hurricane. The bugs stopped moving, their eyes shifting to him as they seemed to notice him for the first time. The Murderhobo wasn't going to give them time to get their bearings: he struck first. Chitin and ichor splattered through the area as his body moved to kill as many as he could access. "Yes! Now we fight! I'll end your presence on this Plane all by myself! You don't get to run away after you stabbed Zed in the heart!"

"Aww, he got us all killed because he *cares* about me!" Zed's voice echoed in the chamber where the only other sounds were the squashing of bugs. "On that note, any idea why we're not all small chunks of meat yet?"

The Preying Mantous remained motionless as Luke worked his way through them. They didn't fight back, they didn't fly away. They just died. Andre's voice reached Luke through his rampage, and he slowed down—but didn't stop—killing the bugs. "They must be a hive mind. Without the thoughts of their leader controlling them, they're just husks.?"

"Are these things going to start fighting me, Andre?" Luke called over as he clapped his hands together and tore the head off another bug.

"Only if you re-open the portal!" the Druid called back. "I think... did we just win?"

"Congratulations, everyone," Taylor called out after another minute without dying. "We saved the desert; time to clean this place up and get to work moving-"

OOooOOmm.

Everyone fell silent as the air itself vibrated and the ambient light was altered. Andre had the best view of the cavern outside the plant, and he finally called over his shoulder in concern, "Hey, all… why any idea why blue light in a shining rock would turn green?"

Zed dashed over and peered out into the open air. "They look fine to me. Green is fine. Green is *lovely*."

Both of them looked inward at Taylor and Luke, but as they did… the lights above went out. Their heads snapped back around to look out, and green light once more suffused the area. Andre was the first to notice that something was different, "The pattern changed? Either different rocks are lighting up, or those ones are… moving."

"Why would the star rocks vanish when you look away?" Luke stomped over, intent on splattering bugs with his feet the entire way. Unbeknownst to them, Taylor's eyes had widened, and her face had gone pale. Her words were only a whisper, but they caused everyone to turn to look at her.

"Fear the caverns, for they too have teeth. The stars are gone when you look away, but they… can still see you."

The world went dark once more, only the light emanating from Cookie allowing them to spot the vines of the behemoth plant reaching for them.

CHAPTER FIFTY

Luke was the first to react by a long shot, his open distrust of foliage saving the team as he Bum Flashed over and swept them into the open air. The plant connected to itself with a clashing that would put thunder to shame, sending them rattling through the turbulent air with enough force that there was no doubt that they would have *absolutely* died if they had been caught.

"If you are hearing this recording," a voice boomed, following the mind-shattering noises of the plant striking itself blindly, "then congratulations: you are the first Druid to get this far. I am sorry that you were caught up in this tragic story, and as an apology... I'll let you know that you will live if you leave immediately using a personal portal. It will take a few minutes for the Draco'inversionem esse naturae to wake up."

"No abyssal *way*," Andre managed to choke out before the group hit the muck far below. Luke swam for the surface, accidentally getting some of the stuff in his mouth.

You need to Stop... has reached level two!

Bursting out of the raw sewage, Luke bellowed in disgust even as he internally cheered that he had been correct. "I'm *unhappy* that resisting disease was the correct answer!"

A pillar of slime crawled out of the revolting pool and onto a more solid area, then rapidly transformed into Taylor as the film was eradicated. She stared up at the green-lit ceiling, where the plant was awakening. "Andre, I need to know what that thing is and how to kill it. I need to know now."

"It's a *Corrupted Nature Dragon.*" Andre didn't bother to sweep the filth off his face as he watched the creature in pure awe. "Nature Dragons are *extinct.* There haven't been true sightings of them in over three millennia. They're spoken of as the highest-level *theoretical* creature a Druid can create. Even then… it takes a Tier-*ten* first, second, *and* third circle Druidic Ability to do it, because they're equal parts plant, mineral, and animal. We need to leave; we need to leave right now."

"We can't let that thing get out of here, Andre," Taylor informed him with all the force she could muster past her trembling lips. Even though her voice trembled, her face remained calm and collected.

"You don't understand." Andre's mind was already on the verge of collapse as the Dragonic plant continued awakening. "This thing is twice as bad as that. It's a *corrupted* Dragon. That means that it went against its nature. In other words, it went against *nature itself,* since its nature *is* nature. It can kill us in passing. We can't kill *it.* Taylor, I have access to *one* Tier-ten Domain in my world, and it ensures that *nothing* in the area around it can die. *Think* about that for a moment."

The voice they had heard moments previously spoke again, sounding sad this time. "If you are hearing this… you have chosen a futile path of resistance. I admit… I love you. Your willingness to sacrifice yourself means everything to me. I wish I was you. A better person than I am. Better than what I have been turned into. I admit I'm bitter, and vengeful, but I can't stop what is in motion. As a reward for your love of this world, I'll tell you what you can do to stop my revenge upon a world that… I wish I had never created this beast within."

"Hey, that's convenient." Zed let out a sigh of relief as he pulled himself onto dry land. "By the way, I nearly drowned under something like fifty feet of bug poop; thanks for thinking to pull me out of there. Oh, *wait*, no one *remembered* their poor Bard?"

"Zed, hush." Taylor pointed upward as the voice echoed out again.

"I corrupted my faithful companion to act as a last line of defense against the Kingdom that had forced me to grow their wealth in a literal way." The person in the recording had begun sobbing lightly as he spoke. "I, Mega Druid Kiefer, hailed as the Druid most loved by the universe, have turned against it."

"I have a bad feeling that he's gonna talk for a really long time, and we're gonna die before he tells us how to kill this thing." Luke judged the distance between himself and the plant, reluctantly deciding that he was too far away to put his Skills to use against it. For the moment.

Andre reached into his pockets and started throwing seeds around. "Just realized that the bugs aren't an issue anymore! Luke, I need a *killer* amount of mana!"

Luke looked at the stern face of his friend, then back at the Dragon-thingy. "I don't want to rain on your parade here, but I think plants are the *issue* here, not the solution."

"Not just plants; I'm working on a fallout shelter in case that thing drops ten miles of stone on top of us," Andre informed him calmly. "I'm not at all thinking that anything I can do will be able to impact that creature. Nature will protest and fight, but ultimately bend to its whims, even if it *is* a corrupted beast. Also, if the lore on this thing is accurate, those 'stars' are actually teeth attached to vines, so let me know if they start moving downward."

"It's able to bite us at a *distance?*" Zed yelped as he stared at the green-glowing gems that completely covered... no, were closing in on the main beast. "Uhm. I think it's starting to pull itself together up there."

Luke tossed a waterskin to Andre as the weeping Druid-voice calmed itself enough to continue speaking.

"All you'll need to do to stop Hamlin is..." The weeping

turned spiteful and vicious. "Ha! All you'll need to do is destroy the Earthen Node he's been draining for however long he's been trapped here! Do it, Druid; turn against nature as I once did, and doom this world as surely as my creation would! Fools... this world needs to be eradicated! The people are filth, and the planet a waste! Once Hamlin reaches another Node, the chain reaction will corrupt the entire planet and force it to Descend! Your only saving grace...? None of you will be around to see it!"

"Ah. He *was* fully insane," Zed acknowledged sagely. "I see. Any of that useful?"

The voice continued rambling and shouting, but Luke tuned it out as he mulled over the instructions. "So this planet is probably dead, is what I'm hearing. What do you guys want to use as our next base world? I'm thinking we should pick up our families before we get outta here; might be hard to come back if it Descends. Andre, your world seems nice. Can we live there for a while?"

"You think the portal back would turn orange?" Zed inquired as the two of them searched for a tunnel entrance. "When this world Descends, I mean."

"Can the two of you stop that, *please?*" Taylor seemed tired when she made her request, but her eyes drifted to Andre. "Anything?"

"What do you mean?" Andre continued motioning like a conductor at an orchestra, growing and directing plants. "This stuff is *amazing* fertilizer. Celestial feces indeed, you know?"

"So all of you just... gave up?" A tear rolled down Taylor's cheek for an instant before it, too, was whisked away by her passive spell. "We aren't going to try to save all the people that thing is going to kill? We *literally* have a chance to save the world-"

"That's just *it*, Taylor!" Andre's bellow took them all by surprise. He was on his feet now, his hands trembling. "We *don't* have a chance! That monster may as well be level *thirty*! As far as we're concerned, that thing is a *god*. It will literally crack this planet apart over time, just by *existing*. You think I don't *want* to save this place? That being represents a perversion of *everything* I stand for!"

"We can beat it!" Taylor yelled back, her facade broken by Andre's emotional display. "The crazy Druid told us how to do it; he just doesn't believe we *can*. What's a Node? He said we need to break it, but can we *fix* it?"

Andre scoffed and sent a wave of sludge at her with a twitch of his finger. "You're so full of feces on the inside, the outside should match. You don't even know what a Node *is*, so of course you listen to the long-dead Druid taunting us with impossibility."

"Well?" Taylor demanded as the muck vanished from her clothes. "Tell me what it is, and I'll go do it myself!"

"You're *incorrigible!*" the Druid raged, turning his mind back to his plants with a growl. "You know what a ley line is? A path for the planet's natural power, the mana of nature that empowers all of humanity? Without a ley line, that mana pools and stagnates; opening Scars and twisting nature into abominations and monsters. A *healthy* planet will have ley lines that work together to eventually Ascend the planet. Now, *sometimes* those lines will cross. If *three* lines cross, an Earthen Node can form a well of power that keeps the pooling mana healthy and natural."

"So this thing has been eating all that power this whole time?" Zed joined the conversation, more to keep it going than for any other reason. "It damaged the Node, or destroyed it?"

"Sounded like it was damaged, judging by the level of crazy that voice seemed to be." Luke offered his viewpoint. "Damaged means fixable."

"You guys..." Andre shook his head furiously, but went limp as they stared at him with bright eyes. "I have no idea how we would even make an attempt on it."

"Wait for the beast to start leaving, fix the Node, and... what, does that kill it?" Zed waved at the plant that was actually starting to exhibit draconic features. "Celestials, look at that thing. Vines for muscle fiber and tendons, metal bones, teeth, and claws, and a super-predator's meaty mind. Where can *I* get one of those?"

"That wouldn't kill it." Andre closed his eyes and thought back to the theories he had once explored with Xan, his mentor. "The sheer amount of mana required to create a Nature Dragon means that their very being is tied to an Earthen Node. If a creature that is *literally* an incarnation of nature becomes corrupted, that means that the Node had to be damaged *after* the creature was made. So... repairing it would... it would... uncorrupt the Dragon?"

"Would you then own a Dragon?" Zed stared at Andre with feverish expectation shining in his eyes. "Andre! This is an important question! You answer it right now!"

Szzz!

Sharp sounds like flaming arrows being fired resounded through the cavern as glowing chunks started raining into the muck all around them.

"What was that?" Andre frowned as one of his plant weaves was abruptly cut through from top to bottom. "Don't let them hit you!"

The falling 'teeth' didn't seem to be targeting them, which was good, since they struck like tiny meteors made of razor blades. The Four watched with growing horror as each impacted area turned into a tiny whirlpool that sucked in the nutritious muck. When the mixture stilled, they had a moment of hope that this was the end of it. That hope was dashed as wooden bodies started erupting from the depths; and the humans got their first look at a creature that hadn't been seen in the local multiverse for centuries.

"*Corrupted Dragon Tooth,*" Andre recited numbly. "I forgot. The Dragon itself won't attack us, because it won't even notice our presence. Abyss, it wouldn't even retaliate if we threw everything we had at it. We're less than ants to it... the creatures that it creates just by *existing* will bring it all the nutrients it ever needs to grow. They'll eat the resources, ravage the earth, and stockpile all life in their guts."

"Andre. I need to know." Luke held Cookie firmly in his right hand, repetitively smacking her top into his left palm as he stared down the shambling Teeth. "How much Potentia do you think those are worth?"

CHAPTER FIFTY-ONE

"Lamprey face with teeth made of metal that spin clockwise on the outside, counter-clockwise with the inner, twelve legs that propel the creature through the water as easily as on land, the Corrupted Swamperling Tooth seeks your flesh and bone," Zed intoned in a too-loud voice.

"*Why?*" Taylor sent a sharp query at Zed as she took the initiative to send a Shatter Shot at the closest Tooth. It hit the creature and blew a chunk off, but the creature merely screamed and initiated regenerating its wood and ivory carapace.

"Gotta get the story right, and saying what I see out loud will help! Any further information on them will be much appreciated for the epic saga I'll be telling one day," Zed explained as he started edging toward a hole in the wall he had noticed earlier. "I think that will get us back to the tunnel system; there are a bunch of bugs just sitting in there!"

Luke appreciated the fact that Zed was using his head. He really did. It mattered. However, the Murderhobo had no intention of leaving right now. "Cookie, you wanna see what we gotta do to kill these things all the way dead?"

Cookie responded by lashing out and smashing through the metal teeth of the Tooth, taking the entire top of its head off. Luke laughed and swapped his mana-weapons to his trusty Battering Ram Knuckles, then threw Cookie at another monster and jumped on the regenerating Tooth, beating its brutalized body over and over until only wood chips and ivory shards remained. That sank into the muck, and he called Cookie back to him.

Damage dealt: 2,100 blunt over 3 seconds.

"I've never met something that can take such a beating that I can still kill!" The Murderhobo howled in joy as his first target fell.

"It's *not* dead, Luke!" Andre called as the muck turned into a whirlpool where the wood chips had sunk. "Even if we get them out of this easily digestible fertilizer and beat them to scraps, they'll just take a little longer to regenerate! I have no idea how to kill them permanently!"

"Escape sounds *awesome*!" Zed called as more of the Teeth began propelling themselves toward their location, leaving wakes in the sludge as they swam. "Andre, anything you can tell us, *please*?"

The Druid joined Zed and Taylor, reluctantly followed by the Murderhobo when he realized that his back was about to be unprotected. The Druid regurgitated everything he could remember as they ran into the tunnel that was *packed* with brain-dead Preying Mantous. "They eat *anything*. Animal, mineral, vegetable. Their bodies are hollow, and when they're filled up, they'll bring the stuff to the Node to nurture it and the Dragon. But that's when they're *not* corrupted, so I have no idea what they're gonna do! A Corrupted Nature Dragon is... I don't even have a way to explain how taboo and twisted that is!"

"My guess is that they'll just be mindless destroyers that do nothing to help nature," Taylor shared her grim vision of the monsters that had started following them into the tunnel. It was too tight for more than a few at a time, but they could already hear the grinding of tortured stone as the Teeth began eating to carve *new* paths toward their fleeing food. "What about the bugs? If we reopen the Scar, would they be natural enemies and fight each other?"

"I *just* closed that, Taylor," Luke growled as he brought Cookie down on a Tooth and turned it into mulch and metal triangles. "Second issue: the Scar is right in the center of the Dragon, and I'm pretty sure that path is closed. Even when that beast moves, the Scar will be hanging in the air a mile up. I can't get at it."

"That, *and* the bugs were fleeing. Good chance that opening the Scar would just wake these things up, let them leave, and we get no shock troops," Zed reminded them, of a simple fact. He gestured back down the tunnel, where most of the Teeth were chowing down on the bugs instead of chasing the humans. "Better to leave it closed so that the Teeth go after the easy treats."

They scurried through the tunnels as rapidly as possible, but *thousands* of Teeth had already been created. The inevitable eventually happened: they turned a corner and found the beasts rushing toward them. That was when Luke realized something that he had missed until that point. "They only shine green when we're looking at them!"

He drove Cookie forward like a spear, smashing directly through the monster's mouth and out the back of its head, letting her momentum continue on to impact the Tooth following behind it, and used his fists to break the lead monster apart. A spinning mouth closed on his hand as it drove through the woody body, and the rotating jaws clamped down in an attempt to blend his limb into mulch. He pulled his arm back in the same instant as his armor sparked and screamed a warning.

Damage taken: 0 (14 armor damage).

"It barely *touched* me!" Luke growled in frustration. He grabbed the chunks of the first monster, and used those to wale on the one that bit him. Then he threw that one into its fellows and followed the tunnel branch that the rest of his team was running down.

Potentia gained: 428. (85% kill credit)

That notification almost made him stop in excitement, and he shouted the information to his group, "They die for good if they get eaten by the others!"

"Good to know!" Zed called from right behind Andre, who he was currently using as a shield as they ran. "It'll go in the song! Was there something else? The glowing thing?"

"Yeah!" Luke knew Cookie would be lightly laughing at his forgetfulness; she was great about poking fun at him in non-annoying ways. "We can't trust dark pathways! They're almost silent on dry land, and they only become visible when we look at them."

"As the prophecy foretold," Zed stoically intoned. "Fear the caverns, for they too have teeth. Wait, no. *Teeth.* Capital 't'. Man, those Anarcanists were actually trying to be helpful, huh?"

"They seemed like solid people when I met their leader," Luke agreed with him instantly. "We need to be able to get eyes on all these things at the same time, and then we can work on crushing them and feeding them to their friends. If we know where they are, we can prepare accordingly!"

"You met—no, wait, that's a great idea!" Taylor looked back at him with interest. "I think I even have a way to make that happen. Andre, we need to get back to the main cavern."

"That's what I was thinking," the Druid agreed as they made a sharp turn and the dark tunnel lit up a bright, toxic green. "*Abyss!*"

Luke whizzed past the Druid and used both hands to drive Cookie down, pancaking the Tooth into the floor, where it screamed at him until he smacked it again. Andre waved his hand, and his vines whipped out and tossed the crushed body at the others, where it was accepted and ground down in an instant by the monsters' blender-teeth.

Damage dealt: 1,342 blunt.
Potentia gained: 391.

Andre stomped on the ground, and a wall of stone dropped

and blocked off the tunnel. "This way! I feel the methane blowing in!"

Luke remembered at that moment that the rest of his team was depending on plants to give them air, and took a moment to appreciate the fact that each of them appeared to have a thick, bushy mustache. The double flower that blocked both nostrils... it was too much. A smile appeared on his face, and he and Cookie shared a moment of smug humor at their friends' expense.

They emerged into the open air of the cavern once more, and the previously dark cavern radiated with bright green light as the thousands of Teeth were suddenly *looked* at. All of them —all of the ones that turned green, at least—rotated and looked directly at The Four. Zed made a mental note that he decided to share with the group. "It appears they know where someone is if they're being observed... what a fascinating power they have. Oh, look, they don't like it when people stare at them. So, maybe, *don't* look, right?"

"I'm ready; hold them off." Taylor began gathering her mana, and delight filled her face as she worked with her power. "All of you, I'm sharing my status sheet with you. Zed, tell me what's different!"

Luke blinked away the information that appeared, but it still blocked his vision for a second.

Level: 10
Current Etheric Xenograft Potentia: 4,523/14,400 to level 11!
Body: 8.9

- *Fitness: 9.2 -> 10.5*
- *Resistance: 6.2 -> 7.3*

Mind: 15.75

- *Talent: 14.7 -> 15.2*
- *Capacity: 14.2 -> 16.3*

Presence: 10.05

- *Willpower: 7.7 -> 8.1*
- *Charisma: 12*

Senses: 31.65

- *Physical reaction: 32.2 -> 34.2*
- *Mental energy: 26.4 -> 29.1*

Maximum Health: 123
Maximum Mana: 250.8 -> 342.25
Mana regen: 5.06 per second

"Something's funky with your mana! You have too much of it!" Zed called at her as lightning began to twist out of Taylor and take shape above her head. "You increased everything except Charisma, probably because of the unicorn horn, but even so... too much mana!"

"This is *amazing!*" Taylor screamed with excitement as the Thunder Beast's Eye fully formed. As soon as it was ready, she *pushed* at it mentally. It looked at her, and she continued urging it onward. After a few moments of internal struggle, she convinced the Spell that it was *supposed* to hover in place a few hundred feet above her and watch for targets from that vantage.

The Spell began moving, and the magical eye detected every possible potential target in the cavern *at the same time.* If daylight on the surface were green, it would still be only as bright as the glow in the huge cavern. Exactly as they had hoped, all the Teeth were transfixed by the Spell and tried to figure out how to absorb it for nutrients so it would stop *staring* at them.

Rumble.

For a long moment, the world paused as the group froze in varying degrees of concern as the Dragon above them seemed to react to the spell... but they quickly realized that the abomination wasn't thinking about them, nor its gatherers. It was simply getting more comfortable. Apparently 'comfort' meant that it no longer wanted to spend energy holding onto the ceiling; because it tapped into the natural forces of the world and reversed the point to which their bodies were drawn.

Over the course of several seconds, the gravity in the room shifted and started pulling up not only The Four, but thousands of Teeth, as well as the muck that coated the floor.

The Druid reacted by lashing them together with a vine as they started to float, then pulling a slab of stone out of the wall above them so that they could control their 'fall'. The stone ledge they landed on began ascending, and they slowly rode it higher and higher, continually passed by Teeth that were dropping *far* faster.

A howling breeze hit them a moment after they started upward, nearly throwing them from their precarious perch and out into the open air once more. Zed, trying to rise from his new position of 'plastered against the ground which was also the ceiling', hunted for the source of the attack... only to realize that it *wasn't* an attack. "The Dragon... all it did was *move?*"

Luke studied the beast, trying to find a *single* weak point. Skin had covered the plant-fiber interior, and he was almost positive that the outer layer was some kind of dense metal. Its eyes were made of diamond; chunks of moving minerals coated the new skin and turned the surface layer into a grinder... "At least it can't fly with all that weight."

"No, there is that," Andre agreed as the wind touched down. "But if it can tap into natural forces, that means it has access to the *Fifth* Circle-"

The Dragon moved a claw and touched the ceiling it was connected to, and the earth began swirling and collapsing *upward*. The stone walls of the cavern shook so hard that Andre needed to intervene once more to keep them on the moving platform. The simple vine was replaced by thick restraints of vines strapping them together. By the time they managed to refocus on the Dragon, a quarter of it had already vanished into the newly-forming tunnel. Taylor realized the Dragon was heading for the surface and cursed harshly, calling out, "That hole it's making should have been far too small for the beast! *How?*"

"It *is* nature, even if it is corrupted. Nature forms itself however it wants." Andre's voice was resigned. "Why expend all the power needed to make a hole a mile wide, when something *that*-sized will work and allow it to move through…?"

The Druid's voice petered off as he got his first look at the Earthen Node that had become visible as soon as the dragon moved away. The green light from the Teeth floating through the open cavern faded into obscurity as a triplet of color filled the air.

The Murderhobo summed up the experience perfectly for everyone.

"Wow."

CHAPTER FIFTY-TWO

- ANDRE -

A perfect equilateral triangle—formed of scintillating liquid energy that shifted among a trio of colors—blazed in the air, fed by nearly indistinct veins of power that vanished into the earth around them. The Earthen Node slowly rotated in place, a wellspring of power that displayed no signs of damage at all. Andre stared directly at the light, swallowing dryly and looking away only when his eyes began to hurt from the intensity of the collected power.

"Breaking that would kill the Dragon, right?" The Murder-hobo's blasphemy almost made the Druid throw the man into open air out of pure shock. "How hard do you think I'd need to-"

"It's *energy*, Luke." Taylor, ever the voice of reason, came to nature's defense before Andre needed to do so. "If the colors are anything to go on, it's red for fire, blue for air, and green for stone or gravity. Now, a simple question arises here, Luke. How do you propose we *break* energy?"

"You..." Luke looked to the others for confirmation as he

slowly finished his thought, "…you figure out how hard you need to hit it?"

"No. Just *no*. Please don't try to figure out a way to permanently kill a large section of the planet by removing an Earthen Node," Andre pled with the group at large, who quieted down. As they approached the ceiling, he released the stone slab, and they coasted the rest of the way up. A coiled vine arresting their momentum was sufficient to terminate their descent gently before they landed, removing any chance of damage even for the Bard. "As you can all tell, the reversed falling is just *barely* more powerful than the natural force attempting to reassert itself."

"I can jump pretty high." Luke launched himself up—down —and the Druid coughed as he tried to speak and shout a warning at the same time.

"*Luke!*" Andre groaned as he used his vines to yank the Murderhobo back to the ceiling. "Listen, all of you: a forceful enough jump will bring you all the way down to the actual floor again. We have a few minutes before everything else reaches us up here, especially the swamp muck, but we need to be careful as we close in on that Node. The Teeth will *not* be happy that we're here. Don't fall. I'm removing the vines now."

With all his safety devices removed, The Four could autonomously explore once more. Taylor took note of all the acid-green Teeth coming to rest on the cavernous ceiling, and began to ready her spells. "Andre… I'm fairly certain I have something that could destroy that Node. If we can't figure out a way to save it, I *will* break it. It'll destroy this area permanently, but it'll give this world time to fix itself. Time to prepare. Time that the Dragon will remove if it gets to another Node."

"Your Nullify Spell?" Andre went numb at the mere *possibility* that she could make good on her ultimatum. His mind whirled and settled on 'blank'. He simply stared at this terrible person in front of him until Zed slapped him and nearly got a thorn in his arm for his trouble.

"*Teeth!*" the Bard screeched as he pointed toward the

Earthen Node. Andre shook himself out of his thoughts when he realized that the Murderhobo was already among the near-countless creatures. Various spells were arcing away from Taylor, and he dazedly wondered how she had regained her mana so quickly.

Even with his mind tormenting him with vague hopes, he began setting up his battle station. Roots drove into the stone around him as a vine anchored itself to his Livingwood Staff, and a moment later, the new bushes were providing him with a sustainable arrow supply. Still, he knew that basic arrows weren't going to take down these beasties. Therefore, he had given the arrows a single directive to follow whenever they slammed into the shambling Teeth.

Grow.

His first shot zipped out, swerving slightly as Luke got in the original path, then embedded itself in the leg of one of the timber Teeth. Andre allowed himself a momentary pause as he waited to determine whether he would need to be an active participant in the next step, but a moment later, thick roots sprang out of the impact site and burrowed into the ground, bringing the Corrupted Tooth to a standstill. It screeched and tried to grasp the wound it had previously ignored, but its body couldn't contort enough to-

"Celestial *Feces!*" Andre flinched as the Tooth was swarmed by other nearby Teeth as they sensed the 'natural' plant matter and attempted to get at it.

Potentia gained: 25. (5% kill credit)

"The first successful root canal!" Zed howled enthusiastically.

"Why didn't I think of that before?" the Druid chastised himself as Zed shouted encouragement to the entire team. It was only then that Andre realized that the Bard was also frantically playing his original-design instrument, the 'Ukulele' they had banned in the mountain pass so long ago, so that monsters wouldn't know their exact location. That ban was out of the question at the moment, and Andre was pleasantly surprised to

find that he really enjoyed listening to the instrument. He enjoyed the *other* benefit even more.

Ballad of Vigor is impacting you! Most-used resource regeneration is increased by 25%!

"Keep that up, Andre!" Zed called to him. "I really like the part where they eat each other and not me! Woo! Yes! *Taylor on your left*! Woo-*hoo*, that was close!"

The Druid didn't have time to track all of his teammates; he needed to start clearing their path. He slammed his Staff into the stone and ordered it to fire arrows at anything that moved, except his team. The Livingwood Staff had a *slight* intelligence, really just enough to understand that the three other people it had been around for so long were friends and not targets. Arrows constantly sprouted from the bushes, presented themselves to the Staff, and moments later erupted, from whatever Corrupted Dragon Tooth needed to die the most—at least from the Staff's point of view.

Now having a plan of action, the Druid turned two of the bushes to seed and poured his blood onto them as soon as he scooped them up. With a push of power, he scattered them and repeated the process. In under five minutes, Andre managed to collect *thousands* of seeds using the new template that he had given them, then turned and began sprinting toward the Earthen Node, which was in the exact center of the cavernous ceiling. "Everyone except Luke, follow me! Murderhobo! You get in front and scatter them!"

He wanted to look back at the Bard, if only to laugh at the man as he tried to play, run, and continue chanting encouragement all at the same time. He hoped that his friend would survive, but now was not the correct time to be worrying about a single person. This entire world could die, and that would set the Plane in a downward spiral that would eventually force it to Descend. If the Bard died, but they saved the world, that would be worth... "Feces, I'm acting like Taylor was. Zed, get over here!"

Andre refused to justify the cost of his friend's life for the benefit it *might* have given. Taylor had done that, and until she proved otherwise, it wasn't just him that had lost faith in her. He hadn't wanted to say it out loud before they were done here, but frankly… the team had outgrown her. It was time for her to go.

He didn't even need to do anything overly special. When they finished this mission, they would hide in the desert, start an oasis, and wait for her to go 'looking for something', her code for sneaking away and informing the crown of their mission's success. Then they would vanish to the *true* hiding place they decided on as a trio.

The fact that he felt her betrayal of the team was inevitable made him slightly sad. It was hard to let go of hope that he had kept alive for decades, even when that hope failed over and over again. *He* would not make the same mistake of losing trust, even if it actually cost him the world. "Hold tight, Zed. You aren't gonna like this."

As soon as the Bard was beside him, Andre used his vines to make a seat under Zed and lifted him up to function as a back-pack. He started running again even before the man was fully stable, using the framework of greenery to bear all the weight, as well as propel them both forward. He loved the fact that moving with such ease made him look as strong as Luke, even when his leveling points had almost exclusively been dropped in Capacity. He might not be able to do what the others could, but he could continue forever. Just like nature itself, he would grind down his enemies, remove their defenses, and destroy them with sheer endurance.

The Druid fell in behind Luke and began scattering his seeds to either side as fast as he could grab each handful. The plants sprouted in the rock easily, but only tiny shoots appeared. Zed called him out on it in the same encouraging tone as before, "You're doing *great*, Andre, even if I don't know why your Ability to control plants doesn't seem to be working!"

"It's working just fine," Andre coolly answered as the first of the Teeth closed in behind them. The wooden warrior stepped on his bamboo caltrop-thorns, and the plant hissed as it released its payload into the fresh wound. There were no visible effects, but moments later, the Teeth accompanying the affected Tooth dove at it and began chowing down, revealing a tangled wooden structure growing within the Tooth's body.

Potentia gained: 25. (5% kill credit)

The Druid vomited to the side as he felt his connection to these plants becoming greater, only for them to be torn apart mere moments later. It felt like a perversion of the natural order to do something so barbaric, and he wondered if the Potentia would comfort him during his inevitable nightmares of this moment if they survived.

Zed's strained enthusiasm interrupted Andre's thoughts. "So, yeah, that was my pants, but I think these clothes were ruined the moment we landed in the swamp. Um. yeah, great job! No one can... um. No one can puke on me quite like *you* can!"

CHAPTER FIFTY-THREE

- LUKE -

"You get in front and scatter them!" Andre shouted at Luke. The Murderhobo didn't need to be told twice. He whooped for joy and whipped his hand at a Tooth that was slowly floating closer, sending out his bottle and drilling the beast in its head. The bottle vanished at the same time as the monster flew into the air toward the sludge creeping up toward them, but the Murderhobo had already forgotten all about that attack. He followed up by using Bum Flash to close on the acid-green twelve-legged Tooth leading the charge at his team.

In the next instant, Cookie turned the Tooth into tooth*paste*, and Luke swirled in place to scatter the remains into the group that was still charging. He ignored the Potentia gains, as he knew he was far from a viable amount needed to upgrade anything. He shouldn't have wasted his time: the Teeth were closing around him, and they were *fast*. He lashed out with his Rope after launching Cookie dead center into the thickest group, but the Chain-Blade Rope simply didn't have the needed momentum to do more than give the closest monster a minor Toothache.

Cookie came sailing back, ringing the bell of a Tooth as she tumbled through the air. Luke punched a Tooth in the jaw, using the blades inside its own mandible to slice the upper part of its head off. The body fell, but he knew it wasn't dead. Chancing a look back, he found that the others were starting to gain on him, and Andre was tossing confetti to the sides as he ran. The image of the bulky Druid as a flower girl at a wedding was somewhat ruined by Zed screaming and frantically strumming his instrument from Andre's back while being tossed around, but even so, the Murderhobo instinctively knew that the battle ahead was his responsibility.

"He did say *scatter* them. I can do that." Luke looked at Cookie as she leapt into his hand, then at the creatures that were converging on him from all sides. He heard his team crying out a warning but ignored it as he swung his Rope down at Cookie.

The weapon wrapped around Cookie's handle and tried to dig in. Even though the extended blades failed to find purchase, they *did* provide a tight grip; and he once more threw Cookie at the Teeth. Grinning, he hauled back on his Rope and *twisted*. His angular momentum pulled Cookie to the side, and soon he was whirling around as fast as he could move.

Pristine Balance ensured he didn't get dizzy or lose his footing, and he began using the Source-cerer's Armory ability to increase the weapon size of his Rope. The oversized Greatclub granted the weight and density needed to smack the Teeth hard enough to send them flying away, so he continued for a few dozen steps before coming to a halt. "What's blue, white, and bad for your Teeth? *Cookie*."

"That was amazing!" Zed called as they ran toward him. "We're behind you! Please don't attack us as we get closer to you, m'kay pumpkin?"

Luke grunted. He appreciated the fact that Zed was learning to help him be aware of his surroundings, but he wasn't going to give the smug Bard the satisfaction when he was showing his knowledge as little jabs like that. Taylor sidled up to him and inspected Cookie, who still had a humming blue cord wrapped around her handle. "Did you learn a new Skill?"

He shook his head, deciding that the Mage didn't need to know every little thing that he could do. The Teeth weren't exactly giving them time to chat anyway, their dozen legs sending them across the ceiling at high speed. It appeared that the Druid had caught on to Luke's plans, and was now combining his seed ability with controlling the earth around them, simply smacking upward to send the Teeth up... down? Into the open air above them. Luke thought it was an excellent way to hurry themselves along, so he tossed out Cookie and switched to his Battering Ram Knuckles.

"Wanna see how many uppercuts I can manage in ten seconds? Me too." The Murderhobo dashed forward and ducked, lashing upward and sending the howling Tooth flying away. "One!"

What followed was Luke doing a series of rapid-fire squats, sometimes sending two or more Teeth out into the open air as they piled on him. It wasn't long before he needed to cut down on the whole-body movement, instead using both hands independently as if he were curling dumbbells as fast as he could. "Cookie! *Ah-ow!*"

Damage taken: 38 shredding.

He had stopped moving forward, and one of the lamprey-like mouths had closed on his side before he'd managed to punch the Tooth away. It started disintegrating as it whistled away, his potently poisonous body too much for its regenerative properties. While effective, there was unfortunately not enough of him to go around. Even with all his strategies, he was getting overwhelmed. Countless more Teeth had swarmed their area, and his team was too close in proximity for him to manage another whirling attack. Not without killing the entirety of his team. He could hear a series of *thuds* as Cookie barged through the line toward him, but he wasn't going to-

Z-zap! A bolt of lightning the thickness of his arm melted a hole through the left-hand line of Teeth, and he took the reprieve to Flash out of combat and reorient himself. Zed was calling instructions, and finally, he got to Luke. "Listen! Andre's going to distract the creatures; we need you up front to-"

"*Flame Lance!*" A swirl of flame erupted from Taylor, blasting a solid dozen of the Teeth away.

"-never mind, Taylor just killed us all." Zed moaned, paused, then continued directing Luke. "Somehow we're not all dead, so we need you to get ahead of us and scatter them again. Andre's gonna make a bunch of waving plants, and we're gonna use that as a distraction to run for the Earthen Node."

"No oxygen here! The methane is pressurized; it's flowing upward! Fresh air can't get past that!" Taylor laughed wildly as a whole new range of options opened up for her. "It can't burn without air! This place won't explode!"

"Until the Dragon hits the surface and oxygen starts flowing down, anyway!" Andre bellowed back over the blender-howling of the Teeth chomping down on them. "Or until he hits feeder caverns, and a huge inrush of wind pours down that tunnel it's carving! *Don't use fire!*"

"Abyss." Taylor's mutter was only heard by Luke, and only because his senses were attuned to the maximum. "I really wanted to kill these things with fire."

"I bet flames would make them dead-dead!" Zed shouted in realization. "If Teeth are dissolved upon mastication, fire is the answer to the last equation!"

"He hit his head; watch for a concussion!" Luke called as he started swinging Cookie in a series of arcs. "Here I go!"

The Murderhobo heard a scream as he began whirling, but he ignored it in favor of putting maximum effort into his attack. Ten steps, hundreds of Teeth flying. Twenty steps, over a thousand sent up, and Cookie was buzzing through the air like an angry hornet. At thirty, a massive swath of ceiling was clear, and he turned his attention back to the situation unfolding with his team.

All he could see was blood.

Taylor bore a gaping wound on her side where a Tooth had chomped down and torn out a chunk of flesh before being blasted away. Andre kneeled next to her, attempting to fend off the trailing Teeth while working to patch her up, and Zed slammed his Ukulele into one that lunged for them, destroying the instrument but giving the Druid enough time to send the beast flying. The Lightning Beast's Eye had zipped over when Taylor became embroiled in combat, her attention too divided to keep it away. It had helped Luke, but in doing so had left Taylor with one less blast that she could use to protect herself.

The Murderhobo rushed over and grabbed her just as Andre finished his ministrations. They turned and charged together at the Earthen Node, Luke carrying the Mage and Andre hauling the Bard. The Druid looked into the distance and screamed, "Full avoidance! Get to the Node!"

"Got it. Good luck to you." Luke slammed his right foot down and soared into the air, causing Taylor to screech and pound weakly on his armor. He shook her gently, and she went green as the pain from her wound flared up. "I've got experience with this. Trust me."

"I don't trust any-" Taylor bit her lip and forced herself to stop talking as the ceiling receded, then paled as Luke whirled them around and kicked off one of the Teeth that was spiraling away. The Murderhobo made sure to overcompensate, kicking *way* harder than needed.

Luke had sent so many Teeth into the air, and at such high speed, that he never lacked for a platform to kick off. That wasn't even counting all the other Teeth that had yet to reach the ceiling. He was keeping a close eye on the muck that was still rising upward, slowly closing in on the area where the spell had originally been cast: right next to the Earthen Node. "We need to get there now, or we're gonna be swimming to get at the Node. I'm *not* opening my eyes under that stuff."

"Hey, Luke!" Zed's voice spoke into Luke's ear, almost making him mistime his next kick. "Andre really likes what you're doing, so we copied it! Now we're swinging through the area like monkeys in a jungle! While I have you here, any ideas on how to fix this thing so that the world doesn't… wither?"

"No," the Murderhobo replied instantly. Zed waited for more, but it was Taylor that continued.

"Are we even sure that fixing it would *stop* the dragon?" Her voice was breathy and pained, but it got the point across.

"Andre says 'no', but since the dragon is linked to it, removing the corruption *should* remove the influence on the creature's mind. If nothing else, it will lose all the magical protections it has until it reconnects to a Node again. It'll just be a really big plant coated in metal." Zed let them think, then badgered them after a long moment of silence. "We're running out of time; we need to make a choice."

Luke landed on the ceiling in a squat, absorbing the force by bending so that Taylor wouldn't get jostled. The act caused him to sink slightly into the ground… and power surged into him. It felt like it should have been painful, but it only made the Murderhobo's bones itch. "What did I just-"

Current Mana regeneration: 80 per second.

Luke looked down and saw a deep brown energy sparking into him a few times per second, as if he were being hit by low-level lightning. "Andre. The ground is attacking me. Do I fight back, or is this something you're doing?"

"He says you're standing on an exposed ley line, and to pretty please *not* attack it." Zed passed back a moment later. "He also wants to know if it's hurting you? Apparently, you should be popping into tiny bits like a spore-mushroom that someone stomped on."

"It's just *mana*," Luke scoffed, gently kicking a rock over the spot where the lightning was emanating. It glowed brown for a moment, then melted and merged with the stone.

"Well… yeah," Zed answered him, "Andre is saying that ley lines are just like Mana Channels, but for the world."

That sparked an idea, and Luke checked carefully to make sure it wasn't actually just more lightning hitting him. "Zed… if ley lines are just Mana Channels, then this Earthen Node is just a damaged Mana Channel. Why not just fix it the same way we would fix the issue in a person?"

He hefted his satchel of powdered unicorn horn and patted it twice.

CHAPTER FIFTY-FOUR

- TAYLOR -

The Mage coughed up blood as Luke made his suggestion to throw away their futures in an insane, misguided, most-likely-won't-even-work sort of way. If the blood had been from anger, she would have been impressed and asked the Murderhobo to teach her so that she could do the same to Archmage Dòn. But no: this was just good ol' fashioned internal damage rearing its ugly head.

"Luke... please, no," Taylor managed to squeeze out, even though her body protested the extra motion. A quick glance at her health made her wince in fear; even with Andre packing the wound with healing herbs and binding it with plants, the flesh in that space was *shredded*. She needed a healer that could repair the mutilated area, not some random leaves that had slight medicinal properties. "It might not do *anything*, and we need that powder to secure our power."

Out of the corner of her eye, she saw Andre tense up. It was times like this that she almost wished she didn't have such potent Senses. If she were blind to people's reactions, it would be so much *easier* to just do what needed to be done. Luke shrugged and pulled open the satchel. "I don't care what we do with this. It'll have no effect on me. You decide."

"Taylor..." Andre took a deep breath and swallowed deeply as mana started rushing toward them. Even the Earthen Node flickered like a candle in the wind for a brief moment, and Taylor hoped that she had been the only one to see that. "We have a shot here to make a difference on a scale that I can't even fully explain to you. This isn't even about the Hollow Kingdom anymore. This is... *nature.* This entire Plane of existence could be destroyed if we don't stop the Corrupted Nature Dragon."

"*I* can stop it." Taylor pointed her finger at the Node. "I just need to get over there. I'll destroy that, and the Dragon will die along with it."

A single tear slowly fell from Andre's left eye, following the bridge of his nose and vanishing in his slowly-returning-to-red mustache. "The Dragon is more than a monster, Taylor. It's bound to a representation of life. It *is* nature, at least nature within the territory of this Node. If we destroy this... nothing natural will ever again thrive in this area. The desert will expand. More and more of this world will fail as power is diverted from other ley lines in an attempt to fill this one. But it will never be fixed. There will be a hole in this world... and it will die."

Taylor took several deep breaths as the Druid's impassioned speech hit her like a Greatclub to the heart. "It will give us *time*, Andre. Even if it does work, how long will it take? What if the Dragon gets to another Node in that time and begins eating it? Then we wasted this and *still* failed. If we don't stop that thing... either way, this world is dead. I'd rather us be alive, Ascended, and powerful, instead of frantically searching for something that will give us a *fraction* of what we'd be throwing away, and hoping we win the race against time."

She turned her gaze away as Andre dropped his to the

ground. "I've decided. Luke, bring me in. We're destroying the Node."

The Murderhobo wasn't one for subtlety or emotional tug-of-war. She was his leader for now, and the order didn't hurt *him* at all. He turned and ran at the Node as she scanned their surroundings for potential enemies closing in. They had crossed the distance in record speed, thanks to the aerial movements, but twelve legs meant that the Teeth were coming at them *fast*. Her Thunder Beast's Eye had fizzled out, meaning the only light in the area was coming from the Node and Cookie. Her quick scan caused a pulse of acidic light to appear in a wave as her gaze traveled the distance, but it also meant that she knew she had time.

Enough time to do what had to be done.

The closer they got to the Node, the harder it was for her to breathe. The pressure coming off of the Node was *intense*, and each of Luke's steps caused one of three different-colored lightning bolts to arc off and strike him. Somehow the thick bands of power didn't seem to faze him, and he even chuckled a few times and muttered something about Cookie not tickling him when they were in a serious situation. Taylor shuddered to think that this man was by far the most powerful amongst them. She coughed and felt blood leak from her wounds before getting vanished by Cleanse.

Current Health: 42/123.

Shredded debuff: -5 health per 15 seconds.

This was the real reason she didn't have time to waste. Her friends might hate her forever for destroying the Node, but she was going to die within the next two minutes. There wasn't time for Andre to open a portal for her to his world. There wasn't time to find a healer. There was only time for her to make sure that her team survived, time enough to ensure the world had a chance to evacuate. Her friends would need to be the beacons that humanity turned to, and if all three of them had these 'prismatic' Mana Channels that Luke swore were real, there was a good chance that they could *do* it.

They could save everyone. *Anything* was possible if these three set their minds to it. They just... they just needed the chance. Her determination firmed even as her vision began to fade. "Luke, it needs to be now. Throw me in there if you need to do so, but get me there *now*."

For some reason, the Murderhobo forced his open satchel into her hands before whirling around and bodily *chucking* her at the Node. Andre's howl filled her ears. "No! Going into the Node is death! That much power! You *and* the world will die!"

"It's already too late for me," Taylor whispered as she zipped through the air, suddenly deep in her first memory of rebelling against Master Don and being thrown just like this, low gravity and all. The Earthen Node came closer... closer... then it lashed out at her. A thigh-thick band of power reached out and slammed into her chest, arresting her momentum slowly as it worked to keep her away.

Power *flooded* her, the pure mana that she had been born and raised in as a child. Its touch made her finally understand at a deep level how everything on this Plane was connected by this fundamental energy. This world's... this *Plane's* mana. It was *alive* in a way that she couldn't grasp, against all teachings of mana that she had ever received. It knew she was coming to destroy it. Right now, it was trying to kill her first.

"So this is what it's like to have powerful Mana Channels." The channeled power kept flowing into her, trying to fill her to the point that she would be destroyed, but before that could happen, she began *casting*.

Current Mana Regeneration: 50 per second.

"A full fifty mana per second?" A smile graced Taylor's face for the first time since they had descended into this pit. "At least I'll get to go out with a bang. I've always wondered what would happen..."

Taking a shallow breath, all her body would allow at the moment, Taylor began casting Thunder Beast's Eye. Then she *kept* casting it. All the power flowing from the Earthen Node was directed through her and into the eye as she slowly drifted closer and closer to the source of the mana.

Current Health: 32/123.

"Time flies when you're having fun," she murmured as her health flashed bright red at her. "I only need nine seconds to use Nullify to its maximum effect…"

By this point she was incredibly close to the Node, but the force of the energy had caused her to *almost* come to a standstill. Another full minute passed, bringing her to only twelve health, and she realized she was about to pass out. With a heave, she released the Spell, and the world was instantly awash with green light as the Teeth were *seen*.

Current Health: 7/123.

Thousands. Tens of thousands. All of them closing in on her. It was time. She was already late.

She pulled in as much air as she could, and wheezed, "*Null-*"

"*Please*, Taylor. Please trust me." Andre's arms wrapped around her, pulling the Mage into his embrace.

Taylor choked on her words as she recognized his presence. She stared into his deep green eyes; eyes that were… the exact color of the incoming Teeth? That was when she realized that perhaps this world had been giving them the clues they'd needed to save it the entire time. "I do… trust you. Andre."

She just wanted the *best* for him. But, she realized at that instant, perhaps she should actually trust *him* to know what that meant for himself. Taylor pressed the open satchel into his hands as lighting arced away from her spell to fry the nearest Teeth.

He would have all the time he needed to save the world, she realized. Her Spell, with all the power the world had given her, would keep him safe. "More than that… Andre. I… *love*…"

Current Health: 0/123.

CHAPTER FIFTY-FIVE

- ANDRE -

"You *what?*" Andre's eyes welled up as Taylor went limp in his arms with a soft exhalation. "Taylor? *Taylor!*"

He let go of her, and she continued to float in place, connected to the Earthen Node via a tether of brown energy. He held the satchel in his hand. He looked at it, and it took everything he had not to slap it closed and throw himself into the maw of the Teeth that were closing in. He wouldn't let Taylor's final act be wasted like that.

There was plenty of time to join her when he was done.

"Andre! What's happening? Taylor isn't responding!" Zed's frantic words hit Andre like a hammer blow, and he glanced back at the final members of his team who were rushing toward him. Luke had thrown him after Taylor as soon as the Druid realized what was happening, but they all knew that Zed wouldn't survive on his own if he overshot and landed amongst the Teeth.

"She died, Zed," Andre managed to say it out loud, though he couldn't keep his voice from breaking. As inside, so outside, he supposed. He watched the corpse of his oldest friend hanging in the air... and closed his eyes. "Take care of each other."

"No! *Andr-*" Zed's shout was cut off as the Druid got a firm foothold and forced himself *inside* the Earthen Node. Into enough energy that there was no surviving it. He knew he only had minutes to live, so he got to work.

On the plus side, he knew that entering concentrated power like this was a *quick* death. He had warned his friends about it, but he also knew it was most likely the best option for healing the Node. It wasn't something he had planned to do, but at this point, he'd do anything to succeed... and then he would be done.

Tri-colored light slammed into him, and he didn't try to resist. Instead, he used the extra power to capture the nearby stone and form a bubble of dense rock around himself, the Node... and Taylor. They'd all stay here together. Forever. As more power flowed into him, he used his Capacity to the fullest, and released the power in any way possible. Plants erupted into the open air outside the stone bubble, *almost* reaching the floating eye that was still sending blistering bolts of pure tribulation at the Teeth.

He took another step and was suddenly the first human to view the core of an Earthen Node with his bare eyes. Andre reached forward, but even with all his strength, he was unable to touch the core itself. That was okay with him. He didn't need to touch it. He dropped his hand down, and reached into the satchel.

Pulling out the largest packet of Powdered Unicorn Horn, he shoved it at the core. The gossamer packaging vanished as if it had never existed, leaving only an eruption of potent catalyst that hung in the air, thanks to the low gravity. It sank into the area around the core, stopping just as his hand had a solid inch from the surface. "No! Come *on*! This can heal you!"

QUERY.

The exultant emotion, the tacit understanding, the mind-breaking fact that nature itself had just spoken to him… it filled a hole in Andre that he had never realized was empty.

Ability gained!

Andre ignored everything besides that fact that the earth had asked him a question, and he needed to answer it. "This catalyst might be able to uncorrupt this Earthen Node! Please, *please* take it!"

DOUBT.

Images of another Druid making promises to the earth. Hard facts that those the world had trusted in ages past had not only failed it, they had betrayed that selfsame sacred trust. A Dragon and a Node were corrupted and went insane in a single instant. The world dyed green as sustainers-turned-devourers were unleashed and began following their instincts. A human standing closer to it than any before had done, and asking for *trust* while attempting to imbue it with *something*? It could be *anything!*

Andre knew that words meant nothing to the Plane. *Actions* were the only thing that *might* sway it. "I'm spending my life on this. If you die, so will I."

He dumped the entire contents of the satchel onto the core, then tossed it aside as the mass of powder settled in a perfect sphere around the Earthen Node. Not even pausing to take a deep breath, Andre reached inside himself and felt his current connection to the stone bubble he had created. He *pulled* on it, offering that bond to the Node.

The world accepted the bond with the faintest feeling of confusion. It seemed to realize what that tether meant a moment later: there was no escape for the Druid. With a shiver of fear, or perhaps anticipation, the barrier around the core of pure energy vanished. The powder collapsed inward.

The world went white.

———

- LUKE -

"I... I can't reach either of them, Luke." Zed's voice quivered as they watched stone and plants erupt from around the Node, sealing two of their friends within. "Luke... he said Taylor died. I think they *both* did."

A resounding *crack* caused the air to tremble, and the stone around the Node was replaced with perfectly transparent crystal. Luke's eyes locked onto two silhouettes revolving slowly around the Earthen Node within, and he closed his eyes and let out a deep sigh. He opened them a moment later, watching as crystalline structures raced out from the translucent shell and began following along the ley lines.

A slight curl of disgust touched his lips when he noted that it spiraled exactly like the unicorn's horns had, but he let it go when it began changing further. Faint runes started to appear in the crystal, becoming more complex as the seconds passed. He could have happily watched the transformation all day, but a furious *detonation* of a scream reverberated through the overhead tunnel.

The Dragon.

"Well, here comes Mr. Grumpy!" Zed laughed as though his mind had failed. "I don't suppose he was supposed to just go with the flow and become *uncorrupted*, was he?"

"I have my doubts," Luke agreed with the Bard's assessment. "Pretty sure it's gonna come down here and try to break what we just fixed."

"How... what can we do about it?" Zed half-sobbed as the air trembled. The Dragon was moving *fast*. Fast enough to cause a downdraft that they could both feel. The Bard went stiff, and his voice lowered to a whisper. "Luke... Luke, I think I'm about to have a moment of being useful to the team. We'll probably die, but I think we can win. I just don't want to do it. I'll die in the way I fear most."

"How about you just say what you wanna say, and stop telling us what the end result is gonna be?" Luke growled at the

Bard, already limbering up in preparation of fighting the Dragon head-on. "Not gonna lie, I'm looking forward to this. I wonder how hard I need to hit nature in the face before it begs for mercy? If only I had a whole bunch of trash I could throw in water or something. I bet that would make it weaker."

"Luke! The downdraft! *Air!*" Zed shouted over his friend's inane rambling. "Your bottle weapon! Can it hold anything?"

Luke materialized the 'Mountaindale' bottle and held it up. "I can put stuff in it, yeah. What are you thinking?"

"Take this and pour it in! Spoiled moonshine from the capital!" Zed pulled out a distended wineskin and handed it over. Luke shrugged and popped the top off. There was a sharp retort as the pressure equalized, then he poured the pungent liquid into the bonded container. Zed handed over his prized firestone next. "Drop that in there, and you have an instant-"

Item upgraded! Mana-made Bottle has turned into 'Bottled Fireball'!
Note: this item will revert to a standard bottle after 1 use(s).

"Celestial feces. It worked. I got it, Zed. Get on my back right now." The Bard didn't need to be told twice, and in the next moment, the two of them had reached the edge of the tunnel leading to the surface. Luke was actually thankful that the Dragon had taken the lazy route and gone directly up through a smallish tunnel.

Putting all the strength he could muster into the act, he *jumped* up and away, twisting and throwing the bottle into the tunnel as hard as he could once he was directly over the center. They continued traveling toward the ground as the bottle went off course and hit the wall.

There was a small flare of light, which turned into a conflagration that filled the tunnel with a roar. The pressure rising from below was still stronger than what was coming down, so the flames *raced* upward as a continuous blowtorch. Luke watched as the perfectly-straight tunnel filled with fire, and his enhanced senses allowed him to see the *moment* the blast hit the Dragon.

"Abyss... not like this." Zed sobbed with the conflagration

reflecting off his wide-open eyes. "I don't want to burn. Not again."

He watched the unholy beast fighting through the flames, attempting to control the natural power and failing, since it had lost the connection to the Node, then trying to escape through the wall. That was the moment it realized that it had done too good of a job creating the tunnel it was descending through. The walls had been reinforced, and all exits had been closed off. There was nowhere for the fire to go, except up past the Dragon itself. The seemingly unending blaze *pounded* against the Dragon's metal hide, and it began to glow cherry-red.

At that moment, the colors of the Earthen Node shifted subtly toward red and blue, and the flames the creature was bathing in intensified. Each second that passed increased the depth of the blaze until the flames were white-hot and impossible to look at.

The Dragon opened its mouth to howl in fury, and the Earthen Node shifted slightly toward green. Gravity reasserted itself in the chamber just as Luke and Zed plunged into the muck that had been slowly rising toward the surface. They were only submerged in it for a few seconds, until their momentum carried them through and their exit closed behind them. For the Corrupt Dragon, gravity was not so kind. 'Down' appeared to be a fluid concept, though the beast always seemed to be 'falling' faster no matter which direction it was moving.

Both of the humans were wiping the filth off their faces as they rocketed toward the ground, managing to peel their eyes open just before they made it to the hard stone below. That was when the colors above flashed to pure red, and the runaway reaction of the superheated, compressed gas failed to keep the flames moving upward. The blowback reached the open chamber, and by then, there was enough oxygen that *all* of the chamber lit up - naturally, it was unnaturally concentrated upon the falling beast that had so utterly ticked off this Plane of existence.

Even so, the explosion filled the massive cavern, the air

converting from stable gas to pure *heat* in an instant. The floating muck partially contained the blast at first, but the explosion slammed it down like a wall, the substance nearly solidified from the force that propelled it. Luke managed to guide their descent, and - strangely coated by a glimmer of green light - they slammed into the huge gourd that Andre had used to bring them to the dangling roots of the Corrupted Nature Dragon in the first place.

The force of landing caused them to bounce and rolled the pumpkin over, dropping them unceremoniously inside Andre's fallout shelter. The gourd then became a plug, a rounded shield against the incoming refuse an instant before it impacted.

The detonation of natural gasses instantaneously baked the sludge into stone throughout the cavern, creating a vacuum that sucked the flailing remnant of the Corrupted Nature Dragon down into the chamber. The earth split from the concussive waves, and a bolt of green light from the Earthen Node signaled the first of *dozens* of rockslides that sent multi-ton boulders bouncing off the beast with impeccable aim.

Red flames, blue-tinged air, and green shifting gravity and stone... each of the forces at work had a turn at the abomination, alternating between tossing it into walls, tossing walls at *it*, and throwing what remained into the ceiling, all while explosions continuously shook the space; sending shaped flame and shrapnel to deadly effect.

After what seemed an eternity, the light of the Earthen Node settled into a comfortable tri-colored glow. The gasses were gone, the rocks began to settle with impacts that shook even more rocks loose, and the heat-vacuum sucked fresh air down the massive vent that had been created. The Draconic corpse was allowed to fall to the ground, bouncing off the filth that had turned into heat-dried, packed earth by the flames and pressure.

Smoke and steam rose continuously from the corpse, as well as the still-shifting ground. Any connection the creature had once held to the Earthen Node had been broken. There was no more power sustaining it. As a fabricated creature, it had no way to generate its own life energy. The last bit of its tail gently landed on the ground, a falling flag signalling absolute surrender. The creature had been burned, battered, and destroyed - all by simple, natural forces.

Nature had been tricked into corruption, but even if it had taken centuries...

The World had taken its revenge.

CHAPTER FIFTY-SIX

A fist erupted through the baked earth, sending flakes of muck and cooked pumpkin flying away to release a *hiss* as the pressure equalized between the two spaces. An angry voice shouted, "No, no, *no*! Ahhh! Oh, we aren't burning. *Luke*! What if it had still been on fire up there?"

"I was bored just sitting here." Luke's head popped out of the earth, and he craned his neck, searching for any sign of creatures still moving around. Unfortunately, the entire space was utterly cave-dark. "Fresh air. That's nice."

"That's *another* thing!" Zed's voice was muffled, something Luke greatly appreciated after being trapped in the small space with him for the last few hours. They hadn't wanted to leave until the walls of their gourd were cool to the touch. "We've been down here for most of the day at this point, and you haven't had *any* good air. Even if you can breathe poison for some reason, how have you not suffocated?"

"My body can sustain itself on mana alone. Poison heals me. That's why I didn't bleed out all over you." Luke pulled himself out of the hole he had made and offered Zed a hand up, not that the man could see it. Luke ended up feeling around until he caught Zed's clothes, then yanked him up and out.

"You have a Skill that lets you breathe poison and live on your mana regen?" Zed simply couldn't believe what he was hearing.

"To be fair…" Luke paused as he tried to look around the space again. For some reason, he thought that there should absolutely be light here.

Zed couldn't let the silence stretch after the first few seconds. "Go *on*. I can't wait to hear what you consider fair in this context."

"They *are* different Skills." Luke finished his thought, and Zed threw his arms into the air dramatically, slapping against charcoal and yelping in surprise at the unexpected pain. "I think part of the Dragon fell on us. Follow."

Luke equipped his mana-made sword and started slicing upward. Each swing caused dust to scatter into the air, and a sharp metal-on-stone sound rang out. On the fifth strike, shifting light filtered through a hole, and Luke wasted no time in chucking Cookie up through the space. She blasted a way out for him, then took a sharp turn and slammed into the head of the deceased Dragon, as though gravity had tripled.

Luke hadn't seen her land, but the unexpected sound caused both of the humans to go very still. Activating his Soul Brand, he tried to call Cookie back. For the first time since he had used the Skill, nothing happened. Cookie didn't come back. He jumped up, following her original trajectory, and squinted around in the blinding triplet of light that shone throughout the cavern. "*That's* why I felt there should be light. Cookie wasn't glowing? Cookie! Where are you?"

Now that they were in the main chamber and his eyes had adjusted, the light of the Earthen Node far above revealed the shattered remains of the much-reduced space. Huge sections of the cavern had caved in, signifying a massive shift in terrain. He had no doubt, after taking the wreckage in, that the only reason they hadn't been crushed was that the Earthen Node had done something strange to the surrounding stone, reinforcing or controlling it so it would stay stable.

"Wow... look at this place." Zed whistled in wonder as he extricated himself from the corpse. "Luke, we should have died at least, I don't know, six times there? How did an unassembled pumpkin pie keep us alive under all of *that?*"

"Druid trickery," Luke distractedly muttered. "Cookie? *Cookie!* Where'd you go?"

The corpse under their feet shifted slightly, and Zed let out a high-pitched scream. A thick stench of fried vegetables filled the air as a small section of the remaining metal 'skin' of the Dragon was pulled away. A new source of light bloomed into existence, and Luke raced toward it. He found Cookie half-submerged in the metal as it flowed into her like water falling over a cliff, simply touching her edge and vanishing.

Just as he arrived, the process finished. He studied Cookie carefully, finding that her hue had darkened from bright-blue to a deep sapphire. He reached over and picked her up, grunting in surprise at the massive weight increase. "What have you been *eating*, Cookie? You've gotta be nine hundred pounds!"

"How can you even lift that thing if it's so heavy?" Zed blatantly insulted her, right in front of Luke! "Oh, look! A gem!"

"She's... I'll admit, right on the edge of my physical output. I can do four hundred and fifteen kilos—also known as nine hundred and fourteen pounds—before it'll really mess with me." Luke let her drop, also releasing a hidden gasp of relief. "I'll be able to hit so much *harder* when I get used to this increase. Since I have no upper limit to natural training in Murder World, the more I use her, the stronger I'll get. She's just being helpful."

"Pretty sure your bone just ate a chunk of Dragon, man. You should be careful; who knows what else that thing can do?" Zed lifted a glittering stone the size of his head that appeared to be the same color as Cookie, though it didn't shine from internal light. "Look at *this*. Okay, it'll be harder for the two of us to survive without being found by the Kingdom, but whenever we *do* get caught, we can pull this bad boy out and say we were bringing a gift to the King."

"No." Luke looked upward, where Cookie was pointing. There had been a flicker of stronger light on her surface that caught his attention, and he knew her well enough to know that something important must be going on.

Zed followed his gaze, and both looked up at the Earthen Node as a hairline crack appeared in the new crystal surface surrounding it. A moment later, two bodies dropped out of the stone, and the fracture vanished as if it had never existed. Luke and Zed watched the bodies fall, making no effort to catch them. Lightning shot down and struck the falling people just as they hit the ground.

Luke trudged toward his fallen friends, dragging Cookie along behind him. Zed coughed at the dust that kicked up, giving the Murderhobo a glare that he couldn't see. The Bard snarled lightly and hurried to walk in front of the taller man, "*Neanderthal.*"

They stood over the unmoving bodies of their friends for a long moment. Andre looked *ragged*, his plant-fiber clothes reduced to nothing, body covered in soot and blood. Taylor looked unsurprisingly perfect, and Luke could tell that her Cleanse or Purify spells had stayed active until the end.

"Should we... burn them? Bury them?" Zed offered with a small, teary voice. "We never asked them what they'd want, but... I feel like Andre would want to be buried, and Taylor burned. Maybe burned, then buried, and tossed into the swill over there to become fertilizer for plants? You know what...? Let's cut them up first so that their corpses are easier to dissolve."

"Celestial *feces*, Zed, what's the matter with you?" Andre's concerned voice rang out, halting Luke's mana-blade in mid-motion as he went to cut up the bodies.

"Oh, *I* don't know?" Zed snorted as Taylor and Andre both started moving gingerly. "Maybe I felt like we should get revenge on people that were playing dead so they could hear the teary farewells of their friends?"

"You were going to *cut us up*, Luke? Like... right then?" Taylor coughed a few times, and burned petals fell from her nostrils. "What the *abyss*?"

Luke shrugged and jabbed his thumb at Zed. "He made good sense. Easier to convert smaller chunks. Glad you're alive; confused as to *how*."

"*Feces*." Andre stood and felt his head, where all his hair had been burned away. "No clothes and no hair. Now I know why Luke comes back naked every time he goes for a swim in his world. We're alive for only one reason: the World isn't done with us. It still needs our help. My help. It knew I wouldn't continue on if it took Taylor from me, so-"

"My clothes are unaffected by mana water." Luke informed the Druid. There was a momentary pause as Andre worked out that he said that Luke 'came back naked', but he didn't get a chance to correct his words before Luke's face tightened; and he turned to Taylor. "You. Where's my satchel?"

"Taylor... we-" Andre took a step toward Taylor and reached out, but The Mage dodged away, causing the Druid to freeze in confusion. Hurt filled his eyes, but still she didn't look directly at him.

"Andre, I'd prefer to have a conversation with you *privately* about what our relationship looks like moving forward, but not here, and not while you're very, very naked," Taylor managed to rasp out as the others looked on. "Thank goodness I only got to the edge of the Node... Andre, my senses are so high that right now all I can smell around you is burned hair, and all I can see is... never mind."

A moment later, Andre was surrounded by a 'firefly'. As a seeming afterthought, it swirled around the others in rapid succession. Luke immediately smelled the surroundings at full strength once more, and he grimaced. "Thanks for that. I had gone nose-blind, but now I get to take in rotting Dragon flesh and steamed cesspit again. Where's my *satchel*?"

"This spell is constantly active for me." A small smile creeped up on Taylor's face. "I either smell everything perfectly, or not at all. Trust me, I feel your pain. At least you get to lose your sense of smell after a few minutes."

"She's smiling; are we surrounded by Inquisitors again or something?" Zed peered around nervously, getting a forced chuckle from the Mage.

"Dying and then getting my heart restarted by the planet gave me some... perspective." Taylor shuddered at the memory of so much power pumping into her. Forcing her to watch in silence as Andre gave up on life, due to her actions. Keeping her heart beating, her eyes open, and her mouth sealed as the Druid went still and floated around the Earthen Node. "I can't keep doing what I've been doing. From now on, Andre is the team leader. What he decides is what we do."

"Not a chance." Andre shook his head and crossed his arms. "I have no desire to be the one that needs to make hard choices like that."

"I'll do it," Zed intoned solemnly. "Please listen to my wisdom carefully."

Everyone ignored the Bard as Luke stepped forward and put his hand on Taylor's shoulder. "I think the mark of a good leader is someone that does the right thing, especially when no one is watching. You never asked us to go in and die for you. But you were ready to do it for us. You've got my trust back, if that matters to you."

"Mine too," Andre joined in, though Taylor still shied away when he tried for a hug. "Luke, over there. I see a part of your bag poking out from under that rock."

"Yeah, yeah, everything's wonderful," Zed grumbled in annoyance as the Murderhobo shambled over to a huge boulder and started punching it. "I coulda been an *awesome* leader. Go make pants for yourself; we can all see *exactly* how happy you are to have Taylor in charge again."

The Druid turned and made a rude gesture at the Bard, freezing in place as he stared the man down. The mood slowly became uncomfortable as the gesture remained, hovering all but forgotten under the Druid's shocked expression. As Zed started to shuffle over to the Murderhobo, Andre finally spoke, albeit in a hushed tone. "Zed. What is that you're carrying?"

Zed looked down at the massive gem, then tried to hide it behind his back. "Nothing. Stand away, nudist."

"What is it, Andre?" Taylor interjected as the naked man slowly started drifting toward the Bard.

"I got a new Ability," Andre responded dazedly, "when I was trying to fix that Earthen Node. It's called 'Call of Nature'. It's Tier nine. Not only does it let me understand natural things really well, it also lets me commune with nature in a really powerful way; I can use power directly from ley lines or Nodes to power my other Abilities. There's a drawback, if you can really call it that. I need to *listen* when nature tells me something, or I'll lose the Ability. Right now, I was just told that I need to raise that seed."

"Raise it? Not grow it?" Luke questioned absently as he reached into his satchel and moved something around. The Druid held his breath as Zed reluctantly handed him the shimmering rock; eyes brimming with emotion, he reached out and ran his hand over the orb. "It's a seed. You grow seeds. You raise animals."

"Yeah... but this has two paths in front of it." The Druid rubbed the sapphire gem lovingly, and it began shining in reaction to his mana. "I can either grow it now, and tether it to myself as a Nature Dragon-"

"Yes. Do that," Luke commanded without hesitation as Zed nodded enthusiastically. The Murderhobo pointed at the charred remains of the Corrupted Nature Dragon. "I want *that* on my side, without the whole 'destroy the world' thing going on for it."

"Guys. Stop." Taylor slipped in next to Andre, searching his face as he stared into the depths of the seed. "What else could it become, Andre?"

"It could become a *world*." Andre's voice broke as tears of joy ran down his face. He hugged the crystalline seed to his chest and cradled it like a baby. "When I'm powerful enough, I could plant this in the void and generate a new Plane of existence."

"So… it's a world seed?" Taylor prodded him.

"It's whatever we could ever want, Taylor." Andre's eyes turned and locked with hers, the passion in his gaze warming her to the core. "This could become… *Anything*."

"Question for you both," Luke called, bringing the group's attention to a familiar feeling of mana congregating. "Why did you only use the top layer of powder when you fixed the Node? I thought you wanted to be *sure* it'd work."

Zed leaned over and peeked into the satchel, where over a dozen packets of unicorn horn powder remained beautifully arranged where they had been hidden under a sectioned-off fold of leather. "You know, I think this is going to be the start of a *great* vacation, guys."

"Just *wait* until you see what I'm gonna turn this cavern into." Andre admired what was about to become his *second* underground Grove. "This place is a real fixer-upper, but I have a few ideas you all might like."

Taylor dropped to a knee as her Sigil began blazing with light, and the others followed a moment later. Luke looked skyward, ready to be annoyed, but a grin appeared unbidden as he saw Etheric Xenograft Potentia pouring in like a river. He looked around at the shell-shocked faces of his teammates, and jumped to his feet, then into the air with a wild whoop. "Let's do that *again*!"

EPILOGUE

Zed stood from his seat in the tavern, wiping away a foam mustache after he quaffed the final dregs of his drink. He scanned the utterly silent room, peering into the eyes of the myriad people reliving his experiences, and once more privately marveled at the power of his Masteries. "Hundreds of years of life, and I'm still in awe of what I can do for people. Well... I'm guessing it's about time."

The True Bard masterfully glided past the patrons of the tavern, careful not to jostle them too hard. He wanted them to feel the emotion of the story, to understand the truth of what he had imparted in their minds. Even so, he needed to hurry. He didn't want anyone listening to his stories to get hurt, after all. He reached the door, took a deep breath, then pulled it open and strolled outside confidently.

"Hello, there! Which unit did they send this time?" Zed cheerfully called to the wall of not only Inquisitors, but elite troops from the *much* expanded not-so-Hollow-anymore-Kingdom. "Don't you *ever* tire of this little game we play?"

The person in charge didn't answer with words, instead silently dropping their hand. Spells, arrows, and a smattering of knives were projected at the Bard, reaching him just as a wall of troops charged at him and launched they could to turn the Bard into mincemeat. Dozens of people who had crowded around the tavern listening to the tale of the Bard were reduced to mere stains in an instant.

"I'm sad to see how little you care for the citizens that trust in you. You know, Mirror Moment as a Mastery has no charge up or cooldown time like it does as a spell. Well, not at *this* Tier. Mages are so funny sometimes," Zed called a few minutes later. The entire unit blinked as one, finding that none of them had moved. Even the commander's arm was still raised in the air, waiting to send the signal to attack. "I was just telling the story of the rebirth of the Rocco Nature Preserve. *You* know what I'm talking about, right?"

At that, the commander *did* show emotion: rage. Again the troop charged; this time holding nothing back as they did everything in their power to inflict damage on this renegade Ascender.

"So you *do* know." Again, the scene was reset as soon as Zed started talking. Everyone was clearly exhausted; even the raised arm of the commander was shaking with fatigue from remaining in place for so long. "Now, now. It wasn't *our* choice to be treated like criminals and chased into the desert. It isn't *our* fault that the Kingdom demanded the World Seed from Andre. Who would have guessed that the Sigils could tattle on us like that when great treasures were found?"

The troops charged, and once more, Zed let them tire themselves out before pulling them out of their mental illusion.

"Was it so *wrong* for us to stay there as long as we were able, taking the time we needed to heal that area? Helping the population that came to farm? Increasing the potency of the entire Kingdom's future generations in one fell swoop?" Zed laughed mirthlessly as the commander struggled to kill him all on his own, but was never able to place a jab within *meters* of his body. "What upset you so personally? Was it the fact that Andre gifted that area to nature itself, and not the Hollow Kingdom, that got your undergarments in a twist?"

Again and again, the troops tried, until even the most elite among them slunk to their knees in the exact spot they had held since Zed had walked outside. "That was probably it. Andre once told me something about kingdoms only caring for their natural resources when they could exploit them."

"War criminal Zed the Mindbender. You are... under arrest for crimes against humanity," the commander of the Inquisitors wheezed in the metallic voice that escaped all helmets of that variety. "Under authority of the united world government, I am here to take you in for justice."

"Oh? You and what army?" Zed smirked as he regarded the literal army that had attempted to attack him. "Certainly not this one. Besides, how am *I* the criminal here? I know *exactly* how many times you killed me."

"Your puppets were merely your tools for evading justice." The commander struggled to remain upright on his knees and not directly fall over. "We've found *you*. The *real* you. Every Ascender with ties to the Dynasty will be here by tomorrow."

"What perfect timing." Zed's nonsequitur, or perhaps his smile, caught the commander off-guard. "You know, every Zed that walks this plane... when they die, I get a copy of their memories. I know *you* know this, since you tried so *many* times to break my mind by proxy. A little secret for you... it's a copy. Like a book. I just read it; their experiences never become things I need to live through. A second little tidbit: the Zeds I send out are in each location for good reason; especially the ones that you were allowed to find."

"Allowed...?" The Commander's eyes widened in horror. "There were more than *that?*"

"My *dear* Bartholomew." Zed chuckled as the Commander realized that Zed knew his *name*. "I could make one a week when I *first* got the Mastery. As a Domain Mastery? I'm sure I could remember how much of this world's actual population is me if I tried, but let's just call it... five percent?"

"*No.*" The whisper was so dramatic that even Zed had to lightly applaud. "You *alone* are a skinwalker infestation…?"

"Look here, child. As you can see by the very fact that you still live, I have no interest in hurting you." The Bard sighed as he slowly stopped clapping. "Your King, Vir, just wants me to stop telling people the truth regarding how he killed his father in the middle of a war in an unrepentant power grab. He wants me to tell him how to control the Dryad, so that he can double the size of his seat of power. Or perhaps it's more simple than that, and he wants an accounting from the war with the Dynasty of Dogs?"

At that, Bartholomew's eyes, the only thing visible through his helmet, grew wide. Zed nodded and motioned toward the tavern. "Feel free to join us, for that is the story I shall speak of upon the morrow. The tale of the Archmage, and how three people Ascended in a single moment. Against all agreements. Fully knowing what it would do to the world, and having the world's *agreement* to do it."

"All I've been authorized to ask you if captured…" Bartholomew's eyes flicked around at the gathered troops as he gulped audibly. "What did you do with the Queen?"

Once again, Zed waved at the door to the tavern. "Come in for a drink tomorrow, pay the tab for all attendees, and any questions you have shall be answered."

"You swear? Anything I need to know?"

"*Of course.*" Zed's eyes gleamed as he nodded solemnly at the commander, who suddenly seemed so very, very young. "I'm going inside now. Until we meet again… just yell if you need *Anything.*"

ABOUT DAKOTA KROUT

Author of the best-selling Divine Dungeon and Completionist Chronicles series, Dakota has been a top 5 bestseller on Amazon, a top 6 bestseller on Audible, and his first book, Dungeon Born, was chosen as one of Audible's top 5 fantasy picks in 2017.

He draws on his experience in the military to create vast terrains and intricate systems, and his history in programming and information technology helps him bring a logical aspect to both his writing and his company while giving him a unique perspective for future challenges.

"Publishing my stories has been an incredible blessing thus far, and I hope to keep you entertained for years to come!" -Dakota

Connect with Dakota:
MountaindalePress.com
Patreon.com/DakotaKrout
Facebook.com/TheDivineDungeon
Twitter.com/DakotaKrout
Discord.gg/mdp

ABOUT MOUNTAINDALE PRESS

Dakota and Danielle Krout, a husband and wife team, strive to create as well as publish excellent fantasy and science fiction novels. Self-publishing *The Divine Dungeon: Dungeon Born* in 2016 transformed their careers from Dakota's military and programming background and Danielle's Ph.D. in pharmacology to President and CEO, respectively, of a small press. Their goal is to share their success with other authors and provide captivating fiction to readers with the purpose of solidifying Mountaindale Press as the place 'Where Fantasy Transforms Reality.'

Connect with Mountaindale Press:
MountaindalePress.com
Facebook.com/MountaindalePress
Twitter.com/_Mountaindale
Instagram.com/MountaindalePress

MOUNTAINDALE PRESS TITLES

GameLit and LitRPG

The Completionist Chronicles,
The Divine Dungeon,
Full Murderhobo, and
Year of the Sword by Dakota Krout

Arcana Unlocked by Gregory Blackburn

A Touch of Power by Jay Boyce

Red Mage and
Farming Livia by Xander Boyce

Space Seasons by Dawn Chapman

Ether Collapse and
Ether Flows by Ryan DeBruyn

Dr. Druid by Maxwell Farmer

Bloodgames by Christian J. Gilliland

Threads of Fate by Michael Head

Lion's Lineage by Rohan Hublikar and Dakota Krout

Wolfman Warlock by James Hunter and Dakota Krout

Axe Druid,
Mephisto's Magic Online, and
High Table Hijinks by Christopher Johns

Skeleton in Space by Andries Louws

Chronicles of Ethan by John L. Monk

Pixel Dust and
Necrotic Apocalypse by David Petrie

Viceroy's Pride by Cale Plamann

Henchman by Carl Stubblefield

Artorian's Archives by Dennis Vanderkerken and Dakota Krout

Made in United States
Orlando, FL
01 July 2024

48496925R00245